THE HOOKUP

THE HOOKUP

INDECENT INTENTIONS, BOOK 2

LILY ZANTE

Copyright © 2018 Lily Zante

The Hookup (#2, Indecent Intentions Series)

Ebook Edition

All rights reserved.

No part of this publication may be copied, reproduced in any format, by any means, electronic or otherwise, without prior consent from the copyright owner and publisher of this book.

The scanning, uploading and distribution of this book through the internet or any other means without the prior written consent of the author is illegal and is punishable by law.

This is a work of fiction. All characters, names, places and events are the product of the author's imagination or used fictitiously and do not bear any resemblance to any real person, alive or dead.

AUTHOR'S NOTE

The Hookup, (#2, Indecent Intentions), is a spin-off from the from **The Billionaire's Love Story** (a contemporary romance serial with 9 installments)

This book is a STANDALONE romance, and while you don't need to have read any of **The Billionaire's Love Story, or The Bet, (#1, Indecent Intentions),** it might enhance your reading experience if you do, since most of the characters in this book appeared in that series first.

The Billionaire's Love Story:

The Promise (FREE)
The Gift, Book 1
The Gift, Book 2
The Gift, Book 3
The Gift, Boxed Set (Books 1, 2 & 3)
The Offer, Book 1

The Offer, Book 2
The Offer, Book 3
The Offer, Boxed Set (Books 1, 2 & 3)
The Vow, Book 1
The Vow, Book 2
The Vow, Book 3
The Vow, Boxed Set (Books 1, 2 & 3)

Indecent Intentions:

The Bet
The Hookup
Indecent Intentions 2-Book Set

CHAPTER ONE

"A re you crazy? Ten thousand dollars?" Luke's voice echoed disbelief.

"That's right. Ten thousand dollars that I can get that girl into my bed," his friend declared.

"I don't want you to do anything stupid," Luke warned. He didn't like the sound of this. Flirting with a woman was one thing, but placing a $10K bet in order to get her into bed? That was insane. Even he didn't play that dirty. He looked at Xavier as if he'd lost all commonsense.

"All above board, dude," his friend replied with a cocky grin. "I don't ever use force. She'll want it by the time I'm finished with her."

"Ten thousand?" Luke blinked again.

"You called it."

"No, *you* called it."

Xavier Stone was unbelievable. He threw money around like confetti, and he could be a real dick sometimes. Luke—even if he didn't respect women the way most men should—even he wouldn't stoop so low as to place a bet to get someone into his bed.

Women, dating, sex, relationships; these things were of no importance to him, and often the order in which they came into his life wasn't worthy of much thought. He would *never* waste time on shit like that. But building his business and his real estate empire? That took all of his time and energy.

Xavier's problem was that he needed to be *wanted*.

Whereas Luke didn't give a shit about these things.

"You provoked me," Xavier asserted.

"Didn't realize your esteem was so fragile," Luke threw back at him. But he also felt sorry for the guy. It couldn't be easy being a younger brother to Tobias Stone—the Wall Street genius who could do no wrong.

"It's not," Xavier shot back.

What was the point of even discussing this? Xavier had clearly made up his mind, and he would no doubt spend the next few months chasing this poor girl until she gave in. Still, Luke didn't like the sound of this. He liked Izzy—she was the au pair to Jacob, Tobias's new step-son as of this morning. The billionaire hedge-fund owner had married the boy's mother, here on his idyllic, private island in Fiji. Luke's job, as the owner of one of the most popular and upscale bars in New York, had been to take care of the drinks for the four-day wedding extravaganza.

"Is there a time limit to this crazy bet?"

"A month," Xavier replied.

"What if she's already got a boyfriend?" he asked, hoping to throw Xavier off the crazy idea. Izzy seemed nice enough, and he didn't like the idea of Xavier hitting on someone as naïve as her. She was pleasant, and nothing like the usual airheads Xavier ended up with.

"She hasn't. I overheard her talking to Savannah. Anyway, are you chickening out now?"

"No." Luke eyed him for the longest time, knowing that his chances for dissuading Xavier were slim. "A month doesn't seem like enough time, and I'd hate for you to do something stupid."

"I'm not going to do anything stupid. I don't know what you take me for."

An idiot, thought Luke, but he didn't say anything. Xavier didn't think with his brain, he thought with his dick, and Luke hoped some other tall, thin and vacuous distraction would come along and make Xavier ditch his bet.

"Three months, then, if it makes you feel better," said Xavier, exhaling loudly as if he was irritated. "But I doubt I'll need that long. Watch and learn, dude. Watch and learn."

"You're an idiot," Luke declared, wishing that Xavier would go to bed before he came up with any more hair-brain ideas. "Listen, buddy. How about you go straight to bed *alone?* Try it. You might like it. And when you wake up in the morning you'll see what a stupid idea this was."

"It's not a stupid idea."

This was debatable, but arguing about it wouldn't change a thing. Instead, he seized Xavier's empty glass. "Bed," he said, forcefully, but with a smile.

"Dude," said Xavier, sliding off the bar stool. "I'm going to wake up in the morning and show you how easily it's done."

"I look forward to watching a grand master at work."

"Jeez," said Xavier, rising to his feet unsteadily. "How many fucking tequilas did you give me?"

"I told you enough was enough, but you wouldn't listen. You've had too much, so do me a favor, pal, and go to bed."

Xavier placed his hand around his stomach.

"And don't go throwing up here," Luke complained, walking towards his friend in case he toppled over.

"I'm fine," Xavier replied. "Jeez. I'm going straight to bed."

"Alone," Luke reiterated.

Xavier walked away, raising his hand up, whether to signify that he was fine, or that he was going or what, Luke didn't know. But he stood there watching, checking to see that Xavier walked towards the main villa, and didn't detour towards any women nearby.

The idiot. Luke loved the guy like a brother, but there was a world of difference between him and Xavier, even though they both had older brothers. But that was where the similarity ended.

The Stone brothers were different, and even though Xavier seemed eclipsed by Tobias's success, the two brothers seemed to have a decent enough relationship.

The Hunters were different. There was no love lost between him and that idiot brother of his. Luke had stopped giving a shit about Travis Hunter years ago. His brother could go and burn in the same raging hell he hoped his father would end up in one day.

A vibration in the back pocket of his jeans alerted him, and he fished out his cell phone.

Marie.

He smiled, then glanced at his watch. She was in early today, taking care of things at The Oasis, one of his clubs in New York. She had no fixed start and finish times, but she always did her hours and often worked overtime, too. A single mom with two teenage children, she was probably his closest confidante, as far as the business went.

"Early shift today?" he asked, raising his hand to let the other bartenders know he was taking a call.

"Yes. Is this a good time? I don't want to interrupt the party or anything."

He walked away from the bar towards a quieter part of the beach. Over the other side, it was still busy. Tobias and Savannah's wedding had finished hours ago, and it was almost midnight, but the party was still in full swing and showed no signs of ending soon.

"It's as good a time as any. The party isn't going to wind down yet."

"It'll be a long night, then?"

He looked around at the guests who were everywhere. "Nobody's going to bed yet." Although he hoped Xavier had heeded his advice.

"How was the wedding?" Marie asked.

"Great."

"Care to share any details? Photos even?"

"Not really. You know weddings aren't my thing." Fuck weddings.

"It was wasted on you."

"I'm here to work, not watch the wedding. Tobias is happy with our service and that's all that matters."

"You should have sent me," said Marie.

"Then Tobias might not have been as thrilled with our service."

She tut-tutted loudly. "I would have done a stellar job, and you know it."

He couldn't argue with that.

"And, I could have told you what everyone was wearing, and how they were behaving, and ensured our service was stellar," Marie added, a boastful tone to her voice

"I have no doubt."

"So, uh ... did Savannah have any single girlfriends? Did you meet anyone *nice*?"

And there it was. Marie fishing for information. While she might have been interested in the particulars of the wedding, he knew where her real interest lay. "I wasn't looking," he replied, gruffly. "I was there to work."

"It must have been beautiful?" Marie persisted.

"It was." But he was here to ensure that the drink flowed freely, and he'd done that.

As far as weddings went, this one had been spectacular. Nothing ostentatious, or over-the-top crass, but *beautiful,* but he wasn't about to tell Marie that. "You didn't call to ask about the wedding, did you?"

"I wouldn't waste my time. Besides, you can tell me everything when you get back. Rumor has it that a new site on Canal Street is going to come on the market in a couple of weeks."

Canal Street? "I want it." He had been on the lookout for a building to come up for sale in Tribeca. A bar or club there would never fail.

"I haven't told you anything about it, yet," Marie protested.

"You don't have to. I still want it."

"Even if it's got mold and subsidence?"

"Problems can be fixed." A bar on Canal Street would be a major achievement. Not bad for a guy who had yet to turn thirty in three years' time. He'd already shown his father that he could cope on his own; he'd been doing so ever since he'd been thrown out of the family home at seventeen and had moved in with Travis.

Three years later, after he and Travis fell out over a girl, he left his brother's apartment, too.

"I knew you'd be interested. I'll look out for it and arrange a viewing as soon as it's available."

"Thanks."

Marie was a godsend. Who else would he have left in charge in his absence? It was only because of her that he had been able to go to a private island for a few days, effectively becoming one of the highest paid mixologists in New York, albeit temporarily.

"Everything running smoothly?" he asked, swatting what was probably a mosquito at the back of his shoulder.

"Of course."

"Anything else I need to know about?"

"You've only been gone a few days. Relax," Marie told him. "The Oasis isn't about to collapse. It's in my capable hands."

"I know. That's why I left you in charge."

"Be good," she said.

"I'm always good."

"That's debatable." She chuckled and hung up, leaving him with a grin on his face.

No matter what, he intended to get this new place, even if it meant he'd have to pay through the nose for it. Canal Street was prime real estate. Anything he set down there—a bar and club similar to The Oasis and The Vault—would make money, hand over fist. If he managed to get it, the Canal Street site would be another jewel in his empire and after that, maybe he would have a similar operation in Miami in the summer, and LA at the end of next year.

He looked up, startled by the sound of a kid laughing. Really, *really* laughing.

Jacob, Tobias's new step-son, was walking along the beach with his nanny, Izzy, following behind him with a cocktail in her hand.

She smiled as she walked up to him. "They let you escape from your bar?" she asked, moving the brightly colored cocktail umbrella out of the way, before lifting the glass to her lips.

"I had to take a call." He liked Izzy. She was cool. Easy-going and friendly, but not in an obvious want-to-get-to-know-you better way. She didn't strike him as the kind of girl who had ulterior motives, and in his line of work he'd seen plenty of that around; sexy young women on the arms of Wall Street banker boys flashing their plastic cards.

"What's that?" he asked, curious.

"A Mockmosa, at least that's what the other bartender told me."

"Ah." Mimosa but without the alcohol.

"It's not as tasty as the one you whipped up yesterday."

"Come over to the bar," he offered, "and I'll make you another one." But Izzy was watching Jacob who had wandered over to the tables where Tobias and Savannah were sitting.

"No thank you, this one will keep me going. Jacob's insisting that he wants to stay up all night, but I don't think so."

"He might surprise you." The kid looked happy enough, though he was rubbing his eyes now and sitting on Tobias's lap.

"He's like one of those battery charged bunnies," she said. "I've never seen him this high before."

"Looks to me as if he's fighting his sleep."

"You could be right," Izzy agreed. "I'd better go get him. I'll have one of your cocktails tomorrow, maybe."

"You know where to find me."

"I sure do," she answered, "Goodnight." For a brief moment he was thrown into a quandary. Should he tell her about Xavier's bet? But his loyalty to his friend reared its head and prevented him. He just hoped that Xavier would forget about the ridiculous idea by the time he woke up tomorrow.

"'Night," he said, his eyes fixed on Tobias and his stepson. It was obvious that Tobias was going to make a great dad. Luke couldn't remember the last time he'd spoken to his father, and was certain he'd never had such close contact as that.

Sitting on his father's lap? Never. The only reason he knew the bastard was still alive was because his sister would have called immediately to tell him that he'd passed away.

Luke wasn't so sure he'd be too upset by the news. He could never forgive. Some things were etched on his mind like markings in stone. Hard to shift, hard to erase, impossible to forget.

He preferred to forget, and sometimes, he managed to. Raking his hand through his hair, he looked over at the dance floor and to see Tobias leading Savannah towards the middle of the floor.

He had to hand it to them, they made a nice couple, and maybe they would end up being happy forever. He wondered if his mother had had the same dreams on her wedding day.

Romance was an illusory illness. Some recovered from it, some didn't.

His sister hadn't learned a damn thing. Her head was filled with ideas for her second wedding, and she was all loved up and living on cloud nine, again. Amanda constantly told him he needed to enjoy life, to not work, work, work all the time. But, what did she know?

Something knotted in the pit of his stomach, and he steeled himself for the inevitable family gathering.

CHAPTER TWO

"What a beautiful couple," Kay's mother remarked, her face lighting up with pride and admiration. For a moment Kay thought she was going to cry.

Her heart lurched. She didn't want to hear the inevitable questions. "Aren't they?" she replied, knocking back her champagne. It was the only way to get through this.

Tobias and Savannah were on the dance floor again with eyes only for each other. Everyone watched the beautiful, and so-sickeningly-obvious head-over-heels-in-love couple glide on air.

Kay observed the rapt looks on the faces of her mother and Savannah's parents. She'd made the huge mistake of sitting with them, and had only done so because she'd seen Xavier at the bar and she was eager to avoid him.

Get me out of here.

As much as she loved her cousin, she couldn't help but feel a tiny bit envious. She wanted *that*. Not right *now*, not today, not this month, or this year, but *eventually*. Despite what she said to her friends, and to Savannah, and despite her easy-come-easy-go attitude towards men, what she wanted, *one day,* in the not-too-distant future, was everlasting love, and marriage, and commitment.

She wanted *forever,* even if she wasn't yet putting out the right signals to attract the right things.

She didn't need a rich guy because she wasn't penniless, but if he was rich, it wasn't a bad thing. The security she craved wasn't financial, it was emotional. She was an independent woman with a great career; one which sucked the life out of her, yes, but she partied as hard as she worked to make up for it.

What she needed, wanted and hoped for, was a man to be her counterpart, to support her, and be there for her.

She didn't need a man to rescue her, she just needed him to treat her right.

Of course, the future couldn't be predicted, but who, looking at Tobias and Savannah, would wish anything less for that couple?

She could continue having *fun,* but none of her fun times had ever resulted in meeting anyone who had made her believe that 'he was *the one.*' She needed another single man just like Tobias.

As she set off for the wedding, she'd had designs on Xavier. The younger brother was rich, handsome and undeniably sexy. He'd seemed like the next best catch, especially now that his brother was no longer single. Unfortunately, she had found out the hard way that Xavier wasn't quite the man she had imagined him to be. The testosterone rolling off him in waves should have been a stark warning.

"They look *so* happy together," her mother cooed.

"They would, Mom. They just got married." Kay's insides pinched together as she braced herself for the inevitable question. Would it be too obvious if she got up now and wandered away?

"It would be lovely if you settled down soon. Don't leave it too late, will you, dear?"

It wasn't a secret that her mother's dearest wish was for Kay to settle down. Her mother didn't understand and no amount of explanation seemed to help. Working long hours at the investment bank didn't leave much time for anything else, and working in Hong Kong, where she had spent most of last year, hadn't helped her dating prospects much.

Savannah's parents looked at her apologetically.

"She'll settle down when the time is right, Sylvie," said Aunt Jean.

"You tell her, Aunt Jean."

She wished her mother could be as understanding as Savannah's mother was. Both sisters, they shared similar traits in many respects, but her mother seemed to be caught up in the same happy-envy that had dogged Kay for most of the day. The wedding had long finished and everyone had spent most of the day, and now the night, celebrating the wedding.

The happy couple had invited close family and friends to their beautiful private island in Fiji, and it was impossible not to be in awe of the new world that Savannah had now stepped into through her marriage to Tobias. From his condo, and his homes around the world, his private jet, and this island, as well as the new multi-million dollar mansion home on which Tobias had lavished millions of dollars on in refurbishments, it all seemed surreal.

The splendor of Savannah's new world was unlike anything that Kay had ever read or dreamed about, even in those celebrity magazines which she had stopped reading. She had also stopped following those Most-Eligible-

Bachelor lists, and blindly buying celebrity magazines in order to keep up-to-date with A and B-lister gossip.

"What about Tobias's brother?" her mother asked, after a few peaceful moments had passed.

The apple obviously didn't fall far from the tree.

"Mom!" she hissed, hoping that nobody had heard her. "Stop trying to fix me up." It was one thing Kay herself having an ulterior motive for wanting to get to know Xavier, but it was something else to hear her mother saying it out aloud.

"But why not? His brother is just as good looking."

"No."

No. No. No.

Her insides knotted together, and it wasn't due to the copious glasses of champagne, or the seafood entrees. "Can we not talk about my love life?

Uncle Dale and Aunt Jean were walking towards the dance floor hand in hand. Sweet, she thought, watching them. She could see her mother's sadness written all over her face. Her father had passed away a few weeks before she had graduated from college. The lung cancer had taken him much too soon. Receiving her college degree had been a bittersweet moment, and in the end, her mother had attended, with Savannah's parents there for support. There had been no-one since, and her mother hadn't expressed any interest in meeting anyone new.

She seemed content with her life, and maybe it wasn't so surprising that days like today made her slightly wistful, and wish for Kay to find someone.

"I wasn't talking about your love life. I was only saying that it was about time you—"

"Mom. *Please.*"

Her mother let out an angry breath and looked away.

"They're perfect for one another. Perfect. Why you don't want that, I don't know."

Kay stared in front at the happy newly married couple. Marrying New York's most eligible billionaire was a dream come true, for sure.

No wonder Savannah looked so happy.

Her life was complete and she would never have to worry again. She had achieved the impossible. Not only had she been married before, she also had a kid, and she had been married to a pig. But she had come to New York penniless, and had managed to win the heart of the city's most eligible bachelor.

If Savannah Page could do that, there was no reason why she couldn't.

Not that her cousin had ever worried much about men or her love life. Savannah, in complete contrast to Kay, had worried about money, and debt, and Jacob, whereas Kay had no debt, had plenty of money, worked hard, had a great job.

Yet her love-life was in tatters.

She had experienced a couple of short flings in Hong Kong. They had been nothing serious, and more to help her pass the time with.

But things hadn't fared any better since she'd returned to New York. She'd met up with one of her ex-boyfriends a few times. Dean had been the closest she had ever come to serious, and when he'd called her a few months ago, she'd gone running back instead of heeding Savannah's advice. He had used her for a weekend, and then discarded her just as easily. So much for 'talking', and a possible reconciliation.

She never learned.

A booty call, Savannah had said later, when she had confided in her cousin. So when her mother talked about Xavier Stone being a possible future prospect, it was the last thing she wanted to hear. She had already tried to make conversation with Xavier. Tried and failed. Made out with him too, and failed.

Xavier had spent most of yesterday evening—well, not most, *some*—showing her card tricks, and they had talked and flirted, and had ended up kissing. She had to give him that—the guy was a good kisser.

A great kisser.

Things might have progressed to something else had it not been for Tobias showing up out of the blue. As soon as his brother had appeared, Xavier had dropped her like a dirty stone.

Humiliation washed over her like a dirty rag. He turned his back to her and ignored her completely. She'd left, walked away into the night, back to the beach, and the bar, once more wondering why some girls had all the luck, and why she didn't.

Xavier walked into view, standing on the other side of the dance floor and eyeing up all the guests. The sight of him irritated her. The last thing she needed was for him to come over to this table, or for her mother to notice him and wave him over. She couldn't put it past the woman.

"I'm going to mingle," she announced, getting up from her chair.

It was too early to go to bed, too early to be lectured on the virtues of being married, and too early to sit around with a bunch of old people.

Surely there had to be other good looking guys on the island?

CHAPTER THREE

The cousin of the bride was at the bar again. Yesterday she had been reeled in by Xavier's magic tricks, and no doubt, his charm, but, Luke noted, she blatantly avoided the younger Stone today.

"What can I get you?" he asked. The good mood she'd been in earlier had disappeared and she now seemed downcast and was trying to hide it. But eyes didn't lie, and her soft brown ones gave it away.

"A bloody Mary, please."

"A bloody Mary, coming right up, but," his bartender persona switched into gear and he placed his forearms on the bar top, bringing his head down to her level. "Are you sure you wouldn't want something more adventurous?"

He had an easy way with girls, and he always attracted their attention, even back at The Oasis, where people knew who he was. He was used to the attention, and used to extricating himself from over-eager customers, but it still never stopped the women from making their intentions known to him.

Kay's seemingly melancholy mood, in such stark

contrast to how she had been before, piqued his curiosity. This woman looked as if she could do with some company, and a part of him felt sorry for her. She should have been dancing the night away instead of being at the bar alone.

"I don't know," she replied, picking up the cocktail list he'd put together for this event. "What do you recommend?"

"What do you usually like?" Some liked their cocktails to be like milkshakes, others liked them strong and reeking of alcohol.

"How about a Slow Comfortable Screw Against The Wall?"

He wasn't prepared for that one. She held his gaze as the double entendre slipped through his ears and ignited the fire that would give him a boner, if she carried on talking like that.

"I can get you one of those," he replied slowly, noting the sudden change in her temperament. Whatever it was that had dampened her mood, seemed to have suddenly disappeared.

Her full lips parted into a smile. "I look forward to it," she purred, sending a shooting star of excitement through his body.

She was forward this one, nothing like Savannah. But he was used to it. It wasn't the first time he'd had a customer proposition him with one of those. In his line of work, he got chatted up all the time. "Be careful what you wish for," he replied, returning the smirk. "I'll whip you up one of those and add my unique twist to it."

"Whip away," she replied, leaning forward, the tops of her breasts were pushed up to the hilt and on display in her low-cut fuchsia colored dress. Her dress, and her breasts, were hard to ignore.

She was obviously looking to make an impression.

He got busy, making up her cocktail, and threw her a sidelong glance. She looked as if she had the weight of the world on her shoulders, and he wondered if Xavier had had anything to do with this.

"Here you go," he said, sliding the glass her way.

She took a sip, "Hmmm." She licked her lips suggestively. "It's delicious. Not too sweet, and not overly alcoholic. Nice. *Dangerously nice.* Have one with me," she said, her French manicured nails circling slowly around the rim of the glass.

He shuddered involuntarily, trying to rein in his response. "I shouldn't." He didn't like to drink on duty, even though he could, because he wasn't supposed to be on duty. He had simply chosen to be behind the bar because it meant he didn't get hassled. From behind the safety of the bar enclosure, he could operate in stealth-mode, at a great vantage point, and could easily see and hear most things. It was amazing how much information and secrets people willingly gave up, and how loose their tongues became after a few drinks.

"Please," she begged, squeezing her shoulders and pushing her breasts together. His heart missed a beat, and the visual created a stirring below.

Hell. Why not? It was past midnight, and it had been a long day. Everything had gone well, and, importantly, Tobias had been pleased with the service.

"A drink, then," he said, pouring himself a scotch.

"No Slow Comfortable Screw Against The Wall for you?" she asked, her eyes falling to his arms, and trailing along his tattoos.

"I prefer a scotch. Cheers," he declared, lifting his glass to hers.

"To Savannah, and Tobias, the happy, happy, happy couple," she declared.

"Amen."

"To all the happy couples everywhere," she added.

He paused, then followed suit. "To all the happy couples everywhere." If she believed that shit then who was he to argue?

"Are you one half of a happy couple?" she asked. And there it was. *The question.* The one he got asked almost every night he was at the bar.

"No." At some point during any of his conversations, this question always reared its head. Women always seemed curious about his status.

"You must be freaking kidding me," she shrieked in surprise. "I don't believe you."

He forced a smile, almost gave a half-shrug of his shoulders, and noticed her gaze drift over to his biceps and stay there a few seconds.

"How come?" she asked, clearing her throat, forcing her gaze to his eyes. "How come a good looking guy like you isn't with anybody?"

"I could say the same about you." Not because he was interested, but because, what sort of answer could he give to a question like that? He gave her the once over as he lifted the glass to his lips again. Her honey blonde hair framed her face and hung in waves around her shoulders, and yet her eyebrows were a darker shade. He'd bet she wasn't blonde down *there*. Not a natural blonde.

She was obviously not a shrinking wall flower and it was no wonder that she'd caught Xavier's eye yesterday. If anyone would have been perfect for Xavier, it would have been this woman. He wondered what had gone wrong that

Xavier and Kay weren't even hanging out in the same part of the beach together.

Except now the guy was going after Izzy.

"I don't have a good track record with guys. It never lasts. Or, it never leads to anything." This was the problem with being the guy who served drinks. It made for being a psychotherapist. The keeper of everyone's drunken secrets and mistakes.

"I don't believe you," he told her. Now he was the one flirting, not because he wanted anything to happen, but because he was curious. Some people attracted love, or lust, and some seemed to repel it. He didn't for one minute believe that Kay found it hard to get a guy.

"Why not? It's true. I'm not saying it to get your sympathy."

"I never implied that you were trying to elicit my sympathy," he said, a flash of real sympathy in his voice. She was pretty, and she had a good figure. An image of the Marilyn Monroe poster in his bedroom during his teen years flashed into his head. Kay might not have been wearing a white halterneck dress, nor had her skirt flying up behind her, but there was something Monroe-esque about her, especially when her breasts looked as if they might tumble out of her dress any moment now.

"Well, it's true."

A group of people suddenly filled the bar area and he didn't want to keep them waiting, even though a couple of the other bartenders were serving.

He looked at her apologetically. "I'm sorry, but we're getting busy again." It didn't seem right to walk away now when she seemed to be confiding in him, but he was running a bar, and serving the customers was his main priority. He threw a final glance at her cleavage, then looked away. It wasn't often a woman caught his attention like that. Something about the sultry night air on this damn island was getting to him. "I'd better tend to these people."

She nodded, and took another sip of her cocktail.

It was all hands on deck. People were making the most of the wedding reception, and Tobias's generosity. Out here in the sultry heat, under the stars and nestled in the Fijian archipelago, Tobias and Savannah's wedding guests forgot about their jobs and their busy, stressful lives. They were clearly still in the partying mood, and it didn't matter what time it was. This party was going to go on until the early hours of the morning.

Being a sober guy working behind the bar allowed him to see people at their most raw and vulnerable form. Alcohol did that. It stripped away people's layers and exposed their true selves.

As Savannah's cousin had done.

When he'd finished serving a couple of people, he couldn't help but notice her still sitting at the other end of the bar by herself, looking a little lonely even in a sea of people.

CHAPTER FOUR

Having fun? How's it going? How's the wedding?

Dean's question-filled text message blinked at her. Sitting by herself at the bar alone, feeling awkward and out of place given that most of the guests were paired up, she had been checking her messages.

Close family had been allowed to keep their phones on them, unlike the rest of the guests, and for that she was grateful. A cell phone was like a woman's best friend, especially at times like now when she had nothing to do and nobody to talk to. It was an accessory that made her not look so sad, lonesome, or desperate.

Most of the messages from her friends had asked the same question. Everyone wanted to know about the wedding of the cousin who had married the billionaire hedge-fund wonder boy. She didn't bother to reply to any of the others, and deleted Dean's message.

She stole another look at the bartender who was still at the other end of the bar, serving people. Her gaze lingered over his tattooed arms, and she admired his defined biceps as he lifted his arms to sweep the hair away from his eyes.

The more she looked at him, the more she found herself unable to look away.

"What are you doing sitting here all by yourself?"

She turned around to see Briony, Savannah's friend from work, standing beside her. "Taking some time out," she replied, cheering up in an instant. She had come to know Briony and her girlfriend Max well, and enjoyed their company.

"From what?" Briony asked, then excused herself while she placed an order for her cocktails.

"From people asking me when I'm going to settle down."

"Ouch." Briony made a sympathetic face. "You'll need another drink, then. What can I get you?"

Kay held up her half-empty cocktail glass. "I'm fine for now, thanks." Besides, she would rather ask Luke for another drink herself. No point in wasting an opportunity like that.

"Who's hassling you?" Briony asked, as she waited for her drink.

"My mother."

"Ugh." A drawn out sigh told her that Briony suffered the same. "You too?"

"Is your mom here?" Kay asked, lifting her cocktail glass to her lips.

"God, no!" Briony looked horrified, as the server placed two drinks in front of her. "What's your mom more worried about?" she asked, slipping her fingers around the stems of the cocktail glasses. "Your vagina, or your ovaries?"

Kay almost spat out her drink in shock. She wiped her lips with a napkin. "Huh?"

"Is she worried that your ovaries might be getting old and shriveled, or that you're allergic to men?"

"I think it's both, although I'm not a ... a ... a..."

"Lesbian, I think, is the word you're looking for," offered Briony, helpfully.

Kay faked a smile, feeling foolish, and embarrassed. "Sorry, I didn't mean to offend you."

"You didn't." Briony cracked a smile. "Come and join us later if you want."

"Thanks, I will."

Another text message appeared, from Dean again:

When are you back? Maybe we should hook up?

She scowled, wishing she hadn't run into him at that bar a few weeks ago. The time before that, when she had agreed to meet him because he'd wanted to talk, it had ended up being a booty call. Of course, it hadn't helped that she was useless at resisting the affections of a good-looking, well-built man.

And of course, she hated being alone. It didn't help now that Savannah was paired up. Her singleness could not have been more starkly contrasted.

And sometimes, she needed comfort. Comfort interspersed with some tender, and some downright dirty moments too.

It felt good to be wanted.

Savannah had warned her then, but she had ignored her. Her problem was that she never learned, and she wished she could. If only she could exercise restraint.

Maybe Savannah had a point when she had advised her not to come across and look so desperate. *'You'll earn more respect if you play hard to get.'*

She looked up, and caught the bartender's eye. Her lips automatically flashed him a slow, provocative smile, and pushed her cell phone away. Maybe she would take Briony up on her offer, and go and sit with her and her girlfriend; at least she wouldn't be in any danger of being tempted by Dean. A culmination of pink champagne and too many cocktails was making her feel light-headed and the last thing she wanted to do was sext Dean something stupid while slightly tipsy.

She lifted her head, sensing that she was being watched, and found herself staring directly into the bartender's sparkling eyes.

"Trouble?" he asked.

Adrenaline flooded her brain, and she momentarily forgot how to think, or speak. Freaking hell, this man with his broad, broad shoulders, now held her transfixed with his pointed stare. Her heart did a funny jig inside her chest.

"Something wrong?" he asked, when she didn't reply.

She swallowed, and managed to compose herself. "A nuisance, more like."

"A nuisance?"

"An ex-boyfriend."

"An *ex*-boyfriend?" His question, the way he asked it, suddenly made her feel warm and tingly.

He was making small-talk, and bartenders were good at that kind of stuff, but it didn't hurt to have someone to listen to her, least of all, someone who looked like he did. How had she failed to notice him before? "He's bugging me."

"He's here?"

"No, he's back home."

"And he's bugging you all the way from there?"

"He wants to know how the wedding went."

The bartender snorted. "I didn't think it was such a big deal for a guy to want to know that kind of stuff. My sister's curious about it, which is to be expected. Girls are nosier."

"Curious, I think, is the word you're looking for."

"You're putting words in my mouth," he replied, "I'd go with nosey." He was making her heart fill up with his soft, low voice. Because even though he was saying normal words, his eyes...freaking hell, those glittering blue eyes, they were looking and making her skin prickle with excitement.

Unable to resist, she answered, "I wouldn't dream of putting words in your mouth." Something else, maybe. Freaking hell. Either he'd doubled up on the alcohol shot in the cocktail he'd made for her, or he was flirting like crazy. For a moment his cool expression seemed to slip, and she didn't miss the jolt of surprise in his features.

She smiled, enjoying the power she had in that moment. Savoring the effect her words had on him. He coughed, than ran his hand through his hair, moving the long locks away from his face. It settled back a little, but sooner or later it was going to fall over his forehead again, and he'd lift his arms and do that whole movement all over again. She'd get another glorious shot of his flexed bicep again. "If you knew my sister, you'd go with nosey."

She smiled at his quick recovery. Usually, she'd have a good retort, some flirty-dirty words to volley back at him, but he hadn't reciprocated. He hadn't flirted back. Maybe this one was going to take some extra work, after all, he wasn't Xavier. The thought of taking up the challenge excited her. "Your sister's already called you for an update?" she asked, deciding to take a teeny weeny bit of Savannah's advice and holding back on the innuendo. Although this probably wasn't what Savannah had in mind when she'd advised her to not come across so desperate, but as far as Kay was concerned, this was a good alternative.

"She's super-nosey, wanted pictures and all. I didn't

take any, on account of Tobias's NDA. The reason she's interested is because she'd getting married soon," he explained.

"She is? Awww, that's nice. When?"

"In the new year, sometime."

"Awesome." She finished her cocktail, felt her head slightly spinning, though she wasn't sure if it was the cocktail, or the effect of having this man's total attention, and basking in it. "Is she older or—"

"How comes your ex is calling you?"

She smiled again, a fluttery feeling dancing in her chest at the presumption that he might be interested. It didn't matter that he'd cut off her question.

"Why's he still calling me?" she asked, provocatively, laying a hand on her chest and watching his gaze lower. *Because he knows I'll come running.* That was the obvious answer. Instead she said, "He's obviously not over me."

"I can see that. Someone like you probably wouldn't be so easy to get over."

A guy wouldn't say anything like that if he wasn't interested. She widened her smile and held it there, waiting for him to mirror it and confirm his interest. "You're saying all the right things," she told him when the smile didn't materialize. She leaned forwards slightly, forcing her breathing to calm down.

This man was interested, but he seemed to be fighting it. He was holding back, and given that he wasn't coupled, unless he'd lied to her earlier, or that he was gay—something which her gut told her he wasn't, there was no reason for him to hold back.

He was also holy freaking gorgeous.

How the hell had she not noticed him before? Piercing blue eyes, broad shoulders, and tattoos on muscled arms. He filled out his black t-shirt well. She would go to bed with happy thoughts tonight, recalling it.

"It's my job."

"Oh." His answer yanked her back to reality. "I mean," he placed his forearms down on the bar top again. "You get to know people." This time his head was once again level with hers. With his face so near, she forgot to breathe. He stared at her, his cool, unhurried gaze, raking over her, playing with her. Flirting and teasing, yet without words.

Freaking hell.

"I bet you get to know a lot of people," she murmured, forgetting how to breathe just then. She was vaguely conscious that she wasn't wearing a bra, and that her pebbled nipples might give her excitement away.

"Maybe." He cupped his chin as if he was thinking it over. "It becomes second nature, being able to read people, and get a vibe from them."

She nodded, only because the fog in her brain prevented her from saying anything. He gave her the once over and she instinctively sat up taller, straightening her posture and thrusting her chest out just enough to pull his attention there. His penetrating gaze set off a chain reaction —and the beating of her heart competed with the throbbing between her legs for the most beats per minute.

"What's your read on me?" she asked, "Seeing that you've been eyeing me up all night." Her boldness pushed Savannah's sensible advice into the gutter.

He covered his mouth with his finger, and she couldn't work out if he was laughing at her, or with her. But at least he hadn't denied that he'd been eyeing her up.

"You sure you can take it?" he asked, those cool blue eyes burning into her.

"I can take anything you give me."

"I wouldn't be so sure," he replied. His response, with its subtle challenge, sent shivers scampering along her chest and stomach. She let out a breathless, "Try me."

She wished he would.

"You're not a wallflower, I would say."

"I shouldn't tell you this but my nickname used to be Good-Time-Kay."

His eyebrows lifted in surprise.

"I like to party," she said, dismissing any other notions he might have. He had no idea how stressful her job was, and therefore would never understand her need to have fun when she was out. "Go on," she said, eager to hear more. "What else?"

"You dress to …impress."

"To impress?" she grinned. "You're being polite. You should say what you mean. I can take it."

"For attention, then," he replied, accepting her challenge, yet his gaze didn't lower, as she had hoped. Their gazes locked for a long, sexy, unspoken moment that stretched out into the night. It was a million times sexier than him looking her up and down.

"Maybe," she conceded.

"And tonight, you seem sad." He lifted his head, looked over her shoulder, towards the dance floor, then back at her again. "Because you're alone, and you're happy for Savannah, but seeing it all in your face is too much."

"You're freaking good," she breathed, unaccustomed to a man who she had barely known, being able to see right through her.

"And this ex is hassling you because he knows he can have you at his beck and call."

"Uh, well," she murmured, taken aback because she hadn't yet met a man who could see past her outer exterior, and this man she barely knew, seemed to reach inside and know all there was to know about her. The sadness over Xavier's treatment of her, and her irritation over her mother's comments flew right out of her head.

Her eyes swept over his face, and over his god-like body, and she knew she had to have him. Every part of her was reacting to him and he had done nothing more than look at her. Desire engulfed her, and her mind raced with thoughts of what it would be like to be in his bed.

He stood up, folding his arms, breaking that magic moment in which the two of them had been bound. When he abruptly moved away, yanking that intimately shared moment, she felt as if her oxygen supply had been cut.

She suddenly missed that closeness. "You might be right," she managed to say.

"Is he a recent ex?" he asked, his voice louder, direct, returning to a more casual tone.

Was Dean a recent ex? The question wasn't an easy one to answer. Although they'd broken up before she'd gone to Hong Kong, since her return, twice he'd asked her to meet for drink and to talk about things, and twice she'd ended up in his bed. "Sort of," she replied, vaguely. She weighed up pouring her heart out to him, versus being coy and trying to win him over through the art of subtle flirtation. Though she didn't do subtle the way Savannah probably did.

Still, the bartender didn't need to know all the details.

"Sort of?" he asked, giving her a disbelieving grin.

"He dumped me over a year ago."

"Over a year ago, and he's still trying to worm his way back to you." The bartender looked at her, and she flinched, wondering what he was thinking. "A girl like you shouldn't have to go running back to a guy who dumped you," he said, making her smile.

He understood her, and right now she needed to be with someone who understood her. She sat up, taking notice. Liking the cornflower blue of his eyes, even in the lamp-lit golden light, those eyes were hard not to be drawn into. Like a spell, a hazy, lazy, hypnotic spell, he was reeling her in, and she was sure he had no idea of the effect he was having on her.

"I'm not so lucky when it comes to meeting good men," she told him, allowing herself to open up.

"Maybe you've been looking in the wrong place."

"Maybe."

"Another cocktail?"

Was he asking her because he was interested? Her heart rate sped up and she decided that Max and Briony could wait. She would stay here for a while longer.

"Same again, if you don't mind." She was about to say something flirty, and dirty, but decided against it and watched as he rustled up another cocktail. She examined him slowly, her eyes raking over his body. "Where did you learn these skills?"

He snorted. "Making cocktails is hardly rocket science."

"But, still," she pressed. "Is there a place you all go to learn? Like a school for mixologists?"

"Please do not ever call me that."

"You don't like being called a mixologist?" she asked, amused.

"No."

"It sounds more upscale than bartender."

"What do *you* do for a living?"

She fiddled around with the cocktail umbrella. "I'm a secretary." Most guys could handle that. If she told them she was in investment banker, they probably wouldn't believe her, and then they'd worry she earned more than them. She didn't want to risk scaring this guy off.

"A secretary," he said, slowly, almost as if he didn't believe her.

"Did you not have me down for a secretary?" she asked, curious, and afraid that his x-ray intuition might reveal her lie.

He shook his head. "I'm not sure. That's an expensive bag, high-end, as is that dress. And you obviously take good care of yourself. A PA to some big guy?"

She swallowed, and wondered if she'd got it wrong about him not being gay, since he had obviously noticed every detail about her wardrobe, grooming and accessories. But he had a sister, and maybe that was why he seemed more switched on.

Intrigued, she propped her elbow on the counter, and looked up at him through her lashes. "I don't believe we've been introduced. I'm Kay," she said, "Savannah's cousin."

He snorted with laughter. "I know. It's my business to know who everyone is the moment they set foot on the island."

She raised an eyebrow. He was chatting her up. He was interested.

"It's my job to know who most of the guests are. Four days, one island. It's easy enough to do."

Her hopes deflated as quickly as they'd risen.

"And, you are?"

"Luke."

"So, Luke," she said, sitting back. This time, she caught his gaze traveling south, and hoped he enjoyed the view, but quick as a flash his gaze moved back up to her face again. "How is it that Tobias Stone got you over here for his wedding?"

"Contacts," he said, sliding his sexy forearms across the top and clasping his hands together.

"Contacts." She nodded. "Tobias Stone is the guy to know."

"He is." He swept his hands through his hair, making her heart leap. His hair was long and floppy, long enough that when he ran his hands through it, the locks fell forward, and all she could do was focus on it. It was copper brown with streaks of auburn and for a fleeting moment she imagined her fingers raking through it.

"It's nice to meet you, Luke."

Her cell phone pinged again, and out of habit, she checked to see who it was.

Call me.

It was Dean again. She knew what this flurry of texts meant. He was probably feeling extra horny tonight, and she had no time for him. After all, he was back in New York, and the bartender, well, he was *here.*

"The ex, again?" Luke asked.

She nodded, and deleted the message, and then an idea flashed into her head.

"Would you mind taking a selfie with me?" she asked, "Just so that he can get the message."

A smile curved his lips slightly. "Sure."

She turned around on the stool with her back to him, and he leaned down over her shoulder as she held her cell phone at arm's length, and they positioned themselves.

His hot breath against her cheek was intoxicating. Freaking hell, this man was something else. She turned her face to the side, almost knocking their noses together. "Ready?" she asked, feeling drunk on his closeness.

"Ready," he said, resting his chin on her shoulder, making her heart fill up. God, he was delicious.

She took the picture, then another one for good measure.

He moved away, straightening up as he looked across the bar. "Excuse me," he said, "It's getting busy again." A group of people had suddenly gathered at the bar.

Speechless, still recovering from his touch, she examined the photo on her cell phone, her pulse racing, her insides in chaos. They looked so good together. Like a perfect couple.

Damn freaking good.

A smile settled on her lips. He had done nothing, yet he'd done everything, and he hadn't even touched her yet.

On an island full of men who were either too old, too confident, or too eager, someone perfect had suddenly appeared out of thin air, just like one of Xavier's magic tricks.

CHAPTER FIVE

I t had been a lazy morning. With the wedding over, a more relaxed vibe filled the air. The beach, as well as the pool area was practically empty, and breakfast was still being served even though it was past noon.

Kay had come down to the beach a short time ago, in a bright sunshine yellow bikini that she hoped was hard to miss. It wasn't long before Savannah found her.

"Eye-catching ensemble," Savannah commented.

"Thank you," she replied, moving her beach bag and hat out of the way to make way for Savannah on the enormous beach towel. "It's neon yellow. Like it?"

Savannah sat down. "Izzy's is bright green. You must both shop at the same place."

Kay made a face. "Hardly. This is designer swimwear."

Savannah rolled her eyes. "I'm sure it is, but it's hardly swimwear. It's no bigger than a few postage stamps. It's barely covering you up."

Kay shrugged. "My nun's habit is in for a wash."

Savannah shook her head, grinning. "You said you were

going to be good. This," she waved her hand at Kay, "looks like a mating call for every man within a one mile radius."

"Not true," Kay denied, putting on her best serious face. "Everyone's paired up, and there is nobody around. I'm reading, while trying to get a tan."

Savannah sat back, propping her arms behind her for support, and with her legs sprawled out in front. She looked cute, in her bikini and sarong. "Sleep well?" Kay asked mischievously.

"I slept very well." Savannah looked out towards the sea, completely ignoring the subtle dig.

"*Very well?*" Kay echoed, doubting Savannah's words. With it being Savannah's first night married, she was sure the newlyweds had spent the night doing anything but sleeping.

"Most people are still sleeping," remarked Savannah.

"It's pretty empty," Kay agreed, eyeing the bar area. A couple of bartenders were serving, but the hot one from last night was nowhere in sight.

"Tobias has arranged activities for everyone and there's a boat taking them over to the other side of the island."

"He has?" Kay frowned. It sounded like too much hard work. "What sort of activities?"

"Parachute-gliding, snorkeling. Come along. I've never done any of those things before. It'll be fun."

"Fun?" It sounded like anything but fun, and she was on vacation. "Are you going?"

"Of course. Jacob and Izzy have gone to the waterfall. Most of the guests are coming and it's going to be pretty quiet around here. Come with us."

It sounded like hell. "No thanks."

Savannah looked at her. "What else are you going to do?"

Enjoy the peace and quiet. Think about last night and the dreamy bartender. "I'm going to lie on the beach, sip a cocktail, and get a better tan."

Savannah stared at her suspiciously. "That's all?"

"Yes," she replied, noisily huffing out a breath and not wanting Savannah to get all wise and preachy with her just because she had a ring on her finger.

"Xavier isn't coming with us either," Savannah announced.

"And?" Not that same old warning again. She had learned her lesson with Tobias's brother, and she had so far managed to avoid running into him. "Why are you telling me?"

"Because most people are taking part in the activities, except for you and Xavier. I'd hate to leave you both to your own devices."

"Oh my god!" she snapped back, pushing her sunglasses up onto her head so that she could look at Savannah properly. "Do you think I'm a complete hussy?" She wouldn't touch that man if she was paid to.

"No, but it wouldn't do you any harm to go on a man-free diet for a while."

"A *man-free diet*?" She laughed. "Now there's a new fad I hadn't heard of."

"You don't have to be joined at the hip with a guy. You can have a good time being single, Kay." Savannah stood up.

"Okay," she said, sliding her sunglasses back down again and lying on her stomach. "A man-free diet. Sure. Why not? Now what?" she wailed, when Savannah walked in front of her.

"No texting, or sexting, or whatever you call it."

"Okay."

"No Dean, no Xavier."

She gave Savannah a military salute. "Understood."

Savannah bent down. "We're going to be on our honeymoon for a few weeks, and I don't want to come back and hear more sob stories about another meaningless encounter that you've had, or someone else breaking your heart. I'm looking out for you." She tapped Kay on the nose. "I'm not trying to be an ogre. I care about you."

"I know." Savannah had always looked out for her, and maybe taking some of Savannah's advice might do her some good. Maybe going on this man-free diet might be the thing she needed. "You're right. I know you're right. Go and have some fun, and we'll catch up later."

"Be good."

"Working on it."

She got back to her book, but the sun shining down and warming the backs of her legs and her body, made her feel drowsy, and the soft, fluffy towel beneath her helped encourage her laziness. She lowered her head and lay there, letting the sun kiss her skin softly.

It was heaven.

Peaceful and perfect.

Until she heard his voice.

"I only want one of you at the bar, the rest of you can go and chill for a while. It's going to be quiet around here this afternoon."

She lifted her head, and glanced over her shoulder to see Luke talking to one of his guys. He was topless, wearing nothing but swim shorts, and she let out a soft moan, watching him like a hawk, as he walked towards the ocean. She gazed longingly at the wide span of his back. Since he hadn't seen her, she was able to savor her examination of him, her gaze fixating on his glorious torso which tapered down to a perfect V at the hips.

"Freaking hell," she murmured, licking her lips at the sight.

She lay on her stomach, with a magazine in front of her, so that it looked as if she was reading, but the greater pleasure came from watching him in the water.

For a brief moment, she considered wading into the sea and joining him there, pretending to be surprised to see him there, out in the middle of the ocean. She might even have put this plan into practice if she had been a good swimmer, and didn't have a fear of riptides, and if she didn't mind getting her hair wet.

It wasn't going to happen, so she settled for watching him instead.

The water slowly swallowed him up, and then he began to swim, moving away out into the distance.

He was such a perfect embodiment of a man. Muscles in perfect proportion to his body; not too big and ugly, and not spindly thin. She shivered, wondering what it might be like to lie against him naked. Something warm tingled along her belly, all the way from the tops of her breasts to the tips of her toes, and Savannah's man-free diet died an instant death.

Nothing beat a swim in the ocean. Nothing.

It cleared his mind, helped him think. Gave his body a good workout. He could feel his heart beat racing and the dull ache in his arms as he waded out of the water after a long swim. He raked his hands through his hair, sweeping the long, wet locks away from his face.

At least this afternoon would be nice and quiet, the calm before the final partying and the last meal in the evening. Most people would be returning home tomorrow, and he and his employees soon after that. He couldn't wait to get back home, and return to his business.

Right now, he needed to take a shower, then grab brunch, and then he would take his time getting things ready for the evening.

He still had a few hours left to unwind.

Looking around at the almost deserted beach and pool areas, it was obvious that most of the guests had taken Tobias up on his offer of going snorkeling and paragliding. The place was like a ghost town.

Except for... he peered closer at the woman in a bright yellow bikini. Savannah's cousin lay on her back, wearing sunglasses, and little else. A buxom woman, she was hard to miss, especially in that tiny little bikini that barely covered her.

He looked straight ahead, not wanting to disturb her. With her shades on and her book resting on her stomach, face down, it looked as if she'd fallen asleep.

He walked past, eyeing her up, before looking away quickly. One look at her, lying like that, and he almost had an instant hard-on.

He swallowed, and let out a strangled breath.

After a cold shower, and dressed in denim shorts and a t-shirt, he returned to one of the tables around the pool area, this time with a bowl of fruit, a protein shake, his cell phone, and his notebook.

Swimming helped draw out the business ideas which had been marinating in his head. He also had a heap of things to deal with—mainly emails from work which he hoped to get to now. He started typing out a response to the most important email, before he was interrupted.

"That was quite some distance you swam." He looked up and into the eyes of Savannah's cousin.

"Yeah," he replied, agreeing, then scanning quickly at the half-finished email on his cell phone. "You should try it."

He noticed her hair was still dry, and she was shiny from all the sun tan lotion she had slathered all over her body.

She tipped her wide-brimmed sun hat up a tiny bit. "I don't like swimming in the sea. I was lying down, trying to get a tan."

"I noticed," he replied, putting his cell phone down. "You looked like you were sleeping and I didn't want to wake you." He picked up his spoon and started on his bowl of fruit, though Kay looked as if she was going to start a conversation.

"I wasn't sleeping."

"You looked like you were," he replied, trying hard to focus on his pineapple chunks so that he didn't have to look up at her. Her skimpy bikini left little to his imagination, and though he was usually good at setting a distance between a guest and his physical needs, the Monroe-esque deity standing before him was trying his sanity. "But I didn't want to disturb you."

"Mind if I join you?" she asked, obviously not taking the hint.

He did, but it would be rude to decline. "Go ahead." He moved his belongings to one side, and kissed goodbye to all that quiet time he'd been looking forward to. If she had been a complete stranger, if she hadn't been at this event, and especially if she wasn't the cousin of the bride, he would have thought nothing of taking her to his room and enjoying the rest of the afternoon. Judging by the bullets pointing out of her bikini top, and that look in her eyes, he had a read on her right now, and it told him that they both had the same idea in mind.

"You're a good swimmer."

"I love to swim. I don't always get a chance to back home."

"Your bartending hours don't allow for any down time?"

"It's a lot of late hours." He didn't even need to be at his bar for the amount of hours he was there for, but he liked being in the thick of things. It was the only way to see what worked and what didn't. "I guess you secretaries don't have that problem?"

"It's a regular nine to five for me." Her gaze shifted to his biceps. "I see you work out." He nodded and grinned, then looked down at his protein shake. She was subtly undressing him in her mind's eye as well.

"What do you like to do in your spare time?" he asked, moving the conversation to a safer topic. He couldn't go there; to the place where his mind was at right now. Somewhere in his bed, with her beneath him.

"Me?" she asked, flashing perfectly manicured nails at him as she ruffled her hair. "Work takes up most of it. Sometimes it gets really busy and I end up staying at work late."

"Seriously?" Secretaries worked that hard? Damn. He had no idea.

"Well, uh, you know what these banks are like. It's brutal."

"Brutal?" That was a strange choice of words. He'd never considered that secretarial work could be brutal.

"It's crazy. The corporate world never sleeps."

"I can see why you preferred to lie on the beach, and why you didn't take up the offer to go snorkeling."

"I work too hard to want to do any action adventure things on my time off. I like to take things slow and easy. Most times."

"I noticed."

She gave him the kind of smile that said many things. He knew, because not a day went by in his bar when an interested female customer didn't give him such a smile.

She was interested, but he didn't dare go there.

"What about you?" she asked. "What do you like to do on your time off?"

"I'm just a bartender," he said, guardedly. "I like to sleep a lot."

"Which bar?"

He knew the moment she asked that question, that she would show up at The Oasis, soon enough. Unless he gave her the name of one of his other places that he rarely visited.

But she seemed lonely, and in need of company, and he didn't want to behave like a total douche. Xavier had already done that to her.

"It's The Oasis."

"That rooftop terrace bar?" She sounded as if she'd heard of it. "Is that the place with a club in the basement?"

"It's called The Vault. Have you been?"

"With Savannah once or twice." She lifted her chin and looked up at him through her thick lashes. "Where do you mostly work?"

"At The Oasis."

"I'll have to check it out. Don't be surprised if you see me there in the next week or two."

"I won't be."

She was going to show up. He just knew it.

The flight back had been a bitch and she had a 7am meeting this morning with her boss. Theodore Remington was a slave driver in an Armani suit. But he was also giving her the important Pembroke deal to handle.

She had to get her act together and fast.

Two strong expressos, a breath freshening mint, and she'd be wide awake and fully alert.

"'Morning, Miss."

Damn that over-friendly concierge.

"Arnold," she mumbled, not even looking up to acknowledge him. She was too busy checking messages and emails on her cell phone.

"How was the wedding, Miss?"

"Beautiful." She quickly replied to a text message from one of the analysts in her team.

"Do you have any photos, Miss?"

"What?" She looked up. "No, I don't."

"Oh, really, Miss?" His face crumpled with disappointment.

"Really, Arnold." She eyed her wristwatch. Freaking

hell. She was already running late and needed to catch a cab in the next five minutes otherwise Remington would eat her alive.

Arnold stood in front of her. "But how did Miss Savannah look? And Jacob?"

"They looked good. Great. Wonderful." She hoped that a flurry of superlatives would get him off her back. She rushed out, her nerves jangled and her body still running on Fiji's time clock. Out on the street, she looked both ways on the street, in an attempt to catch a cab.

"I can call you a cab, Miss," said Arnold. He stood on the curb waving his arm at the cab which was coming down the street.

No sooner had it stopped, than she jumped in.

Damn it.

Issuing the address to the cab driver, she prayed for a traffic-free passage. With any luck, she'd make it there on time.

She was seven minutes late and by the time she raced towards his office, with her apology speech ready, Remington's PA told her that he was running late on his international conference call and would be with her in half an hour.

Drawing a breath, she felt her body loosen, felt the tension of this morning slide away.

It had been too much of a shock, waking up in New York on a dull, gray morning, far from the sun-kissed beaches of Kawaya. At least the morning had started well with Remington's conference call running over.

Later, when the meeting did take place, she managed to get through it in a wide awake and fully alert mode.

"I can handle the meetings with the client for the next few days," he offered as they walked back to their desks after the meeting. Her colleague, Geoffrey had been covering for her in her absence, but as the woman responsible for handling it all, she was eager to take the reins once more.

"Thanks, but I'll take it from here, thanks."

"If you insist. Let me know if it gets too much."

"I can handle it, Geoffrey."

"We know you can. I'm just suggesting, what with you just having come back."

She smiled at him and returned to her desk. Remington had charged on ahead, rushing to his next meeting. Kay never saw the guy eat, or sleep. This was how he rolled. He practically lived his life at the bank.

As for Geoffrey, she hadn't liked him much when he had joined a year ago, fresh out of Wharton with his MBA and his I'm-better-than-you attitude. She had been even more reluctant when Remington had put Geoffrey in charge of her work while she was away at the wedding. But, as she had discovered, her worries had been unfounded because he had done a great job. The client hadn't noticed that she had even been away, so she owed Geoffrey a couple of drinks at the end of the week.

The rest of the day turned out to be full-on hectic.

Ordinarily, it would have been a crazy day even if she hadn't been away for the wedding. But now, given that she'd been out of the office for almost a week, and was suffering from jet-lag, it was hard going. This, on top of the Pembroke deal, meant she couldn't afford to set a foot wrong.

"How did it go?" Her friend, Erin, swooped out of thin air and stood facing her. Kay looked up. "Well," she replied. "Considering how this morning started."

"I hate to tell you but you look like death."

"Thanks for lifting my spirits. I'm still jetlagged."

"Lunch later?" Erin asked, pointing her pencil at her. Lunch today wasn't going to work. Lunch anytime this week wasn't going to work. She had documents and presentations to review, and subsequent corrections and recommendations to make. All of a sudden a vision of her lying on the velvety sand on Kawaya flashed through her mind.

It was hell being back here. Hell, hell, hell. The cold, dull misery of New York in October fared badly against the sultry heat, sun and sand, and cocktails.

Talking of cocktails, she remembered the smokin' hot bartender.

Seeing him again would bring a smile back to her face.

"I want to hear all about the wedding," Erin hissed. "Let's go for a drink later."

Kay considered the offer. She wanted to go out but these next few days were crucial and she was mindful of Geoffrey's offer to handle meetings with the client for the next few days while she recovered from her vacation mode.

It was already tough trying to prove she was as capable as any man of doing this job. Working in a male-dominated environment, she had learned to handle the attention, and the dismissive comments, had learned to develop a thick skin and to take these things in her stride. More importantly, she'd learned to hide it when things hurt her.

With the passing of time, her skin was getting thicker, and she was able to withstand a lot more of the pressure, and the sometimes chauvinistic attitudes of her fellow colleagues. Not many things upset her anymore, and she had learned to give as good as she got. Over time, she had learned to deal with men who assumed that she was useless at her job, men who often joked that she had only been given the job because of the length of her skirt's hemline.

In that way, she surprised men. It was easy enough to see the shock on their faces. She was good at what she did, and soon kicked to the curb any hesitation others might have had about her ability to do the job, and survive in the tough world of investment banking.

It wasn't work she sucked at. Only matters of the heart.

"Today's out of the question," she said. "It's going to be a late night." She knew already that she would be having dinner at her desk, and then going over material with analysts and senior bankers. Sometimes these things could go on for hours. She wasn't going to get home before midnight most nights this week. "But Friday might be good. Plus, I need to catch up on my sleep."

"And I need to hear about that wedding."

"I promise to tell you as much as I can," said Kay, staring at her screen and trying to force her mind to focus. Post-vacation blues were a nightmare and the idea that Savannah was having the best time ever on that island—just her and Tobias, and no Jacob—made her more wistful.

"Can't you even show me a few photos from the wedding?"

"We weren't allowed to take any. Sorry."

"Friday, then," said Erin, and spun around on her heels and left.

By the time Friday came around, she was back to her normal self, and the jetlag had worn off. Her productivity levels were high again, and she had caught up on everything. She and Erin were able to leave work early.

They jumped into a cab and headed for the bar where Luke worked, though Kay kept quiet about him. She prayed he would be working at the bar tonight because seeing him would make the end of the working week that much sweeter.

"This better be good," Erin said. "What's this place called again?"

"The Oasis."

"I've heard of it," said Erin, and looked as if she was scrambling for details. "Does it have a club in the basement?"

"That's the one."

A short while later, they were sitting upstairs in the rooftop terrace of the bar. "This *is* cool," said Erin, glancing around the room. Kay agreed. It was. She'd been here once or twice before, with Savannah, but hadn't paid as much attention to the place back when she hadn't even met Luke. She looked around the room, hoping for a glimpse of Luke.

"Why do you keep looking around?" Erin asked. Her friend knew her well, so there was no point lying about it. "Wait," she said, grabbing her wrist and not giving her a chance to reply, "Did you arrange to meet someone here? Am I...am I your gooseberry?"

"No!" Kay replied, then shook her head for emphasis. "It's not a date exactly, it's just that one of the bartenders from the wedding works here."

"*That's* why we're here?" Erin's brows pushed together. "I knew it. Which one?" she craned her neck around the bar, scanning the clientele.

"It doesn't look like he's here," Kay replied, feeling the heavy weight of disappointment. Seeing Luke would have been her reward at the end of a tiring week.

"You had a holiday romance and you've said nothing to me until now?"

Kay turned around to set the record straight. "It wasn't a holiday romance, and there's nothing to tell—except for the wedding details which I'll get onto when we've ordered our drinks." She glanced over at the bar again, hoping that a miracle might have transported Luke to it.

"Why don't you ask one of the servers if he's working tonight?" Erin suggested, examining the drinks menu.

But she couldn't do that. It would smack of desperation. And what if Luke had a girlfriend now? Who was to say he'd been telling the truth on the island? She certainly hadn't been, even though she considered her secretary lie to be tiny in comparison.

When a server came over they ordered cocktails. Kay reined in the temptation to ask when Luke might next be in. Even if she wasn't fully able to strictly follow Savannah's man-free diet, she had to at least give it a try.

While they waited for their drinks, Kay told Erin as much as she could remember about the wedding. "You can't tell anyone. I'm sure people don't care, and it's no big deal, but Tobias is a nice guy, and believe it or not, I feel like I'm doing the dirty telling you."

"I won't tell a soul," replied Erin, with a degree of solemnity that looked fake. The server set down their cocktails and disappeared as discreetly as he'd appeared, leaving Kay to spill everything. She told Erin about the four day wedding extravaganza, and answered the many questions she had.

"Wow," was her friend's response at the end. "You lucky thing. You should have stayed out there for another week at least."

"The newlyweds are using the island for their honeymoon."

"I bet they christened every part of it."

"It's huge," Kay replied, recalling her days there. "It would be a heck of a lot of christening to do."

"She's a lucky woman, your cousin."

"I know."

"But still, it sounds awesome. I don't know how you managed to return to work and get on with things. I know you like to prove you're as good as the guys, but after what you've described. I'm amazed."

"The Pembroke deal is huge, and I'm lucky that he let me have a few days off at least. Plus, I don't want Geoffrey thinking I can't handle it. I have to prove myself every goddamn day."

"I wouldn't want to be in your shoes," said Erin, chewing her lip as if the problem were hers. "How come you're in charge of the Pembroke deal? It's huge." Then, as if she'd realized her mistake she quickly added, "I mean, it's about time, too. He's passed you over too many times."

Kay nodded in agreement. "Maybe he wants to give Geoffrey something big, but he knows I'll kick up a fuss if he bypasses me again. I can't mess this up." Geoffrey was a brown-noser, and Remington, for all his authoritarian sensibilities, seemed to like that.

"You won't," Erin said, reassuring her. "But this is going to eat into your life, as if the bank doesn't already own your soul."

"Tell me about it," Kay replied, sipping her cocktail and draining the glass. There was still no sign of Luke, and she was beginning to wonder if this was a waste of her time, being here, being hopeful.

"What's his brother like?"

"Whose brother?" she asked, looking around the room once more. And there he was. Those tattooed arms were hard to miss, and he was dressed in his usual, black pants and a black t-shirt. She only caught his side profile, because he was talking to somebody—an older woman. The two of them walked over to a table in the far corner, behind Erin, and sat down.

"His brother?" Erin asked. "What was he like?"

"Whose brother?" She forced herself to look at Erin and not let her gaze wander over her shoulder. Luke was in her line of vision. Easy to see, and easy for her to become distracted.

"You're not even listening to me," Erin wailed. "Tobias Stone's brother."

"Oh, him. He's nothing like Tobias Stone, that's for sure." Her gaze started to wander again, and if she wasn't careful, Erin would figure out that the object of her fantasies was sitting only a few tables away. She liked the advantage of looking at him, without him seeing her, and decided to keep the news to herself. The last thing she wanted was Erin to have an orgasmic shriek if she pointed him out to her.

"And?"

She forced herself to shift her gaze from Luke and the woman, and back to Erin. "And...there's nothing more to say. He's not as nice as Tobias. In my opinion, he's nothing but a womanizing douchebag."

"Did you meet him?"

There was no way she was going to own up to making out with him. "It was an island, Erin. I couldn't avoid running into him."

She glanced at Luke again, and couldn't help wondering about the woman he was with. Was she a friend, or a work colleague? And why was Luke sitting down at the table with her, with folders and a pen? Why wasn't he behind the bar? He was also dressed differently from the other bartenders; not for him the standard white shirts and bowties.

Maybe he was the head bartender, if there was such a thing.

She vaguely recalled Erin saying something to her. "Really?" she replied, turning her full attention back to her friend.

Erin set down her cocktail glass. "Who are you eyeballing?" she asked, before turning around to look. She turned back to her. "Who?"

"Nobody. Sorry. I'm really worn out, it's been a hard week. I'm just glad to be here, and not at work. I feel as if I spend more time there than at my own apartment." Then, "What's going on with you?" she asked, giving Erin her total attention. She listened on as her friend told her about the latest gossip in her department. Ordinarily, office gossip would have taken up her attention, but it was difficult to remain interested given the gorgeous hunk sitting several tables in front of her. Every so often, she would glance over at Luke, trying to decode his body language to see how friendly he was with the woman who sat beside him.

"Is that the time?" Erin gasped, looking surprised.

"Why? Are you rushing off?" Kay asked, incredulous. She had planned to spend the evening here. The last thing she needed was to be abandoned by her friend in a busy bar on a Friday night. How desperate would that look, especially since she would no longer have Erin's as a shield to hide behind?

"I'm supposed to be catching a movie with my roommate." Erin downed the rest of her cocktail in one and put her coat on.

"Ugh," wailed Kay. "I was hoping we could catch up."

"Not that you're in the talking mood much," her friend replied.

"Can't you stay for one more drink?" With Erin gone,

Luke would see her, and he would know how pathetic she was to have come here alone.

"Sorry. I was supposed to be at the theatre by 8. Shit, I'm late." She grabbed her handbag. "Have a good weekend. See you on Monday."

Feeling exceptionally exposed without the cover of her friend, Kay ordered a mocktail mojito, convincing herself that the absence of alcohol would help her stay resilient, should Luke come over and say hello. He looked to be deep in conversation with the woman, and given the evidence of the folder and pen, her hopes rose.

Maybe the woman was his boss? It didn't look as if she was his anything, other than work-related. For starters, the woman wasn't remotely fashionable, not with that plain-looking blouse, and dark hair that hung like limp lettuce from her head. And she appeared to be older than him.

The server delivered her virgin cocktail, and she sipped it slowly, becoming increasing conscious that she was alone, and the bar was getting noisier and busier with time. She sat back stretching her legs out under the table, her back sinking into the soft leather of the sofas, and tried to divert her attention away from Luke, and instead looked around the bar.

It was different here; understated gorgeousness, and a breath of fresh air from the usual contemporary looking bars that she was accustomed to. No slick mirrors or polished glass surface, and no shiny tiles. This place provided an exotic experience, with its snug sofas and lampshades. With the cushions and the heaters, it didn't feel as if it was Fall.

Then, she saw Luke's companion getting up. She got her things together and headed for the exit. Luke slowly got to his feet, and checked his cell phone while still standing at the table. Kay watched him, hoping he would sense that he was being watched and look up at her. Instead he glanced at his wristwatch then shoved his hand back into his trouser pocket and continued looking at his phone.

She sat up straight, lifting her body so that she was taller in her seat, but even though she was only a few tables away, he still didn't see her.

How could he miss a woman sitting alone at a table in a place full of people? Was she that invisible to most men?

Maybe that was her problem.

Maybe it was only the jerks and assholes that she attracted.

Instead, he made his way to the bar where he spoke to some of the guys there. Staring at his back, admiring, half-lusting over the span of his shoulders and his upper body, she swallowed. Here, in a normal setting, away from the island, from the sun and the sea, and the sand, he seemed twenty times more attractive to her.

Her heart sank when he then put on his jacket.

He was leaving?

She couldn't let him leave, not without him knowing she was here. As he headed towards the exit, she got up and rushed over to him, meeting him as he walked through the door. She tapped him on the shoulder, forcing him to turn around.

"Hey."

He tilted his head, as if not quite recognizing her at once.

"Luke, isn't it?" *Remember me?*

"Savannah's cousin?" he asked, slowly, angling his head. "Kay, right?

Oh my god, oh my god, oh my god. He did remember her.

The fact that he said her name, gave her some relief.

"Hi," she said, now feeling slightly self-conscious. "Fancy meeting you here."

"Fancy that." The corners of his lips quirked upwards.

"I wanted to check out your bar," she told him. As if she had only come here to admire the architecture and interiors. He wasn't stupid. "I came here with a friend from work."

"Great."

"It's a cool place, this."

"You like it?"

"It's different."

"How so?"

"Sitting here, I feel like I'm in an exotic place, not in New York."

"The owner would take that as a compliment."

"Be sure to pass it on."

"Will do."

She waited for a sign, for something, *anything*. Any sign to indicate that he might be interested in her. Her chest swelled with hope.

"I was curious to see where you worked."

"Yeah, well. This is me. This is the place where I work."

Now would have been his chance to show interest. He could have at least seemed a little enthusiastic at the fact that she had sought him out. He could have asked her why she was curious to see where he worked. In that way, they could have flirted and gotten things moving.

But she was getting nothing back from him. No signs, no interest, none of that flirtation from the island. She felt stupid.

"How come you dress differently from the other bartenders?" she asked, glad to have something not-quite-ridiculous to say.

"I'm in charge of the other bartenders."

"I assumed as much. You seemed busy earlier," she poked the question at him, "I wasn't sure if you were in a meeting or something, with that lady."

"You mean Marie?"

"Marie?"

"She's ... my ... manager."

"Your manager," she replied, sounding happier than was normal for such a reply.

"Yeah. She's a ... she's a great manager."

The conversation was stilted, and nothing like she had expected. On the island he had been so much friendlier, so different. It was as if there were two sides to him. "Good to see you again, Kay, but I need to go."

"Are you going already?" she asked, wondering what time he started his shift.

"It's been a long day."

"I was hoping to catch you behind the bar and ask if you could make that nice cocktail again."

His eyebrows pushed together, and she could tell that her desperate request hadn't exactly left him enamored. "The cocktail?" He'd forgotten already.

"The one you made for me at the wedding reception. The Slow Comfortable Screw Again—"

"Right," he said, cutting her short, making her feel even more stupid for taking up his time. "You want that?" He looked completely disenchanted with the idea. She knew then that she had made a huge mistake.

"You know what," she said, looking at her watch and feigning surprise. "It is late and I need to go." It wasn't late at all, but the conversation had died two minutes after she'd stopped Luke in his tracks, and it was only getting worse. Most guys wouldn't need so much cajoling, but this guy? He wasn't interested at all. Those moments on the island had passed. Whatever it was she thought she had felt, under the influence of pink champagne, and heady cocktails, under a starry sky, with powdery sand between her toes—those moments were gone. And she had been deluded. If he'd given her any time, it was because it was his job. He was a barman simply doing his job. She was completely deluded in trying to recapture the magic from the island.

Not only did he not look remotely excited about seeing her again, but he seemed to resent being asked to make her that cocktail.

He scratched his neck again. "Now that you're here, why not?" His demeanor changed in a flash and she assumed he felt sorry for her. She didn't like the idea of that, and it would have been different if he'd shown any interest when she'd first accosted him.

"Another time," she said, determined to leave quickly. "You seem busy, and I shouldn't have imposed."

His expression softened. "You're here now, and it won't take long. I could do with a drink myself."

CHAPTER SEVEN

He knew she was going to show up, and he'd been surprised she hadn't shown up within the first few days after returning from the wedding.

But, what the hell. It was Friday night.

He should have been annoyed, as he often was when a woman he'd met someplace else tracked him down and assumed he was interested in her. But once again, Kay elicited a touch of pity from him, more than his anger. She always seemed wanting.

"What do you want, boss? I'll get it for you." One of the bartenders asked him as he went behind the bar.

"A friend of mine just showed up," he said, reaching for a cocktail glass. He quickly fixed Kay's cocktail and grabbed a small bottle of lemonade for himself.

When he walked back to her table, she was on her cell phone.

"Your ex again?" he asked, grateful to have remembered something to strike up a conversation about. These kinds of meetings were awkward. Kay had come here because she was interested in seeing him, because she probably had something in mind. Women didn't just turn up, alone, to have a drink and admire the surroundings.

"No," she replied, hastily putting the phone away. "Thank you," she said, as he set the glass down in front of her, then sat across from her. "You're not having a cocktail?"

"No. Cheers." He lifted his bottle and touched her cocktail glass with it.

She took a sip. "This reminds me of the island."

"You like reliving memories, huh?"

She flashed him a flirtatious smile, her mascara'd eyes wide open and shiny. "It was an unforgettable wedding. I had a great time."

"It was work for me," he told her.

"You didn't enjoy yourself *at all*?"

He stared at her, knowing she was fishing for something. What did she want him to say? That he'd had a great time talking to her and that he wished they could take things further. He didn't wish for anything of the sort, but it was what she was probably hoping for.

It was the furthest thing from his mind. "It was work, and I had to deliver. You can't do a job for Tobias Stone and mess it up."

"No you can't. But you did great, and I presume he's very happy."

"He hasn't complained yet." And that was a good sign. Though right now, Tobias was most likely busy doing other things. Relaxing, he hoped. The guy didn't get much down time, and after what had happened to him in the past, it was good to see him having a turn for the better.

"I bet he and Savannah are sitting under the stars and making plans for the future."

"Or they're having a lot of sex," he quipped, getting straight to the heart of it.

She laughed. "That's my idea of heaven."

"Having a lot of sex?"

The color rose in her cheeks. "Sitting under the stars and talking."

Typical woman.

"Anyway," she said, holding up her cocktail glass. "What's in it?"

"It's a variation of a fresh orange juice and vodka and Southern Comfort liqueur and other stuff."

"A slow comfortable screw up against the wall," she repeated, not even blushing as she said the words. Didn't sound to him as if she was naming the cocktail either. This woman didn't bat an eyelid. She didn't hold back or do any of that subtle flirting shit. She was shameless and said it like it was, and he liked that. Though she was going to be hard to shake, and he hoped him having a drink with her—out of politeness, and because she was the cousin of Tobias Stone's new wife—didn't put any ideas in her head. He hoped this would be the last he saw of her, because he couldn't start anything with her, a short-term encounter, or one wild night in bed. While he could break his own self-imposed rules, and allow himself to become temporarily distracted by her, his brain gave him all the reasons not to indulge this eager woman's whims.

He was only being polite. After all, she'd come here with a colleague from work, as she'd said, then hopefully she would bring other PAs and secretaries next, and, maybe, their bosses. This was how word-of-mouth spread.

And he was only going to make small talk and have one drink with her.

"You came here with a friend?" he asked, not sure whether to believe her or not.

"Yes, I told you. I came with Erin." She blinked, then

frowned. "You think I came here alone, don't you?" She looked around the room. "Ask him," she said, pointing to one of the servers. "Ask him if you don't believe me." Something about his assumption had ticked her off.

"I believe you. It's no big deal," he said, not understanding why she was getting so riled up about the matter.

"I'm not that desperate that I'd come here alone, just to see you."

Okay.

"My friend and I wanted to come for a drink, and I thought I'd check out where you worked."

"Okay. I hear you." He lifted his bottle again. "Do you feel better now, now that you've explained?"

"Yes." She let out a sigh as she lifted the glass to her cherry red lips. He hadn't remembered her lips being so red before, and he guessed that she had touched up her lipstick while he'd gone to get the drinks. "She wanted me to tell her about the wedding, and then she left."

A long awkward pause followed, until she asked, "How long have you worked here?"

"A couple of years." He had started building his empire four, almost five years ago and now had a handful of bars, and a club. This place, The Oasis was the only one that had a club. The Vault, in the basement of the building, was an upscale establishment, and entry to it was by membership only.

"And how do you know Xavier?"

"Because he comes here a lot."

She didn't say anything, which was probably just as well, given that she didn't know how tight he and Xavier were. He knew more about Xavier's life than his friend knew about his, and as such, it was often the case that Xavier came to him for advice more than he needed to bother Xavier with his problems. This was how he liked things to be. Just the same way as he was happy for Kay to think he was a bartender. Sometimes girls figured out who he was much earlier, and that skewed the way they saw him. At least Kay seemed keen on him without knowing much about him.

"I wish I'd found this place sooner," she said. "It's given me that vacation vibe again."

"I'm glad you like it," he said, "And make sure you tell your friends."

"I will."

He took a final sip of his drink and threw her a cursory glance. She was conservatively dressed in a dark suit, she looked sharp, and slick. Professional. She looked so much more attractive in her work clothes, all covered up. It gave her a polished appearance, particularly with her breasts not falling out of her top.

He didn't have her down for being an average secretary. Maybe she was a PA to someone high up, because, looking at her handbag, tucked away against her hip on the sofa, he knew a bag like that was expensive. So was her watch, and her hair was done up nicely in a messy bun, not hanging all over her shoulders.

He had a pretty good eye for people, because it was his job to notice these tiny things. "It was good to see you again," he said, making the decision to leave. He'd done his bit. Showed her some attention, made her the cocktail, along with appropriate small talk. He could just as easily sit here talking to her all night, because the more time he spent with her, he realized she wasn't just a vacuous customer talking to him with the intention of enticing him into something.

Maybe she *had* come here with a friend, and was after a few cocktails and nothing more.

She seemed disappointed at his announcement. "It was good to see you."

"Yeah." He wasn't going to say anything else.

She paused, briefly. "I had a good time on the island."

He could tell that she was waiting for him to make a move, or say something. Let her know he was interested. Most women who sought him out here, did the same, but with Kay things were trickier because of her connection to Tobias Stone. He didn't want to rock any boats with the Stones, and he never mixed business with pleasure.

Her eyes met his, and he could tell that she was interested. She was waiting for him to say something, or do something.

But as tempting as she was, he wasn't willing to make that mistake.

CHAPTER EIGHT

The lying rat.

Anger bubbled under Kay's skin, as she craned her neck forward, re-reading the bio on the club's website.

Luke Hunter—that was his name—wasn't a bartender at all.

He was the multi-millionaire owner of several establishments in the city, and he was the son of a Texan oil baron.

Of course, she had also lied, by telling him that she was a secretary and not an investment banker, but it was hardly an *epic* lie.

She sat back, gazing at the photo on the screen, her anger rising to the surface as she wondered why he hadn't shown any interest in her when she had finally turned up at the place he worked, which she now knew to be the bar he owned.

Those same cool blue eyes stared back at her, except this time he wore a white shirt, rolled up at the cuffs, and his hair seemed longer, less copper colored and more blonde, as if he'd been on a surfing vacation. He had the whole-sun kissed thing going on, and she wondered where he'd caught the sun in that picture and who he'd been kissing.

Just looking at his face gave her palpitations. Luke Hunter was the kind of man that women noticed—most women, except for her. Freakin' hell. How had she managed to bypass him for Xavier on the island?

Her curiosity dug deep, and she now found herself wondering why he had lied. Who would lie about being a multi-millionaire?

But he ticked all of her boxes. All of them, and now her interest in him had quadrupled. The problem was, she had to figure out what his hold-up was. Most men liked that she didn't play too hard to get. This guy? He didn't seem to notice her. For all the signals she'd put out, she had received none back from him.

At least she now had a membership to The Vault. She'd paid a ridiculous yearly fee to join, and hoped it would be worth it. It had already proved its worth, thinking about it, because it had been then that she had snooped around the website and found the picture of Luke.

Being a member, she could get a group of her friends to come along. Geoffrey had expressed an interest, and because she owed him for taking care of things during her vacation, it seemed only right for her to ask him along.

And that was how, the following week, a night out at The Vault came to be. She had already made up her mind to go upstairs to The Oasis at some point during the night, in order to seek Luke out and confront him.

Tonight, she was determined to find out, but even as she had walked into the club, into his domain, and knew that she would run into him soon, she suddenly experienced an unfamiliar emotion. A tremor of hesitation slowed her down.

She didn't want to dance around, flirting and talking, and *hoping* he would ask her out, nor did she want a rejection thrown back in her face. She couldn't even talk to Savannah about it on her return from her honeymoon, because she was supposed to be on that man-free diet.

By 11 o'clock on Friday night, Kay had already spent two hours in The Vault. She let her hair down and went straight onto the dance floor, leaving Geoffrey at the table with a few of their colleagues.

She spent the night between bouts of sipping cocktails at their table and trying to make conversation despite the loud music, and dancing on one of the podiums with her colleagues. It was while she was taking a breather, and sipping her drink, that she saw Luke in the distance.

There was something about attraction, some subtle, invisible force that allowed her to pick him out from a group, even in dimmed lighting. She was able to locate him like a targeted heat seeking missile in a place heaving with people.

He was in his familiar black T-shirt and pants—his uniform, she assumed, now that she knew better—and he was talking to someone behind the bar. More than talking, he was laughing, and smiling with a pretty young waitress.

Jealousy pierced through her, and for a moment she froze, not knowing what to do, what to make of this or how to approach him. She wasn't even sure it was still a good idea to confront him about his obvious lie. He owed her nothing, and from the way he had been with her the last time, showing no interest, she was suddenly unsure again.

But he's in his working environment, she reasoned, knocking back another sip of her drink. It was a valid question to ask him. Not many people, in her opinion, would lie about being multi-millionaires.

Anger, fueled by his lie, gave her a devil-may-care attitude which bolstered her further. That, along with a pinch of recklessness that seemed fitting for a Friday night, made her get up in order to seek him out.

"Where are you going?" Geoffrey's shrill voice reached her ears as she stood up. He tried to grab her hand but she pulled hers away, disliking the overfamiliarity. "I've seen someone I know," she said, trying to shake off the cutting edge to her voice, trying to make it sound more blasé. She walked away, not even looking behind her, and her stomach did a peculiar turn as she saw Luke howl with laughter with the pretty little waitress.

"What can I get you?" the girl asked her.

Kay ignored her and looked at Luke, who stood on her side of the bar. "Hi," she said, and watched his brow wrinkle together for a split second. She suddenly feared that he wouldn't even be able to recall her name. The loud music didn't help.

"You found The Vault," he said, raising his voice so that she could hear.

"Yes."

When he said nothing else, she wondered if he even remembered her name.

"It's me, Kay. Savannah's cousin."

"I know who you are. My memory isn't that lousy."

"I brought more work colleagues along," she told him.

He glanced over his shoulder. "I see that. Thanks."

"I should be on commission," she offered, cheekily.

"Maybe you should."

"I applied for membership."

"It's the only way you get to come here."

"Or unless a member invites you," she reminded him.

"Or that." He smiled. "Someone's been reading our T's and C's."

"I read every page on your website."

"That's eagerness for you."

She was tempted to ask him now, about his hidden identity, but the music was loud, and it was busy. She leaned towards him. "I never expected it to be such an exclusive club."

"It works, for our clientele."

The whole conversation had been around nothing in particular. Nothing interesting. She was seriously beginning to wonder if he might be gay because she couldn't detect a single interested vibe coming from the guy.

And yet, looking at him, slowly set her pulse and heart beat racing. The music was loud in the background, and she had to listen carefully to catch everything he was saying, so she touched his arm, and shouted into his ear, not wanting to have that conversation here, or shout her way through the conversation.

"I need to ask you something. Mind if we move over there?" she asked, pointing to what looked like a hallway leading off from one side of the bar.

His puzzled frown didn't escape her, but he moved, and she followed.

"Is something wrong?"

"You lied," she said, hurling the accusation at him. Yet, saying those words out loud made her suddenly conscious about the ridiculousness of her confrontation.

"About what?"

"You're not a bartender. You own this place, and the bar upstairs."

"I own a lot of bars."

"As I've discovered." Damn. She sounded like a gold-digger, and this hadn't been the intent of her accusation.

He lifted his chin, looking defiant. His eyes, the color not as obvious now in the dim light of the hallway, blazed down at her. "Have you been snooping on me online?"

"I was getting membership for the club, and I was curious."

"What were you looking for?" he asked.

"Nothing," she replied. "But what I found was interesting."

"Like what?"

She would have given anything then for the gift of telepathy, to know what he was thinking. A shiver skated over her, and she wasn't sure if it was from a feeling of humiliation she was trying to downplay, or from the way his voice, low and husky, rolled through her, setting off balloons of wishful thinking inside her fickle head.

For she could be fickle, when it came to men, and she had enough self-awareness to know this about herself.

"Like your bio on the website, and the fact that you don't work here, you own the place."

"So I own the place. So what?" His I-don't-give-a-shit shrug left her feeling silly, because he was right. What difference did it make whether he was a bartender or the owner?

He most likely thought she was a gold-digger, and that was so not the case. "I was trying to see what type of club it was, since your membership isn't cheap." It was a desperate attempt to shift the conversation.

"This is an exclusive club . That exclusivity comes at a cost."

"I needed to know that this wasn't a shady BDSM place in disguise."

His brow creased, and he seemed to regard her with a look of amusement. She wanted to disappear beneath the floorboards.

"This is an above-board establishment. If you want that kink, you'll have to go elsewhere."

"I only want to have a good time."

"You want to live up to your nickname, what was it again?"

Heat rose to her cheeks, as their gazes locked. He was humiliating her, and he seemed to be thoroughly enjoying it. "I wish I hadn't told you."

"Don't be like that," he replied, with a smile. "You're a party girl, is what you said. Nothing wrong with that."

"What?" she asked, feeling slightly shy because of the way he was looking at her.

"Nothing." He gave a slight shake of his head. "You came here straight from work wearing that?" He jabbed his chin indicating her outfit.

She looked down and shook her head. "I changed in the washroom at work." No way could she have gone to work in this; a beaded halterneck top and pleated skirt made from shimmery fabric. It was stylish, and sexy, and she knew she looked damn good in it.

"Nice dress," he murmured. "It suits you."

She smiled. It was the first nice thing he'd said to her off the island. "Thank you." Usually, other guys would have made a move on her by now. With Luke? Nothing.

"You don't look so bad yourself," she said, and wished he would do or say something so that they could stop beating around things. She hated the chasing game, hated the will-he-won't he? Does-he-or-doesn't-he-like-me drama of romance.

"I'll take that compliment."

"You should," she said. "That's what it was."

He seemed to hesitate before answering. What was wrong with him? Everything he did, or said, was measured, and he never seemed to respond in the way she hoped. "It hasn't been an easy day," he said, finally, surprising her with his words.

"No?" she asked, her hopes rising that he had shared some slight part of himself with her. "Let me buy you a drink," she offered, "And you can tell me all about it."

She held her breath and waited for his answer, waited to see what this man, this Luke Hunter, the son of an oil billionaire, New York's number four, owner of bars and clubs, and the guy who ticked all the boxes, would say to that.

CHAPTER NINE

Should he let her buy him a drink he didn't need?

Luke resisted the urge to scrub his forehead, the way he often did when he was thinking a problem through. And as tempting as she looked in that bare-backed top of hers, he knew the sensible thing to do was to decline politely.

"That's not necessary," he said, trying to find a way to let her down gently. "I'm a grown-up, I can handle bad days."

"Sometimes it's nicer to talk things over. You helped me when I was on the island."

"I made you a cocktail."

"It helped."

The woman was persistent, if nothing else. The way she looked at him with those big, round eyes filled with longing, pure and simple, it reminded him of his mother. He would see her looking with that same yearning at his father. He had been fifteen years old when his father moved a pretty college intern into the family home. A month later, the dirty bastard moved her into the bedroom he shared with Luke's mother, and moved his mother to another room.

It was obvious what was going on. His poor mother had been powerless, and she could do nothing but stand by and helplessly watch. And accept. He had only been a teenager then, but that wistful look on his mother's face was one he never forgot.

Kay had the same look about her.

"Thanks, but no," he said, shaking himself out of that dark memory. As hard as it was, he had to decline.

"I'd better get back to my friends, before they start wondering where I've disappeared to."

"Enjoy the club," he told her. "You're right. You should be on commission." He couldn't help but give her the once-over again. She definitely looked so much more attractive in her sexy after-work outfit. So much more appealing than the short, skimpy dresses she'd worn on the island. He preferred subtle sexiness as opposed to in-your-face blatant nakedness.

"I'm happy to spread the word. We're having a great time."

"We?" He wasn't sure why he'd asked that.

"My friends, from work. Have you listened to anything I've said?"

"I've listened to everything you've said. I just wondered if you'd come with a boyfriend or something."

Her tongue flicked over her lower lip, as she seemed to weigh up her answer. "I don't have a boyfriend, remember?"

"That was then," he replied, slowly, giving her the once-over. "I can't imagine a woman like you staying single for too long." Later on, he would wonder why he had played the devil's advocate, why he had made that remark, knowing full well that it would only lead the way to temptation.

"Savannah has me on a man-free diet."

"A *man-free diet?*" He chuckled, because it sounded ridiculous. "What the hell is that?"

"Men are bad for me, apparently."

"Says who? Savannah?"

"Says me. She's always there to pick up the pieces."

He nodded, wading in deeper even though his brain was telling him to go home. He shoved his hands into the pockets of his trousers, and turned to the side, leaning against the wall, his gaze sweeping over her face again, drinking in her features, and wondering, once more what that full mouth would feel like on his.

She smiled, maybe because he couldn't help but stare at her, and her smile reached into every cell in his body. He returned the smile, and for a moment they basked in the possibility of what could be. Of where this night could end up, for right now they were at the crossroads of intention. Either he could leave now, as he had planned to earlier, or he could hang around a while, and see what unfolded.

"Do you always do what Savannah says?" The conversation was falling into dangerous territory.

"No."

He suddenly remembered her nickname, Good-Time-Kay. It told him everything he needed to know. Savannah obviously must have had good reason to put this gorgeous, voluptuous creature before him on a man-free diet.

"She thinks I might get back with Dean."

"Aaah, Dean. Why does that name keep coming up? Is it because he's irresistible?" *Or was it because she had no self-control?* It was a good thing she couldn't read his mind, because she blushed. It was the first time he'd ever seen her blush.

"He can be." She bit her lip, and looked down, embarrassment clear to see in her eyes. "And what about you? Still single?"

"Still."

"That makes two of us."

"It does," he agreed.

She looked up at him, all calm and unfazed, but the not-so-slow rise and fall of her chest told him otherwise. He could see himself taking her home, and …

He had to calm his shit, but the blood rushing south wasn't going to calm anything down.

"I'll see you around," she said, twiddling a lock of her hair in her finger, before turning on her heel and walking away.

Leaving him to admire that half-naked back of hers.

The heavy throbbing between her legs was a physical sign of the effect that Luke Hunter had on her. She was hot and sweaty, not because of the club, but because of *him*.

What had possessed her to tell him about the man-free diet, and then mention Dean? She was over him. Had no further interest in the guy, and yet she couldn't seem to keep him out of the conversation. Maybe at some sub-conscious level, she was looking to elicit some sort of response from Luke, even if it might be jealousy.

She returned to their table to find Geoffrey scowling. The club closed at 3am, and the way her friends were dancing, it didn't seem as if they were ready to leave anytime soon. Without saying a word to Geoffrey, she returned to the dance floor, and danced the rest of the night away.

One by one, her friends started to leave until it was just her and Erin. She was suddenly surprised when the DJ announced the last song, and after that, the music stopped.

Erin had found a group of people she knew, and went over to talk to them. Kay returned to their table and found, much to her dismay, that Geoffrey was obviously drunk now. He'd sat here the whole night, not even getting up once to dance. Looking ridiculously red in the face, as well as sweaty, he glared at her. She managed a half-smile, but didn't dare ask him what his problem was, sensing that his dour mood and drunken state might make him turn aggressive.

She got her things together, and waited for Erin. People started to make their way to the cloakroom to collect their belongings. Geoffrey got to his feet just as Erin came over.

"I'm going to catch a cab with my friends," said Erin, kissing her on the cheek to say goodbye. "We live near each other, it makes sense."

Shit.

"Can I squeeze in?" asked Kay, already feeling uncomfortable at the idea of being left alone with Geoffrey.

"It's a full cab," said Erin, making an apologetic face. "Just jump in with Geoffrey."

Easy for you to say, thought Kay. "See you on Monday."

"Catch a cab home together?" Geoffrey asked, placing his hand over her bare skin. She shivered, and moved away, turning around to face him.

"A cab?" she replied, her stomach lurching at the idea of spending a journey with him. "You go ahead," she told him. "I can make my own way back."

"Why?" he snarled, his tone sharp. "It's only the two of us, and Sunnyside is on my way home."

"No," she insisted, having no idea of where he lived, and startled that he knew where she lived.

He grabbed her bag, in an attempt to get her attention. "Why not?" he asked. "You spend all evening giving me the come on and you sit here, letting me buy you overpriced cocktails—"

His words winded her, and she blinked. She never, ever flirted with any of the guys from the office.

"We all paid for them in turn," she said, shocked by his pettiness. "Stop being such a petty little man."

"I fucking looked after your Pembroke account while you were away. It's the fucking least you could do for me."

His words smacked in her stomach. There were too many assumptions in his accusation, and she didn't want to ask him what exactly he expected from her, given that he was talking loudly, and people were starting to look their way.

"You were doing your job," she hissed. "You're drunk Geoffrey, go home."

"Everything okay here?" Luke asked, stepping forward and surprising her.

"Who's asking?" sneered Geoffrey.

"I am," replied Luke. "I suggest you listen to her and leave, or I could have my security men escort you out of the door."

"Go on big guy, do your fucking best."

"Geoffrey!" Kay was horrified by what he'd said. "Okay, let's get a cab. I'll get the cab with you now. Happy?" She didn't want a scene, and he was ugly drunk. Why had Erin left her to deal with this alone?

"You're not getting in a cab with him," Luke shot back at her. "He's drunk."

"You don't get to tell her what to do," sneered Geoffrey, poking his skinny little finger into Luke's chest.

"Don't touch me, pal," Luke warned, his face clouding over. "I'm calling you a cab, and I suggest you get in it."

"I can call my own cab, *pal*." Geoffrey shot back, just as two security men came over. He shrugged his arms, as a warning for them not to lay a finger on him.

"Just go home, Geoffrey. Please," Kay begged. Geoffrey could be a dick, and he was clearly going to be a bigger one now that he had his moment to shine. She turned to Luke, "It's not a problem, I'll get a cab back with him."

"I'll take care of this," said Luke, facing her as he stepped between her and Geoffrey, his tall frame completely obliterating Geoffrey from her view.

"I don't want any trouble," she said, looking up at him, and clearly aware of the potent buzz of electricity that had sparked in the two inches that were between his chest and hers.

He lowered his head. "The guy is drunk, and clearly an asshole. I don't think you should get a cab home with him to keep the peace."

He straightened up, and through gritted teeth said loudly, "Quit jabbing me in the back, dude, otherwise I'll have you thrown out." He turned around. "Get this gentleman a cab, will you?" Luke asked one of the security men.

Geoffrey stepped to the side, flashing her a look of pure contempt, before being dragged upstairs by the security men.

CHAPTER TEN

"Thank you," Kay said, for the third time since they had left the club.

Luke glanced at her from the driver's seat.

"You're on my way home. It's no big deal."

"I could have shared a cab with him."

"Seriously?" No way would he have allowed that. "The guy was drunk, and getting louder by the minute."

"He's harmless."

People behaved like morons, often, when they were drunk. "We see a lot of guys like him, at the end of the night."

"You have a built-in radar, do you?"

"It's a skill of the job." It became easy to read people, in the line of work that he was in.

"I imagine you see all sorts, more than you let on, *Mr. Bartender.*"

"Are you still sore about that?"

"No. I find it amusing."

He said nothing in response to that, then, "Who is he?"

"A guy from work."

He'd heard parts of the conversation between the two of them, and Luke was sure the guy wanted more than to share a cab home. His people would usually step in at that point, and try to defuse the situation, call separate cabs, if necessary. He didn't want any trouble in his establishments, even if his customers were in the process of leaving. Bad publicity could kill a business.

But he wasn't yet sure why he had stepped in, and why he had then offered to drive her home. Yes, Sunnyside, the area where she lived, was on his way, but he was so entrenched in his business rule of not getting involved with the clientele, that this situation now seemed at odds with his rules.

"He has a soft spot for you."

"Ew no!" She cried, bunching her face up in disgust. "Don't say that. It makes me want to throw up."

"You don't see it?"

"I prefer not to even think about it." She turned her face away and looked out of the car window. "He took care of a client deal for me while I was away and he thinks I owe him," she said after a while.

"A client deal? What type of client deals do they have you secretaries get involved with?"

"Uh...oh, just some hospitality stuff," she replied, turning to face him. Her eyes widened, exactly as if she'd been caught in a lie. "Dinner followed by theater stuff."

Dinner followed by theater stuff? She'd thrown a smart leather jacket over her dress, and looked sexy, and smart at the same time. But as nice and as appealing as she looked, he was not going to go there, he reminded himself. The only reason he was giving her a lift home was because he wanted to make sure she got home safely.

He parked up outside her apartment building.

"Thanks for taking me home," she said.

"Don't mention it."

"Would you like to come in?"

"It's way past three." It was beyond late. There was only one reason she was asking that question, and it wasn't because she wanted him to taste her coffee beans.

"It's Saturday tomorrow."

"Some of us have to work," he told her.

"You own the place! Surely you don't have to slave away behind the bar. Surely you don't even have to step foot in the place, unless you want to."

"I'm a workaholic. I practically live at the bar."

"Even workaholics needs to relax."

He could detect the suggestion in those words, and he weighed up the alternative. Her jacket gaped open, the beads on her dress glittering as they caught the light of the lamppost. He was open to having girlfriends, just that he preferred not to get involved with people from the bar, or friends, because he was never one to get deep, or open up. He didn't want or need that kind of vulnerability. Usually, he met women while he was doing the most normal of things; like going out to get groceries, or getting a haircut, or a sports massage. The relationship with the sports masseuse had been his most recent one, and it had soured, when she wanted to know more about him, when she wanted more than just sex. He cut her off, told her it wasn't working for him, and changed his sports masseuse.

Those were the types of women he allowed himself to get close to.

Kay was going to be complicated.

"Are you sure you don't want to come in?" she repeated.

He could drive away now, and let her down, and hope that she would eventually get the message, or, he could give her what she wanted, and to hell with his rules. "Come in for what, Kay?"

"I'm not asking for a date," she said, turning her body towards him and leaning back against the car door. He had turned the engine off, and it didn't seem to her as if that was the sign of a guy wanting to get home and go to bed. "I'm asking if you would like to come in. You've taken me home, and rescued me."

"Rescued you? Oh, right. The asshole."

"Like I said, he's an idiot."

"Perils of the job?"

"Huh?"

"You secretaries must get hit on all the time."

She laughed, more to hide the niggling feeling that he was onto her. She wanted to come clean, for there was no point in keeping up pretenses. He wasn't just a bartender, he was the goddamn king of the club. He wasn't going to be intimidated by her or what she did.

Not wanting to lie anymore, especially now that she had discovered his secret, she confessed. "I'm not a secretary."

"I had a feeling you weren't. Your turn to confess. What are you then?"

"An investment banker."

He nodded. "Why am I not surprised?"

"You're not?"

"You let a few things slip."

"Oh, really?" This surprised her because she thought she'd covered them up well. Obviously she hadn't.

"Why the lie?" he asked.

That was easy. She fanned her face and took her jacket

off because it was suddenly getting hot in the car. And it didn't seem as if he was willing to go to her apartment. She was happy to sit here and talk to him. "You told me you were a bartender. I was afraid that if I told you what I did, it might scare you off."

He chortled in surprise. "Scare me off? Seriously?"

"Some men can't handle it when a woman earns more than he does. Ask me how I know." As soon as she'd told him, she wished she could take the words back, for she had unwittingly let him know that she had been interested in him from the start.

"So you lied and dumbed yourself down?"

"It's not the first time," she told him.

"That's shocking."

"But true."

"Still shocking."

"And still true."

"You always have to have the last word?" he asked.

"I try to make it a point, because most times, men like to, and I can't have that."

"I bet you can't." He smiled, a proper smile, as if he'd suddenly given himself permission to relax. "Are you feeling hot?"

"It's getting hot in here."

"Then maybe I'll come in for a cold drink."

Her heart missed a beat. "You're feeling hot?"

"Looking at you, yes."

That was a move. For sure.

She smiled. "Let me cool you down."

CHAPTER ELEVEN

C ool him down?

She was going to do anything but that.

He had gone to her place out of curiosity, and because he had an idea of how the night would end.

He hadn't gone because he was dying from thirst.

He cast his eyes around the room. It was small but cozy, more lived in and homely than his sparse apartment with its minimalist décor and black and silver color scheme. "Cute place," he commented, watching her heading into what looked like the kitchen. His eyes lingered on her bare back as he followed her.

"Thanks," she said. "Would you like water, or something fizzy?"

"A glass of water, please."

"Drinking and dancing always makes me so thirsty." She poured a glass each and handed him one. She was smoke and mirrors, with that little white lie. Dumbing herself down and making out that she was a secretary, of all things. Yet he understood that, the need to pull back, and not reveal too much. Everyone wore masks and maybe she was more like him than he had at first thought. Maybe it went towards explaining why he seemed drawn to her, why he had offered to drive her home rather than get her a cab, even if her place was on the way home. He never went out of his way like that.

But she was obviously interested in him; maybe finding out who he was and how rich he was might have played a part in that.

He'd been with enough women by now to know that things like that mattered to some. Maybe it did to Kay.

"So thirsty," she exclaimed, emptying her glass and setting it down, her lips wet as she pressed them together. "Did you want something hot?" she asked, noticing that he hadn't taken a sip.

He set his glass down. "We both know I didn't come here for water." He tried to read her face, tried to guess what she might be thinking, and whether this was wise. It was one thing, sitting inside the confines of a car with darkness encroaching from the outside. It was an altogether different thing being here, in her kitchen, with the light on, staring at one another, wondering which one of them was going to make the first move.

"I don't know what you mean," she said, eyeing his lips.

"No?" he asked, stepping towards her and closing the gap between them. He was pretty sure she did, but given the situation, he liked to be 100% sure, even if she was looking at him with eyes shiny with lust. He wondered what those plump lips of hers might feel like against his. He traced his finger down her bare arm. "My apartment is only ten minutes away. I didn't need to come here to get a glass of water, and you didn't have to insist."

"That's true. I didn't. But I'm glad you came up,

anyway," she said, stroking her fingers along the lapel of his jacket. "We could talk."

"About what? The global economy?"

She blushed. "Let's ditch the conversation, then."

"And get straight to it?"

She angled her head. "You don't beat about the bush much, do you?"

"Time is of the essence." He traced his finger along her bare arm, looking into her eyes for signs that this was what she wanted.

"That feels good," she murmured.

"Cold?" he asked, as goosebumps sprang up everywhere he touched.

"Not cold."

He snaked his other arm around her waist and pulled her against him. She looked up, lifting her hands to his shoulders and he dropped a line of kisses along her neck. She moaned and slid her arms around his neck, pressing against him and sighing. She was so responsive, and so appreciative. With her there was no hint of playing-hard-to-get, no wasting time or chasing.

"Just excited?" he asked, letting his hand drop lower, before cupping her breast over her beaded top.

She shuddered in response, her eyes suddenly dark. Bedroom-eyes. She parted her lips, looking up at him, and he couldn't help himself. Dipping his head, he sealed her lips with his, his tongue sweeping into her sweet mouth, tasting, feeling, claiming. She clung to him, kissing him back, her fervor unleashing. Their dueling tongues playing out the frustration that had been kept in check for so long.

His hand lowered, tried to find an opening at the waist so that he could slid his hand under her top, but it was too tight for him to gain access. He needed to touch her; needed to feel her bare skin against his hands.

"You move fast," she gasped between breaths, while he fumbled with the halter tie at the back.

"I can go slow if you want," he replied, his fingers stilling as he pressed his hardness against her.

"I wasn't complaining."

He kissed her again, loving the feel of her full lips against his, loving the feel of her full curves against him. But he still couldn't untie the damned bow. "Did you double knot this?" he asked, his hunger for her making his body pulsate.

"I didn't want it to come undone in the club." She lifted her hands, but he spun her around, eager to do it himself.

His eyes dropped to her bare back, and he pushed her hair to one side before dropping a smattering of kisses all over her bare skin. "You are unbelievably sexy," he bit out, desperate to untie the bow and have her naked.

His fingers clutched at the double-knot and unraveled it. He tugged her top down, his hands skittering over her stomach, then moving up to cup her bare breasts.

Fuck.

She was luscious, and soft, and beautiful. His hands held her firm, pebbled breasts, and his boner turned to steel. He kissed her neck as if he would never get another chance to again, and rolled her nipples between his fingers and thumbs; knowing that they'd moved on from mere acquaintances to something more, into the realm of dark and dirty.

He couldn't breathe, not now, with his hands and lips all over her, zapping the oxygen from his body. She was sheer, overwhelming sexiness, and he toyed with her, taking pleasure and giving pleasure back. The silence between them was broken only by the fast rise and fall of her chest and her throaty moans; the kind of moans that would soon lead to better things. He pressed against her again, desperation driving him. "I need to fuck you, Kay. Do you want me to fuck you?"

"Yes," she begged.

He wanted her no matter the connection to the Stone brothers. For once, business and pleasure *would* mix because, goddamnit, this woman knew exactly what she wanted, and he had every intention of giving it to her.

But, even in the thick haze of arousal, his brain still functioned. "I don't do romance, Kay, or should I call you Good-time-Kay?"

He felt her flinch, and knew he'd messed up.

"You jerk," she answered back, her voice quaking with indignation.

His hands stilled on her breasts. He hadn't been thinking properly. How could he, at a time like this? "Sorry. I'm sorry." He dropped a kiss on her shoulder. "I didn't mean that."

She straightened her back, and for a moment he thought she was going to tell him to go to hell. He dropped another kiss on her shoulder, and another, and another, and slowly, his fingers pinched her nipples gently.

"Don't ever call me that again."

"If you promise never to call me a mixologist again."

She snorted. "Deal."

But he was determined she understood exactly what this was. "I'm not looking for romance, Kay," he murmured, sliding his hands down to her waist, as his lips pressed against her shoulder.

"And I've already told you," she murmured, shakily. "I

don't have time for romance, so we don't have a problem, do we?"

"What do you want?"

"Whatever you're willing to give."

She could say this to him now, in this moment, when she was topless and his hands were all over her? She seemed to have temperament of a man when it came to love and sex, and it was perfectly fine with him because the last thing he needed was a whingy, whiny woman looking for love.

He turned her around, his eyes falling to her breasts, sending a signal straight to his manhood. He swallowed, resting his hand against the small of her back, pulling her towards him. A flicker of surprise flashed in her eyes.

"I want no baggage, no headache, no commitment," he told her.

"Okay."

"Okay?" he asked, surprised. She hadn't batted an eyelid.

"I get it. I understand. I don't have time for romance either, so you don't have to wor—"

He kissed her again, not letting her finish. Kissed her more passionately, this time, his mouth hard against hers, his body pressed just as hard against her. She moaned against his mouth, the lusty sound a signal to his animal instincts.

He needed to fuck her.

She wasn't so different from him, and she didn't seem to be looking for any ties. Nothing permanent. This *could* work. It could be a one off encounter, maybe more, depending on how tonight played out.

When he pulled away, her lips were wet and swollen, her mouth slightly open.

"Freakin' hell," she gasped. "I haven't been kissed like

that in a while. You can kiss me all night long, if you're going to kiss me like that."

"I want to do more than just kiss you," he rasped, turning her around, so that her bottom sunk into him again, and her back was against his chest.

She giggled. He slid his hand under her skirt and shoved it into her panties, surprising her with his speed. She gasped when his fingers sank into her silky wetness.

Fuck. She was soaking wet.

"You're ready for me," he husked, sliding a finger in, and then another. She jerked against him. "Oh, yes," she cried out, as he rubbed her clit. She bit out another dirty groan. "Please," she begged.

"Please what?"

"Please..." she huffed out, almost falling back against him.

"Please what?" His fingers stilled.

"Please fuck me."

"If you insist." He moved his hand away and bent her over the table, intoxicated by her arousal.

"This is a new one, even for me," she giggled, when he lifted her skirt up and bunched it around her waist. His raging boner stripped his mind of all rational thought, and he stopped to admire the sight before him. And to catch his breath.

A strip of a black thong separated her butt cheeks.

"Shit," he groaned, his hard-on intensifying as his hands skated over her satin-soft bare cheeks. Blood roared in his ears.

"You've seen all of me," she murmured, resting on her forearms as she turned her face to the side, not fully able to look at him.

"And it's a beautiful sight," he growled, appreciatively.

"It's not fair."

"Are you complaining?" he asked, leaning over her and bending down so that his mouth was inches from her lips.

"I'm not complaining at all," she said. He planted another kiss on her lips because it was impossible to get that close and not kiss her. "You know what I want," she said, when he pulled away. "It's the same thing you want."

"What's that?" he asked, unzipping his pants, and freeing himself from his boxers.

"To have you inside me."

She was going to be the death of him. He was already on the verge of getting blue balls if he didn't fuck her soon. He pulled down her thong, and admired the view.

"Are you sure you don't want to take this into the bedroom?" she asked.

No way. The bedroom implied intimacy and comfort, and he much preferred this. Fast and dirty. "You said this was a first for you. Are you uncomfortable? I can get you a cushion." He'd seen a few on her couches.

"I can get used to it. It is a first for me. Is it a first for you?"

"No." But he didn't care to give her a further explanation. Avoiding the bed as much as he did when having sex, meant he'd christened most of the furniture in an average home.

"Don't forget the condom."

He never did. He'd already split open the foil packet.

"I won't. I'm careful." He slid it on, then positioned himself at her entrance. She gasped out aloud, sounding out a low, appreciative moan as he started to tunnel in. Grabbing her hips, he thrust in slowly, inch by inch, letting her body take in the size of him. She was so wet as he slid in, his body jolted because she felt so good. She had her forearms down, with her forehead resting on her hands. Undecipherable sounds came from her lips, groans more like, syncing with his thrusting.

He moved faster and faster, her arms now stretching forward so that her fingers gripped the edge of the table.

Her moans encouraged him. Not that he needed any encouraging, but he had almost forgotten how good this was. It had been a while since he'd fucked anyone, and months since he'd been with the sports masseuse.

Kay was a beautiful, welcome relief. She was soft, and slick as he slapped into her, pounding her again and again, each thrust making the kitchen table wobble.

"Harder!" she gasped, making the kinds of animal sounds he loved to hear. He complied, grabbing her hips as if they were a life buoy in a raging sea. Heat and adrenaline coursed through him as he buried deep inside her, then pulled out, and did it over and over and over again.

As much as he wanted to, he couldn't drag it out, because the sight of her naked bottom, and the sound of her moans took him over the edge. His stamina was low, and just like that, after a few hard thrusts, he was done. He grunted as he came, taking the weight of his body onto his arms as he collapsed over her back.

She moaned with disappointment as he pulled away, her face resting on her hands, and her ass still high in the air. "Didn't you...?" he asked, knowing the answer even as he asked the question.

"No."

Hell. He prided himself on pleasing women. "Sorry." He zipped up his pants, guilt washing over him. "I don't know what happened." Except that he did. Weeks of pent-up frustration, and months since he'd last had sex. And this woman was beyond sexy. Somehow she had managed to touch him in a way nobody had. Not since he'd had his heart broken. "Can I use your bathroom?"

"Yes." She sounded pissed off as she lifted her head. He was tempted to run his hands over her tight, pert bottom again, but it didn't seem the thing to do. Not now that he hadn't satisfied her. Beside, all that touchy-feely stuff would imply a level of intimacy that he wasn't comfortable with.

"It's down the hallway." She straightened up, pulling her thong up and turning her back to him as she did up her halter tie.

She hadn't even looked at him once.

CHAPTER TWELVE

S he felt used. He'd gotten his payoff, and left her feeling empty. Cheated of hers.

She'd told him she was fine with this. But *this* wasn't what she'd envisioned when she'd said she wasn't interested in having a relationship.

But this had happened too fast.

She wasn't used to it.

Not that she was crying wolf.

It wasn't as if he'd *made* her.

No.

She had *wanted* this.

But sexual satisfaction at the end would have made her feel he cared about her.

Not *this*.

There had been nothing in it for her apart from the initial excitement of him stroking her bare buttocks, and the few brief seconds of foreplay while his fingers had given her cheap thrills.

But that had been it.

He didn't care about her. He hadn't taken his time or

been gentle and loving. Could she blame him when she had told him that this was all she'd wanted? She was saying one thing, and feeling another. But it didn't take away from the fact that she felt like that tissue he'd used to clean up a few moments ago; good for one thing, then crumpled up and discarded.

The bathroom door opened and she quickly smoothed down her hair, then stepped out into the living room, putting on a brave face as if it were her battle gear. Awkwardness stretched out into the next few moments, and she wasn't sure what to say to him.

He cleared his throat, and she saw his car keys in his hand. They looked at one another for a few seconds, and she found herself unable to speak. Her throat was parched, the moisture drying up and making her swallow. She now found herself in a situation that was alien even to her, and she'd been in plenty of scenarios that had only lasted one night.

"It's late. I should go," he said finally.

She nodded, trying to work out what to say, how to be, what to do. With the others, things had never been this awkward, but this was different. Luke was different. He was unreachable, almost. He'd used her, and now he was set to go. The others, they had stayed around. Some had stayed the night and stayed for breakfast, some had stayed for an hour or so. It hadn't only been sex. But this was exactly how it felt to her, with this man. He seemed to be in a rush to leave. With him there was no conversation, no finding out about him, no discussion. No lying in bed, no holding one another.

"I didn't think it would be like this," she blurted out, unable to hold back.

"Like what?" he asked, not even blinking.

He had to be freaking kidding her. The sex had been one-sided, and now he was leaving? "So fast."

"I told you," he said, slowly, his knuckles tightening as he gripped the car keys. "I don't do all that romancing stuff. I don't stay the night, if that's what you were expecting."

That wasn't quite it. He didn't seem to understand. He hadn't even made her come. Folding her arms, she rubbed the sides, suddenly feeling cold, unwanted and used. "Maybe you should get a call-girl."

"Why the hell would you say that?" His forehead puckered into ugly little ripples. "Are you going to make a thing of this? I told you upfront, I don't do romance or relationships. I warned you."

He had. Numerous times. She'd been the one who hadn't heeded it. But she wasn't going to let him get away with it so easily. "There was nothing in it for me."

She heard his audible sigh. Of irritation, it sounded like. "I'm sorry," he ground out. "I—didn't realize. It won't happen again."

Again?

Staring at him, standing across from her, still looking so handsome, she suddenly felt a twinge of regret that she'd called him out on it. This man was everything she could ever want in a boyfriend; rich and handsome, and enough of an enigma to make her curious. There was more than a hint of trouble beneath that beautiful façade. Unlike Dean, Luke was a closed book, and she, being a greedy reader, wasn't about to let him slip through her fingers until she got to the end.

She bit her lower lip, staring back silently, as she tried to hold herself together. His scent clung to her needy skin, imprinting itself on her body. "Unless you want it to," he said, as an afterthought, or perhaps because he could read her mind. Perhaps because he knew of the effect he had on women. "The sex, I mean. It depends on you, on whether you want to get together again...or not." She didn't know how to answer that, so she said nothing as he walked up to her. Sliding his hands back into his trousers, he looked down at her, and even though they weren't standing too close, she could feel the heat from his body—an electric buzz, something sharp and potent rolled off him and electrified the nerve endings inside her.

"But, you're right," he continued, "It shouldn't have happened like that. I shouldn't have been so greedy. It's not my fault I couldn't control myself because you're so goddamn sexy."

Freaking hell. He was saying all the right things. A charmer, like Xavier, almost, but better. In her books he was better, and sexier. He was perfection, if a little damaged, and hard-to-fathom, and she was a mass of contradictions trying to fight the feelings his words evoked. She swallowed, as arousal stirred deep inside her. Suddenly, she wanted more of him; his fingers, his mouth and his cock, against her, and inside her. "Great," she said, managing to say something. "Blame me, why don't you?"

His brows pushed together, making her focus on the vertical line between them. "It's a compliment. It's been a while since I ...fucked." His words slapped into her, but she somehow managed to stay upright.

Fucked?

Technically, that described what they'd done, but to hear him say it just sounded so demeaning.

Walk away.

Whispered warnings from her gut rose up. As beautiful as he was, as sexy and as gorgeous as he seemed on the outside, Luke Hunter was going to bring a level of mass of complication into her life, if she let him. She didn't need this.

But she ignored her gut instinct. "You have a real way of making a woman feel special."

"I have rules, Kay, and I hinted at them before we fucked."

She winced, hearing him say the word again. "Can you..." she hesitated, not liking the way he threw that word around. "Can you stop saying that? I get it. I *get* that you're making a big deal about not *making love* to me. I get that it's just *fucking* to you."

"It's not to you?" he asked, his eyes serious.

"That's all it is to me, too, but I don't need you to keep going on about it."

"Good, because that's all I can offer. Besides, you made out that you could handle it, otherwise I would never have agreed to come to your apartment."

"I *can* handle it. Don't you worry about that. You and I aren't so different in that respect."

"There are things I don't do," he said, gazing at her intently.

"Go on." She tilted her chin up, letting him know she could take anything he threw at her.

"I don't stay the night, and I won't treat you like my girlfriend, or partner, or lover."

She chuckled, because it sounded so ridiculous. "Did some past girlfriend leave you broken hearted?" she asked, trying to make sense of his constraints.

"I don't waste my time thinking about crap like that. I don't want romance or the emotional fuckery that comes with it."

"How about making me come? Is that also not allowed?"

His lips clamped shut, while tight muscles flexed on

either side of his jaw. "I don't care for the other stuff," she continued, loving the idea that she'd hit him where it hurt, "but an occasional orgasm or two would be good."

"I'll see what I can do, next time."

"Surprise me," she said, as she watched him walk towards the door.

"'Bye." He glanced over his shoulder, then left.

She felt as if she'd just made a pact with the devil. None of her previous encounters had ever required this type of discussion. Could she change him? Fix him, even? For it was clear that this man had issues. As perfect as he looked on paper, there were still things about him that she wasn't sure of.

Maybe she could slowly cajole him into being the type of man she wanted.

The question was, would it be worth it?

The next few weeks flew by and she found herself wrapped up in a heavy workload, sometimes staying at the office until the early hours of the morning and taking the company cab home. On those nights she fell into bed around 2 to 3 am, and would then wake up, and go to work for another grueling day all over again.

Since that night at the club when he'd had to be escorted out by security, she hadn't spoken to Geoffrey much, apart from when it came to work related questions. Sometimes she had sensed that he was going to say something, about that incident, but he never did, and she didn't push it.

Savannah arrived back from her honeymoon soon after and arranged a night out for the two of them to catch up. Kay found herself looking forward to seeing her cousin, but Savannah's suggestion to meet at The Oasis caught her by surprise. All of a sudden, it seemed as if the bar she most wanted to avoid, was most people's favorite haunt.

"Why don't I come over to your place?" she suggested, curious to know why Savannah, who was hardly the type to go out, now wanted to.

"We've just come back from our honeymoon," said Savannah, "and I'm still on vacation mode. Let's go to The Oasis. Besides, Tobias is meeting me there later on."

Damn. That wasn't going to work. "But what about Jacob?" she pressed, eager to avoid The Oasis, and by association, Luke.

"He's got a sleepover at Lenny's tonight. I hardly ever go out, so you should make the most of this opportunity. How come you don't want to go out?"

"I've been working some crazy hours," she said, her gut twisting at the idea of seeing Luke again. He evoked emotions in her that she didn't fully understand. Recalling that night, and what had passed between them both disgusted and excited her. She hadn't called Luke since, not that he was on speed dial on her phone, but she knew how to get a hold of him, and had chosen not to. "But if you want to meet there, we could go."

He hadn't called her either, but each time she thought of that night with him, her body reacted. It could barely be called a night. Rough and feral, it hadn't been a gentle or loving encounter. Yet heat stirred and coiled around inside her, and if she lingered on those memories too long, she was left in a semi-state of arousal.

By not going to that place, she was hoping to wean herself off of him. She was fully aware that she had ignored Savannah's sage advice regarding men, and that it was her fault entirely for being in this predicament in the first place. She had chosen Luke and what he offered—spontaneous and exciting sex—and there were obviously bound to be consequences for making this choice. If she wanted an easier life, she knew what she *ought* do—walk away—but she couldn't. She didn't want to. She could handle what they had.

And so it was she met with Savannah at The Oasis; they'd met outside at the same time, Kay getting out of a cab, while Savannah climbed out of a chauffeured car.

At first glance, Kay marveled at the change in her cousin. This was what a person in love looked like. Savannah's eyes sparkled, her skin was iridescent, and her sun-kissed hair framed her face. She looked beautiful.

Kay suddenly felt conscious of herself.

"I still feel as if I'm on my honeymoon," said Savannah, sinking into the oversized cushions. Their booth, near a window with red drapes, overlooked the rooftop which was busy, and full of tables. There were plenty of heaters around to keep the cold out, but sitting inside, with the amber colored table lamps sparkling like warm jewels, was so much cozier.

Savannah looked more than well, Kay decided. She looked to be glowing, and it wasn't the light from the lamps which was giving her that warm light.

They'd both ordered drinks. She'd settled for a glass of wine, while Savannah had asked for a virgin mocktail. "You look freakin' amazing, Sav. You'll be telling me you're pregnant next," she offered, hiding behind a drinks menu, and hoping that she wouldn't see Luke tonight. Her cousin wasn't one to drink much, but the virgin mocktail hadn't gone unnoticed by her, and the glow had to come from something.

"Before I think about another baby, I want to make sure Jacob's okay."

"Why, what's happened to him?"

"Nothing. Nothing much. Izzy and Xavier did a great job of keeping an eye on him."

"You left *them* to look after him?" Her eyes widened with disbelief. "*Xavier?*" she repeated, unable to comprehend how Savannah could have been so irresponsible.

"Not just him, but Izzy, and my parents. Xavier wanted to help out."

Her brain scrambled for reasons as to why he would have. "Are they an item?" It wouldn't surprise her. Xavier Stone could get lucky with a brick if it had a pulse. The horny little shit.

"No." Savannah laughed as if it was the most ridiculous suggestion. "They couldn't be more different. My parents had Jacob most of the time, but Izzy would come over at weekends, and I think Xavier wanted to help out. Jacob likes him, and I want him to have more male role models in his life. You know how bad Colt was."

"And you think Xavier would be a better role model?"

Savannah sipped her drink through a straw. "He's misunderstood. He's not such a bad guy. But he's off limits to you, all the same."

"As if I had any intention of getting involved with him," she cried indignantly, wanting to put that ghost to rest. She had no plans to get close to Xavier Stone even if she lived to be one hundred.

"How's the man-free diet going?" Savannah examined her face closely. "You would tell me, wouldn't you? If you veered off course?"

Kay put down her glass. "Do I look as if I have time for a man?"

"Good evening, Ladies."

She didn't need to look up to know that he was standing right next to her, so close that she could detect that electric buzz that passed between them. So close that she had no doubt he'd heard what she'd said.

"Luke!" said Savannah, rising to her feet with a smile.

"You're back," he exclaimed. "And you're looking great." She felt a sharp stab of jealousy hearing Luke pay a compliment to another woman. They hugged and exchanged cheek kisses, while Kay remained seated and suffered in silence, feeling even more awkward when he completely ignored her. She hadn't been prepared for this—to see him and have him ignore her.

Savannah remained standing while they continued their conversation, laughing and reminiscing over the wedding, making small talk as she stared into her glass feeling completely left out.

"You know Luke, don't you, Kay?" Savannah asked, pointedly. "He was at the wedding." Kay begrudgingly looked up at him.

"We've met."

"Hello," he said, smiling. "Can I get you ladies another round of drinks?"

"I'll have another one of the same," said Savannah, pointing to her half-empty glass.

"I'm fine," Kay told him. The expression in those cornflower blues eyes seemed cool, almost distant. He seemed to be handling this unexpected meeting better than she was.

"I'll be back with the drinks," he told Savannah and then left, prompting Savannah to comment on how nice he was, and what a wonderful job he'd done at the wedding.

"Your wedding was a fairytale come true," mused Kay. "You're so lucky, Sav."

"I am, aren't I?" Savannah blushed. "It feels so big-headed to agree, but I feel so blessed. After Colt, I couldn't see myself wanting to be with anyone ever again."

"And you hit the jackpot." She hadn't intended for that to sound bitter, but it did. Savannah's brows pushed together, and she frowned. "It just happened, Kay. I wasn't looking for it, and I didn't have any expectations."

"I know," Kay replied, flashing a smile in an effort to over-compensate.

"Playing hard to get wouldn't hurt."

"What are you trying to say?"

"That if you didn't give in so easily to a bit of attention—"

"I don't give in that easily."

"There's no need to get so defensive. I'm just offering advice. If you don't focus on looking for a relationship, you might find it."

"What's *it*?"

"Love."

"Who's looking for love?"

"Do you want to be Good-Time-Kay for ever?"

She huffed out an angry breath, not liking the way even her cousin was perceiving her. "That nickname was because I liked to party. I'd go out and have fun. It didn't necessarily mean I ended up making out with everyone." She wasn't that kind of woman. Not entirely. She didn't readily jump into every man's bed.

"I'm sorry," said Savannah, reaching out and tugging at her sleeve. "I hate seeing you get hurt all the time. I just meant that if you *do* meet someone, then playing hard to get might not be such a bad thing. You give too much of yourself, too soon."

"I'm going to lower my expectations, and be more like

you." Her mouth fell open as she understood how that must have sounded. "I didn't mean—"

"I know." Savannah smiled. "I know what you meant. I had this life plan all worked out, and it was only ever me and Jacob in it." She placed a hand over her stomach and sat back. "And now, I have so much more to be thankful for. Somedays it still seems like a dream."

"Rub some of that magic love potion on me," Kay begged, half-joking.

"Here, you go, ladies."

Shit on a fiddlestick.

He'd heard.

His cornflower blue eyes seemed to see right through her, touching her deep within, making her feel and think things she had never done before. As intense as his gaze was she couldn't look away.

"A virgin mocktail, and a cocktail for you," he said, putting down two cocktail glasses.

"But I'm not drinking cocktails—" She started to say.

"Sorry. My mistake."

"It was."

His eyebrows pushed together, as if he wasn't quite sure what she was alluding to. "Then I'll get you something else," he said, with a smile, "only, you seemed to like it the last time."

Her mind battled to figure out if it was innuendo, or if he was talking about the cocktail. She lifted the glass and examined it. It was the same one he'd made for her on the island. The one he always made for her. "They should rename it to Kitchen Table," she said, dryly.

Savannah seemed pre-occupied with her cell phone, and appeared not to have heard.

"I like it," said Luke. "A Slow Comfortable Screw Against The Kitchen Table."

She wasn't sure if he was intentionally trying to humiliate her, and as such, she didn't know whether to slap him or throw the cocktail at his face. "It wouldn't be *against*, it would be *over*," she retorted, and then cringed at her pathetic comeback.

"You're right," he said, nodding, his eyes dancing with amusement.

"What are you two talking about?" asked Savannah, putting away her phone.

"Nothing," Kay replied, feeling flustered. He seemed to always leave her in some sort of negative state, flustered, or empty, or just unsettled.

He was like a storm barreling into her life, and leaving just as fast, after he had wreaked havoc with her mind and body.

CHAPTER THIRTEEN

He'd assumed she would appreciate the cocktail, but apparently Kay was still pissed off with him.

Post-coital disappointment seemed to linger around her. Yes, he had been greedy, and yes, he had failed to satisfy her, but seriously? Did she need to hold the grudge for this long?

She and Savannah looked to be deep in conversation. Twice he'd gone up to their table and twice he'd caught the tail end of their conversation. It had been worth it, though, to see the look of embarrassment on Kay's face.

He could see right through her. Women were easy enough to read, in his experience, and, despite what Kay said, she was a romantic.

They all were.

And this was the problem.

Even his mother had been a complete romantic, right up until the end, clinging to futile hope even when his father hadn't been interested.

Kay, for all her brash talk, for all her insistence that she could handle the type of relationship he offered—one based purely on physical needs—was not as tough as she tried to make out.

She wanted a connection, first and foremost, and then, love. Women did.

He'd had no intention of calling her after that last time, even though before he had left her, he had implied there might be a next time. The more he thought about it, the more he didn't like the way he seemed drawn towards her. For that reason, it seemed better to cut off with her completely.

They'd fucked, and that was it.

He was over it.

Except that she had turned up in his bar tonight, and damn it if the sight of her in her smart working clothes didn't turn him on. He didn't understand the interest, couldn't even pin it down to him having been celibate for a few months prior. Maybe a tiny fraction of it had been pity. He'd felt sorry for her, alone at the bar, the same way he felt sorry for her when she'd turned up here, her scent of desperation, combined with her curves, making for a tempting combination.

And now that he'd had a taste of her, now that she was back here again, now that he remembered her words, and her claim that he'd left her unsatisfied, well, he needed to make it up to her.

So he spent the next hour half in conversation with some guests at the bar, and half in keeping an eye on Kay.

Now that she was here, he wasn't going to let this opportunity pass him by.

He watched her kiss Savannah, and get her things together. Then he watched her leave. Calm as anything, he strode over to her, meeting her just as she pressed the elevator button to go down.

"You're leaving already?" he asked.

"Yes." Her expression registered a sliver of surprise, but the ding of the elevator made her turn her head. She schooled her expression as the doors slid open, but he pressed the button to close them.

"What are you doing?" she asked, her voice sharp. "I was waiting for that."

"I need to talk to you."

She looked at him. "About?" Those full lips tempting him.

"You're still mad at me."

"No I'm not."

He didn't believe her. "You barely said hello," he challenged.

"That mattered to you?"

"Not too much."

Yes.

Maybe.

He sucked in a breath, then leaned forward, his lips almost touching her earlobe. "I knew you couldn't handle it," he whispered, up close to her ear.

"I *can* handle it," she insisted. "I work with men who are bigger dicks than you."

Her verbal slap hit him hard and prompted a quick comeback. "*Have* bigger dicks, or *are*?"

She let out a strangled gasp of exasperation, clearly annoyed by his blatantly wrong interpretation. "Are you sure you don't have a twin? Because this is not the guy I met at the island," she shot back, clearly pissed at him.

It wasn't the first time he'd heard a woman say that. Something happened to him, when he couldn't handle intimacy. He couldn't help but be a jerk. It was why he had his stipulations, why he wanted things to be a certain way. It was why he didn't want a relationship long-term. He could do nice and friendly, be a good listener, a friend even, but if things went deeper, he couldn't deal with it.

"There's only one of me."

"Just so that we're clear," she said, suddenly standing an inch taller, "I can *handle* it. I work with men who think that because they're men, and because I'm a woman, that I can't handle surviving in a man's world. I can. And I've been doing just fine. "

"What does your work have to do with this? With you and me?" He found himself admiring her neat little up do, and wondered whether he would get a chance to take it out later, and see her hair fall around her shoulders.

She crossed her arms, her brown eyes cold as she glowered at him. "I'm not hurt and I'm not mad at you."

He still didn't believe her. "Even about me fucking you over the kitchen table?" He asked calmly.

She didn't flinch that time. Didn't even bat an eyelid. He swallowed, his eyes falling to her lips, and making him wonder if he could see her tonight. He'd be sure to give her an orgasm or two to make up for the shortfall last time.

"When you fucked me over my table," she said, her red matte lipstick outlining her lips, giving him ideas. She took a step towards him, her temperament suddenly changing. Where just a moment ago she had been surprised to see him, she seemed to have overcome that quickly. "I can handle your rules, and your arrangement. You don't do romance, and you don't want emotional baggage. You don't have to keep reminding me, and the fact that you do makes me wonder if you're the one who's having second thoughts. Maybe *you* can't handle it, as for me, I really don't have the time for all that...*fuckery,* as you say." She rubbed her fingers together, as if she was flicking some imaginary dust from them.

Most women didn't talk back like this, most women were just glad he had showed an interest in them at all, and he had assumed, wrongly now that he was getting to know her, that Kay would be the same. But here she was, twisting his balls, telling her he'd treated her like a piece of meat, and that the experience had done nothing for her. More than that, she was turning him on, throwing back at him the crap he threw at her. He suddenly had the urge to take her in to his office and do unspeakable things with her. Things she would enjoy. Of that much he was sure.

"We're on the same page then," he managed to say, marveling at the way this woman had managed to give him an erection by just talking. It wasn't even dirty talk.

"In case you're in any doubt," she said, chewing her bottom lip and running a perfectly manicured fingernail over his lapel again. "I like sex as much as any man, it's the being treated like a piece of meat part that I have an objection too."

"I heard you the first time," he said, clearing his throat.

"Maybe what you need," she said, grinding her words out slowly. "Is a call girl. One of those high-class escorts, the ones who offer massages with extras. I've heard there are places for men with money, if you don't want to get caught in a strip-joint."

This was not the whimpering, whiny wreck of a woman he had first met. If she'd been like that, he could have given her another pity-fuck, and be done with her. Instead, she seemed to have the upper hand, and he didn't like that.

A part of him still wondered if it was her bravado talking. Sometimes women put on an act because they liked to manipulate the situation. He still wasn't sure what to make of her, and despite her bravado, her saying she could handle the way things were between then, he knew that most women weren't okay with it.

Maybe there was a truth to what she'd said. She probably had balls because she needed them to survive in the line of work she was in, but when it came to matters of the heart, women were soft, and he was sure Kay was no different. In fact, he had yet to meet a woman whose heart was made out of stone. There was only one woman who'd had that title, and it was the bitch he had later discovered was his father's mistress.

"You're not a piece of meat," he said, reaching for her hand and rubbing his thumb over it gently. His other hand slid to the small of her back, and he tugged her towards him, a stirring in his briefs causing his brain to short-circuit. There was something about a woman with red lipstick implying that she had no problem using him just for sex. She was going to give him another boner and all without even touching him. The urge to kiss her overrode his thinking, and he wanted to taste her sweet mouth again. He wanted to lead her into his office and take her on his desk; pleasure her with his tongue first, because women always loved that shit.

"It won't happen again," he said, moving closer but fighting the desire to claim her mouth. His lips were a few millimeters from hers, giving her an out. "If you don't want any of this, I understand."

"I never said I didn't want any of this," she replied. He turned her wrist over and lowered his mouth to it, inhaling orange blossom and jasmine. She didn't flinch, or retract her hand, and so he dropped a kiss there, then another, further up, and another.

Taking her silence as a sign of her acceptance, he lifted

his mouth to hers and claimed it. Her lips parted and he kissed her, softly at first, then, when he felt her hands snake up behind his back, he drove the kiss deeper. She was soft, and warm, and she had forgiven him. Looking into her eyes he saw softness again, and relieved, he buried his face in her neck, inhaling, and breathing in her scent, her essence, her everything.

She moaned, and pressed against him, making him hard again. This was what she wanted, what most women wanted, and he gave it to her. Slow, sensual get-ready-to-fuck kissing, with his hands sliding gently over the fabric of her work suit.

He pressed against her, until she broke the kiss.

"Now that we're clear," she said, moving towards the elevator again. "Let me know when I can pencil you in. Not tonight. I'm busy."

The elevator dinged its arrival, and she got in, then disappeared, leaving him annoyed, and as horny as hell.

She might as well have poured a bucket of ice over his dick.

CHAPTER FOURTEEN

Savannah's advice had worked.

It had actually, truly, definitely worked.

Who knew?

It had given her courage when she had been sooooo tempted to give into Luke that day. She'd been ready to go to his place or hers. Whichever was the nearest. He had kissed her long and deep, and pressed his body against hers, making it obvious as to what he wanted.

Ordinarily, she would have given in. She would have easily succumbed to a man whose need for her was so great that it intoxicated her.

Ordinarily.

But she had heeded Savannah's advice well. The playing-hard-to-get part, if not the man-free diet advice, and it had worked. She was determined to do more of it.

Walking away from Luke that day had been tough, because his need for her had been unexpected. She had no idea how she had managed to walk away and go home.

She had somehow also managed to go through the next

few weeks without calling him. But he hadn't called her either.

Luckily for her, work kept her busy. She didn't have time to think about Luke. So when Erin suggested going to The Oasis one evening after work, with a group of friends from the Legal department, she tagged along, even though she didn't know Erin's friends that well.

The Oasis was quickly becoming a Friday night go-to place for after work drinks.

She had been at the office since 6.30am, and had managed to complete a milestone in the Pembroke deal. Remington—he'd been in the office from the start of the day—told her to go home and enjoy the weekend.

So she did.

Returning to the familiar bar made her slightly anxious again. She caught sight of Luke a few tables away, talking to a table full of flirting women. Seeing him all dressed in his familiar black, looking too-damn handsome for words, made her insides flutter like falling autumn leaves.

She observed him unknowingly. He had a gorgeous side profile, and big, beautiful inked biceps. He walked over to the same old table in the far corner and sat down, then looked through his folder, occasionally checking his cell phone from time to time.

He must have sensed her staring because he looked up and smiled at her. She couldn't help but return the smile.

There was a danger that tonight, if he so willed it, she wouldn't be able to walk away. He had wanted her that day near the elevator, and he would want her now. All she had to do was agree. Any guilt she had about not following any of Savannah's advice, immediately disintegrated as she knew it would. She had never intended to follow it through, for she had needs, as a woman, and this man, even with his rules and stipulations, ignited a fire in her that nobody had ever been able to. Not even Dean, and he was someone she had fallen in love with.

She got up and walked over to him, not caring what Erin and her friends made of it.

"Hello, stranger," she said, smoothing her hand down her pencil skirt. "Mind if I sit down?"

"Go ahead." He closed his folder, eyeing her with an amused expression. "Long time no see, no hear."

"I've been busy."

"I gathered. Is that a business meeting?" he asked, nodding at the table she had vacated.

"Does it look like it?" Erin and the girls had a table littered with cocktails. It was happy hour, and there wasn't a business folder or pen in sight.

"You've been avoiding this place," he asserted.

"Maybe."

"You left me hanging, that last time."

The twinkle in his eyes made her heart stop for a second. Was there a hint of flirtation in that sentence? "Maybe."

"And now you're here again, turning up when I least expect it."

She smiled sweetly.

"I can't figure you out," he said, tapping his fingers on the table a few times.

"I could say the same for you."

"We're not so different, after all," he said. "Sit down," he motioned to the seat next to him. "I don't bite."

She did as he asked, but left a good-sized gap between them.

He lifted his eyebrow at the gap. "I promise you, I don't bite. Not unless you want me to." He patted the empty area, and with a roll of her eyes, she moved closer, but still left a few inches between them.

"So, what brings you here tonight?" he asked.

She waved her hand towards the table she had vacated. "My friend Erin suggested we come here."

"It wasn't because you needed to see me?"

"No."

"You sure about that?"

"Yes." The heat of his stare was making her cheeks turn pink.

"Because," he whispered into her ear, leaning in so close that she could smell his cologne, "sometimes when you turn up, I start getting ideas."

"Ideas?" she asked, moving her head away so that she could get a read on his expression. "What sort of ideas?" She blinked and made out as if she had no idea what he was talking about.

"I can't tell whether you're in or out with regards to our arrangement. We seem to talk about it more than we *do* anything."

"And we both know you're a do-er, rather than a talker."

He gave her a devilish smile. "Exactly."

But it was true. They hadn't signed anything, hadn't discussed anything, apart from his freaking rules. Her showing up at the bar wouldn't have meant anything, but her coming up to him as she had done just now might signal intent. She could see why he was thinking what he was, and now that she was in close proximity to him again, that same buzz, the pull of that familiar connection between them, heightened things further.

She wasn't sitting here having a *conversation* with Luke, as much as she was having an *experience*. The neurons in her brain fired off, putting all sorts of visuals in her brain. He was intoxicating, and as she breathed in his scent, felt goosebumps crawling along her skin, and the familiar throbbing between her legs, she knew it was impossible to walk away this time. Being around Luke was like falling into a raging torrent and getting carried away. She was powerless to stop herself, to save herself and knew that it would not end well.

He was not like the others, not even like Dean who had managed to reel her back a couple of times, much to her detriment.

And sensing things, knowing the warning in her gut, she wouldn't have stopped now even if she could, because she hadn't yet had her fill of this man.

"So," he said, shifting a little closer to her. "Are you in, or are you out?"

She wrinkled her nose up, considering his offer, and surprised also, by his forwardness. "I'll need to think about it." But right now, she was hungry. She looked around for a menu, because there were none on his table. "Does this place do food?"

"Of course, but it's mainly finger food. Canapes and that type of food."

That type of food wasn't going to fill the hole in her stomach. She was starving. "Do you want to get dinner?" she asked. "I haven't eaten all day."

"I'm not hungry."

"I was at the office at six this morning and I didn't even have lunch." It had been another long day in a week of long days, and it was beginning to take its toll. "I had a chocolate bar, on the go, and three cups of coffee," she continued, knowing that something was wrong, but not understanding what.

"That's not healthy."

"I know. Erin keeps telling me I need to get some fruit snacks, or some seeds, and nuts." She sat back, wondering. "So, what about dinner?" she asked. A painful silence followed and it made her wonder. "Or is that one of your rules?"

"I'm not hungry."

"But I *am*." She didn't understand his stubbornness. Probing deeper, wanting to test him and his boundaries, she made a suggestion. "We could grab something quick. I'll need the energy, especially if we're getting together later on," she said, in her best seductive voice.

"Why don't you go get something and come back?"

Huh? "Are you allergic to food?"

"No. Like I said, I'm not hungry."

"Then at least come along and watch me eat."

When he didn't give her an answer, and stared at her as if she'd asked him to go looking for apartments together, she decided enough was enough.

Anger twisted in her gut. What was she doing with this man where even the idea of going out for dinner made him seethe? Usually, men freaked out about the big decisions, about going steady, about making big life plans.

Not about getting something to eat.

Walking away now would be the wisest, sanest thing to do. Heaven help the woman who ever got involved with Luke Hunter emotionally. She was lucky in that she hadn't, that what they'd had was just sex.

"It's only dinner. Just freaking dinner. I'm not asking for long-term commitment."

"I told you to not have any expectations."

Screw you.

She got up.

"You're leaving?" he asked, sounding surprised.

"You expect me to stay?"

CHAPTER FIFTEEN

He wasn't going to chase after her just because she'd had a hissy fit over dinner. Not *over* dinner, but because he didn't *want* dinner.

Seriously?

Women were too goddamn emotional. She wanted a cozy dinner for two, and next she'd want to be staying the night. That wasn't what he wanted.

It was exactly what *dinner* led to.

Expectations.

Crazy expectations.

He had tried to be transparent with her, let her know what being with him meant, and what it didn't mean. It was a hookup, pure and simple.

Why couldn't she get her head around that?

He got up and was about to head towards his office when he saw Xavier set foot into the bar. Approaching him with a smile, he greeted his friend, relieved to have normal male company for a change and grabbed a table just by the bar.

"Do you have an update on your little project?" he

asked Xavier, curious to know how things were working out in that department.

"I haven't had any pussy, if that's what you're asking."

"No?" he asked, surprised. "I would have expected the two of you to have become better acquainted by now."

Xavier made a face. "No fat fucking chance. But, she's coming around."

Coming around? Luke wondered if this was the case, or the way Xavier saw things. Izzy seemed to have way more sense than the usual airheads Xavier attracted, and it wouldn't have surprised him if she'd told Xavier to get lost. Surely the guy would know when to back off? "She is?"

"She'll be caving in soon enough, though," Xavier replied, with his usual sense of smugness.

"Isn't she a student or something?" he asked. They didn't even mix in the same social circles.

"She is, but she's doing some work for me on the side now," Xavier announced proudly.

"Seriously?" Luke couldn't believe his ears. Izzy was working for Xavier? The guy's tactics blew him away at times. He was a real smooth hand when it came to the art of charming women. "How the hell did you manage that? Wasn't she working for Savannah and looking after her son?"

"She's not doing so much of that right now, so she's got time, and I offered her some work."

This was a new development. He could see how clever Xavier had been. Not content to sniff around Tobias and Savannah's place, in the hopes of seeing Izzy, he'd given her some work just to get to spend some time with her. "Are you sure she even likes you?"

"What's not to like?"

He wasn't going to go there. "Are you sure you even like

her that much?" he asked, opting for another angle. "Because I've seen you meet someone for the first time, and then walk away with her less than thirty minutes later. I've seen you do that, here, with my own eyes. And if you haven't even gotten to first base after what, six, maybe eight weeks? I don't think you stand any chance. Maybe it's not so much that she's not into you," he said, phrasing his words carefully, "but maybe your heart isn't in it. Just face it, pal. You're not her type. You might even be too old for her."

Xavier flipped his middle finger at him. "I'm twenty-fucking-seven. I'm in my prime, and I'm making progress, and that's all you need to know."

"Fine. As long as you know what you're doing, and it isn't illegal."

"It isn't," Xavier snapped.

"Good." Luke hoped for Izzy's sake it wasn't.

"Savannah's cousin was here. You remember her, don't you? Kay?" Xavier asked, completely changing the subject.

Luke's insides hardened, and he wasn't sure why the idea of Xavier talking about Kay bothered him. "Yeah, I remember her."

"I think she's pissed off with me."

"Pissed off with you?" Why would this idiot think Kay was pissed off with him? He knew exactly why she was pissed off and Xavier had nothing to do with it.

"She wasn't too friendly when I ran into her downstairs. Didn't want to talk to me."

"Do you blame her?" Luke asked. "The two of you didn't seem to be getting on too well at the wedding." But he was curious to hear Xavier's take on things.

"She's pissed I never called her."

Called her? What the fuck would Xavier be calling Kay for? Luke's stomach hardened like cement. "*Were* you supposed to call her?" he asked, casually reaching out and grabbing two beers for them. He needed something, *anything*, to show he was calm about the bullshit Xavier was spouting.

"I mean, we're practically family now, but even if we weren't, they expect you to, don't they?" returned Xavier. Luke shrugged, his muscles tensing as he forced himself to remain quiet.

"Except, you wouldn't call, would you—Mr. Ice-Cold and Doesn't-Give-A-Fuck?" That title, the first time he'd ever heard Xavier call him that, described him to a tee. He had learned to control his emotions, had learned not to give too many fucks, but this was Kay that Xavier was talking about and, for reasons he couldn't yet work out, it was impossible for him to not be bothered by Xavier's commentary. "Are you going to call her?" he asked, gripping his bottle with more force than necessary. He needed to know whether Xavier had any designs on Kay. They weren't strictly family, and if Xavier thought he stood half a chance with her, he'd go for it. Luke knew what the guy could be like.

Xavier shook his head. "She's not my type."

Luke released his grip on the beer bottle, and a slow exhale followed. "I didn't think Izzy was your type either, but that hasn't stopped you from pursuing her."

Xavier seemed to be thinking about it but didn't give anything away.

"I've said it before, and I'll say it again," Luke told him, "you don't have anything to prove."

"We have a love-hate thing going," Xavier insisted, before breaking out into a mischievous smile. "It's always the prelude to better things."

"Love-hate?" Luke chortled. "It's been *hate-hate* each

time I've heard from you." It was odd how different Xavier saw things. The same could be said of him and Kay. She had only suggested that they have dinner. She hadn't expected a proposal, nor a declaration of love, just goddamn dinner, and he'd behaved like a total dumbass over it. He'd treated her in a shitty way.

He sat with Xavier for a while longer, showing a polite interest in his friend's plans for winning Izzy over, but he soon excused himself and returned to his office.

He hadn't liked it—Xavier talking about Kay. He hadn't liked it one bit. Picking up his phone, he decided to call her, but his finger stayed poised over the *CALL* button. If he called her now, if he sought her out, and apologized, then suggested dinner, what would happen? What signal would that give her? It might give her ideas, make her think he was malleable. Did he need the added complication?

No.

He wanted no baggage, no headache and no emotional connection.

But an image of Xavier's smiling face flashed in front of him. If Xavier didn't get anywhere with Izzy, the guy might be tempted to get it on with Kay. Luke's gut twisted. The fuck he was going to risk that happening.

He called Kay, but she didn't answer. He was about to text her, but he didn't know what to say. If she'd picked up the phone, he could have made a joke about being hungry. A text was different. It was out *there*, and irretrievable. Not only that, but nuances could change the way she interpreted the message.

He had a better idea. Slipping the phone back into his pocket, he snatched his keys from the desk and walked out of his office. He would turn up at her door. He got into the elevator with good intentions but by the time it reached the ground floor, he had changed his mind again.

Going to her place now would mean something, and he didn't want *anything* to mean *something*.

Him turning up now would make her think he cared enough about her to want to change his rules and no woman was worth doing that for.

That wasn't how he operated.

That wasn't what he wanted.

Nobody would ever understand his position, which was why he kept his private life private, and his love life as vague as possible.

He threaded a hand through his hair. He was reacting hastily, instead of taking a step back and assessing things in a calm and level-headed manner like he always did.

Xavier had fucked with his head with all that talk of Kay, and that stupid bet, and he'd made Luke think he might not be able to keep his dick away from Kay.

If it came to that, he'd deal with it.

Which begged the question, if Kay was just a hookup then why the hell did he get so riled up about thinking of her with Xavier?

He ground his jaw. This was bullshit. Good-Time-Kay wasn't going to get inside his head.

He'd only been with her once, and it had meant nothing.

She was nothing, and nobody, and he didn't need to lose his shit over it.

He pressed the button and headed back up to the bar.

CHAPTER SIXTEEN

"You'll be there, won't you?" Amanda asked again.

"Do I have a choice?" He'd been there, just about, at her first wedding, a few years ago. The thought of being in the same place as his family had filled him with such dread that he'd been late to the wedding, and had missed half of the service. As it was, he'd only stayed for a short time at the reception after.

This time, he was determined not to be that big of a jerk. Amanda hadn't ever wronged him and she needed him to be a better brother than he had been.

"Not really," his sister replied. "I'm going to mail the invites out after Christmas."

"I know. You've already told me." At least ten times.

"Bring your plus one."

"You already said." He slipped his finger into the collar of his shirt, a million things playing on his mind, not least of all the bid he had put in for the Canal Street site.

"Well, I'm reminding you," she pointed out. "Since you always forget everything I tell you."

"That's because I'm a busy man." He had more pressing

matters to tend to, but he couldn't focus on them because for the last ten minutes his sister had been rambling to him about her goddamn wedding, telling him about her ceremony which would be followed by a reception at a fancy hotel.

"It's going to be a small and exclusive affair," she'd told him earlier, dampening his spirit because he'd hoped there would be lots of people so that he could get lost in the crowd. So that he wouldn't have to rub shoulders with his family.

"Is that all?" he asked. "I've got a meeting to attend."

"There you go again! What happened to the nice conversations we used to have?"

"We can talk all you want at the wedding." She was already on her second marriage and he wondered how many more times she'd be putting new rings on her fingers. It was just as well that she had no kids.

"Are you coming over for Christmas?"

He scowled. She asked the same question every year, and every year he gave the same answer. "What do you think?" Christmas at his father's mansion. An empty place, full of empty memories. Amanda and Travis might have forgiven and forgotten, but he never would.

"That one day you might change your mind."

"I'm coming to your wedding, Amanda. Be grateful for that."

She laughed. "I am."

"If you don't mind, I'm in the middle of a meeting," he told her, shaking his head at Marie who was scribbling on her notepad, and trying to make it obvious that she wasn't listening, but it was so obvious that she was.

"You didn't say it had started!"

"I didn't think you'd be blabbering on for so long."

"Charming!" she replied indignantly, but he could tell she was smiling. "I'd better let you go, Mr. Busy Business Man. Don't forget your plus one."

"I won't."

"It's nice to have someone to share all that wealth with—"

"Goodbye Amanda." He hung up before she started lecturing on the virtues of dating and finding a woman to love.

"Amanda's wedding?" Marie asked, looking up.

"Yes," he replied, wearily.

Bring a plus one, she'd said. He considered the idea. Maybe he would ask Kay, once things were back to normal between them. Not right now when things were still sore. Not that they *should* have been sore, but it had been a couple of weeks since Kay had been here and neither of them had contacted the other since then.

She'd been even more pissed off than he'd expected. Getting involved with a woman was a goddamn headfuck and this was why he steered clear of that stuff.

"You *are* going to Amanda's wedding, aren't you?" Marie asked.

"She's my sister. I can't get out of it."

Marie knew things about him that nobody did. Not even Xavier. But she didn't know *everything,* just enough, just what he felt comfortable telling her.

"Are you going alone?"

He knew she was going to ask that question at some point. "I might be taking a plus one." Tension crept along his muscles. Talk of Amanda's wedding and the ensuing family reunion always made him feel uneasy. He got up and stretched his arms out, exhaling deeply in a bid to calm himself down. He looked out of the window behind his desk, saw the tables full of people down below. From here he had a perfect view of the rooftop terrace.

"The sports masseuse?"

"She's history."

"Already?"

He shrugged, his brows knotting together at the question.

"You saw her for almost a month," Marie blurted out.

"You've been keeping track?"

"You seemed more relaxed, when you—" She cleared her throat, "When you have a female friend."

"She gave great head."

Marie raised an eyebrow. "Notice I didn't say girlfriend."

"I don't need a girlfriend. Just sex."

She narrowed her eyes.

"Sorry." He fisted his pockets. "Why are you keeping track of who I see and for how long?"

"I have a teenage son. It's a ninja skill us moms possess."

He grinned. Marie was old enough to be his mother. Sometimes, their relationship scuttled into odd corners. Mostly, he was the business man, telling her what needed to be done, but there were times when she cut through all that work bullshit. She was direct and she would say it as she saw it. He was thankful for the guidance. The only problem with Marie being his business confidante and go-to person was that she was a woman, and as such, had a woman's curiosity about her. She'd be asking for Kay's vital statistics next.

"Who's the plus one you might be taking?"

He feigned nonchalance, and picked out a piece of fluff that was clinging on the cuff of his jacket. "I'm not sure."

Her face had disapproval written all over it. "I hope

you're not going to take an escort." She pinned him with a stern look. "Isn't it time you stopped using those people?"

"I use them rarely, and never for sex," he clarified. For one thing, he never trusted where these women had been. But for the purpose of having a plus one to take to the wedding, mainly so that he had someone to talk to so that he could avoid talking to his family, the escort service would do.

Unless Kay turned up at the bar sometime soon and he could ask her. He'd mention that it was no big deal, because women could be fickle and she'd no doubt make something of it, but having her there would make it easier on him. It would be better than taking an escort and pretending they were an item. Men didn't pay attention to these things, but women did. And he wanted to portray the image of someone in a relationship. He wanted to show that he was just fine and Kay was the perfect trophy girlfriend to have on his arm.

"A fine looking young man like you," Marie continued, rising up from her chair with a frown. "I don't understand it."

"I'm not paying you to understand my personal preferences, Marie. I pay you to look after my bars."

"We both know that I do more than look after your bars," she pointed out with a smile. She took care of the accounts, and invoicing, and marketing. She was a goddamn wonder woman but without a cape or a tiara, and he depended on her. She knew that, and sometimes, he sensed, she used this to her advantage, and treated him not as her boss, but more like her teenage son.

"Yes, you do. I take it back, I'm sorry. But you're rewarded well, aren't you?"

She moved her head from side to side, as if weighing up his question. "I never say no to a raise." She smiled.

"We'll talk about that at the start of the year in your next appraisal."

Her smile widened. "Sign here, here, and here," she said, passing over some paperwork to him. He scribbled his signature.

"I'll set up a meeting with the owner." The Canal Street site was highly sought after and had a number of interested parties after it. He and Marie had already scoped it out twice, and he'd taken his architect to get a feel for the work and cost involved in having a complete makeover.

"Do that." Because he was ready to buy it now, before he got into a bidding war with some other savvy entrepreneur . With bars and clubs, location was everything, and he wanted his establishments to be in the best, upscale areas. Places where clients would think nothing of paying upwards of twenty dollars for a cocktail, and thousands to become exclusive members of his clubs.

When Marie left, he turned his attention to his computer but unable to concentrate and still irritated by his sister's phone call, he reached for his cell phone. For the third time that week, he picked it up, and was about to call Kay. And for the third time, he hesitated. It was turning out to not be about the sex. They'd only done it the one time, yet he found himself embroiled in the mental games already, and this was not what he was used to. He was used to having things go his way. With most women, he had the strings, and he controlled when, and how often he would see them.

Not so with Kay. He wanted to see her, but he would have preferred it if she came to him and they had sex, instead of twisting his balls and leaving him high and dry.

The fact that he spent more time than usual thinking about her unsettled him. More so because he'd been hoping to have forgotten her by now.

It had been two months since Tobias and Savannah's wedding, and two months since he had fucked Kay. How was it that he was still sitting here thinking about her? What the hell was going on with him that she had managed to burrow under his skin like that?

Damn.

He'd give it until the wedding. Clearly, he needed to fuck her out of his system properly, and if he could get her to come to the wedding, it would be a fait accompli.

He would call her some other time. Amanda, and the wedding, and all that other stuff—there was too much debris swirling around in his brain. He needed his wits about him when talking to Kay. Now was not the time.

A few days later towards the end of the week, he noticed that a group of people from Kay's workplace were in the bar. He recognized the slime ball, Geoffrey, immediately, but there was no sign of Kay.

Was she deliberately staying away from this place in order to avoid him, or was something wrong? Or maybe it was because of something else, and nothing to do with him?

He called her, and this time the phone rang for a while but then went straight to voicemail. It was the perfect excuse for him to find out what was going on. He grabbed his car keys and left, arriving at her apartment a short while later.

But he couldn't get past the concierge, an old man with a huge gap between his front two teeth.

"But I've been here before," he stated, when the old man refused to let him go straight up.

"Somebody else must have been on duty. I've never seen you before."

Luke frowned. "Can you please just let her know I'm here."

The concierge buzzed up to announce his arrival, then with the phone receiver still in his hands, told him, "She said she's not expecting you."

"It's a surprise visit," he said, gritted teeth. "Tell her I need to talk to her."

The concierge repeated the sentence into the phone, then said, "She wants to know what it's regarding."

What the fuck? "Could I talk to her?" Luke demanded, holding his hand out to take the phone.

"It doesn't sound to me as if she wants to talk to you," the old man countered, refusing to hand the receiver over.

"She will once she sees me. What's your name?" he demanded, so that he could report him to the maintenance manager seeing that the guy was doing his best to piss him off.

"Arnold. And your name, Sir?"

"Luke

"You must be new," Arnold commented. He said 'new' like he was this season's couture line.

"New?" Luke asked, confused. "Look, *Arnold*," he said, drawing in a long breath and puffing out his chest. "I would like to talk to her," he said, slowly. But the old man had put the receiver down. "She clearly doesn't want to see you, Sir."

His jaw clenched together and he walked away, then pulled out his cellphone and called her. She answered straightaway. "Don't hang up, please," he said, "Just hear me out." He paused, then turned around to find the concierge giving him the beady eye from his desk. He turned his back to the man. "I was out of line last time, about dinner."

There was silence at the other end. "I'm sorry," he said, but still, silence. "Kay?" he barked, annoyed that he had apologized and she hadn't even acknowledged it.

"Come up. I'll tell Arnold to let you in." She hung up.

He spun around to find the concierge still looking at him. He gave him his cheesiest smile. "She said I could go up."

The old man barely moved a muscle. "It's on the—"

"I know where it is," he said, tightly as he walked towards the elevator. "I've been here before."

The door to her apartment was ajar, and she was waiting in her living room, standing, with her arms folded, looking as if she was about to bite his head off.

"It would be easier breaking into the Federal Reserve than getting past that old man downstairs."

"Arnold vets people carefully."

"Does he have to vet many of them?" he asked, carefully.

She frowned. "Excuse me?"

Damn it, if he didn't have to watch what he said. "He said I was 'new'. What does that mean?"

"I have no idea."

"How often do you—" He stopped, not wanting to dig a bigger hole for himself.

"How often do I what?"

"Nothing. Sorry. I didn't come here to argue."

"What did you come for?" she asked, her arms unfolding and her hands settling on her hips, as if she was gearing up for a fight. The blood in his veins drained south as he eyed her. Makeup sex was often better than normal sex. His mouth pressed together and he couldn't figure out how to get from this, to the next stage.

"I was worried about you."

"Why?"

"Because I haven't heard from you."

"You were worried about me?" She looked puzzled, and all he wanted to do was get this out of the way. It had been almost two months since that first time, and being here now, brought back potent memories. A throb of excitement surged through him.

"Yes. Your work colleagues have been here but I haven't seen you lately."

"I've been busy," she said.

"I thought it was because of that dinner saga."

"That—" She looked away, shaking her head. "Was weird, yes."

"I told you—"

"Yes, but it's *still* weird. You... have...issues...clearly." She exhaled loudly. "I had to say it. There," she gesticulated with her arms, flailing them in mid-air. "I feel better now that I've said it."

"Issues?" He slipped his hands into his trouser pockets. "I don't have any issues. I just want an easy life."

She stared at him and shrugged. She swallowed. "I found it weird, okay? I don't know what I'm getting myself into, with you, with *this*."

"I thought I'd made it pretty obvious, what I will and won't allow," he replied, unsettled by her words. She was changing her mind, and having second thoughts about their arrangement—it was exactly what he'd predicted. Kay, despite what she'd said about being able to handle it, couldn't.

At least this was one way of getting her out of his

system. It wouldn't take him long to find someone else. It probably wouldn't take her long either.

"You haven't been to the bar lately."

She narrowed her eyes at him, obviously not liking his subtle accusation. "Are you keeping tabs on me?"

"No." She was running rings around him, and it wasn't something he was used to. "Your work people were there, including that arsehole, Geoffrey. I haven't seen you for a while, and you didn't answer my call. I thought something might be wrong."

"So you came to make sure I was okay?" The expression on her face softened.

"I wondered what you were up to? Wondered why you were lying low and whether you were avoiding me."

"I've been busy at work."

"Busy, huh?" She was fine, it was obvious.

"Busier than usual." She flicked her hair over her shoulder, then folded her arms again, unknowingly diverting his attention to her ample breasts.

"Did you want to go to dinner?"

"Dinner?" Her brows pushed together as if he'd said something utterly ridiculous. "You don't do dinner. You have rules, remember?"

"It's only dinner, Kay. Just fucking dinner."

"That's right. That's all it ever was. You're the one who made such a big deal about it."

He looked stupid, especially when she put it like that. "Well, I'm asking you now." He walked towards her, and noticed that she pressed her lips together, as if bracing herself, or getting ready.

"You're asking me about dinner *now*? Is that why you came over?"

"I came over because ..." He missed her. He missed the sex, he told himself. It was just the sex. "I haven't seen you, and it doesn't feel as if we're ...together."

"Together?" she snorted. "You're not talking about a *relationship*, are you? You don't do relationships, remember?"

"We're doing something similar," he stated, letting his gaze run up and down her length. "That is, if you still want in. I owe you a couple of orgasms," he said, "If you still want them."

She bit her lower lip. "Think you can deliver this time?"

"I've never had a problem before. I was...overwhelmed by you that last time." He wanted to fuck her in at least three different positions before he left here, to make up for the downtime he'd suffered, at the hands of her teasing.

"Overwhelmed?" she said, her voice turning softer, more seductive. "Did you mean to compliment me?"

"Take it any which way you want."

He might not have wanted commitment, or long-term emotional baggage, but he wanted her now, even if in the depths of his brain, in the haziness and fog regarding his ideas about connecting to another person, the lines were already blurring. His cock twitched at the sight of her, and of what he wanted to do to her. And Xavier's subtle interest in Kay reminded him he needed to ask her something. It also reminded him that he needed to cleanse Xavier out of her system, in case she might have been interested in him.

"Xavier mentioned he saw you," he said, watching her reaction.

"I ran into him recently."

"Yeah? What do you think of him?"

She frowned. "Why?"

"No reason. Just that he wondered why you hadn't called him."

She snorted in disbelief. "I'm never going to call that douchebag."

"Why's he expect you to?"

"I have no idea!" She folded her arms. "We… shared a moment."

He angled his head. "A moment?"

"We got to talking when he did those magic tricks on the island."

He nodded, remembering. "And?"

"And we …" She struggled to phrase it. "And…then we… made out."

"Made out," he said, nodding.

"Kissed." She shrugged. "And then we got interrupted, and he forgot me after that."

"That was all? Nothing else happened?"

She looked at him closely. "What did he say happened?"

"Nothing. He didn't say anything happened." But he was glad to hear her confirmation.

"If I didn't know you any better, I'd think you were jealous."

"Me? Jealous?" Right now he wanted to bury himself balls-deep inside her so that she knew that this arrangement was between them only. His need to possess her was greater now, than his desire to question her.

"The way you're questioning me, yes."

He walked towards her slowly. "I don't expect you to see anyone else while we're still seeing one another."

"We're seeing each other?" she exclaimed, her tone mocking.

"We're not *not* seeing one another."

"What the hell does that mean?" she retorted. "Double negatives confuse me. Say what you mean."

They had an agreement, even though nothing had been signed, or set in stone. It had been verbal, an agreement of sorts and neither one of them could back out without telling the other.

Seeing her, barefoot, in her smart work skirt and silk blouse, sent a signal straight to his manhood, and he wondered how long it would take before he could get her panties to fall around her feet. He wanted her, and he wanted her right now—and not for a pity-fuck, like last time. This was going to be a claim-me, territorial fuck.

He missed fucking her and he couldn't wait any longer. Hooking his arm around her waist he tugged her closer to him, then slanted his mouth over hers and kissed her. She didn't move at first, didn't part her lips, nor reach for him with her arms, but slowly, as he worked his lips over hers, and his other hand moved to cup her neck, her defenses tumbled. Her mouth yielded to his, and she parted her lips, moaning as the kiss deepened. She had missed him, despite her stubbornness to admit it.

And, god, she felt good.

His heated body pressed against hers and he hardened, making her giggle as she moved her mouth away. Her hands moved down, stroking him over the fabric of his pants, rubbing him gently and making him shudder.

"Shall we get dinner first?" he asked, staring down into her face, his gaze remaining on her moist, red lips.

"You want sex, and you're trying to bribe me by suggesting dinner?"

"I won't lie. I'm horny as hell, but I accept that I was out of line the last time."

He lifted his eyes to meet hers and their gazes locked. "You admit it then?" she asked.

He blinked, in answer.

"You were lucky to catch me home this early today. I haven't been getting home until after eleven."

"Then we should make the most of you being home early."

"We should, because this—" She rubbed him harder, "won't wait."

He growled in agreement.

"And don't treat me like a piece of meat, this time."

He looked at her, puzzled, and then he understood. That first time, he hadn't been the best lover. "I won't."

She rested her hand on his chest. "I know what this is, Luke, and I'm not expecting anything."

"Good," he murmured, leaning close as he took her earlobe between his finger and thumb and pinched it gently. He dropped a small, wet kiss along her neck.

She turned her head towards him, closing off his access to her neck and ear. She was soft against him, and with that silky blouse, he couldn't help but slide his hands over her body.

"Not on the kitchen table this time," she cautioned.

He couldn't help but smile at the memory, his boxer briefs were so tight now that he had to get out of them fast.

"We can do it wherever you want."

It was rare to find a woman who was practical, and didn't need a shitload of romancing before getting down to business. A woman who had needs to be met and was as eager as him to get down to it. They kissed again, the soft, mewling sounds as she moaned into his mouth arousing him further.

How much he had missed this woman. It was going to

take some focus, keeping it like this, purely sex and nothing more. But, Jesus, she understood him in a way he hadn't been understood for a long time, and he liked that.

She didn't make him feel bad, because she didn't expect more than this.

It was the perfect hookup.

CHAPTER SEVENTEEN

She could barely breathe. Her heart lurched inside her chest, and her knees buckled. He only had to kiss her, and touch her, and she would lose her mind.

Silly, really, that her reaction was something a teenager might have, not a grown woman who had had many lovers.

But Luke Hunter had this effect on her, and all she could think of was getting naked and making love all night long. He would call it something else, but she knew what it really was. After all, he'd come back to her, hadn't he?

She'd led him to her bedroom, wanting the comfort of the bed this time. And she'd removed his jacket, he had allowed that, but when she reached for the buttons to his pants, he gently pushed her onto the bed. He tried to hitch up her skirt as she lay there, but the damn thing was too tight and didn't ride up easily.

"It's a pencil skirt," she explained, getting up as he rolled over to the side. The mechanics and logistics of what they were doing suddenly seemed stilted. She stood up and quickly unzipped her skirt, letting it fall to the floor, then turned around to see him lying on the bed, looking up at her.

"That's better," she said, unsure of whether to join him again.

"It's definitely better," he agreed, his eyes roaming over her body approvingly. He was still fully dressed, looking perfectly normal except for that huge tented package in his pants. Her heart pounded, and just when she thought the intimacy of a few moments ago had vanished, he lurched forward, sitting up, his hands encircling her wrists as he pulled her towards him.

Burying his face between her legs, he inhaled her scent, and did no more than that. She let out a low moan, anticipating his next move, needing him to touch her, and take her and give her what he had promised. Widening her stance, she raked her fingers through his hair, grabbing a handful of his silky locks as blood coursed through her fully aroused body. His hands slid to either side of her hips, his fingers hooking into the waistband of her panties. "You don't need these," he murmured, making her gasp when he peeled her panties down, all the way to her ankles.

She stepped out of them, groaning as his nose touched the neatly trimmed hair of her landing strip. His fingers skated over her highly sensitive skin, and she thanked the heavens that she'd had the foresight to have a French wax recently. Her brain fogged over and she couldn't think, or speak. A delicious sliver of anticipation licked her body.

"I want to taste you," he rasped, sliding his fingers over and into her slickness, making her knees buckle. Anticipation crawled all over her, making her skin prickle. She exhaled, panting out short breaths as he took turns, rubbing and stroking, eliciting sighs, like music, from her lips as his fingers strummed her.

"But I need to fuck you first."

She moaned again, as his fingers moved away from her aching mound and under her blouse, skittering over her belly and cupping her bra covered breasts. She longed to be completely naked, but she was powerless to move. Naked from the waist down and fully clothed from the waist up, she felt more turned on than ever. A shiver ran through her as he pulled her back onto the bed and claimed her mouth. They kissed long and hard, as if they hadn't ever kissed before, and all the while, his hands continued to stroke her. Yet, still, he was fully clothed.

"I want you naked," she said, when they took a breath.

He got up, then unzipped his pants and freed himself, and she stared at him.

At *it*.

And gasped.

"So if Xavier showed an interest in you now, what would you do?" he asked, matter-of-factly. But she couldn't drag her eyes away from him, needing him, willing him to move quickly.

"What do you mean, *what would I do?*" she asked, watching him slide on a condom. Her eyes flickered up to meet his gaze.

"You made out once, so you obviously had a thing for him," he replied, climbing onto the bed, and kissing her again, sucking every rational thought from her mind. She lifted her hips, turned on by the feel of his hardness hovering around her slick entrance. "Once," she murmured, loving the feel of his lips, his tongue, and his cock. "Now," she pleaded, wanting him with a ferocity that was new to her.

He held her gaze, not even moving an inch to satisfy her. "You sure you don't have a thing for Xavier?"

"What?" she asked, arching her back, lifting her hips again, trying to entice him into her. "Please," she begged, panting, her hands on his shoulders. "I need you *now*."

"I will fuck you to oblivion, but I need to know first."

"Freaking hell, Luke. What the hell is wrong with you?" she asked, irritated. She squirmed under him, desperate to swallow him up, confusion lining her brow at his hesitation.

"I just need to know you're not going to be tempted by him again."

"I already told you, I can't stand the guy."

And that was all he needed to know. He slammed into her, making her cry out in relief, filling her to the hilt, as he planted a sensual kiss on her lips. He claimed her mouth with the same fervor that he had claimed her body.

"Again," she murmured, her voice pleading, and low as her muscles clenched around him. He was buried hilt-deep inside her, and she writhed beneath him in ecstasy. In the next moment, he reached down and ripped her shirt buttons off.

"You owe me a blouse," she stuttered, digging her nails into his shoulders as he rocked against her. An animal groan escaped her lips, and she heard him moan as he slammed against her, the friction starting to build.

She unfastened the front clasp on her bra, needing to feel his mouth on her, and in the next second, his lips clamped onto one breast, sucking hungrily. Her heart pounded with the same ferocity as his thrusts, and she moaned appreciatively each time he rocked against her; her mind dizzy, her body coiling tight, and building to fever pitch.

Every nerve ending in her body tensed.

"Don't stop," she cried, closing her eyes as the pressure peaked and became almost unbearable, as if she was going to explode. She placed her hand over her breast, before sliding it to her clit. Luke shoved her hand away, staring at her with hooded eyes.

"I'll take care of that," he growled, gripping her wrist hard. Her eyes fluttered open as he brushed his thumb gently over her lower lip before slipping it inside her mouth. She sucked it greedily, looking into the depths of his eyes and finding warmth. This man was sexy, and he was fucking her, not making love, but fucking her. She loved it. Didn't want him to stop.

They were a tangled mess of thrashing hot, sweaty bodies drowning in pleasure. A haze of intoxication swept over her as he kissed her again. She kissed him back, hard, and primal, needing to feel his tongue against hers, while his cock pounded her relentlessly.

He consumed her, body and soul.

She looked at him, loved the way he made her his, the way he owned her body, and used her for his pleasure. Experiencing a oneness she rarely felt, she hugged her arms tight around his body, like the bars of a prison from which he couldn't escape. When he kissed her again, his tongue sweeping against her lips before plunging into her mouth, she clung to him, her arms like a garland around his neck. He claimed her with his mouth, and lower down he owned her with every thrust.

It didn't matter that he only wanted this and nothing more. She would take it. He would be the undoing of her, but right now, she didn't want anything else.

His eyes locked into hers as he thrust hard, evoking a gasp from her with each powerful stroke, and moving faster and faster until her heart beat so hard, she could hear the blood gushing in her eardrums.

And then it came; they reached the point of release at

the same time. She cried out, arching off the bed, digging her nails into his skin because it was too much. Breathless, she felt herself shattering under him, shuddering and splintering into pieces as she came, watching his face contort. His body tensed, and then he jerked inside her, letting out a guttural groan.

At last, his head fell forward onto her breast and she fell back against the pillow. They lay like that, still joined for a few moments, before he moved off her.

He rolled over, and she was about to roll against him, snuggle in his arms, but he got up still fully clothed from the waist up.

"Come back to bed," she said sitting up.

"I need to use the bathroom," he told her, and walked out, leaving her still sitting, and completely naked.

She suddenly felt let down. Discarded, even. Dispensable. There had been no spooning, no holding, or hearing one another's heart beats.

And yet, when they had made love, she'd felt it all, the searing intensity, and the connection; the beating of their hearts as they had come together. This man had owned her, and had claimed every inch of her body as if he had branded his name all over her.

She'd been with enough men to know which ones cared, and which ones only needed the sex. Luke wasn't easy to read but for now, he had made her feel as if he'd needed her.

For all his rules, for all his weird ways, in the end he had sought her out. He was the one who had asked her if she wanted to go out to dinner. He had come looking for her. And that had to mean something.

The meaningless one night stands and empty encounters from her past fell away.

Whatever this thing with Luke was, she wanted to believe it had the potential to be more than a hookup.

CHAPTER EIGHTEEN

They were barely into the second week of December when Savannah broke the news.

"I'm pregnant," she announced, her eyes gleaming, her face flushed.

Kay cocked her head, not sure at first if she'd heard right. "You're what? *Pregnant*, did you say?"

Savannah's face lit up like Christmas, confirming the news, and Kay's eyes fell to Savannah's stomach, as if she could x-ray right into it. She lunged forward and flung her arms around her cousin, hugging her tightly, before springing apart, fearful she might have crushed her too hard. "Did I hurt you? Was that too hard? Are you okay?"

"I'm fine," said Savannah laughing.

"Come over here and sit down." Kay took Savannah's arm and led her to the couch.

"I'm not injured," Savannah protested, "and I don't feel any different, apart from the morning sickness. I'm barely even showing."

"Morning sickness?" asked Kay as they sat down.

"It's not as bad now as it was in the beginning."

Kay couldn't help herself. "Freaking hell, Sav!" she gushed excitedly. "You're going to have another baby. I knew you would. I just knew it!"

Savannah threw her hands up, as if admitting defeat. "Tobias wanted a baby badly."

"This was his idea?" The notion of that man wanting a child suddenly blanketed her in warmth. What would it feel like, loving someone so much you couldn't wait to make a baby with them?

A shard of pain shot through her. Her and Luke's relationship was so different. She couldn't even call it a relationship, because—as he often reminded her—it was just a hookup. What they had was a farce in comparison to the cotton-soft and sumptuous love that Tobias and Savannah shared. It had taken Luke weeks to consider a dinner date. God forbid she ever suggested having a baby. He would spontaneously combust.

"Even before we got engaged," Savannah continued, "He wanted us to try. Last year was such a whirlwind, a baby wasn't anywhere on my radar, but when he said he wanted a baby, oh…" She put her hand to her chest, making Kay squirm. To see someone so in love when her own situation was so far removed was painful. She forced a smile, even though the comparison hurt. "I can't describe it," Savannah continued, "Something inside me melted and I wanted to have a baby for him so badly."

"You must have had a lot of fun trying," Kay offered. She couldn't ever imagine Luke suggesting anything like that. Hell would have to freeze over first.

"We did," Savannah replied, the huge grin on her face still there.

"How are you feeling?" Her gaze dropped down to Savannah's belly again. No wonder her cousin had worn a loose fitting A-line dress. "Apart from the morning sickness."

"I'm feeling great." Her cousin proceeded to tell her all about her experience. "Well, I wanted to tell you in person before you heard through the media. We told our parents yesterday."

"I won't tell anyone."

"It's going to break in the press in a few days' time anyway, and then everything will go haywire for a few more weeks. It's something I have to get used to."

Kay gave her a sympathetic smile, but Savannah looked so happy, so glowing, and content, as if the world was her playground. It was hard to imagine that there was a baby inside her, maybe not a fully-fledged baby yet...but *life*. Soon there would be a tiny little baby for everyone to fawn over, a second baby for Savannah and a sibling for Jacob.

Uncle Dale and Aunt Jean would be over the moon, she was sure, and her own mother would, too. Any day now her mother would probably call her to lecture her on the ticking time-bomb of her ovaries.

With a shiver, she thought of what lay ahead. The comparisons between the girls would continue. Future events filled her with dread. There would be the christening, and the baby's first Christmas and first birthday, then other milestones in the baby's first year. She couldn't stomach it; the disappointment in her mother's voice at future family get-togethers where Savannah would be surrounded by her doting prince and children, and she would...*not*.

She wondered whether she would still be with Luke, or was that expecting too much, several months down the line? Would she still be single, or still having short-term flings? One thing was clear. Time was marching on and she was getting older. Maybe she was already too old to be doing what she was with Luke. This thing with Luke—it would have ended had he not sought her out, but now that he had, now that they had been together, and the sex had been amazing, she couldn't think of walking away. The connection between them felt more intense than anything she had yet experienced with another lover.

If they were going to part ways, the directive would have to come from him. "And Jacob?" she asked, not wanting to dwell on these things too much. "How did he take to the news?"

"He can't wait."

Kay beamed at her, a wave of profound happiness settling over her. This *was* wonderful news. The best. Now that she thought about it, it wasn't that surprising that Savannah was pregnant. She knew Tobias was going to make a wonderful father, especially after seeing how he was with Jacob.

"You don't look too big. When are you due?"

"May."

"So you were pregnant when you got married?" She'd been so wrapped up in her own drama with Xavier at that time that she hadn't paid much attention to the bride.

Savannah nodded. "Could you tell?"

"No. I had no freaking idea." She recalled the wedding day. "You looked amazing, Sav. Are you sure you were pregnant then?"

"Positive."

"I was sure you'd make a baby starting *that* night, especially the way you two were around one another."

Savannah giggled. "Were we embarrassingly loved up?"

"You couldn't keep your eyes off of one another. You should have seen the way you were on the dance floor."

"I've never been happier."

"I've never seen you looking happier. I knew you'd get pregnant, but it never occurred to me that you'd *already* be pregnant."

"It happened so quickly." Savannah sat back on the couch, curling her knees up and making herself at home. "I came off the pill, and within the month, it happened."

"Just as well you were on the pill then. Otherwise you'd have gotten pregnant as soon as you met."

Savannah blushed. "We didn't have sex for months," she confessed, sweeping her hair away from her face again.

"For *months?*" Kay echoed, guilt slicing through her, and with it a sense of shame when she thought of that first night in her kitchen. If Savannah had any idea what had happened between her and Luke, she would be shocked.

"He was my boss," explained Savannah. "Not my direct boss, because I reported to Briony. He was her boss."

"Oooh," Kay squealed. "You had an office romance with the CEO!"

"It was not like that," insisted Savannah. "I never set out to get involved with him. I didn't see him in a romantic light at first."

"Why the hell not? Didn't you think he was good-looking?"

"I thought he was rude."

"Rude?" She couldn't imagine Tobias being rude to Savannah, ever.

"And it was Jacob he took a shine to, more than me."

"So you had the cute little boy thing going for you?"

Savannah shrugged. "Jacob helped, yes, but I didn't use my son to ensnare Tobias."

"I'm kidding, Sav. Where's your sense of humor?"

"Sorry. I get asked all sorts of stupid questions from women who still think I'm a gold-digger."

"Bitches."

"Yes, you'd be surprised at the reaction I get from some women."

"Go on," Kay prompted. "You didn't think he was good-looking at first, so how did things develop?"

"We had months of ... moments."

"Moments?"

A smile lit up Savannah's face as if this conversation had picked her up and set her back in those early heady days of getting to know Tobias Stone. "We shared those looks, those smiles, those quiet moments...it was all unspoken, so sexy and yet so frustrating at the same time, trying to figure out if he could see, and sense what I was feeling and thinking."

"What were you feeling and thinking?"

"That he was an intense man, he was cold, and stand-offish, and yet he was so gentle and caring with Jacob. He drew me in slowly. I wasn't desperate to find a partner. I didn't focus on any of that. I just wanted a better life for Jacob. My son had seen so many nasty things, I wanted happier times for him. He was my focus, my everything. That's all I wanted."

"And you ended up with everything. The perfect man, the perfect life. The perfect future. Married to a billionaire, for goodness sake, Sav!"

"It was never about his wealth and status. You knew more about him than I did!" She fiddled around with her glistening rock of a ring on her finger. "Because even if all the riches fell away, and the external trappings were gone, it wouldn't matter to me. I would be happy with Tobias wherever we were. I was happy with Colt, once, at the beginning. Even in our cramped little apartment, with both of us struggling to make ends meet, even when he still had a job. I was so happy."

Kay understood that, to a degree, but she had never been short of money, and had never needed a man to give her security. Having the kind of body that interested men, it was her experience that they often didn't know what to make of her. Men couldn't handle beauty and brains, and her ample breasts completely confused them. She had to fight for her corner at work just to prove that she was good at her job, when often the danger was that men saw her as nothing but eye candy.

It had stemmed from school, in her teenage years. Her fast changing body had made her one of the first in her class to warrant attention from hormonal and spotty teenage boys.

Somewhere along the line, after college, that message had become engrained. It was easy enough to get attention, but after a while something told her that *that* type of attention was a hindrance, not a help.

When she got interviews for prestigious jobs, it was her brain that got her a foot in the door, but it was her figure and looks that often got her noticed by men higher up. She would be lying if she said she hadn't used her flirting powers to her benefit. But once she was in, it was her brain that ensured she was seen as a formidable employee.

"But how did you know?" she pressed. "How did you know he was *the one?*"

Savannah's smile lit up her face. "Because of things he did. Because actions speak louder than words, *always*. It's not what a man says, it's what he does for you."

It's what he does for you.

Luke hadn't done anything for her, not anything

romantic. She swallowed and looked away, fearful that her cousin might look at her and see what she was trying to keep away from her. She had a crazy notion that Luke would change and see that she was worthy of being loved, but hearing Savannah talk like this about her own experience, sowed seeds of doubt in her head.

Savannah patted her arm, as if to reassure her. "You'll get your Mr. Right, too, especially now that you're not looking for him. Maybe it's a blessing in disguise that you're so busy at work right now you don't have time to think about anything else."

"Some days I don't see it as a blessing."

"But you still love what you do?"

She had always loved her job, had always seen herself as a career woman, but lately, more so after Savannah had gotten engaged, she'd started to think about wanting more. "It's something to do, isn't it?" At the end of the day, her job was a means to an end. She didn't hate it, she didn't always love it, but there was something missing from her life, and looking at Savannah only served to make that void larger than ever.

"You wait and see, the right man is out there, Kay. He might even be waiting in the sidelines right now. It's a matter of timing. And, if you don't go chasing him, you might find he comes looking for you."

Savannah was so Pollyanna about romance, it sometimes made Kay want to retch. She wanted to tell her that things didn't always work out well for most people but she didn't say anything. Savannah was over-the-moon happy, annoyingly so, and there was no point in having a debate about real love, or asserting that it wasn't possible for everyone.

But she wondered what her cousin would think if she

ever found out about her and Luke and the arrangement they had. What would Savannah think if she discovered that Kay was with a man who was so inaccessible, that he couldn't give her anything of himself, except his body? Everything they had was purely physical.

Luke couldn't commit. *Wouldn't* commit, and that was what she was up against.

Whose fault was that?

She had not experienced those moments which Savannah spoke of. She had no sweet, or flirtatious texts, no phone calls, no future plans. She didn't even have much in the way of conversation. She had nothing to indicate that she meant anything to Luke outside of sex.

She'd told him once she was happy with it, and that she could handle it, but she wasn't so sure anymore.

Chances were, soon, a few months down the line, she and Luke would move on. Dean might come back, or a few more years might pass, with more meaningless one-night stands and short-lived relationships. She would eventually meet someone who was *enough*. A guy who would tick enough boxes so that her aging self would think he was 'the one'—but he wouldn't rock her world.

He would just be enough. And, like most women, she would settle for that.

"Why are you asking about me and Tobias?" Savannah looked at her suspiciously.

"No reason. I was curious, that's all, especially now that I'm on my man-free diet."

Savannah tilted her chin up.

"It's given me the time to think about what I want," Kay continued, hoping that it would be enough to convince her cousin.

"I knew this would help you," said Savannah, smugness

creeping into her tone. "You were starting to worry me when you were jumping from one man to the next without a moment alone."

This was how Savannah saw her? "It wasn't like that," she replied, her face feeling hotter by the second. "I didn't sleep with *everyone*. Some guys I just made out with."

Savannah blinked, and then a second time, but didn't say anything.

"*Sometimes*, it only happened sometimes. I didn't like being in Hong Kong. It was all work, work, work, and I didn't have my circle of close friends around me, so I had to start all over with work people."

"But you're back now," Savannah said.

"And having you and Jacob here is the best thing for me," she agreed. Luke had a tiny place in her life, and once she figured him out, once she unraveled the broodiness beneath the mask he wore, she hoped he might be some kind of constant in her life. A dubious constant, but a constant all the same.

While she wasn't lucky to have a guy who professed his love for her, or bought her chocolate, or pampered her after a hard day at work, he was still around, in the background, a phone call or text message away. It wasn't ideal, hooking up just for sex, but it was better than nothing.

"A new baby in May," said Kay, cleverly changing the subject before Savannah probed too deeply.

"A new baby, and we're moving a month or so before then."

"How come it's taking so long?" She'd seen pictures of the massive property. It was huge. Too big for a family of three. And she could only imagine how many millions it must have cost.

"It's Tobias. He wants to build extra rooms. He wants

me to get a live-in nanny, but I'm not sure about that. Not for the first year, I don't think."

Was this woman crazy? "Take all the help you can get! Isn't the first year the hardest?"

"Yes, but I don't think I need a nanny at all. I had Izzy helping out while we were away, and I was going to have her do more hours for me, but I don't want to neglect Jacob. He's going to get neglected when the baby comes, for a while, anyway. I managed to look after Jacob, and I worked, and I had Colt to contend with and all that nasty stuff, and I had no nanny then, except for my parents who looked after Jacob when I went back to work." Savannah laughed. "I had no money either, with which I could have paid the nanny, but we did fine."

"Yes, you did, hon." Kay's heart swelled with pride, knowing everything Savannah had been through, and to see her now, all her dreams had come true. Except that marrying a billionaire and living the jet-set life had probably never been Savannah's dream. She had only wanted the best for her son, and she had wanted out of that awful marriage. "We'll have to throw you a baby shower," Kay decided.

"A baby shower?" Savannah laughed.

"We should go out and celebrate," Kay suggested. "It doesn't feel right sitting here and doing nothing."

But Savannah didn't look too enthralled by the idea. "Can we not?" she pleaded. "I can't stand people noticing who I am. I can't even shop in peace, at the moment. I'm hoping it's because of the wedding, and I hope the news will die down soon, but the pregnancy news will probably come out soon, and it will all start up again."

"We can go somewhere discreet. I'll give you a hat and sunglasses."

Savannah made an unhappy face. "I have a fundraiser event next week, and then Tobias's yearly Christmas fundraising event for the adoption centers. I expect the baby news will have broken by then and things are going to get crazy for me again. Please...can we stay here, and veg, like we used to in the good old days?"

"Is it really that bad?" The way Savannah spoke of it, she made it sound like such a tortured life.

"Worse. It means you can't ever have a bad day. You can't. Even if you've got a headache, or you've read some salacious piece of gossip written about you, you have to be out in the public with a smile on your face. I completely get why Tobias loathes the press."

Kay patted Savannah's arm. "Fine, we'll stay here, and we'll veg, and talk, and eat, and catch up. How long do I have you for?"

"The whole day."

"Perfect." A girlie day just hanging out at home was probably a good thing for her, too.

"You can tell me all about how your man-free diet is coming along. I'm hoping you haven't given in to any more of Dean's texts."

"Dean," said Kay, thinking of her ex for the first time in a long time. If there had been a huge plus to her arrangement with Luke, it was that she had managed to erase Dean from her memory. "That loser?"

Savannah's face brightened. "You're calling him a loser now?"

"He was using me," she said, sitting back, and tucking her legs under, "So, yes. He's a loser."

"You don't know how happy it makes me to hear you say that."

"I do listen to you sometimes," said Kay, not even flinching as she said it.

"You actually took on board what I said?"

"Why do you sound so surprised?"

"Because you hardly ever listen to me."

Kay swallowed. If Savannah had any inkling of what she was really up to, she would be disappointed, and disgusted. While she hadn't managed a man-free diet, she had managed a Dean-free diet, and she was sure that Savannah would be pleased about that.

"I want to go downstairs later and spend some time with Arnold."

"Arnold? Whatever for?"

"He wanted to ask about the wedding. In fact, I need to bring Jacob over one day because he said he wants to see Arnold."

"And talk about what?"

"We just want to see how he's doing."

"Why do you care?"

Savannah looked momentarily puzzled by the question. "Why don't you?"

"Because I have other things to think about...like my job, and getting to work on time and ..." She shook her head, confounded by Savannah's reasoning.

"Arnold is a lovely man!" Savannah cried, defensively. "Jacob and I always loved chatting to him. He's such a sweetie."

"I don't have the time," said Kay. "But you should go and speak to him. He keeps on hounding me for details about your wedding, and I never have the time for him."

"Awww," gushed Savannah. "I miss him."

"I bet you don't miss those days," Kay muttered, "He's a

concierge, for goodness sake." She got up and walked into the kitchen.

"I wouldn't care if he was the janitor. He's such a caring and considerate man," replied Savannah. "He always looked out for me and Jacob."

Kay paused for a moment and recalled that time when Arnold had vetted Luke before he allowed him upstairs. He could have let him go up without giving him too much of a hard time. She had come home in a foul mood that day. Remington had been pissed off, and she'd taken the hit for a presentation that one of the analysts had messed up. She'd come home and been short with Arnold, and yet he'd still looked out for her.

"Well," she said, pulling open a bag of chips. "I'm always rushed in the morning, and I've been doing crazy hours lately." Besides, she had never had the time to make small talk, with anyone, least of all the concierge. She filled some bowls with chips and pretzels and got out a box of chocolates.

"What are you doing?" Savannah asked, leaning against the countertop.

"We need snacks, for now, and we'll get some food in later."

CHAPTER NINETEEN

As he watched Xavier and Izzy leaving The Oasis, Luke envied the ease with which his friend charmed women. He knew Xavier had brought Izzy here to show him that he was making progress with the bet.

And yet, when he left, Luke couldn't help but wonder why Izzy had agreed to go anywhere with Xavier. The girl was sensible and down-to-earth. Surely she could detect bullshit a mile off?

How she had even agreed to work for Xavier was beyond him. Xavier often said whatever came into his head, without filtering, and he wondered what Izzy would make of that.

Even now, after having seen them together, Luke was none the wiser as to what was going on between the two of them. Only time would tell. Either Xavier would boast about winning the bet, and no doubt tell him about his conquest, or he would go quiet, because Izzy wasn't stupid and she wasn't going to give him the time of day.

Seeing them together made him think of Kay and he

was tempted to see her again. He was in no mood to be alone. In fact, since their last encounter, he hadn't been able to stop thinking about her. It should have spelled danger for him, but he chose to ignore it, and preferred instead to focus on the release she afforded him. She was the perfect solution for late night comfort.

He pulled out his phone, and texted her.

Are you free tonight?

He grew restless when she didn't reply immediately. Checking his phone, he saw that not only had his text message been delivered, but she had read it.

And still she hadn't replied. Irritation scratched his skin like an itch that couldn't be ignored.

Growing increasingly irritated, he called her, and his heart skipped a beat when she picked up.

"Hi," she said, sounding surprisingly bright, surprisingly upbeat.

"You didn't reply to my text."

"You sent a text?" she asked, acting surprised.

You know I did, because you read the message. But he didn't say anything because a disagreement wasn't the way he wanted to start the evening.

"Are you free tonight?" he asked, wondering what she was wearing, and how soon he could get to her.

"No. I'm busy, actually."

His mood deflated in an instant. "Doing what?" She was being eerily evasive and even though asking her risked him sounding nosey, he was keen to know.

"Savannah's over, and we're catching up."

Fuck. When girls got together they didn't stop talking

for hours. "That's the rest of your evening taken up. Will you be free around 10?"

"I'm not sure. Why, is this a booty call?"

"Maybe."

"You miss me, don't you?" she asked.

"I miss certain *parts* of you."

She giggled. "They're parts of me, so theoretically, you miss *me*. Why don't you just say you miss me?"

"I miss fucking you."

The line turned eerily quiet. She didn't giggle. "I guess you do, huh," she said, finally, as he struggled to find a way to put that right. "I miss more than that—", he started to say, but she cut him off.

"I need to order take out."

"Cool." The frost in her voice was hard to miss. "You must both have a lot to catch up on."

"We do."

It was odd, how the same evening that Xavier and Izzy had been at The Oasis, Savannah had gone to see Kay. "Xavier and Izzy were over earlier," he said, relieved to find something neutral to talk about.

"And that's why you wanted to see me?"

"What?"

"Because you're still hung up on me and Xavier?"

It wasn't such a neutral topic after all. "I'm not hung up on you and him. You said nothing happened."

"It didn't."

Silence rolled across the airwaves.

"I fucking miss you, okay?" he said, hating that what should have been a normal phone conversation had turned to this. Fuck. Why was it that he could experience a multitude of emotions just trying to call her to meet up? He wasn't falling for her. He wasn't. Not like that. Not like it meant anything, not like he needed to make her happy, or not make her mad. It wasn't *that* kind of happy. He was just mad at her because the sound of her voice made him want to see her. That was all.

"You do miss me," she replied, whispered almost, as if she were in shock. "I'm free tomorrow, if you really, *desperately* need to see me."

"Do I sound desperate?" Slinky minx. That voice, that tone. She was teasing him.

"It's why you called, isn't it?" she replied, and he imagined her grinning.

"Is Savannah there?" he asked, wondering if she was eavesdropping on the conversation.

"She's gone to see the concierge."

"Arnold?"

"She has a soft spot for him."

"Will he let me in if I come tomorrow?" he asked.

"I can ask him to be extra gentle with you."

"Any requests for tomorrow?" he asked, "I think I delivered last time."

She giggled. "You did, yes."

"No complaints?"

"Absolutely none. Oh, wait, maybe you could—"

What did she want now, he wondered, a delicious stirring started in his groin. "I could what?"

"Nothing."

"I could what?"

"I don't want to break one of your rules."

"Tomorrow then," he said, not probing further. He wanted to possess her. Take her to bed and fuck the living daylights out of her. The thought of her luscious body aroused him faster than any woman had before.

This was new.

He didn't usually think about someone like that. Obsession over sex was a waste of time. He had better things to tend to.

CHAPTER TWENTY

They'd been at it non-stop. He'd arrived a few hours earlier, and she had been ready and waiting, as eager to see him as he obviously was to see her.

No sooner had he walked through the door, than they'd rushed at one another, a mesh of hungry mouths and hands.

He'd pinned her against the wall, his hands on either side and devoured her with kisses. Leaving a trail from her lips down her belly, and lower, unbuttoning and unzipping her clothes as he worked his way down. Then, he'd sunk to his knees and pleasured her, making her forget everything but the feel of his tongue on her.

When her knees had buckled, when she couldn't even stay standing, he'd pushed her onto the couch and they'd ended up having sex right there. Their frenzied lovemaking leaving them both breathless.

The next time had been in her bedroom.

"Aren't you tired?" she asked, casting her eyes on his back. He had turned away from her, almost as if he didn't want her to see him naked.

"No."

"Why don't you turn around?" she asked. "I've seen it all before." It seemed silly to get all coy now, when they'd seen one another naked, and had been intimate with one another. He lifted his head to listen, but didn't turn around. She longed to lie in bed with him, feel his naked skin against hers and talk. Hold hands at least, like lovers did, but he always seemed in a rush to leave.

"What's the rush?" she asked. *Why can't you stay?* She had almost been tempted to ask him to stay the night when he'd asked her yesterday if she had any complaints.

"I have some proposals to go through," he said, before sliding his t-shirt over his head.

"It's the weekend," she exclaimed, holding the bed sheet loosely to her chest. "Don't you ever rest?"

"I just did." He turned around, as he pulled his t-shirt down his finely sculpted body. A body she'd had the pleasure of stroking earlier, and now her fingers itched to do the same again.

She climbed out of bed, covering her body with the sheet. "You work too hard," wanting to touch his face. The intimacy, she noticed, only lasted as long as the act. It was as if he couldn't bear to let his guard down once their lovemaking was over. Even now as she stood in front of him, it felt odd that she couldn't stroke his cheek, or take his hand. He used those things only as a prelude to sex, never after.

"You work hard, too," he countered, rolling down his t-shirt and giving her one last peek of those beautiful abs, before his cotton shirt covered them completely.

"Then surely we both deserve to stay in bed, and hang out. Eat pizza in bed, and do whatever comes naturally."

"What are you doing in February?" he asked, ignoring her suggestion completely.

"February?" Her mind snapped to attention, and the words *Valentine's Day* seeped slowly into her brain. "Nothing much, business as usual. Why?" She tried not to raise her hopes.

"Are you free around the second?"

Her heart began to thud. Maybe he had planned a getaway. "The second?"

"My sister's getting married, and she said I can bring someone."

The disappointment that it was nothing to do with Valentine's Day was replaced at sonic speed by the offer of a wedding invitation.

He was inviting her to his sister's wedding? She didn't even know he had a sister, let alone that she was getting married.

"I didn't know you had a sister."

"I do."

"Tell me about her," she said, trying not to let it bother her too much, that he was ready to leave right after sex.

"You can meet her at the wedding, and find out for yourself," he said, sliding his shoes on.

"Why can't you tell me about her now?" she asked, prying deeper. She sensed that he didn't like it but she couldn't help it, and she didn't care.

"She's my sister, what more is there to know?" he asked, expelling irritation. "Can you come?" he paused, then, "Do you want to?"

Of course she wanted to. This man was hard to gauge. He'd just used her for sex, and now he was inviting her to his sister's wedding. What was she supposed to make of that? He was being dismissive of her, yet his action said otherwise. Inviting her to his sister's wedding wasn't something she could take lightly. It was a big deal in her books. "I'm pretty sure I'm free then, so yes."

"Great."

The lack of enthusiasm in his voice, prompted her to question him. "You don't sound too excited about it. Are you sure you want me to come along?"

"I asked you, didn't I?"

She had no idea why he was getting so worked up, but given that he'd made such a commotion out of dinner, should she be surprised?

"You don't sound too excited about going, and you don't have to ask me to come if it bothers you. I'm not even sure why you asked me in the first place."

"Because I'd assumed it might be fucking nice for you to come along."

"OK. I'll come. At least I get to meet your family, huh?" The idea secretly thrilled her. Perhaps it would help shed some light on this man who was still a closed box to her, but he didn't reply.

Whatever happened, Luke obviously felt something for her—enough to ask her to a family wedding.

These things couldn't be dismissed as easily. She sensed he had a difficult time with his family, and that this would be an eye-opening event, but at least he felt close enough to her to ask her to accompany him.

Nothing could take that away from her.

CHAPTER TWENTY-ONE

The Oasis and The Vault were bursting at the seams. With only a few days to go until Christmas, people were getting together for a final drink before going home for Christmas. There were also the usual last-minute get-togethers with friends. Luke liked seeing his bars packed to overflowing.

It made for good business. This time next year the new Canal Street site would be up and running. He'd put in a successful bid for the place, and it was now his. Workmen were ready to go in and start working on it towards the end of January. His life was going to get pretty busy soon, and thrown into the mix was Amanda's wedding. Still, with Kay on his arm, things would be bearable.

She'd come to the bar with her work colleagues earlier. Theirs was a large group and they took up two tables. She hadn't yet come over to him, and looked busy in conversation. Adrenaline gushed through his veins at the sight of her, because seeing her always made him want to claim her.

It was going to be a good night. Again. Things between them were good, and he preferred that they stayed that way.

He disappeared into his office, in order to tend to some business and when he returned, almost half an hour later, he saw her standing near the bar with someone.

And the guy had his hand on Kay's arm.

The breath stopped in his throat. He didn't like it. He didn't like it at all. Kay's back was to him as he walked up to her, just in time to hear the man next to her ask, "Why don't you come over and say 'hi?' You know everyone."

He wasn't the type of man to indulge in public displays of affection, but he slid his arm around Kay's waist so that she was forced to turn and look at him. When she did, he hugged her closer, their lips barely touching. "Hi," he said, in what was probably his first daring public show of affection.

She looked flustered, and surprised, as she should, for they both knew this wasn't him. This wasn't how their relationship rolled. "Hey."

"Did I interrupt something?" he asked, moving his head back, and even though he could see the man's face over Kay's shoulder, he kept his eyes trained on her shocked face.

"Are you feeling okay?" she asked, as his other hand held firm against her hip.

"Now that I've seen you, yes."

She angled her head, not understanding. He had to admit, this show of affection was confusing. "Am I interrupting something?" he asked again.

"I think you did," the other guy said, in a snarky tone. "We were talking." Luke momentarily afforded him a nano second of his attention.

He turned to Kay. "He says I did," he echoed, looking directly into her eyes, needing to read her reaction. Had she been flirting with this loser? Or had she just been talking to him?

"You didn't interrupt anything," she said, resting her hand over his hand that lay around her waist.

"Good."

That guy, whoever the fuck he was, vanished. "I need to talk to you about something," he said, talking directly into her ear, and catching a dash of her perfume. Bottled musk and flowers. A rush of blood surged through his veins, speeding up his heart beat, his pulse, and turning him steel hard. "In my office."

"In your office?" she cooed, her lips moist and seductive. She could be a real tease without even trying. Seizing her hand, he tugged her away from the bar, through the doors and down the hallway to his office.

"Where are we going?" she asked, as he pulled her up a small flight of steps.

"You'll see," he said, throwing open the door. "My office," he announced, letting her enter.

He closed the door after her, and watched as she walked around the room, her gaze taking in the dark tan leather sofa and his bookcase. She walked up to it, then looked through the shelves.

"Greek philosophy?" she asked, giving him a surprised look.

"It passes the time."

"So does Hustler magazine, apparently."

"Maybe for pubescent teenage boys."

She shook her head, grinning, and slipped the book back in its place. "What did you want to see me about?" she asked, walking over to his cherry wood desk, and running her finger over the Bankers Lamp. "Not a speck of dust."

"I keep my desk tidy. I hate clutter," he told her, still

standing with his back against the closed door, and watching her.

"You do seem organized."

"I am. I only have on it what I need."

"Hmmm," she said, then turned to look out of the window. "You can see the rooftop terrace from here."

He walked towards her. "Nice view, don't you think?" he asked, standing directly behind her.

"You can see everyone."

"Yes." The busy tables on the rooftop terrace were easily visible from here. It wasn't an entire floor down, barely half a floor, for the building was constructed in a haphazard fashion, but from this vantage point he could see into the rooftop terrace without leaving his office.

"Can they see us?"

"Only our head and shoulders, if they look straight up. Many people don't even notice." He inched forward, pressing the evidence of his arousal against her back.

"Oh," she said, reaching behind her, touching him there, making him jolt. "You're excited to see me."

"I'm always excited to see you," he replied, unzipping her skirt and letting it fall to the floor.

"Do you spy on people?" she asked, leaning back into him, deliberately, pressing her rounded bottom into his hardness deliberately. "No." His teeth grazed her earlobe, while his other hand skated around her lower belly then slipped into her panties. Touching her like this made him want to fuck her to heaven and back. He could barely contain himself.

"No?" she asked, but this time her voice was soft, and dreamy.

"If I want to know what's going on, I go into the bar and sit at my table."

"But all the same," she continued, arching her back against him, shaking as he rubbed her clit. "You have a pretty good view of people."

"I do," he agreed, sucking her earlobe. She rested her head against his shoulder, sighing.

"Who was the guy?" he asked quietly.

"Which guy?" She arched off of him slightly, and moved her hand between their bodies, stroking him over the fabric of his pants, catching him off guard.

"The guy you were talking to," he said, plunging his fingers inside her.

"De—an," she gasped, jerking involuntarily.

He palmed one of her breasts, loving the feel of it over the fabric of the silk work blouse. She turned her head to the side, exposing her neck and he dropped a kiss along it.

"You always know how to make me come so fast," she whispered, shakily.

"You're so responsive."

"Only with you."

He dropped another kiss on her neck, loving her answer. She was like an instrument he could play with his masterful fingers and mouth.

"That was Dean?" he asked, irritation putting a dent in his plans when her goddamn pantyhose constricted the movement of his hand. He wanted to claim her pussy, feel it in the palm of his hand as if he owned it.

"Yes. Are we going to do it *here?*" she asked in a husky voice.

"Why not?" He slipped his hand under her blouse then forced it under her bra until he found her nipple. When he tweaked it, harder than usual, she squealed, arching her back even more. He couldn't take her top off, couldn't strip her from the waist up, in case anyone looked up. "So that was Dean?"

"Huh?" she asked, sounding dazed. Faraway.

"That was your ex—the one before me?"

She nodded, might even have whispered a 'Yes,' he couldn't tell. She quaked as he continued to rub her between her legs, the law of cause and effect enacting in front of him.

"He seemed happy to see you."

"We were only talking."

"I think he still likes you."

"Nothing going on between us..." she sighed, pressing her pussy against his hand.

"I know. I just don't like seeing him with you." He rubbed her harder, making her moan as he slipped two fingers inside her.

"He doesn't mean anything," she whimpered, then turned her face to the side, trying to look up at him. He kissed her hard, taking pleasure in fondling her body, and relishing that she was here and in his arms now, not in Dean's. The need to possess, and claim overriding everything.

"Stand up a minute," he ordered, when she had gone limp against him. He tugged at her pantyhose, the second-skin like garment stuck to her hips and legs like glue.

"What if someone walked—" She placed her hands on the window, her forehead pressed against the glass.

"They won't. I locked the door." He peeled her pantyhose and panties down her legs, getting them only as far as her knees. "I don't understand how you women can wear this shit," he complained, before standing back up and freeing himself from his boxer briefs. It would be better if he bent her over his desk so that he could bury deep inside her, or turn her around so that she was facing him, but he couldn't wait. Not seeing her had been hard enough, but seeing her with the asshole earlier had lit the fire.

"I wouldn't have worn panties, if you'd told me we were going to—"

But she didn't get a chance to finish. He rammed into her in one push, and she gasped, her head falling forward so that her forehead rested on the window.

"That feels *sooooo* good," she stuttered, between pants, her hands splayed out against the window. He slammed into her again and again, his orgasm building, thrust by thrust.

"I love you inside me," she said, between short breaths.

"Just you and me, Kay. Remember."

"Just you and me," she ground out, and he could feel her muscles clenching around him.

Together, they were the whole, and perfect and complete. Her soft exhales the perfect symphony for releasing his bottled-up emotions. Like this, they were so intimately connected, that he never wanted to let go. His pent-up anger and jealousy had melted, and now he was fueled by nothing but lust, and the need to make her his.

The air turned to steam and painted the window with a veil of condensation. It was only when he burst inside her, that he recognized the heightened feeling, and the cause of the intensity.

Crap.

He'd gone in bare, and hadn't used a condom.

"Damn," he said, pulling out and reaching for the box of tissues on the desk. He heard her disappointed moan. "Damn it," he hissed again.

"What?" she asked, turning around slowly, her face flushed.

He zipped up his pants. "I forgot to use a condom."

She wiped her hand over her cheek. "No," she gasped.

"Yes. I'm sorry. I got carried away." It was his fault, but with her, he lost his mind, couldn't think straight.

"I'm on the pill. Don't worry." She pulled up her panties then smoothed down her skirt. "I'm not going to present you with a secret love-child nine months down the line." She looked up at him with a worried frown. "But ... the others. I mean, your other hookups...the ones before me."

She was worried about *him* giving her something? Maybe he should be the one to worry? After all, how many men had she been with? And who knew what she had been up to in Hong Kong?

"If you're worried about me being clean," he said, clenching his jaw at the absurdity of what he was going to say next. "I'll get checked, and show you that I'm clear."

"Okay." She looked uneasy herself. Despite the lurid nature of their relationship, talking about sex and the consequences of it, still felt stilted. He wanted similar reassurance from her, that she was clean. But just as he was thinking of the polite way of asking her to do the same, she said, "I'll get tested, too. I'm not the slut everyone thinks I am. I don't screw entire baseball teams."

His lips turned up at the corners. "That's a relief."

She threw him a stony look.

"I'm kidding. I'm allowed to joke with you, aren't I?"

"Having just screwed me up against the window, you're allowed."

"You liked it."

She smiled in reply.

"Who was the last guy?" he asked, curious for confirmation about Dean. He didn't usually care with others, and hadn't had a clue what the sports masseuse had been up to because he had always been careful, but this recent slip up now gave him cause for concern.

"Why does it matter? This is personal stuff," she stated.

"And what we did just now wasn't?" But he caught her drift. They fucked. That's all they did. They didn't talk about their emotions and feelings, or any of that other stuff. It had suited him fine, until now.

If he wasn't careful, they were going to end up having another disagreement. With Christmas and New Year around the corner, this might be the last time he saw her for a while, and there wasn't long to go until Amanda's wedding. He didn't want to risk upsetting things too much.

Besides, sex with her was always great and something about her always made him want to keep going back for more. She wasn't the usual stick insect he'd been used to, and her curves, and ample boobs made a change from hugging a skeleton.

"You said you were over him."

"I am."

"Your turn," she said. "Who, and when?"

He blew out his cheeks, buying time, wondering how to answer this without coming across all uptight. He wasn't used to being questioned like this. "A sports masseuse."

"When?"

"A couple of months ago."

"And after her?" she asked.

"There was nobody else."

"And then you found me?" she challenged.

"*You* found *me*," he clarified. "

"Are you glad I did?" she asked, and lifted her hand. She was about to touch his face but she stopped.

"What do you think?"

This time she actually touched his cheek, grazing it with the back of her fingers. He was powerless to stop her. She stroked his lower lip with her thumb. "I've got something for you," she said, looking at him with shining eyes.

"For me?"

"Wait there," she ordered, and rushed out, leaving him standing there, curious.

She returned moments later, slightly breathless, clutching a shiny gift bag. "Don't get angry," she said, handing it to him. "It's Christmas, and ... you know ..."

He felt like a douche taking it, knowing that he hadn't bought anything for her, that he hadn't had the foresight to think about it. Actually, that was a lie. He'd walked past Victoria's Secret last week, and had seen something he knew she would look great in. But he had walked past, and dismissed the idea.

He opened the box. Inside were two key-shaped cufflinks. "Keys?" he asked, looking puzzled.

"They're not the keys to my heart," she said, pre-empting him, "So don't go getting moody or anything. But they only had dice, and cars, and globes, and I figured you'd have all of those."

"These are cool," he said, looking at her, smiling. "You shouldn't have."

"I wanted to."

"Thank you, but I feel like a bag of shit because I didn't get you—"

"It's okay," she said, shaking her head. "I don't give to get.

"I don't have keys, you're right."

She stood there looking at him like a puppy dog with shiny eyes. "Savannah's pregnant," she announced.

"I heard." He'd found out days earlier, when one of his waitresses had mentioned it to him.

"She says she was pregnant when they got married."

"I'm not surprised Tobias wanted to move fast," he answered, slowly, feeling uneasy with the way Kay was looking at him, as if she was checking his reaction.

"That's what she said. Isn't it sweet that he wants to have a child with her so soon?"

Marriage and baby talk didn't interest him, and he didn't want her to think that they were on the road to that journey, not now, not anytime ever.

"Nice for them."

"A new baby," she cooed, "Someone for Jacob to play with."

"Nice for Jacob." He put the gift box on his desk, not wanting to stand around talking about these things.

"I should get back," she replied, obviously noticing that the atmosphere between them had suddenly chilled a few degrees. "My team will be wondering what's happened to me."

CHAPTER TWENTY-TWO

She was glad to have escaped from New York. Going home to see her mom over the Christmas break had been lovely, but as the days passed, and she settled back into the fabric of her life before she had ventured to the Big Apple, she realized many things had changed. Or rather, *she* had changed.

Within a day, she felt out of place, out of touch, and restless, especially when her mother couldn't help but gush over Savannah's pregnancy. It made it difficult being around her, because there was only so many times Kay could say again that she hadn't yet met anyone, that her career consumed her, and that she wasn't interested in men, and, *yes,* she would get her priorities right, one day.

As if that wasn't bad enough, meeting up with some of her high school friends didn't fare any better. Most of them were already married and had settled down. A couple of them already had more than one child. One had recently become engaged, which left only Kay as the only one not in a relationship. At least, that's what she told them, otherwise, she would be lying.

Listening to her friends exchanging baby tips and the best recipes for bread, she felt out of place and out of touch. She was restless—as if she had an itch all over her body. She felt out of place even at home. Her mother, glad to have company, seemed to want to be around her all the time, never allowing her time alone with her thoughts. It wasn't nice to think it, but she soon felt claustrophobic and, after a couple of days trying to relax at home, walking around the edges of conversations she wanted to avoid, she returned to New York earlier than planned.

But the restlessness continued, and she couldn't figure out what it was.

There had been no correspondence between her and Luke, but he had told her that he was in Miami and LA on business, looking at potential sites. She wondered if Marie had gone with him.

She found herself people watching more than ever, but seeing couples holding hands as they strolled along Fifth Avenue, or sitting in coffee shops and restaurants, laughing and talking—was like a knife to her belly.

She had none of this.

A tide of self—pity washed over her again, and she couldn't shake it off. Christmas and New Year were the most miserable of times for single people. Even if she wanted to call and talk to Savannah or any of her friends here, with a view to meeting up with them, she wouldn't have because she knew they would all be busy with their partners, and she would be a hanger-on. She couldn't allow herself to be that person.

Work saved her. She worked soul-killing long hours to make up for the emptiness of her life. Nothing was more important than proving to Remington that she had this. And once the Pembroke deal was over, she would use that as a milestone to take stock of her life.

For now, Luke was the perfect antidote to her hectic working life. The sex was great, but coming home to an empty bed wasn't. She felt hollow, cheated, almost as if she was suddenly starting to see that what she had wasn't the foundation to anything strong, or worthwhile. There was no chance of anything long-term evolving from this.

Once the wedding was over, she would strongly consider taking Savannah's advice and going on that man-free diet. It would help her wash Luke right out of her skin, and soul, and heart.

Luke, unlike Dean, unlike most men she had been with, wasn't transparent. He could be tender one moment, and cold and distant the next. Sometimes, the dichotomy of his being wore her down.

She missed him, in her quiet, lonely moments and in her mind's eye she embellished the type of man he was; she made him out to be someone who loved her, and in her imagination she saw them having Sunday brunch in a café near Central Park, then having drinks and dinner after work before going home together.

Maybe it was not seeing him for a few weeks that distorted the image she had of him, for she spent far too much time thinking about him than she should have. She was now starting to see the error of her ways. He was unreachable, and she barely knew any more about him now than she had that first time she'd met him at Savannah's wedding.

But when he called her, a few weeks into the new year, the sound of his voice filled her with joy.

"I haven't seen you at the bar," he said, the words hanging in the air, like a question.

It was obvious why he'd been looking out for her.

He wanted to have sex.

She should have refused. Should have made an excuse, but the wedding was a few weeks away, and she needed to honor that invitation.

"I'm clean, by the way," he announced. "I had the test done. Everything's fine. I can show you the letter, for proof."

"I'll take your word for it," she told him. "I'm clean, too." She'd had her results, and she was clean. Now her only worry was that she might be pregnant. She'd told him she was on the pill, but with all the late nights and her crazy work schedule, there had been a few days here and there when she'd forgotten to take it. It had only ever been a secondary backup to ensure she never got pregnant, because she never had unprotected sex. Never. And the idea that she might be pregnant filled her with dread, and a little hope. Each time she thought about buying a pregnancy kit, she pushed it to the back of her mind. It frightened the hell out of her, to find out for sure—because her whole world would change. And Luke would lose his shit.

"No back to work drinks for you and your team?" he asked.

"No time." She laughed a little, to hide the disappointment. Why couldn't he tell her he missed her, or ask her out to dinner, or ask her how her Christmas was?

All that time she had been away, she'd been thinking of him. Not of intimate moments, but of conversations, disagreements, *moments* they had shared. She wanted to make him happy, always, in her daydreams about him, and if that wasn't love, or a semblance of it, wanting to bring happiness to someone, she didn't know what was.

"Come and meet Marie. She wants to meet you."

"Marie who wants to meet me?" This was new.

"She wants to see that you're real and not an escort."

"Why?"

"Because I told her about you. Besides, you've been curious about her for ages."

"I have not been curious about her."

"Could have fooled me."

She was stoked that he wanted her to meet Marie, his erstwhile business confidant. Could it be that while she had spent her vacation thinking of all that was wrong with their relationship, he had spent it realizing that he wanted more?

"I'll see if I can pass by in a hour or something." She'd been here since 6am, and tonight she could have an early night.

"Okay. See you later."

She put away her cell phone. So much for starting to distance herself from him. There was no point in doing that now, with the wedding only weeks away.

True to form, when she walked into The Oasis, Luke was sitting at his table in the corner with Marie. The two of them looked up at her as she walked over. Smiling, she put out her hand as Marie and Luke stood up. "So you're Marie?" she asked, shaking the woman's hand.

"Nice to meet you," Marie replied. "I'm sure I've seen you here."

"I come here more than I should." They smiled at one another, then Kay looked at Luke, he looked at her, and there was a moment of extreme awkwardness. Neither of them had had to navigate a welcome greeting in front of other people before, and she wasn't sure how to go about it. Should she kiss him or hug him?

"Hi," she said.

He leaned forward and kissed her cheek, taking her by surprise. "Hey." He tugged her hand, so that she sat down alongside him, a display that had been solely for Marie's benefit.

Marie sat opposite Kay and gave her the kind of smile that settled all her initial fears. Something about her was so homely, so endearing that Kay's previous jealousy fell away. It also helped that Marie seemed to be a good deal older than Luke.

"So, you're the business manager?" Kay asked, feeling comfortable around this woman now.

"I don't know that that's an apt title," said Marie. "I do anything he asks me to do, within reason."

"Is he a good boss?" Kay asked.

"Careful," Luke cautioned Marie, with a grin.

"He's not bad," Marie replied.

"She's not a bad employee, either," Luke retorted.

"I have two teenage children to bring up," said Marie, "so, I'm kind of stuck."

"Stuck?" he exclaimed, his tone jovial. "You have a generous employment package here, and you'd be foolish to consider working for anyone else."

"It's true," Marie told her. "If anything this guy is upfront, and I trust him. He might look too young, and he might look like a total layabout, but he's smart."

"Layabout?" Kay asked.

Marie nodded at his tattoos, so blatantly obvious for everyone to see, especially when all he wore was mostly plain black or plain white t-shirts.

"He does give the first wrong impression, doesn't he?" said Kay, quick to agree. Her gaze trailed over his muscled arms, beautifully inked.

"Why are you smiling?" he asked.

"I was admiring your tattoos."

"Most girls do," said Marie, and they both turned their attention to Luke, and eyed him up.

"I'm beginning to wish I hadn't introduced you to one another," he replied, putting a hand to his neck.

"He's feeling sorry for himself today," Marie announced.

"He is?" Kay asked. Then turned to him. "What's wrong?"

"Nothing."

"Nothing," mimicked Marie, making a move to get up. "That's his typical response. He probably over did it at the gym, I expect."

"It's nothing," Luke said. Though she had to admit, now that she looked closely. He didn't seem to be his usual perky self.

"You okay?"

"Fine. I'm coming down with a cold."

"Told you," said Marie, winking at her. "He's after some sympathy. Expect full-blown man flu." She glanced at her wrist-watch. "I have to go. Nice to meet you, Kay." She turned to Luke. "Don't forget to reply to those emails I sent you."

"Slave driver," Luke called out after her as she left.

"Are you sure you're okay?" she asked him, peering closer.

"It's a cold. I don't do man flu."

"Don't worry. I'll look after you if you're ill."

"I don't need anyone to look after me," he leaned towards her. "I just need you for sex."

She bit down on her teeth, managing somehow to still smile at him, even though the constant reminder of why he was always so keen to see her, hurt. "Marie seems nice," she said.

"She's reliable, and hard-working, and I trust her."

"She must be good," said Kay. "It's not like you to trust many people. "

"Good observation."

"Easy enough to make," replied Kay. She knew the bare minimum about him, and likewise, he never asked her much about herself, except when it had come to Dean. Thinking about it further, they really were no more than two strangers who shared physical intimacy. Something about that didn't feel right to her. Not anymore.

But sitting here, next to him, like this, and him having introduced her to Marie, she felt as if she had somehow been included in his inner circle. She let the feeling sink over her, because it wouldn't be long before her bubble would burst.

"Am I that transparent?" He knocked back his scotch.

"On the contrary. I'd say you were hard to read."

"Hard to read," he repeated, as if the words were new, and surprising.

"Did you think you were an open book?"

"I don't know what people think of me."

She would have found this to be an odd comment, but knowing him as she did now, it made perfect sense. He didn't give enough of himself away. He never shared, he never went deep. He never put himself in a position where he was vulnerable.

She understood what they had, because—as Marie had said—he was upfront, but he never gave enough of himself away. She *knew* him, but she also didn't know him, for Luke Hunter had hidden demons and after nearly three months of being with him, she was no closer to unearthing them.

"The first time I saw her, I figured she was your girlfriend."

"People make that stupid assumption from time to time."

"Why's it stupid?"

"She's much older than me."

"Would that stop you?"

"I tend not to fall for women who are older than me. And I've never seen her in that light."

"But still," Kay persisted, trying to get into his mind, trying to unravel his thought processes. "Sometimes you can't help who you fall in love with."

"Who's talking about falling in love? She's good at what she does and that's all."

His reply startled her, but something pushed her to challenge it. "No-one's talking about falling in love, but I'm talking about people in general. What if you met someone you liked but they were a few years older than you, and you didn't know? Then what would you do?"

"I don't ask people how old they are, but clearly, Marie is old enough to be my mother."

Kay laughed out loud. "I never saw her as your mother. I think she'd be hurt to know that's how you see her."

"Nobody can replace my mother."

"Moms are irreplaceable," she agreed.

"Yes, they are."

"I'm looking forward to meeting your mom and your family at the wedding."

"My mother's dead."

She rushed her hand to her mouth, to stifle the shock. "I didn't know. I'm so sorry."

He shrugged, looking straight ahead, not making eye contact with her. She had questions, a million of them, and wanted to ask him but he looked faraway, his expression hard to read.

She couldn't ask him. Couldn't go there, because even if she dared to, she knew that he would close up and not give her the answers she sought. Worse, he would remind her that these things weren't part of their arrangement. She felt together yet apart, sitting with him here, most of the time, except when they were making love.

This was not what she wanted.

Yet to anyone sitting here in the bar, seeing her and Luke at the table together, they might be forgiven for thinking here was a normal couple, in love, together.

How different the truth was in comparison.

"You can meet my father and my sister, though," he said, turning to face her. His expression was still hard, and even the smile that he forced on for her benefit—the smile she could see right through—didn't fool her.

"I'm looking forward to it. What about a wedding gift?" she asked, knowing how lousy he was with gifts. "Have you got any ideas about a wedding gift? I'll contribute my share—"

"It's taken care of."

"Oh." That was the end of that. She didn't bother asking him what it was, or whether he would buy and sign the card. He'd deal with it.

The wedding was two weeks away, and he hadn't said a thing. She had no idea where it was, how long they were going for, what to wear. "It's only a few weeks away," she said, touching on the subject. "What should I pack?"

"Nothing. We're driving up for the day only."

It was just as well that she had asked. "So I only need to take one day off work?" Remington wouldn't give her such a hard time over one day.

"Yes."

"That's good to know. I'm glad I asked you," she said.

And there would be no overnight stay. As jovial and as easy-going as he had been moments ago, while Marie was here, he'd turned in an instant. All of a sudden she wasn't so excited about the wedding. Luke seemed to want it over and done with and if this conversation was any indication of what she could expect, she was already beginning to dread it. "Where is it?"

"New Haven."

A couple of hours drive there and back. She braced herself. "And it's formal wear, I presume?"

"It's a church wedding, with the usual wedding reception after."

She gritted her teeth together. "Why don't you show me the invite? Then I wouldn't have to interrogate you about something so simple."

His brows pushed together. "I threw it away."

Shock swept over her like a gust of wind, forcing her to close her eyes as she absorbed his words. She opened them again, and blinked. *"You threw away your sister's wedding invitation?"*

What kind of a man did that? And his sister was the one member of his family he claimed to like.

"I have the address, I know the time. I know where we have to be."

She couldn't believe what she was hearing. He was insane. Talk about totally dysfunctional. This was going to be a family gathering from hell.

"It will be nice to meet your sister," she said, being sincere, meaning it. But also because she didn't know what else to say. Surely his sister would be normal? How much more dysfunctional could she be?

His expression seemed to relax then. "Amanda's not so bad. I've never met the guy she's marrying, so I can't comment on him but I hope this marriage will last longer that her last one did."

"She's been married before?"

"This is her second wedding."

"How old is she?"

"Twenty-five."

Another one, she thought. Luke's sister was a few years younger than her and on her second husband.

She was going to ask him how his mother died, and when, and how old he was, but she didn't dare go there.

"I'm going to head home," she said.

"But you haven't had a drink or..."

She shook her head, sliding her arms into her jacket. The last thing she wanted was a drink. It had been a mistake to come here. Lately, either her rose tinted glasses had come off, or the stark reality she had realized during the past few weeks had made her question and examine each and every interaction with Luke more painstakingly than ever.

He was nothing like the carefree and friendly man she had met at the bar on Tobias's private island. If anything, he was so Jekyll and Hyde that it sometimes made her uneasy. This wasn't a hookup, as much as it was a mistake, and as soon as his sister's wedding was over, she was backing out of their arrangement. She could have dumped him now, but she didn't like to let people down.

That was her downfall, her Achilles tendon.

He looked pensive, as if he was on the verge of telling her things, but right now, she had neither the patience nor the energy to want to hear it.

"I don't like talking about my family."

"I noticed."

"You'll meet them soon enough."

"I know." She slid out of the booth and stood up. "It was good seeing you," she said. He looked so lonely as he sat there, not even getting up for her. Not that she expected a hand shake or anything, just an acknowledgement that she was going.

At least she knew that the kiss on her cheek when he'd seen her earlier had been solely for Marie's sake.

CHAPTER TWENTY-THREE

"We're late!" Kay cried, for what must have been the fourth time that morning.

He floored the gas pedal. "We'll get there in time." *Just in time.* He'd planned it so that they would be the last ones to arrive at the church. So that they could sneak in the back once everyone was already seated.

"But the wedding starts at eleven."

"We'll get there."

"But it's…"

He slammed his foot on the accelerator. "We'll get there. It's no big deal if we're a few minutes late. Don't stress me out, Kay." She fell silent.

He winced as a spurt of pain shot along his neck. It was becoming more frequent now. Pressing his fingers to it, he felt the pain intensify. Maybe he should have returned the doctor's call after the blood tests for the STD check had come through. The doctor had wanted to run a few further tests, but Luke didn't have time. Miami and LA had been more important then.

It wasn't ideal, but he already hated the idea of coming face-to-face with people he would rather not ever see again.

He reminded himself that he was only doing this for Amanda. On top of the family headache, he had a pain in the front of his neck which was spreading up towards his ear. A blasted wisdom tooth, no doubt, or he was coming down with something.

He had considered staying at a hotel near the wedding venue, because the four-hour round trip, coupled with the stress of seeing his father—and dealing with all that other stuff—was too much to deal with on top of his pain. But the idea of staying over made his stomach roil, and he decided to go with his original plan of driving to New Haven and back in one round trip. No matter what, he was determined to see the wedding through because he owed Amanda that much.

He glanced over at Kay who was completely silent. Damn it, he didn't want her in a mood. The whole point of bringing her was to make things easier for him, and he didn't need for her to look like a sour puss on his arm.

"We might be ten or so minutes late," he said, trying to get a read on her mood. "It shouldn't be a problem. Amanda's hardly going to be at the church on time." But Kay didn't say a word.

Maybe his plan was going to spectacularly backfire. Maybe he should have hired an escort, because at least she wouldn't have gotten pissed. Nor would she have complained that they were running late. And unlike Kay, an escort wouldn't have been interested in meeting his family. She would have seen today's wedding as payment for a day out. Kay probably thought it was a step up in their relationship.

In the end, they *were* ten minutes late. As they got out

of the car and headed towards the church entrance, he saw his old man. Silas Hunter stood at the top of the short flight of steps. He was an imposing sight. Even in his early sixties, the man was fit, and large, and as terrifying as ever. Luke inhaled deeply, forcing himself to hold it together. His father liked to screw with their minds, and he'd screwed with his mother's mind the most, chewing her emotions to mincemeat before spitting her out. A shiver rolled down his spine. After all these years, the big bastard still had the power to make him feel like a frightened teenager again.

The next few hours, he told himself. *Just get through the next few hours.* Reaching for Kay's hand, he smoothed down his tie as they rushed towards the church. His father eyed them as they walked up the steps. "Luke," he said, stretching out his hand.

Bitterness flowed through him, chilling his veins. He was loathe to take the proffered hand, but he knew it would only show his father that he was weak, that he was afraid. His father didn't care that Luke hated him, but he would see the weakness in him.

So he reached out and shook his father's hand hard, as if he wanted to crush every single bone in it. "Silas," he said.

"Amanda will be pleased," the old man said, turning his attention to Kay, his eyes widening. The slimy, old bastard hadn't changed one bit.

"This is Silas," Luke said to Kay. "This is Kay."

"Nice to meet you," said Kay, but he could tell from her voice that she was wary, as if she wasn't sure how to address the old man.

"Delighted," his father replied, taking her hand and kissing it. Luke balled his free hand into a fist, wanting to sock it to his father's big ugly face. Instead, he fought for self-control, and stopped himself.

It took less than thirty seconds, the greet and go, but it seemed to last a lifetime. There was nothing more to be said between them, and with his hand still firmly holding onto Kay's, he tugged her and walked towards the church door.

"Amanda wants you to sit at the front, with the family," he heard the old man say, as they walked away.

At least it was done, one of the things he'd been dreading. The whole of today was going to be one big obstacle course. At some point he'd come face-to-face with Travis and his wife.

"You okay?" he asked Kay. She'd been quiet in all of this, and he squeezed her hand, grateful that she was here with him.

"Yes, are you?" she asked, the earlier disagreement quickly forgotten.

"Couldn't be better," he muttered, guiding her towards one of the pews towards the back, purposely disregarding Amanda's request.

"Didn't your dad say that—"

"I don't care what he said." He ushered Kay in, and followed after her, choosing to sit near the aisle. Craning his neck, he looked around to see his brother and his wife, and some of his extended family occupying the front few rows. Unease, heavy as lead, settled in his stomach. He'd only been in a church a couple of times in his life. Once for his mother's funeral, and a few years ago for Amanda's first wedding. He hadn't attended Travis's wedding.

He turned to Kay, needing a distraction, eager to block out everything. She looked at him and smiled, and in her soft eyes he found a sea of calm. He took her hand in his and she squeezed it gently; that one simple, unspoken act, lifting his spirits and providing a reassurance that he needed.

She seemed to understand.

And she didn't ask too many questions.

This was why she had been the perfect choice to bring to the wedding. It was why she was perfect *for everything*.

Their arrangement worked.

It was the perfect no-strings-attached type of arrangement that he preferred. He'd been worried that it wouldn't be possible with Kay, with her being a friend of a friend, and him breaking his rule of getting involved with people he knew. But she was low maintenance—not in the way she dressed and carried herself, for he could see she was sky-high maintenance there, but in the way she didn't bug him too much. She was always busy at work, and this he counted as a blessing. Kay was that rare thing—a woman who liked sex and didn't care to hide it, and who also didn't seem too bothered about commitment.

It was perfect.

They worked.

She nudged him, pulling him out of his thoughts and bringing him back to the present. People were standing. Amanda walked down on her father's arm, a veil covering her face. His little sister couldn't help but smile as she walked down the aisle with her father.

I t was all so odd.

This was the conclusion Kay had come to as she stood with Luke outside the church after the wedding ceremony had finished.

The wedding had been such a strange contrast compared to Savannah's wedding, not in terms of extravagance, but in how different the atmosphere was, how different the family dynamics were. She had been prepared for some kind of friction, but not this. Luke had been edgy from the moment he had picked her up in the morning. He'd been late, and she had been ready an hour before he had arrived, risking his wrath and calling him twice to ask him what was taking him so long. He'd been miserable even before he'd reached her.

He was dragging it out, as if he didn't want to go, as if this was a visit to the dentist for root canal, not his sister's wedding.

Added to that, the relationship with his father seemed especially strained. While she didn't always see eye to eye with her mother, she loved her unconditionally, and would do anything for her. But Luke, seemed to find it difficult to even look his father in the eye.

"Who's that?" she asked, staring at the woman who was on his father's arm. She was obviously so much younger.

"Bitch number three," Luke replied coldly.

Startled, Kay stared at Luke. "Who?"

"His wife." Quiet rage dripped from his words.

"Oh," she remarked, squeezing his hand harder. He had let her hold it today. In fact, he had been surprisingly tactile towards her. Holding her hand as they had walked into church earlier, and now he'd slipped his arm around her waist. She couldn't figure out if he was trying to make a point, or if it was just that he needed the comfort of having her near. Either way, it made her feel special.

"Come and meet my sister," he said, when the new bride and groom finally walked out of the church to the sounds of cheers and clapping.

They walked towards the newlyweds, still holding hands.

"This is what it takes for me to see you?" Amanda

asked, as he kissed her on both cheeks. She looked radiant, and her face lit up even more on seeing her brother. "I didn't see you in the church. Where were you?"

"At the back."

"But I wanted my family to sit at the front—"

"Does it matter?" he asked, cutting her off. "We were there." He congratulated the groom, and introduced Kay to the couple.

Amanda's eyes grew large as the two women met. Something about her expression, and the quick glance she threw her brother told Kay that his sister was more than a little surprised to see her.

"We don't get to see him much," Amanda told her. "And I am so happy that he asked you to come along. It's *so* lovely to meet you."

"Lovely to meet you, too," Kay replied.

"Don't rush to make it number three," Luke said to his sister.

"Hey," the newly married groom retorted. "There will be no number three." He kissed his new wife on the lips.

"No there won't," Amanda said, happily. "You're on Table 1," she told Luke. "*Please* make an effort to be nice."

"Of course." Luke bowed his head, acknowledging the request.

"Would you excuse us?" Amanda said, "We'll catch up later."

Make an effort to be nice?

"What did she mean?" Kay asked.

Luke's face clouded over. "She's gone and put us all on the same goddamn table." She patted his arm, trying to reassure him. "It's going to be fine." She had no idea what she was trying to reassure him about, but clearly, something was amiss.

But Luke didn't say a word. His jaw clenched, and she could see the muscles on either side of his face tighten.

"When was the last time you saw your sister?" she asked him.

"Two years ago."

"Two *years* ago?" Her mouth gaped open. She barely went six months without seeing her mother.

"And your father?"

"Five years ago, at Amanda's first wedding."

Five years?

She had questions, even more so now, than she'd had in the morning.

"Luke." They both turned to see a man and woman standing in front of them.

"Travis," Luke said, stiffly. The man held out his hand but Luke refused to take it, the action causing a ripple of discomfort between the group. She had no idea who these people were. The man, tall and dark-haired, had more than a passing resemblance to Luke's father. The pretty and svelte woman standing next to him stared back at her.

"I'm Travis," said the man, calmly ignoring Luke, and offering his hand to her instead. She had no option but to take it, even though she sensed the animosity rolling off in waves from Luke's body. "Luke's brother."

Luke's brother? Shock spiraled through her. Luke had a brother? He'd never mentioned it. "It's a pleasure to meet you," she said, and hoped that she had managed to successfully mask the surprise announcement

"This is my wife, Maggie," Luke's brother said. She acknowledged his wife and the two of them shook hands while Luke's face was turned the other way. Kay jabbed him in the ribs, but he didn't turn around. He was purposely refusing to acknowledge them.

"Hi, Luke," the woman said, pointedly staring at Luke. The situation was getting so embarrassing that Kay was compelled to jab him in the ribs again. "Luke!" she said sharply.

This time he turned his head. "Maggie," he ground out, squeezing Kay's hand for comfort. Catching the hard edge to his voice, Kay looked up at him. A fake half-smile was plastered to his face, but he didn't shake the woman's hand or kiss her on the cheeks.

"You look well," the woman commented. "It's good to see you again, Luke."

"Is it?"

"Let's keep things civil," his brother said. "For Amanda's sake."

"Let's hope Amanda doesn't get married again," Luke replied. "Otherwise we'd have to do this all over again."

Kay looked at them, trying to connect the dots and failing.

"We're at the same table," Maggie informed her.

"Oh," Kay replied, forcing a smile. She had no idea what this meant, or what Luke would say, but a polite smile from her seemed to be fitting. Maggie seemed equally as uneasy, as the two men beside seemed desperate to avoid the conversation.

"Are you staying at the hotel?" Maggie asked her. "Silas blocked out a whole floor for family."

"Uh, no, I don't believe we are."

"We're not," Luke stated.

"There you go. We're not." She gave Maggie an apologetic smile.

"That's too bad. Well, we can catch up at the reception."

"We're not staying," Luke replied.

"Not even for the reception?" Kay asked. Since when had he changed his plans?

"That's low," his brother said. "You don't have to take it out on Amanda."

As she looked from one brother to the next, and saw the way their faces twisted in hate, Kay wondered what exactly was going on.

Luke fixed his brother with a cold stare. "I'm not."

"Don't do that, Luke," his sister-in-law interjected. "Amanda will be upset."

"She'll understand," he growled.

Kay squeezed his hand gently, and even though she knew she'd wouldn't have much chance of getting him to change his mind, it was worth a try. "Why don't we stay for a while?" To leave now would only make things worse—though things already looked pretty bad to her. "Your sister looked so happy to see you."

"No."

"But we've come all this way and it's your sis—"

"We're not staying," he ground out, touching his neck. She noticed he'd done that a few times today. "What's wrong?"

"Nothing."

"Don't ruin this day for Amanda," Maggie said.

"I'm not. She understands, I'm sure."

"We can switch tables," Maggie persisted. Kay stared at her, and at Luke's brother who still remained silent. If Luke's relationship with his father was weird, things were a whole lot stranger between the brothers.

"As if that's going to help," he said, his voice low, and cold. "Come on," he said to Kay. His hand slipped from her waist to her hand again. He gripped it hard. "We're leaving."

"Now?"

He didn't even bother to say goodbye as he tugged her hand and started to walk away. She quickly nodded her farewells and rushed to keep up with him.

"What are you doing?" she asked. "I thought we were going to stay for the reception."

"Changed my mind."

"Shouldn't we at least say 'bye' to Amanda?"

"She's busy."

"This is rude, Luke." They had walked away, leaving the sea of wedding guests behind them, and she turned around, to take one last look. "Let's stay, at least for the first course." She was sure he was making a mistake, and she didn't want him to. Family was family. You were stuck with what you had, and you had to make it work, no matter what past disagreements there might have been. Blood was always thicker than water and she feared that in years to come, Luke would regret it.

"Amanda will never forgive you."

"I'll make it up at her next wedding."

"That's just cruel."

"Mark my words."

"You don't need to voice something like that at her wedding," Kay hissed, appalled by his insensitivity.

"She can't hear me."

Her mouth fell open. She knew he was jaded. Knew something in his past had shaped him, but this wasn't healthy, this level of cynicism. She studied his expression for a long time, confused thoughts flying around in her head like circling bats. Before her stood a man battling some inner demons, and she couldn't do a thing about it.

"Don't make a mistake you'll regret, Luke."

He let go of her hand as if it was made of hot iron.

"You don't have a fucking clue," he snarled. "We're not staying, and that's final."

Her heart jolted, him speaking to her like that. She'd rather have his coldness than his rage, and as ready as she was to argue back, even she could see that this wasn't the time.

Something else was going on, something below the surface, something she wasn't aware of. She wanted to reach out and comfort him, for it was obvious that he was hurting, that he was bitter about something, but Luke was hard to care for, hard to reach, hard to soothe.

She felt like superfluous baggage, not like his plus one.

CHAPTER TWENTY-FOUR

The entire journey back was steeped in stony silence.

She had so many questions, but he looked so miserable that she knew better than to get him riled up even more, especially with the crazy speed he was driving at.

Not once did he turn and look at her, or start a conversation. Maybe he was waiting for her to say something, but knowing his moods, she didn't want to rock that boat tonight.

So, she said nothing.

She had hoped that meeting his family would have given her the missing pieces of the puzzle, but instead, she had been left with even more questions. If it was any consolation it was knowing that Luke Hunter had a problem with most types of relationships. It wasn't just with her.

"Did you mean for me to come back to your place?" she asked, as he parked up in the underground parking lot of an unfamiliar place. She wondered if he had been so deep in thought that he'd almost forgotten to drive back to her place.

"Yes."

They took the elevator up, and he showed her into his apartment. Even though she was still in the dark about his family dynamics, seeing them had given her a better insight into the man who now stood before her; the man who stared at her with his cornflower blue eyes. He loosened his tie and tossed it onto the couch. But if he wanted to have sex, she wasn't in the mood for it right now.

She wanted answers first. He flung open the door to his bedroom, then strode in, taking off his jacket, and started to unbutton his shirt. Slipping off her shoes, she perched on the edge of the bed, purposely putting some distance between them as she watched him take off his cufflinks.

"You wore them," she commented, pleased to see that he had, and to such an important occasion.

"They were on my dresser," he replied, carelessly tossing them there. She nodded, understanding him a bit better now and realizing that his filthy mood made it impossible for him to just say 'Yes'. It was easy for him to taint even the simplest of comments with a streak of nastiness.

"Why didn't we stay?" she asked, refusing to be daunted.

"I didn't want to." He pulled down his pants.

"But it was your sister's wedding, and we drove all that way. She would have wanted you to stay. Your brother and his wife even asked you to—"

"I don't want to talk about it," he growled.

"Maybe you should. Maybe you should let out whatever it is that's bothering you."

His eyes blazed as he stood there in his boxers, a silent tower of simmering emotions.

"You can't keep running away from your issues, Luke."

"Who says I'm running?"

"I am." She threw him a conflicted look. Could he be so blind that he couldn't see? He strode over to the closet and pulled out his sweatpants and t-shirt, then put them on. She stood up, determined to keep pushing and probing, deciding not to let him off so easily this time. "Explain it to me, then," she said, softly, walking towards him. "So that I can understand the crazy set up in your family and you can—"

"Take off your dress," he said, interrupting.

"No," she replied, standing her ground. No sex until she had answers. "Is this why you drove home early?"

She placed a hand on his bare chest, just as he slipped his head through his t-shirt. When he rolled it down, her hand was caught between his skin and the fabric. She stroked the ridges of his abs softly. "Tell me," she murmured. You're all worked up about it. Get it out of your system, and then we can have sex."

If it would make him feel better, she'd let him, because instead of his usual stony countenance, he seemed restless tonight. Irritated and weak, half the man she was used to being with.

He sat on the edge of the bed, and she did, too, taking one of his big, strong hands in hers. He let her, even though this was too intimate a move for them, this subtle indication of caring.

"You took me to the wedding, you made me meet your family, and then you dragged me away. Don't I deserve some answers? I'm not asking you for commitment, Luke, only answers."

Lines formed on his forehead, wrinkling his otherwise smooth face, and she felt sure that at any moment now he would tell her to go to hell.

"My father..." he ground out slowly. "...He moved his

mistress into our house while he was still married to my mother."

"His mistress?" She blinked, processing the news in shock.

"We didn't know she was his mistress at first. He said she'd just joined the company. He said she was a new employee in one of his companies, and that she didn't have a place to stay, and he was putting her up for a while until she found somewhere. But she started hanging out with him. Going for a swim in our pool with him, sitting in the hot tub. Pretty soon, he moved her into the bedroom. The one he shared with my mom."

She stifled a gasp. "What did your mom do?"

"She moved out."

"Did you know what was happening at the time?"

He shrugged. "Not at first. Not until mom moved into the spare bedroom."

"How old were you?"

"Fifteen."

"And your brother and sister?"

"Travis is a few years older, and Amanda must have been eleven. I don't think she knew what was going on."

"And your mom?"

"She still lived there."

"How old was the mistress?"

"Young. *Very* young. Straight out of college almost."

Kay recoiled in disgust. The age gap was as disgusting as the cruelty inflicted on Luke's mother by his father. She stared at him, clutching his hand harder, watching his face twist and harden. ""But didn't your mom object, or give him an ultimatum?"

"What could she say? She had no voice in that house. He was the big boss. The big man. The fucking oil billionaire. He was a tyrant, and he was a pig to her. It was obvious what was going on. His mistress had no shame."

"And *nobody* said anything?"

"Nobody *could* say anything. He was the patriarch and we couldn't question what he did."

"Why didn't your mom leave?"

"Because she believed he would change. Who knows? I'll never know why she didn't. She couldn't say a thing. She still loved the bastard."

"That must have been so awful for your mom."

"It killed her." He pulled his hand away and clasped his hands together.

Her insides filled with dread. "What do you mean?"

"She ended her life."

Kay clasped a hand to her mouth. "What?"

He turned and stared at her with darkened eyes; eyes which often undressed her just by looking, without him even touching her. Now he looked lost, and unreachable, and she couldn't help but put her arm around his big, broad shoulders.

"Oh, Luke," she cried, leaning into his body. He looked so defeated, and so broken. "How...how ..." She couldn't bring herself to ask.

"She lay down on their bed—the bed she had once shared with my father—and slit her wrists."

"What?" She gasped, pulling away, horrified. "She killed herself?"

He stared at the floor, and gave the slightest nod. "I was the one who found her."

The room spun around her as the shock of his confession hit. She couldn't imagine it, a teenage boy walking in on that. And now, as he opened up to her in a way he had never before, she felt suddenly protective over him, as if she couldn't bear for him to be hurt again in the re-telling of something that clearly still haunted him. A person never recovered from something like that.

Never.

He was living proof of that.

She had gained an insight into his pain, and an understanding she simply had never had before.

No wonder he hated his father so much. No wonder his relationship with Travis seemed so fractured. An event like this must have smashed through the entire family like a deadly hurricane, uprooting all their young lives and their world, and changing it forever.

"Take off your dress," he ordered, issuing the command roughly. She had more questions, and needed more answers. She wanted him to talk it out, to let it all go because she could see he'd had it locked up inside him. But that could come later. Sex was his go-to, and if it helped him through his dark moments, who was she to withhold it?

She wanted to obey, to give him what he wanted, but on her terms. She stood up and unzipped herself from behind, then let the dress fall to the floor. He sat up, his hungry gaze roaming all over her body. Instead of removing her undergarments, she knelt on the floor, inching forward until she was between his legs. Placing her hands on his thighs, she leaned towards him, boldly, brushing her lips against his, seeking, judging, feeling tentatively, before pushing her tongue into his mouth and gently exploring.

She was blatantly disobeying him, and taking charge, doing what she wanted, for a change. And he was letting her.

Her hand trailed along his inner thighs. Reaching between his legs she placed her hand on the fabric of his sweatpants, making him gasp out as she stroked the length of his hardness. This was a rarity for her, she who had always let him take her however and whenever he wanted, now she was doing things her way.

"Lie back," she ordered, freeing him from his sweatpants and boxers, pulling them down, hearing another loud sigh escape from his mouth. But it wasn't a 'no'. He didn't stop her.

She wanted to make him forget the pain of his past, and this was the only way she knew how. Curling her fingers around him, she stroked him slowly, while sliding her other hand over his inner thigh.

He didn't stop her—most men wouldn't have—but with Luke she could never tell. He liked to be in charge, and he never freely gave her power in bed. This time he was letting her have her way. She pumped him slowly at first, and moved her thumb over his silky tip. He jerked, and she stole a look at his face, eager to see his reaction. A sigh, more like a sound of deep appreciation, escaped his lips and his contorted expression, his closed eyes and relaxed face, told her he was deep in the throes of his ecstasy. She licked her lips before gliding his length into her mouth slowly, and was rewarded with a curse and her name falling from his lips.

She started slow, then picked up in the pace, moving faster and faster, her own arousal building from the sounds of his appreciative groans. His hand raked over her head, yanking a handful of hair, but she lost herself in the moment, wanting to pleasure him to the end, knowing that he needed it.

The speed and ferocity of his release, when it came, consumed them both. She wiped her mouth as he let out a sigh, his chest rising and falling, as if he'd run a mile.

"Sorry," he said, breathless. "I didn't mean to—"

She scooted onto the bed and kissed his chest. "I wanted to," she said, easily, the happiness inside her rising like a soufflé, knowing that something she had done had made him feel better. He opened his arm, and she slid in, nestling her head against his chest. All those other times they'd met for sex, this was what he had denied her, and she had hungered for it.

She lay alongside him, still in her bra and panties, while he was fully clothed. The mask he often wore guarded his inner feelings, but she had seen it stripped bare this evening. Holding her, his defenses seemed to have crumbled, and the weight somewhat lifted. Now he looked relaxed, and it made her happy to know she had done that for him.

They lay like that for the longest time, and her cocooned in his arms, him holding her close as if he needed her.

She hugged him without thinking.

"What?" he asked, kissing the top of her head.

"Nothing," she replied, kissing his chest. She was happy, that's what, and as much as she wanted to tell him that, something made her hold back. If his mask had slipped, it would only be a matter of time before he put it on again, and she didn't want to risk messing things up. She didn't want to presume too much, and as much as she wanted to lie here all night, she couldn't.

She soon had her answer when the sound of soft snoring told her he wouldn't be able to rise to the occasion again; therefore the only alternative was for her to go home, even though she was loathe to leave him.

Silently, she moved off the bed.

"What are you doing?" he asked, opening his eyes. He lifted his head up as she slipped her dress over her head.

"Getting ready," she replied, trying to do up the zipper at the back.

"For what?"

"To go home," she replied, puzzled.

"You don't have to."

"But..." She didn't know what to say, because that had been the arrangement. He'd told her from the start. "You always want me to go."

He got out of bed and walked towards her. She didn't dare to breathe. He was so changeable, she never knew where she stood with him.

"Stay with me tonight."

"You want me to stay?" she asked, making sure even as her heart seemed to miss a beat. Maybe it was starting to happen—that this was turning into more than just sex. She *was* beginning to matter, and he was beginning to care. She pulled the zipper up slowly then switched her arms to pull the rest of it up with her other hand, but he came up behind her and stopped her.

"Yes," he said, standing so close behind her that she could feel his breath against her neck. "Stay, not because I'm asking you to, but because you want to."

Her mind fought to make sense of it all. Too much had happened today. He wanted her to stay. Things *could* change. Things *were* changing. He cared about her, and she now understood more about him.

"I want to fuck you."

And with those words, her hopes and happiness plummeted.

Her head fell to her chest as she closed her eyes at the blow. Who had she been kidding? "I should—I should go," she said, scrambling to pull herself together, forcing her voice to sound louder and steadier than she felt.

Why couldn't he ask her to stay because he *wanted* her to stay, because he wanted to be with her? Why did he always make it be about the other thing? She longed for the romance, for softness, and seduction, not for being treated like a whore.

"Why?" she asked, giving him another chance to redeem himself.

"Why, what?" he asked, grazing her neck with his lips. He slowly pulled the zipper all the way down again. "Why do I want to fuck you?"

"Why do you want me to stay?" She willed him for another answer, willed him not to see her as Good-Time-Kay for she no longer wanted to be that woman.

Today, he'd shown her his wounds, and she'd started to believe she could heal him and help him to change. She could do all these things, because *he* was slowly starting to change. His request just now was a remnant of his usual self. In time, he would come to see that he needed her for more than sex.

"It's cold outside, and it's warm in my bed." He nuzzled her ear some more, and pressed his body against hers, and this time she felt his hardness against her back.

"I'm tired," she said, fumbling around with the embroidered beads around her neckline, distracting herself from the harsh reality that his words had subjected her to. He had reminded her once more that what they had wasn't normal, and that she still played along with this lewd arrangement, even when, most days, it was no longer enough.

He planted a wet kiss along her nape, nibbling her delicate skin between his lips, making her shiver.

"You want this, don't you?" he whispered, mistaking her reaction for arousal. Now it's my turn to pay you back." He moved her hair to one side then kissed her neck with a gentleness that was rare. There was nothing fast, and urgent now. He was taking his time, drawing tiny, wet kisses along her neckline while his fingers stroked her jaw.

She should have been happy. He'd let her take care of him, as daring a move as any she had ever made, and now he was asking her to stay. He was a master at raising her hopes then shooting them down. And now she was caught between giving in, and giving him up; a thought flashing through her mind of the rollercoaster ride she was on with this man.

"But what about your rules?" she questioned, finding the courage because he had a chink in his armor and she had nothing to lose.

"Screw the rules."

"Why now?" she asked, as he slipped the dress off her shoulders. It pooled around her ankles.

"It's been a trying day for me," he said, stroking her shoulders gently. With her dress off, his manhood jabbed her in the back. He pressed in harder, teasing her, letting her know.

She was expecting too much, if she hoped that Luke Hunter was falling in love with her, but this gentle way he had, right in this moment, of touching her and talking to her and pleading with her to stay, made her think there would be better times ahead.

This man made her happy when he was happy, and he made her miserable when he was not, and there wasn't a thing she could do about it.

"And you make things better," he moaned, his hot breath warming her neck.

"Better?" she asked, sounding hopeful, giving in and sinking back into him. He was familiar now, each cell in her body recognizing everything about him, from the scent of his aftershave, to the feel of his arousal against her. His fingers on her and inside her, like his mouth all over her body—every part of him had already imprinted onto her.

She liked that he wasn't rushing things, liked the way his hands circled around her hips and waist, slowly moving lower. Liked the way his lips made slow, sensual love to her neck and shoulders.

"Why didn't you tell me you had a brother?" she asked, suddenly remembering. He lifted his mouth from her shoulder, his hands stilling around her hips but he remained silent.

"Because it wasn't important."

This was going to take digging. "Why don't you both get on?"

"Because we don't."

"But you do with Amanda."

"Yes."

He wasn't giving her much. "What about—"

"I don't want to talk about it," he said, unclasping her bra, then peeling down her panties. She heard the soft shuffle of him undressing quickly behind her before his arms came down around her and he pressed his naked body against her. She sighed, throwing back her head as she sank back against his chest. He pushed her back to standing, then quickly made his way down her body, still behind her before falling to his knees and pleasuring her with his fingers and mouth. She barely managed to keep standing, her knees threatening to buckle beneath her. She had barely managed to catch her breath when he pushed her onto the bed on all fours and thrust inside her.

And just as fast, he pulled out. "Condom," he muttered,

leaving her feeling cold, and exposed while he moved off the bed.

Her heart raced, and blood surged through her veins. In her fully aroused state she was about to tell him that the condom didn't matter. That she might be pregnant. But before she could say anything, his cock slammed into her, and she cried out in ecstasy, and gratitude, and relief.

Her insides were like a raging forest fire as he owned her, pounding into her relentlessly, the let-up never coming. She could feel the tight pressure building in her belly, heat radiating outwards from her core, tipping her almost over, over, over, and just as she was on the precipice, he pulled out and turned her over onto her back. He thrust into her again, staring at her with an intensity he had never shown before. There was no ending of her body and his. They were one, and that was all that mattered. She needed him the way a fish needed water; without him she ceased to be. She was just an empty vessel, going about her day, but in his arms, she came alive.

She brought her knees up, opening up, letting him sink balls-deep inside her, making her moan in ecstasy. They came together, a tangled mess of heat and sweat, of hearts beating furiously.

Later, as they lay in bed, on their sides, his chest against her back, and holding her, she felt special. For one foolish night, she pretended that this was where she belonged.

CHAPTER TWENTY-FIVE

She could give a man a hard-on in a stiff breeze.

Kay's back was turned to him when he opened the door, and a puff of steam rose past him. She spun around. Rivulets of water trickling down her hair and shoulders. "I didn't want to wake you. I hope you don't mind me using the shower—"

Seriously? "Why would I mind you using the shower?" He pressed his lips together, contemplating her words. "Am I that much of a monster?"

"I wasn't sure, that's all."

"Do you mind?" she said, covering herself with her hands as best as she could.

"I've seen everything, no point in hiding it."

"You have, haven't you?" she replied, letting her hands slip to her sides so that he could see everything. He struggled to remain to stand still and do nothing. He'd made love to her last night; it hadn't only been pure animal rutting, he'd experienced something deeper, more fulfilling. And waking up with her had been just about the best thing. It sure beat waking up alone.

He rubbed the back of his neck, contemplating the turn of events. The whole goddamn tsunami of events that had happened this weekend. If he didn't watch himself, he was going to get hurt. He had become so adept at placing women and relationships on the periphery of his daily life, far removed from his life goals and dreams, that Kay's effect on him, her ability to make him sit up and take notice, was troubling.

For her, he had a craving the likes of which he hadn't known in years. This weekend he'd allowed himself the indulgence of enjoying her without thinking too much.

"Did you sleep well?" he asked.

"I don't remember us sleeping much."

He couldn't help but smile at that. "No." *He* had slept well, though. Maybe it was something to do with her being there, next to him. Her body warm, and soft, and comforting.

"You're beautiful," he murmured, his compliment slipping out unchecked, because she was, and because he felt something for her. He looked at her, staring right into her eyes. It had been another lifetime ago that he'd felt this close to someone. Sex had served a need, but this woman filled something deeper than that. It unsettled him, as much as it anchored him.

"Do you mind!" she cried, half-laughing as she tried to cover her breasts, ignoring his compliment. If she was as shocked by his compliment, as he had been to say it, she hid it well. He didn't say these things to women. He had learned to keep his thoughts to himself, just like he had learned to push the good ones away.

"No, and neither should you," he said, staring right into her eyes. "You *are* beautiful, inside and out. I guess I'm lucky I met you."

It was an awkward moment, one in which he had dared to be bare and transparent with her. She looked as if she didn't know how to respond, and so she turned to the side, lifting her hands to her hair as the water ran down it.

"I'm making coffee." This was another first for him in a long time, having someone stay the night. After yesterday, seeing the family after so many years, having Kay over had been his salvation. "Did you want some?"

"You're asking me to stay for breakfast?" Her mocking tone was hard to miss, even over the sound of the shower running.

"Not breakfast, just coffee," he replied, jokingly.

"I thought so."

"I'm kidding. I'll make breakfast. What will you have?"

That simple question seemed to have stumped her. "Just coffee."

"Why don't we go out and get breakfast? Or maybe even some brunch later?" he suggested. His goddamn neck was still sore, and he'd have to pop a couple of pills, but still, having her around for breakfast was better than having breakfast alone.

"I have to go to work."

He blinked, slowly, trying to decipher if this was her way of backing off. "It's Saturday."

"I know, but I have to go in. There'll be lots for me to catch up on."

"Just because you took one day off?"

"What can I say?" she said, throwing her hands up, directing his attention to those beautiful ample breasts. She turned the shower off, and he handed her a towel.

"That's too bad." *Too bad.* He didn't want her to go so soon, and it got him thinking if she really was just looking for an excuse to leave. He worked every day and there were things for him to look over daily, but they could wait.

He remembered that he'd bought her something. A second gift. After she'd given him cufflinks for Christmas, he'd felt foolish for not having anything to give her in return. He'd gone back to that lingerie store and picked up some sexy lingerie for her. Then, thinking that it was tacky and might send the wrong message—he didn't want her to think that she was merely a plaything to him—he'd bought her a bracelet later as well. He'd noticed that she wasn't a necklace or earrings girl and that she wore a watch and usually something thin and elegant around her wrists. So he had bought her a pretty diamond and platinum bracelet.

It was back in the office. If it was here, he could have given it to her. It would have been the perfect time to give it to her now. She knew more about him than anyone. The stuff about his mother? He'd never told Xavier, or the sports masseuse or any of the others. Nobody knew about that shit, not even Marie. His past was locked away in a cold and dark corner of his heart, but Kay had somehow managed to unlock it.

"I'll put the coffee on," he said. "Take as long as you want."

The aroma of fresh coffee filled the air.

"That smells good," she said, walking into the kitchen later, still wearing the dress she had worn to the wedding yesterday. She didn't like wearing yesterday's clothes and underwear, but not in her craziest fantasies had she ever imagined she would be spending the night at Luke's place.

She hopped onto a stool next to him, at the breakfast bar.

"Are you sure you don't want to eat anything? We had a crazy night last night."

Her stomach fluttered at his words. It wasn't like him to talk about these things. Usually what they did was cut and dry; they met, had sex, and it was done with.

It filled her with a sense of joy, him saying what he had. "We did, didn't we?" she agreed.

"I liked that you stayed the night."

She had to school herself not to grin outright at that. Memories of him making her come all night danced inside her giddy brain. This was unexpected. Not just last night and staying over, but this morning, *now*. She'd half-expected the magic dust to have disintegrated, and that he would have been eager for her to leave, that she would be walking out in last night's clothes with last night's mascara running down her dirty face, but everything about him this morning indicated otherwise.

She hadn't expected *this*.

"I liked that you asked me to," she replied. His barriers had slipped so far down and he seemed to be saying what was on his tongue. It was eye-opening.

She wondered if this was what people like Tobias and Savannah experienced, this heady feeling of wanting to smile all the time because every cell in her body tingled with joy. Joy that came from being near him, doing nothing more than sitting here and drinking coffee.

"How's your throat?" she asked, her gaze dropping to his jaw. "Is it your throat? Or your neck?"

"I'm not sure. It hurts to swallow."

Poor man. She almost lifted her hand to his face to cup it. It had been easy enough to do last night, but she wasn't so sure this morning how to be around him. "I didn't know you weren't feeling too good."

"I've had this pain for a couple of weeks. I think I need to go back and get it properly seen to."

"Don't leave it any longer" she cautioned.

"It'll be fine," he said, dismissing her concern. "I might have forced myself to stay for the party if I was feeling 100%."

"You left because you weren't feeling well?" She didn't quite believe him.

"I'd been popping pills all morning."

"In secret."

He shrugged.

"You should call your sister and explain. She seems nice."

"She is."

"And your brother?" she asked, tentatively broaching that sore subject.

"Let's have a good morning, and not talk about him."

"Okay," she said slowly, reluctantly abandoning the list of questions she had about him. "You should try and make it up to Amanda, somehow."

"Take her out to dinner, you mean."

"You don't do dinner."

He raised an eyebrow. "Can we let that go?"

"Are you breaking all your rules for me?"

He looked away. It wasn't the reaction she had expected.

"Forget I said that," she added, hastily, not wanting to push things.

"It's forgotten." He tapped his fingers on the table. "Maybe we could all go out as couples for dinner?"

She tried not to show her total surprise. "Amanda and her new husband, and you and me?"

"Didn't realize you had to spell it out quite like that, but yes."

"It feels as if I'm looking at a new you. It's like your brain got partly rewired after the wedding."

He was so full of surprises this morning, so nice, and loving, and caring. She much preferred this nice version of Luke, and now she found herself holding her plans in check. She had considered ditching him after the wedding because she couldn't do this any longer, but she had seen that he could be different. That once she had probed deep enough, once he'd let her in, she had discovered his frailty, his softness, his decency. She understood that he sought comfort in his sexual interactions, but the way he was talking to her now made her feel less like a sex object and more like a girlfriend. It made what they had seem more like a relationship than a hookup.

He turned sideways on the stool, so that his entire body was facing her, reminding her of what it had been like to lie snuggled up against him last night. "The rewiring has nothing to do with the wedding," he said.

"No?" She took another sip of her coffee, trying to suppress the hope rising within her.

"Seems like fucking you in every conceivable position did that."

Her smile dropped as fast as her hopes had risen. He might as well have ripped her heart out.

"It's your fault," he continued, not noticing her silence, "you being so goddamn sexy. It's hard for a man like me to keep his hands off you."

She was speechless, and it was suddenly hard to breathe. His words had sucked the air right out of her lungs.

"That's what they all say," she replied, finally, as her built-in survival tactics kicked in. "It's a miracle I can walk straight this morning."

"You weren't complaining last night," he replied, flashing her an I-can-make-you-come-all-night smile. Her heart had already plummeted to her ankles by the time she'd drained her coffee cup. "It was pure, filthy, dirty sex, and you know how much I love that," she said, returning his wide, full smile, even though she was dying inside.

"We must do it again sometime," he told her, the light in his eyes suddenly dimming as she stood up. His brows lifted, as if he didn't quite understand something.

"I'll see when I can next pencil you in," she said, looking around for her handbag.

"You're leaving?"

She couldn't get out fast enough.

CHAPTER TWENTY-SIX

"You look pale," said Marie, sitting across the desk from him.

"Been a tiring weekend." It could have been a lazy weekend. At least, a lazy Sunday, had Kay not rushed to leave so quickly yesterday. Maybe he shouldn't have been as direct about the sex and about how she made him feel. He wouldn't have, had she not reminded him that he was starting to break his rules for her.

"You shouldn't have driven there and back," Marie suggested, giving him a disapproving nod. She hadn't been happy when he had told her that they had left soon after the wedding. "Not staying for your sister's wedding reception. That's unheard of."

"I saw the wedding," he maintained, trying to keep his cool.

"And would it have killed you to stay for the reception?" she asked, fueling his simmering anger. He'd been annoyed with himself before he'd come into work this morning. Sunday could have been so much better if it had worked out, if he'd managed, for once, not to lose his shit over things.

Coming to work and dealing with a pissed off Marie made things even more shitty. "Can you drop it, please?"

"Family relationships are hard," she held a finger up, mom-style, making him snap his mouth closed. "It was your sister's wedding, Luke. Her *wedding*. Would it have killed you to sit down for a couple of hours?"

He swallowed. Marie didn't know what she was talking about, and he was beginning to lose his patience.

"Quit going on about it, Marie. You're as bad as Kay."

"She said the same thing to you?" asked Marie, her voice lifting. "I like that girl. She seems to give you a run for your money."

He picked apart a large paperclip, bending the thin wire out of shape.

"What did she think?"

"Of what?" he asked, looking up, his mind had completely switched off for a few moments there. His mind had backtracked to him and Kay having coffee, and how differently things might have turned out had he not been careless with his words.

"Of the Easter Bunny," replied Marie, her face deadpan. "What do you think?"

"She was glad she came with me," he replied, vaguely, his thoughts distracting him again.

"I'll have to ask her myself. At least that way I'll get an honest answer."

"We have more important things to deal with, and Canal Street is our main priority right now." Work would soon begin on the new site, and he had a shit ton of contracts and legal paperwork to deal with.

"You should go over there today, and check it out,"

Marie told him. "I need to catch up with work here at the office."

His neck was hurting again, and he'd made an appointment to see the doctor later today. "I'll go over tomorrow." He had every intention of keeping an eye on the place while the builders were working on it, but just not today.

"Let me know next time that girlfriend of yours is here," said Marie, getting up and walking towards the door.

He wanted to see her again. Only, he had stuff to deal with first. He was feeling tired again. The wedding had drained him, seeing his family had emotionally drained him, but physically he was feeling tired, too. The only time he had forgotten all the tiredness, the only time he had felt truly alive was when Kay had been around. Having her next to him in bed and holding her through the night had been comforting. In her he had found the kind of peace he hadn't found in anyone, and then he'd gone and ruined it.

Opening his desk drawer, he looked at the gifts still lying inside. He had no idea when Kay's birthday was, and it occurred to him that he could give her these gifts for Valentine's Day.

But that would risk him making some kind of statement and it wasn't in his DNA to take a good thing and run with it.

Even if that good thing had helped him to somehow bury the past. Meeting Travis and Maggie hadn't been as difficult as it usually was. He'd dreaded that moment, but it had lost its impact on him.

Maybe he had moved on. This was all Kay's doing. She was helping him erase the hurt from his past, and she didn't even know about it.

He picked up the jewelry box and fingered its embossed

gold signage. For a guy who avoided commitment, he was going about things the wrong way.

Unless he was no longer that guy.

He had slapped her back to reality with a sentence.

Perhaps that hadn't been a bad thing, otherwise she would have continued to wrap herself up in grand delusions about their passionate night together.

Luke was so changeable, like a chameleon, and maybe her impressions of him had been right all along.

As the days passed, she found herself confused about the state of their relationship. As much as she wanted to end it, she found herself unable to walk away, especially now that she had a window into his soul and had glimpsed some of his demons. She wanted to help him, but he wasn't an easy man to help, or love, or be with. This much she had learned.

Spending that night with him after the wedding had convinced her that he was starting to change. Their intimacy had deepened, and waking up the next morning in his bed, with his arms around her, had given her hope that the relationship she had secretly been wanting all along, might slowly come to be.

She had seen a gentler, more considerate side to him, as well as an intensely troubled side, too, and his revelation to her, about his mother and her subsequent death, and his father's mistress, had caught her off guard. It was as if the stress of seeing his family again had brought down his barriers, and softened him enough so that he could open up to her.

If she had been dreading the morning-after

awkwardness, his actions the next day had completely surprised her.

It had all gone so well, him talking to her, and opening up, and suggesting they go out and grab something for brunch later on. And then he'd gone and ruined it all by reminding her of the reason he wanted to be with her.

For sex, and nothing more.

She had left his apartment wondering if that was how men like Luke Hunter rolled, and she reminded herself that she had been on the brink of splitting up with him before, and that she had only put it off because of the wedding.

She had been torn. One moment thinking that it was possible to move beyond the hookups, and the next moment, convinced that she was being an idealistic and hopeless fool for thinking this way.

But that had been a week ago, and she hadn't heard from him since. No text or email, nor a phone call. It was Valentine's Day tomorrow, and she would have expected at least a text or something by now, because he had no idea how much he'd upset her, and he would have assumed that everything was still fine between them. Besides, it wasn't as if she was expecting a present from him. Christmas had taught her that the guy wasn't into exchanging gifts. She already knew not to have any expectations, and had forced herself to forget that night with him, but it was hard to when Luke Hunter's sense and smell were still imprinted all over her.

She could no more *not* think about him, than she could not breathe. Forgetting him was impossible, and was made more so because of his total silence. She didn't know what to think. She wasn't sure if he was ignoring her because he regretted making himself vulnerable, or whether he was just busy. He'd mentioned that work would soon be starting on the new club he'd recently bought on Canal Street, but the truth was, she just didn't know what to think.

So when Erin suggested that they go to The Oasis, she found herself in a quandary, particularly since she didn't know what face to show the friend who was so excited for her 'new romance.'

"Why not?" Erin whined, when Kay made up another excuse for why she couldn't.

"I can't," she replied, pretending to busy herself in work. She had plenty to do and had done a few fourteen-hour workdays lately, but that was because her mind hadn't been on work as much as it should have been.

She hadn't had her period either. Unable to wait, she'd taken a test, but it had been negative. She was treading between the two possibilities. One in which she carried Luke's child, and one in which she didn't. Only time would tell. Maybe she'd take the test again in a few days' time.

She had no desire to step foot inside Luke's bar just yet. Back when it had been just a hookup, things had been different. *Easier.* She hadn't given of herself as emotionally back then.

But there was more than just her reputation to think about now, it wasn't just about what Erin, or Geoffrey, or Savannah might say, if they knew. It was about protecting her heart. Unable to help herself, she had entertained the idea that she and Luke could have something more, that he needed her, even if he couldn't say it in as many words. Her feelings for him had changed.

If he had at least tried to get in touch this past week, she might have taken Erin up on her offer, but going to the bar now, given Luke's silence, might anger him. *She* had good reason to be angry with him—she had come to demand more from the relationship and now she knew that he didn't. For him it was what it was; convenient sex between two like-minded people. She couldn't understand his reasons. Perhaps he couldn't handle it, those broken rules and the revelation about his past and his mother's story. Those things might have been too big a step for him to take.

"Just for a couple of drinks," Erin insisted.

"No," she replied, looking up at Erin somberly.

"Have you both had a fight?" her friend asked. "I noticed you've had your head down lately."

"In case you hadn't noticed, Remington is looking to me for results. I can't mess this up."

"Not even for a couple of drinks?"

"Maybe next week." She would wait it out. Let Luke come to her. Or make the move and split up with him now so that the thing was done soon. Anything was better than dealing with the mental trauma of being in this type of situation with that type of guy.

CHAPTER TWENTY-SEVEN

"Do you want to get a beer or something?" Xavier asked him soon after he had arrived at the Canal Street site.

Luke was happy to see him, but getting a drink was going to be impossible. "I could do with a couple of beers, but I can't today. There's just too much going on." He did a double take because his friend looked like shit. In fact, Luke was pretty certain he didn't look so good himself. After his visit to the doctor, and a subsequent ultrasound, he'd discovered that the doctor wanted to run more tests.

"Why? What brings you here?" he asked, because something was clearly up with his friend. They hadn't kept in touch lately, so the fact that his friend had turned up, told him things were dire.

"She found out," said Xavier, looking miserable. "Izzy found out about the bet."

"She what?" Poor girl. That couldn't have gone down well at all. He swiped a hand on the back of his neck, staring at his friend. Xavier looked as if his easy-come-easy-go world had imploded. In the background, the continued banging and drilling noises, as well as the workmen's loud, gruff voices, filled the air.

This wasn't the place to have *that* type of conversation and he could see that Xavier needed someone to talk to. He was about to suggest they go someplace quiet, when Xavier spoke. "She found out. She knows, and she hates me for it."

"How the hell did she find out?"

"I have no fucking idea." Xavier glanced at him. "Wasn't you, was it?"

Luke had to blink a few times to make sure he wasn't dreaming. They weren't close *close*, like in your face close. Xavier didn't know anything about him, or even that he'd been to his sister's wedding, or who he was dating—if you could call what he and Kay had *dating*. But this surprised him, that his friend would think he'd been the one to snitch on him. "You're really asking *me*?" He glared at Xavier in disbelief. Shaking his head, he said, "I never said anything. You know I wouldn't, right?"

"I don't know how the fuck she found out, then."

"Wasn't me." He couldn't believe Xavier had continued with that crazy, lame-ass idea of his. A $10K bet to bed a woman? Who the hell did that kind of thing? "You didn't seem to be getting anywhere pursuing her, and I thought you'd forgotten about it."

"I *wasn't* getting anywhere, and I *did* forget about it."

"So, what's the problem?"

"Things changed," replied Xavier, in a dull voice.

"Things changed? Like what?"

"I like her."

Luke blinked, trying to digest what Xavier had just said. Was it possible that Xavier had fallen for Izzy—as impossible as that seemed?

"So what's the problem?" he asked again. If he liked her,

surely he could find a way to explain his crazy ass idea to her. At least, he could try. It had been a hell of a stupid idea in the first place and the guy seemed to be getting his karma returned.

"I meant to tell her."

Oh, hell yes. The need to come clean. Xavier *had* fallen for her. "Why? I wouldn't have told her, and she would never have found out."

"Doesn't matter. She knows now. It's all blown up."

No wonder the guy looked like shit. It wouldn't have mattered much if he didn't care, but having the girl you like suddenly find out that you put a price on bedding her, so *not* a good idea. Perhaps he shouldn't have been surprised that Xavier had feelings for this girl, especially if he'd had to work hard to get her. "I've never known you to *not* like pretty and sexy, and Izzy seems to be the perfect combination, but what made her warm towards you?" This was the million-dollar question. How a sensible girl like Izzy could fall for a playboy like Xavier.

"Stuff," said Xavier. "Maybe she saw my better side."

"You must have done your best to charm her?" he asked. It must have been something big because, as far as he was concerned, Izzy and Xavier had nothing in common.

Xavier Stone was like a walking hard-on. His affinity for women, for being known as the stud, and for being so blatant about it, always surprised Luke. They were both so different in that respect, even though they both worked their way through plenty of women. Xavier openly chased after them—the guy loved women and he loved pussy. He seemed to make a game out of it. But Luke didn't chase them. He didn't need women in the same way Xavier did, and he could just as easily do without them for long periods of time. That is, until he'd met Kay, and now he didn't know what to think.

"I didn't play her," replied Xavier, defensively.

Luke understood. Xavier had fallen for Izzy in a big way —otherwise her finding out about the bet would never have been a problem. He didn't want to hurt this girl, but by virtue of her finding out what he'd done, she would never forgive him, and he couldn't handle that. "And what we had," he continued, "wasn't based on trying to get her into bed."

Yet the guy was smiling. The girl he had fallen for had just found out that he'd placed a bet on her, and he was grinning about it. Either his feelings weren't as deep as he professed, or he was using laughter to disguise his pain. "Why are you smiling?" he asked. "Is this still a game to you?"

"No. *No.*" Xavier shook his head. "I'm crazy about that girl."

"How crazy, exactly?"

"The kind of crazy I've never been."

Seriously? He took a closer look at his friend's miserable face. His eyes gave a clue to his suffering. Luke whistled. "Shit."

"You see my problem?" snapped Xavier, throwing his hands up in the air. "She found out about everything. About the bet, about the money, and that it was you and me who talked about it."

Hell, no. "She knows I'm implicated?" He hated Xavier for that. As far as Luke was concerned, he and Izzy had gotten on fine on Tobias's private island. Luke had harbored no such feelings for her.

Xavier's eyes narrowed. "Tell me you don't have any designs on her?" he demanded, making a second ridiculous accusation in the same conversation. Seriously? Was this guy for real?

Luke didn't go looking for women. They came to him. And Izzy was a student, for fuck's sake, she was still at college—even if she'd expressed an interest in him he would never have hooked up with her.

"You idiot," he muttered. The guy was obviously in love because his brain had turned to mush, and he wasn't capable of thinking straight. Why else would he make such unjust accusations? "I'm not interested in your girl." It was sad to see, what the green-eyed monster of jealousy could to do a man, and then he remembered that night around Christmas time when he'd caught Kay's ex making a play for her. He hadn't been able to handle that too well, either.

Jealousy was a bitch.

"You sure?" Xavier asked.

"Calm your shit," said Luke, mildly irritated, and understanding his friend's turmoil. "I'm *not* interested in your girl."

"Okay."

And in case he and Izzy ever discussed where this ridiculous idea came from, he said, "The bet wasn't my idea, pal."

"It was my fucking stupid idea," agreed Xavier. "So now, tell me. How do I get out of this mess?"

"You've tried to explain to her?"

"Yes, I've tried. I've texted and emailed and left long messages on her phone. She won't talk to me."

"I can see why. You were an idiot, and it was a crazy thing to do." Winning Izzy back after such a big fuck-up wasn't going to be easy.

"Who's side are you on?" Xavier growled.

"On yours, you idiot. I'm just trying to think it through, figure out what your best plan of action might be."

"I was drunk. I thought I had something to prove, and I believed she was acting all not-interested, and that it was going to be easy to make her see."

Luke nodded, and expelled a hard breath of air. "Make her see how awesome you were?" he asked.

"I hate hearing you describe me like that."

That sounded about right for Xavier. Twisted thinking that had nothing to do with Izzy's feelings, and was based purely on his.

Come to think of it, the same could have been said for him, and Kay would probably agree with that. His needs had been paramount to her feelings, especially when they had first gotten together. And then later on, his initial reason for asking her to accompany him to the wedding.

He'd been no less a jerk than Xavier.

"Luke?" He turned around when he heard someone shout out his name. It was one of the workmen. Raising his hand, he indicated that he'd be over in five. This wasn't the time or place to be having this kind of conversation. The bar looked like a demolition site. "I can't talk. My men need me. But look, here's the thing, pal. You have to give her time. You have to stop pestering her. You have to wait for her to come to you, but it depends."

Xavier looked up. "On what?"

"If she was really into you in the first place."

"She was."

She must have been. Izzy Laronde wasn't the type of girl to give any guy—no matter how interested he was in her —the time of day.

"Then you have to give her time to find her way back."

One of his guys came up to him again. "We need you to take a look at this wall now, boss."

"I'm coming." Luke turned to Xavier. "Sorry. I need to go. Now's not a good time."

"I appreciate it," said Xavier. At least he didn't look as worried as he had initially. Maybe talking things over had helped. "We'll get together sometime," Luke promised.

"Yeah. You call me. I'm not as busy as you." He left, and Luke walked over to his construction guys.

Later, he returned to his office to finish up on some paperwork and saw that he had a couple of calls to return, including one from the hospital. It was too late to make the calls now, so after tending to some urgent emails, he freshened up, and changed into a clean pair of clothes.

The conversation with Xavier was still fresh in his mind. His friend had surprised him. He'd done the impossible and had managed to win the heart of a sensible college student. Of course, he'd lost her just as quickly, by the sounds of it.

People changed. The impossible became possible. Rules were not set in stone. He and Kay weren't complete opposites—they were similar in more ways than not. He used women for comfort, the same way she used men.

Women like Kay could deal with the type of relationship he was willing to have, for he didn't only screw women physically, he knew that he probably screwed with their minds. Despite what some women said, they couldn't handle a meaningless fling—not one that lasted more than a couple of nights. And unless you were a hooker charging by the hour, no woman was willing to be someone's fuck buddy, and be happy with it long-term.

But now things were changing even for him, and that was a problem he needed to take care of. Something had changed between him and Kay that night, and he'd reacted the only way he'd known how to afterwards, he'd ignored her completely. He'd been condescending to her over coffee, when he could have been genuine. He could have asked her to spend the day with him, tried harder when she'd made excuses about having to go to work.

Maybe she was confused with the way he was being around her all of a sudden. He could have told her he enjoyed her company, maybe even told her that it meant something having her with him at the wedding. But he'd gone and spoiled it all by playing up the sex part of their arrangement.

It wasn't love. Absolutely, definitely not. But it no longer felt like just a hookup, either.

He hadn't called her since that night after the wedding, but not a day had passed that he didn't think of her. He'd purposely stopped himself from getting in touch because the feeling of getting used to having her around scared him.

But he didn't want to end up like Xavier, not realizing what he had until he risked losing her. And now, the idea of seeing her, or making it up to her, made his heart beat faster.

He opened the drawer and saw the gifts he'd decided to give her for Valentine's Day. He didn't *do* Valentine's Day, ordinarily. But he could mention that he'd bought them just after Christmas, confess that he'd felt like a real douchebag that he hadn't gotten her anything. Whatever. He'd use it to try and put things right.

He slipped the jewelry box into his jacket pocket, and picked up the dainty gift bag. Grabbing his keys, he considered texting her to see where she was, then decided against it. She had avoided coming to the bar, and he hadn't been in touch. Things between them were probably a little icy. It would be best to turn up unannounced at her place, and unless she had found another watering hole, he assumed she'd be at home.

Twenty minutes later, he was at her door with a gift bag and a bottle of the best champagne.

But no flowers.

Damn.

He'd forgotten the flowers.

This looked like a typical booty call, and today of all days. Just as he was about to turn around and leave to get the flowers, she opened the door. Her face was a picture of surprise and shock, but she seemed to compose herself quickly. He was starting to wonder if this had been as great an idea as he had first envisioned.

"Hey?" She said it like a question, and stared at him with a *what-the hell-are-you-doing-here* expression.

"Hi." He smiled, tilting his head slightly, trying to gauge at which end of the in-deep-shit scale he was at. On a scale of 1 to 10, with 10 being the worst, it seemed he was at a 10.

"You should have called," she remarked, stiffly, reminding him that their hookups had never been spontaneous.

"I wanted to surprise you." He handed her the gift bag. "For you," he said, noting her hesitation in taking it.

"What is it?"

"Take it and you'll see," he insisted, dangling the bag in front of her. She was cold, and understandably so, but he had plans to fix that.

"You shouldn't have."

"I wanted to."

She shrugged as she took the bag. "Thanks, but you shouldn't have..."

He followed her in and briefly wondered if he'd caught her

at a busy time, that she might have been working, but there was no obvious paperwork or laptop in sight. She placed the gift bag on the table, and walked away without looking through it.

Things were not looking good.

"Sorry," he said. "I should have called, first. Is this a bad time?"

Her face turned slightly pink. "I can't," she said looking away, "It's my...I'm on...my period."

He remained rooted to where he stood, her words confusing him and derailing his thoughts completely. The whole moment was steeped in awkwardness, as they stood a foot apart, in her living room.

"I...I..." He didn't know what to say, especially since his motive for coming here tonight hadn't been to have sex. "That's too bad."

Her brows knotted together, and he realized too late that it had been the wrong thing to say. "I mean," he said, fumbling around trying to find a way to redeem himself. "It's okay, it's not why I'm here."

She folded her arms, and stared back at him and he wished she would say something but she didn't. She seemed to be waiting for him to speak.

"Do you need anything?" he asked, hating the silence, and for once feeling as though he didn't have control of the conversation. "Can I get you anything?"

"I'm on my period, Luke. I'm not sick."

"I know." He coughed lightly. "I know that." What was he supposed to say? *Get better?* She'd only bite his head off. "I'll—uh, I'll see you around. Call me." What an idiot. Why had he gone and said that? She seemed so hostile, and so unwilling to even give him a shred of a smile, that he couldn't find a way of salvaging the visit.

She clearly didn't think anything of the gifts. Escape was his best option.

"Call you? When I'm able to have sex again, you mean?"

Her words hit him like an axe slicing clean through him, and he couldn't work out if she was mad because of her time of month, or because she was just generally annoyed at him.

"That's not...that's not what..."

"But you've come here for a reason, *for sex*," she said, spitting the words out as if they tasted bitter. "Why else do we see one another? What else do we have?"

Goddamnit. Talk about walking into the eye of a hurricane. A sinking feeling collected in his stomach. This was the last thing he needed, after the kind of week he'd had. Who the hell needed this shit? Not him, that's for sure. Not when he'd done the decent thing and come to see her, with gifts and with the intention of making it up to her.

She hadn't even given him a chance.

Every instinct in his body told him to turn and run, but her standing there, looking so miserable and pitiful, made him feel sorry for her again.

Why couldn't she be like the others? Playful and laughing.

A tease.

Why couldn't she be the way she had been on the island, and in the earlier days when she had come to the bar looking for him?

"What else do we have?" he asked, incredulous, his anger beginning to rise. "You knew what this was going in," he flung back at her.

"Yes I did, and, like I said, I'll call you when I'm fuckable again."

He jerked his head up in surprise, his eyes settling on

her face. She never usually swore, and right now, she looked pretty pissed. This wasn't at all how he had expected this evening to go. Gritting his teeth together, he considered going over to her, and comforting her. And then he wondered if women routinely turned into banshees when it was their time of the month, or if they merely showed their true colors.

"You do that."

He left, closing the door behind him and walking away as fast as he could, even though it didn't feel right to be walking away when she was obviously hurting about something.

Turn around, make it better. Don't leave her like this.

But if he turned back and apologized, and tried to be there for her, she would think of a happily-ever-after future, and that was not in his life plan.

Christ, it was difficult enough acknowledging that his feelings had changed, but too many moments like this, full of conflict and headache, made him wonder if he could go the distance.

He wasn't ready for the emotional landmines. Couldn't suffer more of the explosions blowing up his world all over again.

Emotional involvement? It had always been a no-no, it *should* have been a no-no even now. He didn't need this level of complication in his life, and he should have walked away. Even after that first pity-fuck.

***

She wasn't pregnant. She'd started her period last night, and the hope she had been carrying around with her had died at the sight of her blood. She hadn't realized the depth of her sadness until now; hadn't realized how deep her desire had been that she might be pregnant. It didn't matter that it would have been Luke's—given how she felt about him now, but the idea that she *could* be pregnant had given her an inner strength she had started to cling to.

And just like that, her hopes had crashed and burned. She'd been in a dark mood even before Luke had arrived at her door.

She should have ended it. If she'd had her wits about her, she would have, but the truth was, she couldn't think straight. Luke arriving at her place had made things difficult. Complicated. Unbearable. If he'd had any regard for her feelings, he would have stayed with her, and it was clear that he had no feelings for her at all.

He'd come here to have sex. Nothing more.

She had been so wrong to think he was changing, that he was starting to feel something for her. The wedding had hit a nerve, and weakened his defenses. That glimpse into the type of man she liked to think he was, was just a glimpse, nothing more. The real Luke was this man—callous, and selfish, and inconsiderate.

She wanted intimacy, but he wanted sex.

A gargantuan void stood between them, and the gap would never close.

Maybe it was just as well that she wasn't pregnant.

What sort of toxic foundation would that child have? It was hardly the fairytale world of the Stones.

How could she have ever believed that their loveless relationship, based purely on need and desire, could ever end well?

If he had stayed, if he had even given her half an hour of his time, it would have given her hope, especially now, in the wake of her wretched sadness.

But he hadn't even given her that.

It had been exactly what they had agreed to. Two people getting together for a physical connection. She had been stupid to ever think it could be something more. The gift bag on her coffee table caught her eye. Inside was a flimsy parcel wrapped in thin tissue paper. She unwrapped it and lifted up the black and peach-colored bustier. The lace was so wispy and thin, it felt like gossamer against her skin.

This was how he saw her.

This was what came to his mind.

This told her exactly how he saw her as. A sex object. And he expected her to put that on, and spend the night with him. The old Kay might have done that in a heartbeat.

But now?

She wanted more, because she was a woman, and not a whore. She wanted a man to love her, for her, and because he wanted to be with her, not for his release, but because she was so much more than that.

She tossed the flimsy garment carelessly to the floor, not caring that it was a designer label, or that it had cost a ridiculous amount of money.

This was what he wanted to see her in, because *this*, and everything that followed once she put it on, was the basis of their relationship.

CHAPTER TWENTY-EIGHT

"It's the best cancer to have."

That's what the doctor had told him. He remembered looking at the man, waiting for the punchline of what was definitely a god awful joke.

Seriously?

"Then I'm a lucky son-of-a-bitch," he'd replied, in a sarcastic voice. "What do I get at the end of it? A fucking ticket to Hawaii?"

"It's natural to be upset, Luke, but trust me on this. Papillary thyroid cancer is one of the most curable of all cancers. And, after the treatment, there's a 95-99% chance that it can be treated without recurrence."

"Aren't I the lucky one?"

The recent biopsy had confirmed his doctor's suspicions, and he now needed surgery quickly to remove part of his thyroid. He'd then have to stay in the hospital for a few days, followed by home rest for a few more weeks, where he had to avoid strenuous activity. Later, he'd have to undergo more treatment, and would be left with a small scar on his neck.

Life was a bastard. Or a bitch. Didn't matter, since it didn't have a gender, but fuck. This news was shittier than shit.

Should he have felt grateful that he had 'the best cancer'? Because returning home later that day, he surfed the internet, and read up for hours, soaking up everything he could find on it. Getting sucked up into the dark vortex of cancer survivor stories left him feeling scared shitless, and he went to bed feeling as if he'd been hit by a train.

Cancer was cancer, regardless of whether it was the best cancer or not, and this shock, this bolt straight out of the nowhere, hit him hard.

He was so numb that he couldn't feel anything. He couldn't think. One moment his mind was pre-occupied with Canal Street, and then next, he was making plans to visit Miami.

He called Marie and told her he would be working from home for a few days, and left it at that, while he moped around, trying to sort himself out.

How the fuck could he, a healthy twenty-seven year old who watched his diet, ate well, exercised and had always been well, how the fuck could he be diagnosed with cancer?

The best fucking cancer.

The day before his surgery, he returned to work, and told Marie.

She took the news well, especially when he told her not to tell anyone, not even the bar staff. He also didn't want Kay to know.

He needed to get through this himself. No emotional baggage, no other person to rely on. While moping around at home a few days ago, he'd pulled out the jewelry box from his jacket pocket, realizing that he'd forgotten to give her the bracelet. The gift bag he'd handed her only had the lingerie.

He had no time to worry about any of that now.

Given the circumstances, and how things had been between them that day, maybe it was time to let her go.

As with most of his life, being a closed book had served him well. He had learned his lesson about people a long time ago. Even those who had once cared and loved you let you down.

So it was better to avoid it all in the first place.

"You should tell Kay," Marie said again, trying to convince him, but he refused to give in. "She doesn't need to know. I don't *want* her to know."

"You can't go through this alone."

"I'm not alone. I have you. It's the best fucking cancer, Marie," he snarled viciously. "I can handle it."

She stared at him, her mouth twisting, and he could see she was fighting the urge to tell him off, that she was holding back because of the news he'd just revealed.

"Don't you want someone with you at the hospital?"

"No."

"Have you told Amanda?"

"She's on her honeymoon."

"And what about the rest of your family?"

"No."

"You're making a mistake. At times like this you need your family around you."

"No, I don't." Christ. That was the last thing he needed. It didn't matter if he had been dying, even if he'd had the worst type of cancer, there was no way he would tell his old man or his brother. In those circumstances, he probably wouldn't even tell Amanda.

According to the doctor, he'd be fine to return to work

after three weeks, and then have regular check-ups. This was a minor glitch in his life. The last thing he wanted was for someone to profess their undying support and loyalty to him and then fuck off. It had happened before, and he wasn't going to let it happen again.

Cancer or no cancer.

CHAPTER TWENTY-NINE

"You're not fun anymore. How does your boyfriend put up with you?"

He doesn't. "I've had a two hour meeting with the client," Kay explained, trying not to sound as irritated as she felt. "I'm up to my eye balls in work and I wouldn't be good company."

"Are you avoiding that place?" Erin asked.

"No!" The woman had too much time on her hands. Not a day went by when Erin didn't suggest they go to The Oasis. Kay regretted introducing her work colleagues to a place she was now desperate to forget about, like its owner.

"One drink."

Kay put down her pen and massaged her temples, slowly thinking about it. "Remington's on my back, the client's on my back. Geoffrey's being a jerk—"

"What's his problem now?"

"Don't ask."

"Just look at you, Kay. You're so stressed out you're going to have a breakdown if you're not careful. I bet your boyfriend isn't too happy that you spend so much time working."

"He knows the score." She wasn't about to let Erin know of her personal troubles.

"Why's Geoffrey being a jerk?"

"Because he's Geoffrey." The more she thought about it, she saw that Geoffrey had been distant with her ever since she'd landed the Pembroke deal. At first she had thought that he was just being a dickhead because she'd snubbed his advances at the club, but as time went on, she was starting to think otherwise. He hadn't hidden his displeasure when Remington gave her the account, but she was used to it; used to having to fight harder to get ahead in the corporate world.

But Geoffrey was as ambitious as she was, and he no longer masked his simmering resentment as easily. She had heard from others that he'd made a few chauvinistic remarks on the sly. She would have challenged them, had she not been too preoccupied by her current workload.

She didn't want to mess up the Pembroke deal, and all her attention and energy were directed there. Even Luke ceased to take up any of her thoughts.

Too many late nights weren't good for her, and Erin was right. She wasn't going to finish all her work overnight. There would be other fires to put out tomorrow. The work never stopped. Geoffrey, or Remington, or both of them, and others, would put more obstacles in her way.

"Let's go," she said, suddenly deciding to do it now. Why have the weight of splitting with Luke hanging over her head? Why not just sever the ties now?

"You've changed your mind?" Erin asked, clearly perked up by this sudden turn of events.

At the back of her mind she was already working out

her strategy. If she showed up with Erin now, she would feel empowered to do it.

She had convinced herself that she was busy at work and couldn't have a social life, but the truth was she was being a recluse. She could have made time, just like she had before, but she was choosing to hibernate in her office. Not facing Luke, not even going to see Savannah, she had avoided contact with others. This current funk had to stop. In fact, more than Luke, it was Savannah she felt the urge to visit, not only because it was her perspective and sage advice that she needed the most, but because she needed to offload, and she couldn't do that with Erin. But Savannah would also be bitterly disappointed in her if she confessed about the current state of her life.

She would figure out how to approach her cousin later. There was a more pressing issue that she had to deal with, and tonight Erin would be her wing woman.

An hour later they were sitting across the table from one another, on the usual big comfy couches she had come to know so well.

She had lied when Erin had asked her how her Valentine's Day evening had gone. She had lied through her teeth and said Luke had come over, and bought her some expensive lingerie. Erin had made a crude joke, which she had ignored.

She craned her neck and looked around the semi-crowded place, hoping to get a glimpse of Luke, but he was nowhere in sight. Her hopes deflated. It would have been the perfect time to confront him. The bar was relatively quiet, and she could have said what she needed to him here in public, but away from prying ears, and then she would have been done with it.

But if he wasn't around ...

Disappointed, she looked around the room again and caught sight of Marie, sitting with her back to her. Kay was surprised to see that she was still here because Marie had mentioned that she didn't often work late. It made her wonder if Luke had gone away on business.

The sneaky little rat.

That would be typical of him, to go away for a few days and not think to tell her. She excused herself and strode across the terrace to Marie.

"Hey, Marie." She tapped the woman's shoulder. Marie turned around, and she looked wary. Dark circles under her eyes gave her the expression of someone who hadn't slept well.

"Hey," Marie replied, her tone quieter than she last remembered. "How are you doing?"

"I've had better days. My friend dragged me here."

"Dragged? I didn't think we had to drag you here. I noticed we haven't seen you in a while."

"Work's manic," Kay replied tucking her hair behind her ears, getting fidgety. "I was looking for Luke but he's not around. Is he away?"

"He's ... busy."

"He's always busy," she laughed, her insides going all smooshy. She'd felt tense from the moment she'd set foot in here, and just wanted it all over with. "Where is he?" She would go to his apartment if she needed to, otherwise she wouldn't be able to sleep well tonight with this unfinished business hanging over her head like a dangling sword.

Marie opened her mouth but didn't answer straight away. "He's been...uh... busy with the new site."

Kay sensed Marie's hesitation and wondered if Luke had said something to her. Her reply at least indicated that he was still in town. This was worse; knowing that he was here, in New York, and still hadn't bothered to call her after that last awkward meeting. It proved to her that he didn't care.

She stared back at Marie's impassive face, trying to decipher the hidden meaning behind her expression. Had the slimy toad ditched her without having the balls to tell her to her face? It might explain why Marie was looking at her with something that bordered on pity.

Folding her arms, she asked, "Is he in his office? I need to speak to him." There were still some things she needed to say to him, even though he'd beaten her to the splitting up.

"I'll get him to call you."

"Is he avoiding me?"

Marie sat up and leaned back against the chair. "He didn't call to tell you?"

"Tell me what?" *That he was splitting up with me?*

"I'll get him to—"

Something was definitely off. "He doesn't want to see me anymore, does he? Is that why you're being so awkward with me?" she asked, getting defensive.

"What? No?" Marie cried. "Goodness no. He never said anything like that."

"If he's in his office, I'd rather just go and see him myself." Did he have someone else in his office? She had a good mind to march in there and see for herself. "You don't have to be his bodyguard, Marie. I'm old enough to handle the truth." She smoothed down her blouse, that mere act telling her body to brace itself for an unpalatable truth.

"He's not here, Kay."

"Then I'll go over to his place."

"He's not there, either."

Marie seemed to be stalling. More than that, she

seemed uneasy. Kay sensed an ice wall between them, and she wondered what it was she was keeping from her.

He had surprised her. She hadn't had him down for being such a coward; she'd expected a more manly response. A terse phone call, or text at the least, maybe even a final rushed, frenzied night of passion before he dumped her. That would be more his style.

"He's in the hospital."

"In the hospital?" It was so unexpected. The words took her completely by surprise. "Why? What happened?"

"I didn't want to tell you, and I..." Marie shook her head as if it was a chore to get the words out, "I don't think I *should* be the one to tell you."

"Tell me."

"He's not well."

"What do you mean he's not well?"

"He's in the hospital, and they're operating on him tomorrow."

The news was like a wrecking ball to her gut.

"Surgery for what?" she asked slowly, thinking of the worst. Luke was so young, and so fit and healthy. There had to be a mistake.

"He should be the one to tell you, goodness knows I've already said too much."

Kay shook her head. "Tell me, please tell me," she urged, a sixth sense warning her.

"He's got thyroid cancer."

She stumbled back a step, and her back hit the wall as the weight of the words fell on her. "What?"

When?

How?

She'd only seen him last week. She stared at Marie completely dazed.

Thyroid cancer?

Was it fatal? She didn't even know what a thyroid did.

But it was cancer.

And that was always bad news.

"He didn't want you to know. He didn't want anyone to know."

"I'm not anyone." It didn't matter what he thought of her, how he saw their relationship, and what boundaries she crossed. The guideposts to their relationship had shifted.

How could someone like Luke have that? He was so young, so fit, so healthy. In an instant, all her hostility fell away. "Where is he? I need to see him."

Marie's face tightened. It looked as if she was caught between a rock and Luke's hard face. A man like Luke would have demanded her loyalty, and already she'd turned him in. "You have to tell me," Kay begged. "You wouldn't have told me if you didn't think I needed to know. I know what Luke's like. He's a hard man to care for, but I care for him."

"He's not going to like you turning up unannounced—"

"I don't care what he likes or doesn't like. Please, Marie. You and I both know he's alone. He isn't going to tell anyone, not even his family. You and I are the only ones he has."

"Get some rest now," the nurse told him, as she poured him a glass of water.

"I have no choice, do I?"

"No, you don't, young man." She handed him the glass. This woman was a matronly version of Marie, he decided. She was jovial enough, strong and robust, where Marie was efficient, business minded, and slender. "We'll take you to the operating room first thing."

How fucking lucky was he? "I can hardly wait."

"Get some rest. It will be over before you know it."

"Don't worry," he told her, "I have no plans to hit the bars tonight."

"Not tonight," the nurse replied, her face deadpan, and he liked that. "Maybe a few days later."

He'd been here since yesterday when they had carried out some pre-op procedures. To think that a week ago, he would never have envisaged that he would be in the hospital, getting ready for cancer surgery.

Shit could happen in an instant.

He would have been meeting with his construction

manager, and ensuring that the building work on Canal Street was going as scheduled. He *should* have been in meetings with Marie, taking care of the business. And somewhere in all of that, he might have found time to see Kay and sort things out. Make it up to her for behaving like a douchebag.

It was a recent thing. A new thing, him even thinking that he needed to apologize. Because she was starting to matter. He wasn't making the transition from not giving a shit, to caring, too well.

It didn't seem to matter much anymore.

In his absence, Marie would have to handle business matters, and as far the personal stuff? That could wait.

A knock at the door, was followed by it opening slowly and then he saw her. Kay's face peeked out through the gap.

What the hell was she doing here?

"Visiting hours are over, I'm afraid," the nurse told her.

But Kay stepped inside quickly. "I need to see him, just for a minute, *please*."

She stepped inside, and he lay on the bed, hating the fact that she was here, seeing him like this, with his vulnerability bleeding all over the place.

"Visiting hours are over," the nurse repeated, blocking Kay's entry.

"Why didn't you tell me?" Kay asked, craning her neck and peering over the nurse's shoulder.

"Didn't you hear me? Visiting hours are over," said the nurse, her voice stern.

"I'm his girlfriend," Kay replied, addressing the nurse for the first time.

The nurse turned around and looked at him, for verification presumably due to his lack of enthusiasm.

"She's not," he replied, shaking his head. It wasn't easy to say, but necessary.

He heard Kay gasp.

"Apparently you're not," the nurse said, turning to Kay. "And if you don't leave now, I'll call security."

Even from where he lay, he could read Kay's face as if she was only inches away from him. She looked mad. Or hurt. Sometimes he couldn't tell which it was.

"I'm not his girlfriend, but we meet for sex, mostly when he wants it. That must count for something."

Seriously? She'd really gone *there*?

The nurse stared at him in disgust. "Is she your girlfriend or not?" she asked. If looks could kill, he would have died already. At least he'd have been in the right place. He didn't answer her, but looked at Kay. "You shouldn't have come here," he muttered. He didn't want her to see him like this. He didn't want anyone to see him like this apart from Marie, because Marie was the only one who had never let him down, and he was too jaded to expect more of Kay.

"Please give me a few minutes with him. I've only just found out now. *Please*," Kay begged, looking distraught and appealing to the nurse with her newly found helpless-woman tactics.

"Five minutes," the nurse replied, and left, looking none too pleased.

Kay rushed to his side. "Why didn't you tell me?"

"Who told you?" Though he already knew where the leak had come from.

"Who do you think?" She fixed him with eyes that were softer. "Why didn't you tell me?" she repeated. Her whole demeanor had changed, as if she had let the hardness fall to her feet. Now she was full of sympathy, and pity, and all that other shit he didn't want, or need.

He didn't want or need other people being worried about him. He could handle this perfectly fine by himself.

"Because I didn't want you to come."

"Why not?"

"Because I can't have sex with you here."

He saw her face tilt, saw her visibly move back a few inches. Then she smiled. "I know what you're doing," she said, nodding her head. "I'm not going to let you push me away."

"I don't want you here. You should take a hint." It was easier to be a bastard when he was lying in bed feeling sorry for himself, and hating life and the universe. A pity party wasn't going to undo the cancer, or make things better.

"I'm slow like that," she countered.

"Yeah, I know." Damn it why couldn't she just leave? "I don't know why you came."

"Because I needed to see you."

"You've seen me now, so, you should go."

Her mouth twisted, and she looked to be at a loss for words. It wasn't like her. She always had a retort or two to hurl back at him. "I know you're scared," she said slowly, as if she was addressing a child. "You don't have to be scared. You're not alone, and you're going to be fine."

His gut hardened. This was the kind of shit he didn't want to deal with. "Marie should have kept her mouth shut."

"She was worried about you. I'm glad she told me."

He didn't want her around. She didn't know what he knew, and she hadn't been let down the way he had. She was digging her claws into him, trying to lay claim, hoping to turn that neediness of hers into something. Well, he had a thing or two to say to that.

"I don't need you, Kay. Don't feel obligated to be here because you think it's the right thing to do. You really should take the hint and go, especially when someone begs you to. I can take care of myself."

"Of course you can," she said, smiling as she looked at him, holding the gaze for the longest time. Her eyes looked glassy, or maybe it was the medication, and the after effects of the various tests they had done on him today. "I know we only use one another for sex, but didn't I deserve to be told?" she asked, surprising him with her candor.

He was silent, and listening to her voice, having her here, made a welcome change from the doctors and nurses he'd been seeing all day. "No," he said, trying to hold firm. It was nice and all her being here, but he didn't want her around. He couldn't let himself rely on her, or let her think she was going to help him through this. "Fuck buddies have no obligation."

"Why are you doing this?" she asked, her shaky voice revealing her hurt.

His neck was still hurting from the needle biopsies, and it hurt to swallow. If he hadn't been given the double dose of painkillers to help him over the pain, he probably wouldn't have been able to say any of this to her as easily as he could. But perhaps this was a way to be done with her. His recovery wasn't going to be instantaneous, and did he really want her hovering around him? "You were like a leech, so fucking clingy," he said wincing as he tried to shift himself into a more upright position in the bed. "I couldn't shake you off if I tried."

She swallowed then, and her hand shifted to her chest for the briefest moment, before moving to her handbag—as if she needed the support of something to hold on to. "Shake me off?" she asked, her voice dropping almost to a whisper. "What are you talking about?"

"About you, chasing me."

She shook her head. "It wasn't like that. We were only talking back then, on the island."

"And yet you showed up at the bar the following weekend."

She didn't say anything, but blinked slowly as he twisted the knife deeper. "And then at the club, when you found out who I was. When I took you home."

"I didn't ask you to take me home. You insisted."

"You were desperate."

"I was not. You asked me a number of times. You did insist."

"I know what you women are like," he hissed, the momentum increasing. Now that he had started, it was easier to spew it all out. He needed it done, so that she would never come back here again.

She didn't say anything, but blinked, very slowly, and he knew this was it. Time to twist the knife bone-deep. "Like a leech," he said, again. "I didn't know how to shake you. I figured one quick fling might do it."

Her brows pushed together as viciousness ripped from his lips. "Might do what?"

"I hate to break it to you, Kay, but you were a pity-fuck." He tore in. "You did everything but practically beg me to fuck you that night."

Her lower lip trembled, and she stepped back, visibly shaken, but silent. "You're evil."

"I'm telling the truth."

"You don't have to do this."

"Just being honest."

Her face crumpled, and he could see she fought for composure, still shaking her head in disbelief. Her brows creased and held there, an angry mark on her face which, until a minute ago, had been bathed in softness and concern for him. "You don't mean it. You're doing this because... because of what you've been through."

He laughed. "Oh great," he chuckled. "Now you're analyzing me. Make it mean whatever you want, whatever makes you feel better about yourself."

"You're heartless," she said, her voice shaky. "I don't know why you're doing this. When we got together, it wasn't like that. You know it wasn't."

Tell her it was. Tell her. Do it now. "Who are you kidding? It was *exactly* like that. I knew that if I fucked you, and humiliated you like that, you'd have enough dignity to know you didn't want to come back for more."

Her eyes glassed over, and she fought back tears.

"But I couldn't shake you off," he said, watching the tears in her eyes and hating himself. But he took that hatred and turned it back at her. "You settled for it. You agreed to it."

"It was never like that. *Never.* You're scared, and you're lashing out, and you don't mean what you're saying."

"I *do* mean it, and I'm doing you a favor by telling you now." He attempted a shrill laugh. "Your nickname is written all over your forehead. *Good Time Kay.* Guys see you coming a mile off. If you played hard to get, you might get some respect from guys, instead of letting them do what they want to you, and you pretending you're okay with it."

She gave him one final mournful look—a look that told him he'd all but destroyed her. And then she slipped out of the room.

He would never forget the look on her face for as long as

he lived. It reminded him of his mother, and how she had looked at the man who had all but killed her.

The room fell silent then, leaving him feeling more wretched than ever. He had taken her goodness, and her concern, and turned it to dust. He sank back into the bed, wanting to double over, regret and anger racking his body.

Reality struck, like a bolt of lightning. He'd gone too far this time.

⸻

He'd taken a sledgehammer to her heart.

She couldn't get out of there fast enough. Flying out of the double doors of the hospital, she ran straight into one of the doctors, knocking his folder to the floor.

"Sorry," she gasped, her mind a riot of confusion as she bent down to pick up the file.

He bent down at the same time, looked directly into her tear-stained face. "Are you okay?"

She straightened up. "I'm fine," she replied, clasping a hand over her heart, hoping to still her heartbeat.

"You don't look so well," the doctor remarked. "Let me get you a glass of water—"

"No," she replied, forcing the breaths to still in her chest. "I'm fine. I was visiting ... a friend." She attempted a smile. "It was the shock of seeing him." She tried to pull herself together, but it still hurt. He'd stabbed every vital organ in her body, and she was starting to shut down.

"Some visits can be like that."

"I wasn't prepared for the shock," she told him. Only when she was outside the hospital, did she stop by a wall to catch her breath.

A pity fuck?

Her mind was in disarray, and a montage of their entire time together suddenly flashed into her head.

It hadn't been like that. *It hadn't.*

Luke had ripped her heart away with his cruel words. He'd spoken with so much vitriol, that she had felt physically attacked.

It took a few moments for her to collect herself, before she could walk towards her car, get in, and drive away.

CHAPTER THIRTY-ONE

"How are you feeling?" Marie asked.

Like shit. "I've never felt better."

Marie gave him a sad smile.

"Quit looking at me like that," he said slowly. "Like you feel sorry for me."

"Me? Feel sorry for you?" She quirked an eyebrow, but he knew her. Knew she was concerned. "How was the surgery?" she asked.

"Better than sex."

She glowered at him. "I'm going to pretend I didn't hear that."

He closed his eyes, and smiled. He wasn't sure why he said that. The nausea had subsided, and the effects of the general anesthetic were starting to wear off. Even the surgical site wasn't that painful, but the nurse had warned him that it would feel tight as the skin healed.

"What time did Kay leave?"

"Soon after she got here." He opened his eyes to take in Marie's response.

"Why? What did you do?" she asked in a disapproving voice.

"Just told her a few home truths."

Marie angled her head, looking distinctly annoyed. "What did you do?" she asked carefully, as if he'd left an explosive device in a public area.

"Told her what she needed to hear."

Marie shook her head. "You upset her, didn't you?"

"My neck hurts," he replied, closing his eyes, not wanting to think about it.

***

"What the fuck happened?" Remington's voice cut through the air like a heat-seeking missile.

"I—I got the dates messed up. I'm sorry."

"Jesus Christ, Kay. What's the matter with you?"

She swallowed. "It's turned hectic all of a sudden—"

"You're fucking paid to deal with hectic," he roared.

"It won't happen again."

"It fucking better not," he growled, "because if you mess up again, I'll take you off this so fast you won't know what hit you, is that clear?"

"Yes."

She couldn't sleep last night. She couldn't get Luke's nasty, vindictive words out of her head.

A pity-fuck.

That's what he'd told her she had been to him. She had been wide awake until the early hours of the morning, watching the clock blinking in the new minutes one by one.

She had gone over every conversation, and every interaction with Luke from the moment they had first met.

The logical part of her brain told her that he was lashing

out. That Luke was angry, and bitter over his illness, but her heart told her otherwise. It convinced her that he was speaking *his* truth, that this so-called relationship of theirs, the one where she had hoped to change him, and slowly win him over—had been nothing but a farce.

The truth came out when people were in a corner, and right now for Luke, it was the worst corner he could be in.

It seemed unfair, and her heart ached for him, but her sadness came in jolts because every now and then she would remember what he had said, and how he had said it all while lying in his hospital bed.

She had looked it all up online, wanting to understand what he was going through. The search engine results wibbly-wobbly through her tearful eyes as she dug deeper and deeper into the dark bottomless pit of the 'net. She found herself wading through graphs and cancer stories, fearing for Luke even though this was supposedly a common and curable type of cancer.

Luke would be fine.

He wasn't going to die.

And yet she was afraid, and hurt, and upset. She was torn between feeling sympathetic towards this man who was so hard to love, and equally as hurt by the way he had treated her yesterday.

She had gone to bed in tears, and had completely forgotten to look over the reports for the client; reports which contained a few errors that had been picked up by one of their analysts. Remington had had to apologize on her behalf because she'd woken up late and missed the 7am meeting.

She didn't cry easily—a hardened woman like her. She was used to surviving in a man's world and considered herself to be as able as the men. She had assimilated a man's way of thinking because she'd had to in order to forge ahead with her career.

But last night had set her back, and her mind was a barrage of torn emotions. She had rushed to the hospital forgetting the slights she had suffered at his hands, and had felt only concern that the man she had started to have feelings for, the man who was so wrong for her, might be gravely ill.

And she had left that same hospital room deeply hurt by the nasty words Luke had hurled at her.

She had gone in worrying about him, and thinking long-term, as if he was her boyfriend, as if they had promised one another eternal life and togetherness forever.

And he had told her that he'd seen her as nothing more than a pity-fuck.

Against a background of such things, she couldn't focus, at work, or at home. At work she was all over the place, and this morning it had culminated in Remington shouting at her across the open plan office environment because she had messed up big time. He'd yelled at her, ordering her to come into his office immediately. She'd rushed past the desks, feeling the heat of her colleagues' stares on her face.

Once inside, she was sure they had all heard his continued yelling, and the walk of shame back to her desk had been pitiful.

She couldn't afford to mess up again.

And yet, Luke had his surgery today, and he didn't want her anywhere around him. It didn't mean that she didn't worry about him.

"What was that about?" Erin had crept up to her desk, and stood looking down at her.

She wasn't in the mood to talk. "I'll tell you later." She wanted to be alone, to get on with her work, to find something to focus on so that her mind didn't hover over the dressing down to the dark places, of Luke in surgery.

"Did you mess up bad?"

"Yes. I didn't check the reports before we sent them through."

"Ouch." Erin made an appropriately sorry face. "We could hear him shouting."

Kay glanced around the open place office, and saw a few heads turn away quickly. "I hate it when he does that."

"The guy's an ass," Erin agreed. "He's real mad."

"I messed up. It was my fault. It's an important account." Remington was level-headed, for the most part. She'd messed up bad, and she had to suck it up and make up for it.

Only, it was almost impossible to focus.

How could she?

She wanted to speak to someone. She wanted to talk to Savannah, wanted some of that simple, no-nonsense advice that her cousin seemed to dole out by the bucketful. Only, this time, it wasn't advice she wanted. She wanted to confess. Spill her guts out, and have Savannah make her feel better. Luke had humiliated her. He made what they had had seem shameful, and her out to be shameless.

She was hurt by the difference in how they both viewed the same event.

Trying to hide the sadness—for him, and for what he had said, as well as the work pressure, was killing her.

If she wasn't careful, she would implode.

But even though Luke Hunter could be cold and uncaring, deep down she knew that the man who'd told her she had been nothing more than a pity-fuck was also an angry and frightened man.

"Let's go for a drink tonight," Erin suggested.

"You seem to want to go for a drink every night." She lowered her head, trying to still her mind.

"We all need a place to go and unwind. The bar is the perfect place."

"I can't. I really can't. I've got too much to do. You heard him. You all heard him. Remington's going to be watching me like a hawk, and I can't afford to mess up."

Erin didn't force the issue further. "I don't want to get you in more trouble," she said. "Maybe another time."

"Another time," said Kay, hearing her cell phone go off, and answering it.

"I need to see you." It was Marie. "I have Luke's cell phone. He's out of surgery."

She let out a breath she didn't even know she had been holding. "He is? How is he?"

"Heavily sedated, and completely out of it."

She could picture him now, sleeping, with his eyes closed, and that beautiful mouth, capable of inflicting the cruelest torture and the sweetest rapture. "So, it was successful?" she asked, suddenly overcome by a burning desire to be by his bedside. When she had woken up this morning, her initial thoughts—those first few fleeting moments devoid of yesterday's memories—made her think of him, and she'd had the urge to rush to the hospital. Until she remembered how things had ended last night.

"It seems to be. When are you coming?"

"Ugh." This was going to be awkward to answer. "You are coming to see him, aren't you?" Marie asked.

"I don't think he wants me there."

"You have to learn to ignore him, Kay."

She gave a subtle nod of her head, her eyes downcast. "He doesn't want to see me. He made that perfectly clear."

"I know something happened, but he's not so bad. He didn't meant it, I'm sure that whatever he said—"

"If you'd heard him, you wouldn't doubt that he meant it."

"Don't be like him. He has nobody else."

CHAPTER THIRTY-TWO

She returned to the hospital room she had fled yesterday.

Marie gave her a tired smile as soon as she walked through the door. She rose from her chair. "Thank goodness you're here. For a moment I was worried that you might not come, being busy at work and all that." Walking towards her, she gave her a hug. "I was hoping he hadn't scared you away. I'm glad he didn't."

"I had to finish some things off," she explained, walking towards the bed. Luke had opened his eyes at the sound of her voice.

"See," Marie said to Luke, returning to her seat by his bed. "I told you she'd come."

Kay looked at him, and he stared back, his face impassive. Hard to read. "I don't think he wants me here," she commented.

"Nonsense," replied Marie, dismissing her comment with a chuckle. "He can't talk much at the moment, otherwise he'd tell you how happy he was to see you."

"He can't talk much?" she asked, beaming. "Oh, what a shame. How was the surgery?"

"According to the doctor, He's got a sore throat, and his voice is a bit hoarse, swallowing food is going to be hard, but he should be fine in a few days' time. Then he'll be ready to go home and recover." She pinned her gaze on Luke's face. "No going into work or working from home for a couple of weeks. The doctor advises complete rest."

Kay searched his expression to gauge his reaction. A man like Luke didn't sit still, *couldn't* sit still. He was always on the go. She wondered how he would cope. Silent rage tainted that face of his, still so handsome despite him looking gaunt and helpless.

"Is he in pain?" she asked Marie.

"The nurse says he's on heavy pain killers."

"He looks angry," she said, enjoying the power she had over a silent Luke.

"I didn't want him to be alone, but now that you're here, I need to go. My kids will need feeding, and goodness knows we're low on groceries."

"Sure," Kay replied, setting down her bag on the chair. She slipped her coat off. "I'll stay a while."

Marie reached for her coat and her purse, then said her goodbye to Luke who nodded.

"I'm glad you came," she said, in a low voice, turning to Kay, and placing her hand on her arm. "Even though he can't say it, I'm sure Luke's glad you're here."

Kay doubted that. She turned to him when it was only the two of them left. "You're not happy to see me, are you?"

His eyes met hers for the briefest of seconds and a flash of anger flickered across those cornflower blue irises. It was strange how angry a man could seem, even when lying in bed post-op.

She had to have her say. "I came because I wanted to see you," she said, holding onto the side of the bed and as she towered over him. "I came because I wanted to know you were okay, even though Marie told me the surgery had gone well. I came, because I care, and I'm not afraid to say it. We had something. You called it a pity-fuck, I called it a connection. I'm not hard and callous, like you, and you're not the man I thought you were, but it wasn't going to stop me from coming to see you. I might not have come today, had Marie not guilt-tripped me into it, but I would have come in a day or so, because guess what, Luke? I'm not a bitch, and I'm not cold and unfeeling like you." She paused, searching his face for signs of his reaction, and yet at the same time finding it odd that she was talking and he could not say anything back.

He turned his face to hers and stared, then opened his mouth, but either the pain was too much, or he was still weighing up how he was going to respond, because he said nothing.

She felt slightly silly, and yet emboldened. For too long, she had given way to this man, let him dictate the way their relationship went. For too long she had given in to him, letting him have his way, whenever he wanted. This was her chance to say it as she saw it, to let him know that she wasn't a pity-fuck. Her esteem wasn't that far in the gutter that she would willingly let a man use her and abuse her. She had seen something in Luke, something tortured, and dark, and understood now where that darkness came from.

She had believed she could help him get over it, and help him heal, but just as there were moments when she thought they could salvage something together, she also harbored doubts.

Now that this had happened, it allowed for some resting

time. Breathing space. A time to assess things. She wasn't going to abandon him now, not like this, but she wasn't sure if she could save him, either.

The nurse walked in again, the same one from yesterday, only this time, she glared at Kay as if she was in the wrong place at the wrong time.

"How long will he be here for?" Kay asked.

"A few more days. Could be another day, could be a few more. It depends on when the doctors want to discharge him."

Kay turned to Luke, not daring to hold his hand, but stroking the side of it with her finger.

"And how long before he's back to normal?"

"A few weeks, could be more. It all depends on his progress and how he heals. If he rests up, his recovery will be quicker. If he doesn't, he's only going to make things worse." The nurse replaced the pitcher of water with a fresh one, and left.

"You're going to be fine," Kay said to Luke. She waited for him to say something, but he didn't. "I don't know if I prefer you like this, not saying anything."

"It... hurts...," he croaked, then made a face as if it had been painful.

"You look like you're in pain. Don't," she cautioned.

He gave her a withering look.

"I prefer you when you don't talk," she continued, gaining more courage the quieter he remained.

Once again, he made a face, then tried to open his mouth, but winced.

She was enjoying this. "It's best if you don't talk. Your voice is going to be hoarse for a few days. It might even be gone for a few weeks." She made an exaggerated woe-be-gone expression. "You might even lose it for a *month*." Her smile widened. "That would be freakin' awesome. Nobody would have to listen to you spouting nasty garbage."

He scowled at her, and she smiled back. "This is going to be so much fun."

CHAPTER THIRTY-THREE

"I'm so glad we're sharing this," Marie declared, when Kay turned up at Luke's apartment a few days later. He had been discharged from the hospital and Marie had brought him back home.

"I don't know if sharing is the right word for it," she replied. She'd come straight after work on a day when she'd managed to leave earlier than usual.

It soon became clear, that just like that, she and Marie had assumed the roles of Luke's caregivers—whether he wanted them to or not. Marie had taken on the motherly role and she, she assumed, was the dutiful girlfriend.

"We both care about him," Marie said.

"It's not like he's got anyone else," Kay told her. She placed a couple of cartons of freshly made soup into the refrigerator. Marie had offered to bring him food until he was able enough to cook for himself and since she didn't cook much, she let Marie handle that side of things while she picked up food from the supermarket.

"What's his family like?" Marie asked, lowering her voice again.

"Uh...well..." She didn't know where to start, and she didn't want to divulge too much in case Marie didn't know everything.

"Pleasant," she replied, unable to come up with a better word.

"He cares about you more than he did the others."

Kay balked, not knowing why Marie was saying all of this now, and maybe it would be better if she put her right. "I—I'm not sure that—"

"He's been different lately," Marie said, interrupting. "Trust me, I know what he can be like. I can see the difference you've already made. It's been a while since he's had a regular girlfriend on the scene, one that I know of, anyway. He likes to keep his personal life personal. I try and pry out what I can, but he's not always willing to humor me."

"He's hard to read," Kay agreed. She frowned, then looked around, worried that Luke might hear them. "Where is he?" she asked.

"He's taking a shower."

She breathed easier. "What makes you think he cares about me?" Marie obviously wasn't aware of Luke's dark and twisted side; the side he reserved for those he became intimate with.

"He's never taken anyone to meet his family before, for starters. You should take that to mean what you want," Marie replied, glancing towards the hallway. "I expect he'll be out soon. He's been in there for ages."

He was taking his sweet time, and she hadn't even seen him yet, not since that day when she'd said all she had needed to say to him. Now she wondered if that had been wise. Her insides knotted just thinking about it. She hadn't gone into the hospital after that, either, needing to place distance between them, but now that he was back at home, it didn't feel right to her not to at least look in on him.

Marie obviously didn't know anything except what was on the surface and by coming to see Luke, Kay had unwittingly led Marie to think she was happy to do this. A normal girlfriend would, and Marie obviously didn't know any better.

She didn't have any other choice, though, did she?

It wasn't as if she was going to turn a blind eye towards him when he was recovering from cancer surgery.

"It will only be this week we'll have to keep an eye on him," Marie said. "I know you're really busy at work, so I'll come by during the day time. I can work from here, so it doesn't matter. I presume you'll be here after work?" She looked up at Kay, expectantly.

"I'll come by in the evenings," Kay replied, slowly. Of course she was okay to check in on him. Marie expected that she would stay the night, but no. That wasn't going to happen. Doing this was hard enough, but this wasn't the time to tell Luke that it was over, not when he was recuperating after surgery to remove cancer cells.

It would be heartless of her, to walk away now.

"I have to go," said Marie, closing down her laptop and gathering her things together.

"You're leaving already?" she asked, alarmed. She liked the idea of Marie hanging around, liked the security of having a third-party to absorb the stoniness that would no doubt be present once Luke came out.

But Marie had walked away towards the shower. She knocked on the door of the bathroom. "How long are you going to be, Luke?" she asked. Kay couldn't make out his answer. But in the next second, she heard a door open and then he stepped into the kitchen.

"Hi," he said, still sounding hoarse. "When did you get here?"

"Not too long ago." Her heart missed a beat when he looked into her eyes and they locked gazes. The hard barrier she had been determined to erect between them didn't even stand a chance.

Today things were different.

Now he wasn't lying in a hospital bed without a voice, nor did he look as weak. Now he resembled the old Luke, with his lips quirking up at the corners. He stood before her, barefoot, and disheveled with his damp hair, looking nothing like the cool, controlling businessman in his suit.

Tender, ruthless and bittersweet memories rose to the surface, and she melted. For right now, he was hers to have, and she was here to care for him.

"I have to go now, but Kay's here," Maria told him. She sounded optimistically happy, and Kay wondered when she should burst her bubble and let her know that things weren't so great between them. "She brought you some soup, so you can have that for now. I'll be over tomorrow. I'm sure you'll be glad to have her company instead of mine."

"Thanks for coming over," he said, his voice so rough that it barely sounded like him.

"It was good of her, wasn't it?" Marie agreed. "Now stop talking and try to get your voice back. See you tomorrow," she said to Kay, and hugged her goodbye. Kay wondered when and how their relationship had suddenly elevated to bestie level.

"Are you hungry?" she asked when it was just her and him. It would help if she was busy doing something, so that she didn't have to stand around awkwardly. This was a new role for her, and for him—something neither of them had envisaged; her being the care-giver and him being vulnerable for the first time since she had known him. A position he probably found as odd as she did.

"I can do it," he croaked.

"You can barely talk," she said.

"You don't have to do this."

She picked out two of the cartons, ignoring him. "Which one?" she asked. She'd gotten two different flavors. He nodded to the one on the right. Asparagus soup.

"I'm sorry if Marie's put you—" he coughed as he tried to get his words out. "If Marie's put you—"

She put a finger to her lips. "Shuush," she said. "Can't you even be quiet when you're told to?"

He scooted onto the breakfast bar stool and watched her instead. She could feel the heat of his gaze on her back as she looked through the cupboards, trying to find a saucepan.

"That one," he said, pointing. "And the wooden spoon is in that holder there, on the countertop."

She nodded, and set to heating his soup up. Glancing around briefly, as she pulled out the spoon from the said drawer, she saw that he'd perched himself on the bar stool, and sat facing her, his hands clasped in front of him on the kitchen island. It turned awkwardly silent.

"About...about the other day," he said, gruffly.

She didn't turn around. "What other day?" Though she knew perfectly well what he was alluding to.

"When you said all those things."

"I shouldn't have said all that." She still had her back to him. "Not yet, anyway. I should have let you recover first." The soup was beginning to bubble, so she turned the heat off. She searched through his cupboards again, and found the bowls. Not saying anything, she poured his soup into a bowl, got him a spoon and put the bowl in front of him.

"Thanks." He looked slightly sheepish. "Don't you want any? I can't eat alone."

"I'll rustle up something when I go home."

"You're not ..." his eyes snapped shut momentarily, it was so brief, that had she not known his moods and his facial expressions as intimately as she did now, she might have missed it. He'd expected her to stay over. Probably something that Marie had told him, based on what normal couples did.

She didn't say anything. Now would have been the perfect time to remind him of his rules, to throw that in his face, but she wasn't that cruel.

He stirred the spoon around the soup, making the steam curl and rise. His brow knitted together and his lips were drawn into a straight line, as if he was thinking, and the thoughts weren't easy ones. "I—" he looked up at her, his open mouth telling her he was struggling. "I'm sorry about...about what *I* said to you the other day."

"When you called me a pity fuck?" she asked, eager to see how he was going to explain himself.

"It's not..." he croaked then shook his head as if it was painful to get the words out. It probably, literally was. Luke Hunter didn't possess much tact. She could see that he wanted to apologize, but there was no point when he was like this.

"You should try not to talk," she advised. She wanted to know, but there was no point in him being so vulnerable when telling her, because she wouldn't be able to fight back, and she needed to fight back. She needed to let him know how much he had hurt her, and how it *still* hurt, hearing him say what he had.

As much as she needed to have it out with him, she

couldn't do it now. It would be a one-sided fight, and she liked to fight fair.

"Don't feel you have to do this because Marie put you up to it," he said slowly.

"I would have offered to, regardless."

"Do it because..." he winced, lifting his hand to his neck. "Because you want to, not because you feel sorry for me."

"I'm not doing this because I pity you," she told him. "I'm doing it because I care."

A tiny muscle along his jawline tightened.

"You can explain all you want later, when you're feeling better." She slipped on her jacket. It seemed too soon to leave, but he was going to carry on trying to talk if she stayed, and things weren't comfortable enough between them that they could sit in silence and just be together.

It was best if she left.

"You're leaving?" His expression was one of disappointment.

"I've got a lot of work to get on with."

"Do it here, I've got Wi-Fi."

Everything about this set up was forced. She didn't understand how he expected her to continue, to pretend they were in a cozy setup when they so obviously weren't. "I'd rather go home. Is there anything else you need?"

He shook his head, looking weak and sorry for himself, and nothing like the Luke she knew.

CHAPTER THIRTY-FOUR

She was being squeezed in every direction. Everyone wanted a piece of her. Remington wanted updates. The client wanted the best deal. Her team always had questions, and then there was Luke.

"*Who's* keeping you so busy?" Savannah asked.

"No-one."

"Then why didn't you ever call me back?" Kay swiped a hand over her forehead, feeling guilt wash all over her. "Sorry, Sav," she said, clutching her cell phone tightly. "I know I've been pathetic." Savannah had called a couple of times during the last few weeks, and each time, Kay had promised she'd call back in the evening but she'd either been busy dealing with the final stages of the Pembroke deal, or, since last week, she'd been going over to Luke's.

"You've been impossible to get a hold off."

"I've been drowning in work."

"Work, work, work. It's always work with you."

"You know me," Kay replied.

"Still, at least it keeps you out of mischief, I suppose," Savannah said.

"Sorry." She felt doubly awful now. Especially given that Savannah only had a few months to go before she had her baby, and Kay had only seen her a couple of times. She'd spent more time with Luke, and was certain that her cousin deserved her loyalty more than Luke did. "Things are just so full on right now."

"I hope you'll be able to make some time for me once the babies come."

"I hope so. May, right?" She rubbed her neck, and wondered when she would have time to schedule in an all over body massage. Her body was falling apart. Long days at work and checking in on Luke made life stressful. She was always rushing around.

"Early May," Savannah replied.

"I'll try and come over and see you before the baby comes," she promised, making a mental note to herself to spend some time with Savannah. "I *will* make it up to you. I'll do lots of babysitting." How had time slipped by and she saw less of her cousin even though they lived in the same city?

"Before the *babies* come."

"Right," she doodled some circles in red biro on the draft copy of the report she was checking. Tonight, she hadn't gone to see Luke even though passing by his place was becoming as familiar as going home to her own apartment.

Luke's hard edges had softened. He seemed almost a different man in some respects, and she wasn't sure if it was the illness that had given him a new perspective on life, or that he was just more tired, and not as blunt anymore. Either way, she definitely preferred the new him.

"You're not listening to me, are you?" Savannah asked.

"I am," she insisted, putting down her report. "Of course I am."

"So the news about the twins doesn't have you excited at all?"

Twins? "What?" She sat up, then sat forward, then stood up, holding her hand to her forehead wondering if she'd heard right. "You're expecting *twins?*"

"Yay!" whooped Savannah. "It only took three tries."

"Twins?" Kay repeated, trying to wrap her head around the idea of two babies, and failing. "How? How…"

"I know, unbelievable, right?" said Savannah, in her most calm and level-headed voice.

"You must be huge!"

"Like a whale, and then some."

She paced around the living room, imagining Savannah's world being turned upside down by three children.

Freaking hell.

Married, and with three children already.

Her mother was never going to stop talking about this. Come to think of it, it had been a while since she'd called her mom to catch up on things. She had let everything go, all her closest relationships, and spent the most time with a man she was going to ditch the moment he recovered. She was getting used to the calmer, more laid back Luke, but she wanted a future, and she wasn't sure he was the man who could give her one.

"Has Briony managed to get a hold of you?" Savannah asked. "She was asking me for your number again."

"Ugh," Kay groaned, rubbing a hand to her forehead. Briony had called and left her a message, which she had listened to and promptly forgotten about. "She did call, and she left a message…" Freaking hell. She was neglecting everything. At this rate she'd have no cousin or friends left. "I'll call her, I promise."

"I'm glad to hear it's not only me that you've forgotten."

"I haven't forgotten you," Kay replied defensively. "I've been...busy."

"Come over," Savannah offered. "Come over and we'll catch up. No point me waddling over to your place. Come tonight."

"I can't. I have..."

"So much going on," said Savannah, finishing her sentence for her. "You sound like Tobias did when I first met him."

"How is he?" she asked.

"Good. Happy, and excited about the birth."

"Typical man." She wondered how happy and excited he would be if he'd had to squeeze out a watermelon from his private parts.

"Seeing that you're so busy you don't have time to fit me in, I'll let *you* tell *me* when you have an available slot for your heavily pregnant cousin."

"Don't be like that," replied Kay, feeling lousy, and guilty at the same time. Savannah had her life together in a pretty package while she was trying to hold hers together. "I'll have more time soon, I promise."

Luke was due to have another treatment soon and once she had seen him through that, she would walk away.

And then she would definitely go on Savannah's man-free diet.

CHAPTER THIRTY-FIVE

He was still tired.

Bone-fucking-tired.

But then Kay walked in, and everything looked so much better. Up until her arrival he had been skulking around the apartment, he'd eaten dinner alone, and he hadn't expected her to come, not with it being this late.

"I didn't think you would come," he said, walking towards the door. His mood had suddenly lifted.

"I said I would." She seemed more cheerful these days, not as wound up as before.

"Give me those," he said, taking the grocery bags from her. "You're too good to me." He was realizing only now. Better late than never.

"I know. But I also didn't want to be on Marie's bad side." She cut him a cheeky grin.

"You're doing this for her, is that what you expect me to believe?"

"Marie thinks I'm a model girlfriend…" She stopped, the flustered look on her face telling him that she'd slipped up. "I mean, those were her words, not mine."

He wanted to tell her she was, but he didn't. He took the bags into the kitchen and started unloading. "You don't have to get this stuff," he said, pulling everything out. "I can shop online."

"You need lots of fresh fruit and vegetables," she announced. "You'll need your strength, plus I had to get a few things for me."

He huffed out a slow breath, not liking this turn of events in his life. All of a sudden he was the sick patient. The guy who could spend hours in the gym, and then swim a hundred lengths, the guy who could keep a woman entertained most of the night, the guy who had never so much as had the flu before was now a sorry walking shadow of his former self.

"Did Marie come today?" she asked.

"No. She said she had too much to do at the office."

Marie had told him she had too much going on at work, and checking in on him as well as looking after her kids, was tough. They were in regular contact many times during the day, though, and she popped in with a couple of home-cooked dishes a few days ago.

Apparently, Marie said Amanda had called at work a couple of times. She was back from her honeymoon, and was trying to get a hold of him. She'd called him on his cellphone but he'd ignored it, not wanting her to ask him a million and one questions about his voice sounding odd. It wasn't as hoarse as before, but different enough that she would notice, and he didn't want to tell her about the cancer.

She'd be over like a shot, and he didn't need that.

"Have you eaten?" Kay asked.

"I ate earlier." He'd waited as long as he could, before having his dinner. If he had known she would come, he would have waited. "I called, but your phone went to voicemail. I figured you were busy."

"I was."

"I saved you some leftovers."

"I had dinner at work."

He forgot. She'd mentioned how they ordered in food when they had lots of work to get through.

What he wanted was for her to come over and have dinner with him, for a change, and then stay the night. Stay in the guest room if it made her feel better. That was what he wanted, but he never asked her, because their relationship was different now. He liked this new easiness they had going on between them especially now that sex was off the agenda. He still missed the sex, but that was a conversation for another day. He had a lot of groveling to do before then.

At least things weren't worse, though it felt as if there was a storm coming. After her outburst at the hospital that day, he sensed that Kay wasn't yet done, that she still had things to say, and he was just going to have to wait for her to say them. Each time he'd tried to have a conversation about that night, and the night before that, when he'd said some despicable things to her, she refused to discuss them, saying these things would have to wait. The tables had turned because there had been a time not so long ago when she had wanted to talk, and connect, but he had denied her that, and now she was having her revenge by treating him in the same way.

He couldn't fault her at all. Kay had been amazingly good to him. The two weeks after the surgery had stretched on like a goddamn month, and had it not been for Marie and Kay coming in to see him daily, he'd have been out of his mind with boredom.

He had still managed to keep an eye on the business, managed to keep on top of his emails and other pressing matters, and he'd kept in daily phone contact with the workmen at the Canal Street site.

Marie took care of all other business matters, and Kay—she was the best part of his day. It was her visits most evenings that he looked forward to the most.

Things became easier between them. She came, she talked, and then she left. And this was how he got to find out more about her. Thinking back on it now, he could see exactly how empty and how meaningless what they had had before had been. Back when it had been just pure physical sex without the emotional connection.

Now, he was slowly making that emotional connection, strengthening it with every new morsel of information he discovered about her. He had come to know more about her than he had ever before, about her growing up, and her getting her scholarship and then her high pressured job. He learned about her boss Remington, and the new client deal she was leading at work, and he marveled that she found the time to fit him in despite all of that.

He was humbled, and embarrassed, and determined to make it up to her. His voice was getting back to normal, but he wasn't given the all clear yet. There was one final part of his treatment left, and which his doctor recommended.

"It will kill off any more living cancer cells that the surgery didn't catch, Luke," his consultant had told him. "I would advise you to have it."

It was a radioactive iodine treatment. It wasn't a surgical procedure, but required him to ingest the radioactive iodine which would make his body slightly radioactive. For the first few days, he'd be in a single room without visitors. Once the radiation levels in his body came down, and he wasn't considered a risk to anyone, he would then be allowed to go home.

The fuckers who told him that this was the good cancer, didn't tell him that taking away part of his thyroid gland meant it would no longer produce the hormones he needed. That the absence of a fully functioning thyroid would make him feel off balance and less than functional, that even if he looked normal on the outside, he would never be 100% the same. That, unless he took his medicine every single day, he would suffer from poor muscle tone, depression, weight gain, and brain fog; there was a whole list of things he would have, things he had taken for granted, things which were working just fucking fine before he'd had part of his thyroid gland removed.

But life had also given him Kay, and she seemed to have stuck by him in spite of everything. He could never make up to this woman for the way he had treated her. And that, he had decided, during many of the free hours he'd had to sit back and reflect on his life, was what he was going to fix as soon as he could .

"Are you ready for it?" she asked a few days before the treatment. They were sitting across the kitchen island from one another. It was their safe place, away from the couch and the bedroom.

He was. "I sure am. I want it over and done with." He did. He wanted this part of his life behind him. He wanted to forget he ever had it, but the chances of that, the doctor had told him, were zero. He would have to take replacement hormone tablets for the rest of his life, in order to prevent symptoms of an underactive thyroid.

She reached across the island, and took his hand. The sudden, unexpected gesture stealing a beat of his heart.

"You're going to be fine," she told him, as she had the night before his surgery.

He smiled, basking in the warmth of her reassurance.

"We'll get it over and done with," she said, making his heart burst. She'd said, '*We*'.

Once this was all done with, he'd explain, he'd make her see and she would understand.

"Thanks," he said, rubbing his thumb slowly over the back of her hand. He waited for her to move her hand away, but she didn't. "You don't know what it means to me to hear you say that."

Things were going to get better.

CHAPTER THIRTY-SIX

I solation stank.

He'd taken his pill and had stayed in an isolation room at the hospital for the first three days because he was a risk to others. His body was literally giving off radiation as if he was a nuclear missile.

After that, he'd driven himself back home and spent another four days in solitary confinement.

'Five to ten days, to be completely safe,' the doctor had told him. "You won't kill anyone, but it wouldn't be a bad idea to wait it out." He'd told Marie and Kay not to come over.

He was expecting to stay in isolation for another few days, but when one evening, on day eight, the door opened and Kay walked in, it physically knocked him back. He'd given her a set of keys to his place a few weeks ago, but seeing her walking through his door as if she lived here was like a burst of sunshine in a cloud of grey.

He liked the idea of her coming home to *him*, of this being *their* place, but he wasn't sure it was such a good idea, him being a walking, talking bundle of radiation and her being this close to him.

"Hey," he said, taking a few steps back. "You shouldn't be here. I'm still radioactive." He took a few more steps back so that he was in the corner of his living room as she watched him, still hovering near the door.

It didn't matter how low the doctor said the levels would be by now, radiation was still radiation. This woman had some guts. "You shouldn't come any closer," he warned.

"I like dangerous men," she replied, giving him the kind of smile she used to give him when he would initiate sex. "You should have come with a warning," she replied, nodding, "But I'm a big girl. I can take care of myself."

"I know you can, I'm not implying otherwise." She had still come through for him when any other woman in her shoes would have told him to go to hell. His entire opinion of her had changed the more he had gotten to know the real her. She had it all—the looks, the chutzpah, the heart of a saint and the body of a Greek goddess.

And she cared about him.

She was his path to redemption and she didn't even know it.

"I love you being here, I really do, but I don't want to put you in any danger."

"The doctor said it was fine, and I trust his judgement over yours."

"Which doctor?"

"Dr. Santini, at the hospital."

He frowned. The dark-haired guy he'd seen before his surgery? "I spoke to another guy and he told me to wait it out." After a while he asked her, "When did you get talking to Dr. Santini"

"At the hospital. He said you'd be safe after a week, they

only add in the extra days as a precautionary measure. And since I'm not pregnant, and we don't have kids, there's no big problem. You should be thankful I came."

"I am. I am thankful. You have no idea," he said quickly, not wanting to push her away. While he didn't want her to become ill on account of him, if the doctor said it was safe, he wasn't going to argue about it. "I'm really, *really* glad you came. I haven't even heard from Marie."

"That's because she's in Miami, checking out some potential properties you told her to look at." She peered at him, craning her neck forward. "Didn't you know? You're the one who sent her."

He swiped his hand over the back of his neck. "Right," he said, nodding, "I keep forgetting a whole heap of things."

"Are you okay?" she asked, putting her bag down and walking over to him.

"Yeah," he replied, taking in the sight of her, because it was so welcome, after so many days of almost solitary confinement.

"I love that you came," he said, not bothering to rein in his words. She cared, and she was doing this for him in spite of all the bullshit he'd given her.

She looked momentarily puzzled.

"What?" he asked, wondering what he'd said.

"That's way too cheesy, especially for you."

"But I *do* love that you're here."

"Only because the doctor said."

"You didn't have to come, though." So, by his deduction, she had come because she had wanted to, only she wasn't going to say it. He was about to remind her that she had a lot going on at work, and he knew she was ducking and diving to slice time out for him, time she didn't owe him and yet, here she was. But he didn't say any of that. It wasn't his intention to get into any type of disagreement with her. He was grateful for her company and as much as he wanted to fix things, he wasn't quite sure she did. She was here in the capacity of a Florence Nightingale, not as someone he'd been intimate with, and while sex or intimacy were the furthest things from his mind, he was eager to talk, to plan for the future, to try and figure out if they even had a future.

"Marie's away for a few days, and Dr. Santini said you'd been alone for over a week—"

"Do you have a hotline to Dr. Santini?" he asked, something uncomfortable settling in his belly.

A flicker of indignation crossed her face. "He was your consultant. I needed to know what I was letting myself in for."

"Letting yourself in for?"

"Are we going to have a disagreement again?" she asked, looking none too pleased.

"No. We're not." He needed to drop this like a hot stone. She was here. For him. He had to remember that the past didn't have any say in his future and he had to stop acting like it did.

He still felt like shit. The metallic taste still lingered in his mouth, and he didn't feel his usual self. Maybe he never would feel completely 100%, and that was something he was going to have to deal with. But he smelled like shit too, and hadn't bothered to shower today. If he'd known she would be coming over, he would have made a concerted effort to clean up.

"Good," she said, appraising him as she lifted her head. "You don't look too good," she said, walking towards him. "It's fine," she said, when he put his hand out in front, trying to halt her.

"I feel like shit," he confessed.

She sniffed. "Have you been sick?"

Fuck. She could smell it on him. He took a few more steps back. "It's a side effect."

"You don't look well at all." She took off her jacket.

"I don't think this is a good idea, Kay." Seeing him when he didn't feel so great was one thing, but seeing him when he didn't feel so great *and* looked *and* smelled like crap was too much even for him. He hated that she was seeing him at his worst, and even though she seemed to brush it off, as if it didn't matter, it mattered to him. It made him wonder if he would have done this for her had the tables have been turned.

"I'm going to take you up on that offer," she said, taking out her laptop and setting it on the table.

"What offer?"

"To use your Wi-Fi."

"You're working tonight?"

"I have some things to finish off by tomorrow."

"I'm going to shower up and go to bed. Sorry, I'm not going to be good company."

"Go ahead," she said. "You might feel better after it. I've got some things I need to look through."

"I don't want to get in the way of your work. I know you're under a lot of pressure."

"You won't get in the way if you go to bed," she replied, giving him a solution he wasn't keen on. He couldn't go to bed knowing she was here, in his living room. He *didn't* want to go to bed. He wanted to talk to her, wanted to get back what they'd had before. Wanted to make some in-roads at least. It begged the question why she was here anyway, when she could just as easily have gone home.

Unless she wanted to be here. Unless she was holding

back. Unless she had realized that they could build on something, after all.

"Don't worry about me. It's fine. I've got this."

She was the real deal. The whole entire, beautiful package, and he'd been blind the whole time. He didn't leave straightaway, couldn't help but look over at her and be thankful that he had met her.

"What?" she asked, looking up and catching him staring at her.

He'd missed her, and with all this goddamn time on his hands, he'd had more time to think about things. "Thanks for coming. It's been weird, being in isolation."

"Even for you?" she asked, "The man who doesn't need anyone?"

He ground his teeth together, smarting at the reminder. "It's my experience that people always let you down, but you never have, even when I've been a total jerk to you."

"Don't go getting all sentimental on me now," she said, throwing her hands up in the air and making light of the situation. It didn't matter that the doctor told him he'd be cured, and be able to continue with his life, he couldn't help but think about mortality, and things going wrong. The cancer spreading, or coming back, of his life changing.

It had been a sobering few days of reflection, but in between the darkness had been the one thought: he was still alive, and even though this vile, deathly, malignant thing had been growing inside him, he had overcome it. He was still walking through that dark tunnel, but he was going to make it. He was going to come out the other end. And he had plans for how things were going to change. Plans to be done with the things that he had held on to for too long— things that had damaged his twenty-something year old self.

He had flipped it around, and in his own twisted way

had come to see his cancer as a gift. A wake up call. Something which had sobered him up and forced him to look at life without the shackles of his past.

"I've had a lot of time to think about things."

But she was shaking her head. "Not now, Luke. I've got an urgent report to look at."

He nodded. She was punishing him for all the times he'd made her feel like dirt. "I think I'm one of the luckiest guys alive."

She didn't smile, but let out a deep breath, as if she was waiting for him to leave.

It dawned on her that she had what she had wanted all along, for Luke to need her.

But things had changed, and he could no more unsay what he had said to her, than she could forget.

She reminded herself that he was a sick man who had nobody else apart from her and Marie, and this in itself made her indispensable to him. If he said nice things to her now, it was because he had nobody else; she needed to remember that, and not be lulled into a false sense of his feelings for her. A sick man being nice to you was not a barometer of the strength of a relationship.

She made up her mind to stay for a few hours, reading up on her reports, and making the necessary changes. A couple of times at work, her guard had slipped. It had been tough juggling work and Luke, especially with her ever-changing feelings about the man. She had managed to hold it all together in the meetings, and Remington wasn't on her back as much, but privately, at her own desk, she would often sit back and look at the path her life had taken lately.

If Luke hadn't been so brutally honest with her, if he hadn't lashed out and told her what he had really thought of her, she might have found a way to believe in them. She could never forget what he had said.

The old Kay would have. Good-Time-Kay would have taken anything that was offered, but she wasn't that person anymore. She didn't want to rectify a relationship that had started off on the wrong foot with the wrong intentions. Theirs had, and there was no way back.

She was overwhelmed and tired. Things were slipping through, and all because she was fighting to keep her A-game on at work, and be there for Luke.

Even Geoffrey had noticed that something was up with her.

He'd been surprisingly helpful lately and even though she kept her private life private, she had let it slip out one day, about Luke's illness. He knew of Luke, and he'd caught her at a time when she was on a low. It had just seemed easier to open up to him. She'd told him that Luke had recently been treated for cancer, and that she was taking care of him. That she was juggling her work commitments, as well as taking care of him.

This evening, after the last meeting with Remington, Geoffrey had passed by her desk and asked her what she was still doing here so late. He told her to go home and have an easy night for a change. He had stepped up and told her he would take care of things in case Remington asked.

She sat back and rubbed her eyebrows. Tiredness had seeped into every cell of her body, and she was desperate for sleep, feeling suddenly overcome with the need to close her eyes because she had sat down.

But she fought it, and opened her laptop, and got to work. Halfway through her report Luke's landline rang. She stared at it, waiting for the ringing to stop, but it went to his answering machine instead.

"Luke! Why didn't you tell me?" The voice sounded familiar, and she sat up, trying to place it. "Pick up, pick up, pick up, or I swear I'm going to come over right now."

Kay looked up, wondering what to do.

"Pick up will you! I'm worried sick."

She jumped up and picked up the phone.

"You took your time!"

"Amanda? It's me, Kay. We met at your wedding."

"Oh...*Kay?*" Amanda's voice burst with surprise. "I was so worried when nobody picked up. What's happened to Luke? He hasn't returned any of my calls. I finally got a hold of Marie and she said he'd had surgery."

He hadn't called to let his sister know?

But then again, should she really be that surprised?

This was Luke all over and his closest relationships didn't matter to him. She, of all people, knew this.

"He did," she replied, slowly. "But he's fine," she said, not giving anything away. "You should really get him to tell you."

"I called and you answered. Where is he?" Amanda asked.

"He's taking a shower," Kay explained. "And he's really tired."

"Marie said he had something wrong with his thyroid."

"He did, but he's been treated for it and he's fine. It might be better to call him over the weekend, because I don't think he's in the mood to talk right now." She would rather Amanda spoke to Luke directly and let him tell her. She knew how things with his family set him off. It was better not to get mixed up in the dynamics and politics of the Hunters.

"Why not?"

"He's recovering, and he's still slightly weak."

"Feeling weak?" Amanda asked in a worried voice. "He's going to live, isn't he?"

"Oh, god, yes. He's going to be fine."

Amanda made a low whine. "I don't know why he didn't tell me. He could have told me. He's such an uptight moody bastard, but he's my brother, so…"

"I understand." Of course she did. She got up and wandered towards the bathroom. She could still hear the shower running. Not wanting Amanda to go to sleep worried, she divulged some more information and explained that he'd only just recovered from the surgery, and then he'd had to have the radioactive treatment a few weeks later. "He's not really been in any state to call and tell anyone." She was lying here. He could have picked up the phone, but for some reason, she found herself making excuses for him.

"I'm glad he's got you to take care of him," Amanda remarked. "Marie says you've really been there for him."

Kay winced. "It wasn't only me. Marie has been here a lot. She's cooked his food for him. That's much more than I ever did."

"Well, I'm just glad you were there."

"I'll let him know you called."

CHAPTER THIRTY-SEVEN

It was the weekend, and Kay had come over. 'For a few hours,' she'd told him.

He would happily take a few hours, a few minutes, whatever slice of time she offered. Her being here had made his illness all the more bearable.

She'd gone grocery shopping again; with Marie away, he sensed that she was doing double duty to make up for it. Together, they were taking things out of the bags and putting them away. He liked this—her being here, and them putting groceries away as if they were a normal couple, running chores on the weekend.

When his doorbell rang, he looked up, pensive. He hardly ever had any visitors, and at this time, in this condition, he hadn't been expecting anyone at all.

"I'll get it," she said, setting down the jar of olives. "Were you expecting anyone?"

"No."

She disappeared out of sight, and then he heard voices. Not just one person. He strained his ears, and felt the color drain from his face. He cocked his head, his ears straining to distinguish the voices.

Seriously? What the hell were they doing here? And why had *she* come?

Amanda walked into the kitchen, then raised her hand to her mouth. "Why didn't you tell us?" And before he had a chance to reply, she rushed over to him. As he reacted, while trying to school his anger, he saw Kay standing there, looking slightly sheepish. And beside her was Maggie.

"I—I forgot to tell you," Kay said, putting her hand to her forehead.

He angled his head. "You knew about this?" he growled.

"I—I meant to tell you that Amanda called…"

"I wanted to surprise you," continued Amanda, breaking away from him and oblivious to what was going on. He didn't know what to say. Didn't have the energy to speak, because it was all sucked up into a knot of anger.

"You should have called," he said, turning his back to Maggie.

"I *did* call—"

"And I forgot to tell you. I was busy with my report," Kay answered, looking slightly flustered.

"What does it matter? We're here now. You could have at least told us *something*." Amanda's eyes were beginning to well up.

"I didn't want you to worry."

"It's cancer, for goodness sake. Of course we were going to worry. We had a right to know, don't you think? *I* had a right, even if you don't care about Dad and Travis." The rising anger in her voice filled the air with tension.

He didn't want to upset Amanda, but it wasn't helping having Maggie in his kitchen, looking at him as if she gave a shit. "I didn't want to worry you," he said, finally. "I would have told you eventually. I didn't know you were back from your honeymoon."

"You didn't even listen to any of my messages?" Amanda shrieked. "Because if you had, you'd have known that we returned weeks ago."

Christ. He swiped a hand over his face. What a train wreck of a morning this had turned out to be.

"I left you so many texts, and called you," his sister continued. "But they always said you were busy, at the new site, or something. I could never get through. Thank goodness for Kay. If it hadn't been for her we'd never have known."

The two of them smiled at one another. He ought to be glad that his sister and Kay seemed to be getting along, even though they had hardly spent any time together.

"We've all moved on, Luke." Hatred curled around his heart, impossible to unpick. The sound of that voice cut into him and cut deep. Maggie had finally spoken. She was the last person who should have come here. He turned around and faced her, this woman who had smashed his heart into tiny, tiny pieces. He looked squarely into her eyes, needing to confirm that she had no hold over him.

"It was cancer," he said, not even blinking. "I had surgery. I'm fine. You didn't need to come." *A phone call would have done.*

"Why don't we all sit down," suggested Kay, "Let's go into the living room and get out of the kitchen."

He watched her herding them out, and wondered why the hell hadn't she told him?

They sat on the sofas; he and Amanda on one, and Maggie and Kay on the other one.

"That looks nasty," Amanda commented, staring at his scar.

"Thanks."

"No, I mean, it looks serious," she said, with a laugh, attempting to lift the atmosphere which had plunged by about fifty degrees.

"Cancer is," he replied.

"Travis wanted to come," offered Maggie.

"Good job he stayed away," he replied, touching his scar lightly.

"We thought it would be better if he didn't come," Amanda chimed in.

"Then why did you come?" he asked Maggie.

"Daddy sends his regards. He was worried," said Amanda.

He said nothing, biting down on his teeth, holding back. The last few weeks had imbued him with a sense of calmness that he hadn't known before. Time away from work, thinking about life, and his own mortality had been sobering. But this sudden unexpected appearance from Amanda and Maggie was too much. Even though he loved Amanda, and even though Maggie no longer inspired feelings of hate in him, it still bugged the crap out of him that she was here and ruining his morning with Kay.

Mention of his brother and father made staying calm more difficult with each passing moment.

Amanda took his hand. "I just wanted to come and see you." Her worried gaze swept over him again, and every now and then it settled on his scar.

"How was the surgery?" Maggie asked. He tried to stay calm, tried to ground himself. He thought he was over this fucking shit. Instead, he pointed, shot-gun style with his fingers, towards the ugly scar on his neck. "Done, and dusted."

Maggie's eyes narrowed, the same way they used to

when she would examine something. He knew that expression well, just as he knew she felt uncomfortable now. At least at the wedding they had been in a big room, surrounded by lots of people. Even at Amanda's first wedding, he'd been with Ginger, the escort he'd hired so as not to go alone.

This was tricky, being in a confined space like this. The more she sat here, the more it brought the past back and he didn't need that, not when he was pushing past it and needing to move on. Seeing her again took him back in time to that warm, hazy summer's day when he'd arrived home early from the warehouse where he worked. Feeling sick, and unable to work the 8-hour shift, he'd come home only to walk past his brother's room, with its door half-open and his girlfriend, Maggie, in bed with his brother.

He had walked in, shocked and broken, and they had looked up. That sight, the smell, and the sounds—music playing on the radio, her giggling—he could hear it even now. And the sheets, a crumpled mess, and the smell of sweat and sex in the air. The image was stamped in his head, but over time it had become interspersed with the image of his mother lying on the blood-red sheets of the bed where she had died, bleeding out on the bed she once shared with his father.

"Will it come back?" Amanda asked, shaking him out of that nightmare.

He looked at her, confused. "Will what come back?"

"The cancer."

"I don't want to talk about it, if you don't mind," he replied, a growing sense of unease spreading all over him.

"Sorry."

"It shouldn't come back," said Kay, stepping in. "But

he'll have to have lots of checkups along the way just to make sure. Apparently, they call it the good cancer".

"The *good* cancer?" Maggie asked, and the three women laughed lightly. The conversation was so awkward, and the silences like barbed wire, that he wished he was back in the isolation room.

"Why did you come?" he asked Maggie, unable to hold back. He felt nothing for her, and knew he would never have visited her had the situation been reversed. Why had she come?

"Luke!" Amanda and Kay's voices rang out in a chorus.

"No, I really want to know. Why did you come? You didn't need to."

"I was worried about you, we all were, and I wanted to see that you were okay." Her voice was hard, determined, as she held the stare. The silent seconds stretched out for what seemed like days.

"It's good of you to come," said Kay, making an attempt at conversation. "Oh my goodness," she cried in the next breath, and stood up. "Please excuse my bad manners. Can I get you anything to drink?"

Both visitors nodded their heads in unison. "We should go," said Amanda, raising a slight smile. "I had hesitations about coming, but I needed to see you, and I'm glad we came."

He could have handled Amanda. He didn't mind his sister being here, but Maggie? She was so out of place, so superfluous, so *unnecessary*. This was supposed to be a relaxing Saturday afternoon with Kay.

Now Maggie had gone and ruined it.

"I'm glad you're okay," she said, standing and getting ready to go.

"I'm fine, Maggie. I'm just fucking fine. Now, run back to my brother, won't you?"

"Luke," cautioned Amanda.

He stared at her and shrugged. "She didn't need to come. Even *you* know that."

Kay looked at him, then, her face questioning, and her mouth slightly parted, as if she had only now pieced it all together.

"We're going," said Amanda in that over-the-top cheery voice of hers. She kissed him on the cheek and gave him a gentle hug. "But I'll be back with Kyle when you're better."

He frowned. "Kyle?"

"My husband," Amanda retorted. "And I'll have to tell you all about our honeymoon."

He groaned. "Looking forward to it."

CHAPTER THIRTY-EIGHT

He looked as if he was going to explode, and she knew he was all riled up again. "Why did you ask them to come?" he asked her.

"I didn't. Why are you so mad? I thought you liked your sister?" She could see him biting down, could see the tell-tale muscles twitching along his jaw. Any moment now he was going to lose it.

"I do like my sister," he ground out quietly.

"So what's the issue?"

He didn't say anything, and she could see him struggling not to erupt in anger. For he was angry. She'd been watching him the whole time. Had heard and seen his interaction with Maggie.

And finally, she had understood.

She was merely biding her time.

"Amanda called here a few days ago, and you were in the shower. I'm sorry, I forgot to tell you."

"You forgot to tell me?" he snarled, his voice full of sarcasm.

"I was working on my report." He had no idea what it

had been like. No idea at all. Sometimes she wondered why she'd done it, why she'd agreed to keep an eye on him, when she didn't have to. She could have owned up and told Marie the truth, but she hadn't. She'd chosen to keep the farce going. Maybe she'd even loved seeing the new Luke unravel. Maybe that had been a part of it, too.

"You know how fucked up my family is. You should have warned me."

"You're not even listening to me. I *forgot*. I've been juggling a lot of things."

"I'm sorry." He paced around the room, as if he was trying to keep it together. "I didn't mean to snap at you."

"I didn't know Amanda was going to turn up. She didn't say she was." Her voice was rising in pitch and she could feel her own anger grow. His temper was like quicksand—hard to avoid once you happened across it. She had forgotten it, almost because being with him during his recovery had dimmed the memory of what he could be like. She remembered the bartender she had first come to know over a few cocktails, and found it difficult to reconcile the man she now knew, with the man she had first believed him to be.

And just like quicksand, her feelings for him were hard to hold on to. She wasn't sure how to be around him, which Luke he was at any moment. Today's episode had shown her that the old Luke was never far away. Any interaction with his family riled him up, and her patience was disappearing fast. She did not need this headache.

"I didn't need my family to come here."

"But I had nothing to do with that. If you want to blame me for anything, blame me for forgetting to tell you. It's not like I didn't have another million things to take care of apart from you."

"I didn't ask you to look after me."

Anger hurtled through her like a hurricane. The ungrateful douchebag. "*You* didn't, but Marie did."

That startled him. His expression bordered on disbelief. "I wish she'd mind her goddamn business. I don't need anybody to look after me, and I sure as hell don't need you."

"Really?" The audacity, the sheer, unbridled ingratitude of the man. "You could have fooled me."

But he seemed too caught up in his own troubles to notice her shock.

"Actually, that's not entirely true. I didn't only do it because Marie asked me to. I wanted to make sure you were okay. I did it because, despite you being the biggest asshole to me a lot of the time, I thought I caught a glimmer of the *real* you, a new you, sometimes."

"You don't know the real me," he replied, looking completely miserable as he sat on the sofa. He leaned forward, holding his head in his hands. She could see that the morning had taken its toll on him. The arguing was only going to make things worse.

"That's because you can't share yourself. You won't open up," she said, keeping her distance across the room from him, and folding her arms. "You're a tightly wound up ball of emotions, sometimes, and trying to reach inside you is impossible."

"If that's what you think then I don't know what you're doing here," he shot back.

"Because I—" she paused. It wasn't love. She didn't know what love was. She really didn't. Not the type of love that Savannah knew. But she had liked taking care of him. She had liked knowing that he needed her, because nobody had needed her before the way Luke had needed her now.

"Because I was trying to be like most normal decent people. I was trying to do the right thing."

"Why?"

"Why?" Because she was starting to think he might be changing for the better. "Because sometimes you *can* be nice."

"Nice?" he scoffed.

"I do care about you, even if it's not the same anymore."

His eyes flashed dangerously. "What do you mean it's not the same?"

"You know it's not," she replied, and before he could question her, she remembered something she had been meaning to ask him. "Why does Maggie annoy you so much?" She wanted to know why he'd fallen out with his brother, but that could wait. Her need to find out about Maggie was more pressing.

"She just does."

"And your brother?" She sat down next to him, not close, but with enough space between them that he wouldn't feel she was intruding. Any conversation about his family seemed to hem him in, and she wanted answers. She'd let it go too long, watching, saying nothing, and yet it was clear to her that the biggest problems he had stemmed from them.

"Don't ever talk to me about my brother."

She pressed her lips together. "You hate Maggie because she married your brother?"

He looked at her as if she had stumbled across a secret. "Did Amanda tell you?"

She *had* stumbled across a secret. She remained quiet, letting him think what he wanted, then, when he didn't let up, "Your sister said she was surprised and pleased to hear that we'd been together for a while."

He squeezed his eyes shut, as if doing so would block out everything. "I needed someone to go with me."

She frowned, not understanding. "Go where?"

"To the wedding. I would have hired someone, but you were on the scene, and you seemed different."

She swallowed, still not understanding where this was going. "Different?" she asked, hoping to coax it out of him.

"With your banking background. I knew you'd make a better impression on my family, in case you were unlucky enough to get into a conversation with them."

"To make an impression on your family?" she asked, alarm bells going off in her head. She shifted, twisting her body towards him. "Who were you trying to impress, your father?"

"That piece of shit." The mere mention of the man seemed to make Luke's muscles freeze up. Lifting his hand to his neck again, he gingerly touched below the scar. "I think I impressed him the most when he caught me screwing his whore."

Her eyes nearly bugged right out of her head. "You... you did *what?*"

"I wanted to get my own back," he said, staring at the floor, his hands steepled together. "After my mom killed herself, I knew the only way to get him back, to hit him where it hurt was to show him what it felt like when the person you loved screwed someone else."

Sadness swirled around her, leaving her tied up in ribbons of pity and love and hurt. She felt for this man, felt his pain as acutely as if it were her own. He turned to her and smiled. "Turned out, she was only seven years older than me. So we ended up in bed."

"She seduced you?" Kay asked, horrified. .

"*I* seduced *her*. Wasn't hard. I was a fumbling teen until

I met her."

She tipped her head to the side, forgetting to breathe.

"She didn't take much persuading either," he continued, "After sleeping with a shriveled old prune like my old man, she was desperate for someone more her own age."

She couldn't find the words to voice her shock. The scene played out in her head and the idea of Luke as a motherless teenager seeking revenge upset her in so many ways. "But you must have been underage."

"It's no big deal. Sex is sex. I was almost of age. And at least I wasn't a virgin anymore."

Now she understood it all, his coldness, and contempt, and the way he had sometimes treated her. This man was messed up, and he was hurting, and none of it was his fault. She leaned towards him, putting her arm around his waist. "You wanted to impress your father's wife? Is that it?" she asked, not quite understanding his quest for one-upmanship."

Luke laughed cruelly. "This new one's wife number three. He married the one I screwed, and then he threw her out the day he caught us. I'd been fucking her for months by the time he found out."

"You poor thing," she murmured. Her head was spinning out of control; the thoughts, the images and the sadness of it all, of how his young life and family had shattered. She wanted to hold Luke in her arms and cradle him.

"It was the same day he threw me out, and then I moved into Travis's apartment."

"There was nothing more between you two?"

"Hell no. I didn't *love* her. I didn't even care for her. I *used* her. She was a means to an end, and it worked. It almost destroyed him when he found out."

It still didn't make sense.

Who had he wanted to impress?

"I wanted Maggie to know I was doing fine."

"What's ... " She had started to ask what Maggie had to do with any of it, and it took a moment, maybe three or four moments, before she pieced it all together.

"She broke my heart," he said, his voice tapering off as he looked away. "I walked in on them one day when I came back from work early," he told her. "It must be hardwired into my DNA, walking in on people having sex."

It was there, starting to rise, the bile, and acid, and feeling of nausea. Rising from the pit of her belly, a slow, heaving monster ready to push upwards. She could feel the room spinning around her, as if a tornado had gobbled it all up.

"But she's married to your brother."

"She was my girlfriend first."

Maggie had been the one who'd left him broken-hearted. Kay remembered back to that first night, when he'd mentioned his rules. She'd hit on the truth without even realizing.

"Maybe she preferred him to me. Maybe I need to treat women better than I do. Have respect for them, but you tell me, how the hell am I supposed to do that?"

He was blabbering on, not even realizing.

"So it was Maggie you wanted to impress?"

He nodded.

And that was why he'd asked her along to the wedding? All along she had foolishly believed he'd invited her because he was starting to feel something for her.

She couldn't have been more wrong.

She scooted a couple of inches away from him, as if she was seeing him with new eyes. She had given him her all;

her body, her time and her attention, and all for nothing. For a moment she was powerless to move. Paralyzed to say anything, or fight back.

The shock of what he had told her reverberated inside her head, in her belly, in every fiber of her body. She had lied when she'd said it was because of Marie that she had stepped up to take care of him. The truth was, she hadn't done any of this because she expected a medal. She'd done it because she had genuinely cared for this guy; for this selfish, twisted man with issues. A man who could not love, and could not allow anyone to love him.

When was she ever going to learn that love didn't come from these types of connections?

"Where are you going?" he asked, as she got up without saying a word.

"I need to go."

He reached for her hand, and missed. "It's not like that now. Maggie's in my past."

She folded her arms together. "But you used me. You took me to the wedding not because you cared, but because you had ulterior motives."

He looked puzzled, but didn't answer back.

"You wanted to impress her, even after all these years that she's been with your brother. You still have feelings for her."

He opened his mouth to speak, but the denial was too hard to make. She didn't need his validation of it. She knew, because of his actions, it was clear.

He was so messed up he couldn't even see it.

She nodded. She was done with his bullshit.

Nothing he said to her now would make a difference.

The man needed a psychotherapist, not a girlfriend.

CHAPTER THIRTY-NINE

She had been so incredibly blind, and so incredibly stupid.

Tears threatened to fall again as she rushed into her apartment building, only to find Arnold standing in front of the elevator. He turned around on hearing her footsteps, and she couldn't hide her blotched face.

"Miss," he said, moving out of the way, but resting his hand on her arm. "Why are you crying?"

She shook her head. *Not now, Arnold.*

"Did someone hurt you?" he asked, looking cross.

She shook her head again, praying that the elevator doors would open so that she could shoot right in.

"Miss." This time he placed himself directly in front of her so that she would have to swerve around him to get in. "This ain't like you."

She huffed out an irritated breath, and then stopped herself. Just because Luke had put her in a foul mood didn't mean she had to take it out on anyone else. That would be stooping to his level. "Not now, Arnold. It's...it's not been a good day."

"I can see that," he said, nodding his head, listening.

"It's...I'll get over it," she said, choosing her words carefully.

"One minute, Miss," he said, when the elevator doors swooshed open. He rushed over to his desk, grabbed something, then rushed back. He held out a large, unopened bar of chocolate. "This'll make things look better. Won't fix anything, but ..." he nodded, shoving it further towards her as she resisted taking it. "Take it."

She chuckled, and it felt so odd that she could laugh about something in this moment. Her eyes welled up, in gratitude.

"Thank you, Arnold." She didn't know what else to say. His offering overwhelmed her. It was such a simple gesture, yet full of care and concern. Worth its weight in gold. This man whom she had practically never acknowledged, had lifted her spirits when he could just as easily have ignored her. "This is...," she was choked up by his kindness, "this is so sweet of you," she managed as she stepped into the elevator and watched his grinning, toothless smile while the doors closed.

With Luke, she often felt that he was the taker, and she the giver. She was the one who cared, and many times she was the only one who hurt, and loved and had feelings. She had pretended it wasn't one-sided, when she should have known from the start.

She should have put Marie right, and not gotten involved even when she found out about the cancer. She might not have ever discovered the truth about Maggie, and he might not have revealed more of his past, but would it even have mattered if she had already walked away? Ignorance would have been bliss.

He wasn't boyfriend material, and she had been sucked

in, once again, into believing he was more. But that stopped today. They were done. She didn't need to go and explicitly break it off with him. She had suffered enough, mistakenly thinking she could fix this man and make him love her. Luke couldn't love anyone because he couldn't even love himself. He was in complete denial of his issues, and there was no hope in helping a man who couldn't see that there was anything wrong with him in the first place.

She deserved better things. A decent man, and a relationship that had a future.

***

"How are you feeling now?" Amanda asked.

He was mildly irritated and hoped she wasn't going to make a habit of calling him daily just because he was a cancer survivor. She'd only seen him yesterday. "The same as yesterday," he replied.

"Kyle said he'd like to come and see you sometime."

"He doesn't have to," he said quickly. Did he need to remind her that theirs was a dysfunctional family? That they weren't exactly regular visitors to one another's houses, even at times like this.

Weddings, yes.

Funerals, yes.

The next time would be whenever his old man kicked the bucket. If he could be bothered to go.

"We shouldn't be strangers, Luke."

He scratched his brow. God, no. He didn't want to listen to this now. "We're all busy, Amanda. This works for us."

"I would like my kids to know their uncles. Is that a lot to ask?"

His head jolted back in shock. "Don't tell me you're pregnant," he said. Because he wasn't sure it would have been wise, her coming to see him when he was still radioactive.

"No! But we're going to start trying soon."

"Already, Amanda?" She was immature, and stupid to be making such moves so soon. The ink hadn't dried long on their marriage certificate, and she was looking to get knocked up already. What if this man turned out to be Douchebag Number 2? "What's the rush? Shouldn't you wait and see how married life works out?" And why the hell would she want a kid, anyway? He was never going to make that mistake.

"What's wrong with you?" she asked, sounding downcast. "You were in a lousy mood yesterday."

"I've just had surgery for fucking thyroid cancer."

"I know. I'm sorry. But I *know* you, Luke. You *never* look relaxed. You're always so wound up."

This was exactly the thing that Kay had said to him. He said nothing.

"Maggie said you looked well."

"She thought I looked well?" He blinked a few times, mulling over the sentence. She could hardly say he looked like shit, could she? "Why did you bring her?"

"She wanted to come. Marie told us you were at home, and recovering from that iodine treatment—"

"Marie told you?"

"How else were we going to find out?"

"Kay never told you?"

"No. Kay told me to speak to you, but then she said you were resting. She was pretty good at being evasive. If anyone understands you, it's her."

He ran his hand over his stubble, thinking. It wasn't

what he wanted to hear. The huge argument with Kay yesterday had wiped him out, not just physically, but emotionally and he'd felt drained ever since she'd stormed out. This morning he'd lain in bed, not caring to do anything. He hadn't even bothered to shower.

"I asked Marie a few days later," Amanda continued, "and she said you could do with some cheering up, and that you'd be fine by the weekend. She said you'd be less radioactive."

Dammit.

He'd blamed Kay for it. She had tried to tell him, but he hadn't believed her, and she'd taken the brunt of his anger. "Funny how you didn't mention it at the time."

"I was too worried hoping you wouldn't go off on Maggie."

"I wish you hadn't agreed to bring her."

"Whatever's happened, it's in the past, Luke. We have to get on, otherwise what's the point? Besides, I like your new girlfriend."

He was about to say something, but decided it would be better not to.

"She's nice," Amanda continued. "Even Maggie said she was nice."

"I don't give a flying fuck what Maggie said."

Amanda, like his family, knew about him and Maggie, but time erased all wounds, and they had obviously forgotten the pain and the scandal.

"Daddy says if you need any money—"

"No."

"For the best treatment—"

"I can afford the best treatment. I don't need his dirty handouts." It was laughable, his father trying to buy his affection back now. It was too late for any bridges to be built between them.

"It's not a dirty—" she started to protest.

"Don't..." Amanda hadn't seen their mother on the blood-red bed. Neither she nor Travis had experienced what he had, and neither had they ever suffered the way he had.

While they probably hadn't been able to forgive, they had most likely forgotten.

It was going to take him time.

"Okay, fine," Amanda said. "I get it, Luke. I just wanted you to know that you're not alone."

Whatever. He was in no mood to get into a discussion with her about that now.

"Maggie feels sorry for you."

"She shouldn't. I have a great girlfriend, and I'm moving on." Except that he didn't, and he wasn't. "Next time you decide to bring Maggie over, warn me at least."

"I didn't bring her. I know the score, Luke. I'm not stupid. She insisted."

"She's wasting her fucking time."

"All she wants is to get on with you, and move past this."

"She should have thought of that before she decided to jump into Travis's bed."

"She said it just happened. She said you were a real asshole."

His lips curled up into a snarl. "The two of you bonded on the way here, did you?"

"Maggie and I get on," Amanda insisted. "I hope me and Kay will too, one day."

He didn't say anything.

"Maggie said you used to be nasty to her, that you

weren't a great boyfriend. She said you used to mess with her head."

He frowned, not remembering it quite in the same way. Sure, he wasn't so lovey-dovey, and he might have said some spiteful things to her, not told her he loved her, and all that other stuff girls wanted to hear. But he never hurt her. Never laid a finger on her.

"She said that Travis listened to her, and he tried to tell her that you were a little messed up. He never made a move on her, she said, and he tried to steer her back towards you."

He rubbed the back of his head, mentally clearing the cobwebs that enshrined events that were buried so long in the past. He tried to remember that time, but it was a haze of messed up emotions. It had been an angry, red hot, tumultuous time. He didn't have counseling, didn't talk to anyone, and kept everything bottled up.

Maybe Maggie was right. He might not have been a great boyfriend.

"She said it wasn't too difficult for her to fall out of love with you and fall in love with Travis."

"He can have her," he said, roughly. "I've moved on."

"I know," Amanda cried, happily. "I hope you don't mess things up with Kay, Luke. She cares about you. She really does."

"Yeah, well." Maybe it was too late for that.

He hung up, after what ended up being mostly a one way conversation.

But at least he had managed to postpone Amanda's next visit.

CHAPTER FORTY

"Geoffrey's taking over the Pembroke account."

"What?" She was sure she hadn't heard right.

"The Pembroke account will be looked after by Geoffrey from now on," Remington stated.

A ball of anger exploded inside her. "But why? That's my account."

"It *was* your account."

"I was taking care of it, Theodore," she said, her stomach sinking lower, and blood-red rage coursing through her veins.

"Were you, Kay? Were you *really*?" Remington asked as he stared up at her, his coupled hands resting over his desk.

"What's that supposed to mean?" she shot back, a bitter taste in her mouth suddenly making her feel nauseous. "You know I was."

"You *were*, Kay," he replied. He was infuriatingly calm, and she much preferred him when he lost his shit, because he somehow seemed more human then. "But given the circumstances, we need full concentration and focus. Do not forget that we are talking about a big client and a huge deal is huge."

"What?" she shook her head. "What do you mean by that? I have given it my full and undivided concentration and focus from the moment you gave me the account. What's going on?" she asked. Because clearly something was. Something had been decided while she had been away. This news had ripped a hole through her chest.

"I beg to differ."

Excuse me? What was he talking about? Her eyes widened in shock, and she tried to think fast, tried to make sense of what he was saying. She already knew that there would be no convincing him to change his mind; the man was like a pit bull once he determined a course of action, but she deserved an honest, no-bullshit answer. "I haven't taken any time off. I've handed everything to the client on time—"

"The report he received a few days ago contained errors."

Her face crumpled in disbelief. She had fixed the errors at Luke's place, and had emailed it to Geoffrey to hand in. He must have sent the wrong document back. She looked out of Remington's glass window, at the open plan office. Where was that back-stabbing shitbag? "I fixed the errors," she said, turning to face her boss again. "I double checked everything, and I emailed it to Geoffrey to scan in and send it on. He must have sent them the wrong report."

"I also recall you went home early that day."

She frowned. She'd gone to Luke's place and made the changes there.

"I understand the stress you've been under," he continued. "You should have told me."

She looked at him in surprise. "What stress?" She never

let her stress show at work. Just like one of the guys, she could, and did, soldier through it.

Remington exhaled slowly, as if he was trying not to raise his voice. "Your boyfriend is seriously ill, I hear. It's only natural that your mind has been elsewhere."

She crossed her arms, fighting back the urge to punch something. His face, even. Unbelievable. After everything she had done, not forgetting the hours she had put in during her time here, giving the bank her life and soul, they were taking away her biggest client. She shook her head in disbelief. "I've been up to date with everything. I haven't fallen behind on anything. It wasn't Geoffrey's business to mention anything about my personal life."

"But your boyfriend does have cancer, am I right, or not?"

Boyfriend was obviously not the right word, but she had to play along. She almost choked at the idea of explaining the details of their hookup to Remington. "We're dealing with it."

"Look, Kay. Don't fight me on this. Geoffrey's dealing with this client now, and everything goes through him. That's my decision, and it's final."

Geoffrey had stabbed her in the back, and now she'd lost her account. Her chance to shine. Worse, Remington saw her as a liability. Heat surged through her body, and the blood in her veins turned to magma. Anytime now she was going to erupt. "This isn't fair," she ground out slowly. "I haven't taken any time off. I've forwarded Geoffrey the correct report. If the client received the wrong one, it's Geoffrey's fault, not mine—"

Remington scratched the side of his face with his index finger, and his shiny white platinum cufflinks shone as the rays of sunshine hit it. "The decision is final, Kay. Cut out the hysterics and get on with business as fucking usual. We're in the banking business, for fucks sake." The good old Remington was back, curses and all.

And just like that, the Pembroke account was taken away, and with it, her chances of promotion.

She had given this company her blood—almost. Her blood, sweat and tears. She had worked around the clock, staying until way past normal hours, and taking work home. She had cajoled, and worked, and negotiated, and drank, and joked with the best of them, but in the end, it had taken a pathetic little whiny-voiced man, a man who hadn't been able to handle her rejection, to stab her in the back while she had been at her weakest. In a moment of vulnerability, she had let down her guard, and mistaken Geoffrey for a friend.

After the weekend she'd had, with Luke, and his sister and Maggie, and the shock of all she had discovered, this announcement from Remington just about broke her. It was everything she had worked for, everything she had put her heart, blood and guts into. He couldn't just take it away from her like that. It wasn't fair. She went for one last attempt. "Look, Theodore. It doesn't make sense to take me off this now when we're so close to making the deal. You just can't—"

Remington looked up at her, his eyes widening as he raised one eyebrow. "I can't what?" he said, quietly. "Can't what?" he cupped his hand to his ear, in what she saw as a final humiliation. She thanked her lucky stars that there was nobody around to witness this.

What did he expect her to do now?

As if reading her thoughts, he said, "Engelmann needs assistance with the client deal he's running. I've told him he can expect you to help out."

Engelmann? The guy who had only joined less than a year ago? She was supposed to help him out? And she'd been here three years. Talk about a slap in the face, a way to make her feel she wasn't worth jack.

"As you wish." She spun around on her heels, and left Remington's office.

Back at her desk, she forced herself to put on a coat of armor, to remain stoic and strong, and to not fall to pieces, especially because she knew everybody was watching her.

They had known before she'd set foot in the office, what was going down today. She willed Geoffrey to come to her and say something, anything. She eyed the pair of scissors in her desk tidy and considered, fleetingly, the possibility of sticking it in his back.

Erin often asked her if she wanted to go to lunch and she almost always turned her down, but today she needed to get out of the office. An hour later, she and Erin were sitting outside one of the sandwich shops, only her mind was elsewhere. She was trying to come to terms with the way both her personal and working lives had been turned upside down.

"How is he now?" Erin asked, having expressed shock and disappointment that Kay hadn't said a word to her about Luke's illness before.

"He's recovering."

"I can't believe it, Kay," her friend said in a whiny voice. "You meet a guy this hot, and fall in love—"

"Who said anything about falling in love?"

Erin looked surprised, the half-eaten bagel still in her hand. She looked at Kay as if she'd asked her an idiot question. "But you've been looking after him, and you lost the account over him. If that's not love, I don't know what is."

"I didn't *intend* to lose my client deal," she said, looking away. "Geoffrey used it to his advantage. Slimy little snake that he is." She couldn't help but wonder how easy it was for Remington. He didn't need to give her client to Geoffrey. He knew how hard she'd worked. Maybe that one time she slipped up was one time too much.

It still hurt hard, and she wasn't entirely sure what she was going to do next. Working alongside Engelmann wasn't appealing, and to her ambitious mind, she saw it as a demotion.

"It was a shitty thing to do," Erin agreed. "He's met your boyfriend, hasn't he?"

She flinched at the label. Luke would vomit if he heard anyone use that term to refer to him. Besides, that hadn't been the way she'd seen him, not before, not now and not ever. "Why? What's that got to do with it?"

"You would have thought he'd understand."

"Geoffrey?" *Understand?*

"He might have had the hots for you before, but that was a few months ago. He's seeing someone from the fifth floor now."

Kay looked at her in disbelief. "Lucky girl," she said sarcastically.

"You should be happy!" Erin countered. "At least he's over you."

"Good for him." She didn't care about Geoffrey, or his love life.

"You did what?" Marie asked, her voice shrill, the anger burning in her eyes.

"I told her I didn't need her anymore."

Marie set down her briefcase and fixed him with a look of complete disdain. "She's not your nurse, she's your girlfriend."

"That's right. And I told her I didn't need her anymore."

Marie tut-tutted loudly and threw him a pissed off look. "You messed up again, didn't you? I swear to god, Luke. You have an in-built self-destruct button."

"She was feeling sorry for me."

"She cared about you."

"She was in the way."

Marie choked at that. "She took time out of her working life to be here for you," she cried, angrily.

"I don't need her. I don't need anyone."

She looked away, shaking her head in disbelief. "You don't know what you don't know."

"What's *that* supposed to mean?"

"That you're a bigger idiot than I thought."

Her words winded him. Marie had never spoken to him like that–as if she was talking to her teenage boy. "I'm fine now. I don't need you or her to check in on me. I'm returning to work next week."

She looked at him, then gave him the once-over. "You don't know a good thing when you see it. I don't know what happened to make you like this, but whatever it is, you're ruining the best chance you ever had."

He didn't want to hear it. "You never met the sports masseuse," he replied, hoping to annoy her further.

"Thank goodness for that."

CHAPTER FORTY-ONE

She didn't want to go to Savannah's baby shower, but there was no way she could avoid it. She *had* to turn up, and she had to look happy. She already looked bad enough as it was, because she hadn't organized any of it. Briony had taken care of it all.

It had been weeks since she and Luke had spoken. He'd tried to get in touch many times, but she had ignored all of his calls and messages. She didn't want to risk feeling sorry for him, for his recovery.

She didn't want to risk making another mistake.

So far, she had managed to keep it together. Even last week, when she had gone over to see Tobias and Savannah, to congratulate them in person about the twins, she had put on a brave face.

Luckily, neither Tobias, nor Savannah had suspected what a wreck she was.

But she had been desperate to talk to Savannah, to offload, and confess, and have a close friend who would show her the error of her ways, and who would also tell her what to do to move on. Only, this time, she would take her advice.

She had focused for too long on the wrong things, and in the end, none of it had been for her own good. Not the hours she gave every day to her former investment bank, nor the time and energy she had willfully given caring for Luke.

Savannah, the person she should have been there for, the one who could have helped her, had been the one she had neglected. And even today, with the baby shower taking place, she was still running late.

"Sorry," she said, breathless, as she arrived at Max and Briony's apartment, feeling as if she'd messed up again. "I tried to get here as fast as I could."

"Don't worry," Briony replied, hugging her as she walked in. "It's only the four of us. Izzy couldn't come."

"Oh?" Kay asked, setting down her huge bag of baby gifts. She slipped off her jacket.

"Apparently, she's got exams. That's what Savannah said."

"That's a shame." She had been keen to meet Izzy and to find out what she was up to.

"I did leave you a couple of messages," Briony remarked, "asking if there was anyone else Savannah might want to ask along today."

Kay blushed a guilty shade of pink. "Sorry. I've been ..." She threw her hands up, indicating overwhelm. She had done nothing for Savannah. How selfish of her, therefore, to think she could go to her cousin and offload all her problems. "What about the school moms?"

"They're doing their own thing for her, thank god," said Briony, rolling her eyes. "I couldn't handle hours of listening to women talking about babies and children."

"Me neither." And, with it just being a small group of

friends, she already felt at ease. The idea of walking into a room full of women she didn't know, didn't appeal.

"No baby talk, okay?" Briony reminded her, wagging her finger.

"So we're not talking about the twins? How can we not talk about them?" she asked lowering her voice as she followed Briony into a room. Max got up and rushed towards her as soon as she entered. "Glad you could make it," she said, giving her a hug. "Briony says you've been impossible to get a hold of."

"I know, I know. I'm sorr—" She stopped, speechless when she saw Savannah sitting on a couch. She looked enormous. "Freaking hell, Sav," she cried in undisguised shock. "You're huge, and I only saw you last week!"

"Thanks," Savannah replied, looking slightly flustered. "I love you, too."

Kay rushed over, grinning. "You're supposed to be big. I think it's the way you're sitting," she said.

"That's a relief to know," Savannah replied as she bent down to give her a hug, being extra cautious not to press against her stomach, which was hard, given that it was almost a bump the size of a toddler, it seemed like. They pulled apart and Savannah's hands went to her stomach. "I feel like a pregnant blue whale," she whined.

"It must be getting uncomfortable, with two Stones in there," Kay commented.

"It's starting to." Savannah smoothed her hand over her bump. "I get breathless quickly, and I can feel the strain on my back, but this is still easier than when they'll be out, I suppose."

They all laughed.

"You're going to have your hands full," Kay replied.

"You two carry on," said Briony. "Max and I are fixing things in the kitchen...and we have a surprise."

Kay looked over her shoulder as Briony and Max disappeared out of sight. "A surprise?" She looked at Savannah. "What surprise?"

"I think I have an idea. We'll have to wait and see."

"Briony doesn't want me to talk about babies too much," Kay told her.

"The less said about that the better."

"But we're at your baby shower, and you're obviously pregnant. What are we supposed to talk about?"

"They're still locking heads over adoption," Savannah whispered, looking in the direction of the door. "It's a delicate subject."

"Noted," said Kay. "How are you feeling?"

"Slow, and heavy. They're going to induce me a few weeks early. I cannot wait. Anyway, tell me what you've been up to," said Savannah. "We couldn't talk much when you came over."

It was true. Tobias had been lurking around Savannah like an overprotective bodyguard and their apartment had been full of boxes, because they were getting ready to move to their sprawling new mansion.

"I'm sorry I've been off the radar lately. I've been hard at work," she explained, not completely lying, but not telling the truth either. She could feel heat slowly crawling up her cheeks. "You know how crazy things get for me sometimes." She decided against telling her cousin about her recent decision to change jobs. She was going to be extra diligent about where she was going to work next, and was taking her time to find a company that would suit her better.

She had tried to prove herself to Remington, and she

thought he'd taken note, but if it had only taken Geoffrey's pathetic and vindictive actions for him to give someone else the client account she had so badly wanted, it wasn't worth staying here and killing herself doing crazy hours. She wasn't valued enough, and she wasn't putting up with it anymore.

"It's always been that way for you," Savannah replied. "I don't know how you do it." She paused, then, "Is everything else okay?"

"Everything's good," Kay replied, laughing nervously. Even if she started to tell Savannah everything, where would she start? Not that this was the right time or the place for it, and hell would freeze over before she ever told Savannah about her and Luke. Still, there it was, on the tip of her tongue, the whole sorry mess, waiting to be unloaded, and cleared off her chest.

But she couldn't. She couldn't tell Savannah that she had lied, that she hadn't even taken heed of her advice from the start, that her need to be with someone had started back at the island. Her cousin didn't need to hear all about her romantic woes all over again. Especially when Kay had been lying to her about her so-called man free diet.

"I lost a major client deal," she said, finally.

"Nooooooo." Savannah expressed the right amount of shock, and sympathy to make her feel better. "What happened?"

"Well," she said, stumped for an explanation. "A whole lot of things."

"But I don't understand. You loved your work."

"It hasn't been an easy few months."

"Why, what's going on?" Savannah rubbed her stomach lightly. "I wish you'd told me. I've been so wrapped up in my pregnancy, and the new house, and the move. I should have turned up on your doorstep when you didn't respond to my messages."

"No, you mustn't feel bad." She attempted to put on a brave face. "It's nothing major. Nothing that can't be fixed." While she hadn't shed any tears over Geoffrey backstabbing her, she had shed plenty over Luke.

"I know that look," said Savannah, peering at her in concern. "You're upset. Tell me." She squeezed Kay's forearm gently, this woman who was overflowing with mothering hormones was going to extricate everything from her if she wasn't careful.

"It's really not a big deal," she said, fighting to keep her voice steady even though her eyes were welling up. She forced herself to toughen up, because this cousin of hers knew her better than most, and would soon discover everything if she wasn't careful.

"That's not nothing," pressed Savannah. "Kay," she said, her voice tender, her hand squeezing gently again. "You're worrying me. What's going—"

"Ta-da!" said Max. She walked in hugging a snowy fluffy ball of fur in her arms. "The newest member of our family."

"Awwwww!" Savannah cried gleefully. "Such a cute little dog!"

"It's a French Maltese," declared Briony, looking ecstatic.

"He's what we've settled on for now," added Max. "We've still planning to adopt a child, but *someone*," she rolled her eyes as she said it, "needs more time to get used to it." She set the dog on the floor, and he padded around, sniffing at Kay's gift bags. The atmosphere in the room suddenly turned prickly.

"What's he called?" asked Kay, hoping to diffuse the tension.

"Fondue," Max replied.

"What?" Savannah laughed as Fondue started to sniff around her ankles and she reached out to stroke him. "Don't let Jacob see him," she begged. "He'll want one."

"He'll have two siblings to play with soon enough," Kay interjected.

"True," said Savannah, stroking the dog again. "Though I could totally change my mind about getting one of these. He's adorable, and Jacob is forbidden from coming here."

"He's cute, isn't he?" asked Briony, lifting the puppy to her arms and kissing him. "I think we're going to have our hands full looking after this little one."

"There's no reason we can't have both." Max eased herself down on the couch next to Savannah. "We've got some games to play later, and then you can open your presents." Max gazed at Savannah's stomach. "You must be so excited," she said.

"Relieved more like," Savannah replied.

Kay turned to hear Briony sigh, and leave the room.

"She's not ready," said Max. "She's *still* not ready. She thinks Fondue is going to win me over, and that I'll forget about needing a child, but I won't forget."

"It's a big decision," Savannah told her. "Both of you have to be on board, but I'm sure you'll figure it out. Briony needs time, and a baby is a big commitment, but I'm sure she'll come around."

"She's always loved being hassle free," grumbled Max. "I'm trying to understand her viewpoint, but I have needs too. And my motherly instinct seems to have gone into overdrive lately. Around the time you and Jacob showed up...or maybe before that. You having twins has made it even worse, not that I'm blaming you," she added hastily.

"Well, you're both welcome to babysit for me, as much as you want, to get a feel for things," Savannah replied. "Tobias and I are spending a month back in Kawaya. You're welcome to come out then."

"I'll be the first in the list." Max grinned. "What about you?" she asked, turning to Kay. "Are you desperate to have a baby?"

Her question took Kay completely taken by surprise. "Errr... no." She shook her head vehemently. "No. *Definitely no.* I don't even have a boyfriend."

"You don't *need* a boyfriend," Max shot back. "A sperm donor can do the job just as well."

Kay felt herself blushing.

"Kay's on a man-free diet," replied Savannah proudly.

"A *man-free diet,* huh?" Max asked with interest. "I highly recommend them."

"She's definitely a heterosexual, Max," said Savannah, intervening.

"Why a man-free diet?" Max asked.

Kay paused, and hoped that Savannah wouldn't be able to see through her. "Savannah suggested I try that because of all the bad relationship choices I seem to always make."

"Boy, was that a true statement." She swallowed, knowing that she was as guilty as ever, and that she hadn't learned her lesson at all.

"Bad choices?" Max looked intrigued.

Now she was stumped. "Well...I ...I think I tend to rush into things."

She could see Savannah nodding her head in agreement, "and I had this idea about how a guy would be, you know, when I fixed him and made him perfect, and so I didn't really care too much what he was like upfront." Something about the way Max gave her all her attention, about the way she leaned forward, listening, made her feel not so bad about spilling her guts. She had held all of this back for weeks, and it seemed easier to tell someone who wasn't so close to her, than it was to tell someone like Savannah.

"Do you think you projected your ideal of what he was *supposed* to be like on him?"

"I'm not sure. Maybe. When he didn't fit that ideal, I ditched him, or he ditched me. It didn't usually take that long."

"I thought taking a break from dating might do her some good," Savannah chimed in.

"And has it?" Max asked, looking rather dubious. Kay shivered, feeling slightly uneasy, as if Max could read her mind.

"I've been too busy at work to even think about guys." She forced a wide smile, hoping to convince them.

Max looked up as Briony returned, but Savannah looked at her as if she didn't believe her.

"Did you invite Izzy?" Kay asked, even though she already knew the answer to her question. She was eager not to have the limelight on her any longer.

"I did," replied Savannah, "but she's busy, too. She said she had exams."

"She could have come for a couple of hours," Kay retorted. She had been looking forward to chatting to Izzy, because maybe she could have gotten the low down on Xavier, and by extension, Luke.

"She thinks we're too old for her. I mean she's still a student, isn't she?" asked Briony. "Maybe she felt out of place."

"I doubt it was that. She's mature for her age," replied Savannah, "And she's a good laugh. You'd be surprised."

"She probably had better things to do," suggested Max, in a sultry voice. "Maybe she's spending the weekend with her boyfriend."

Kay looked up in surprise. This was news. "Who's her boyfriend?"

"They're speculating," replied Savannah. "They don't know for sure."

"She's got an internship at Stone Enterprises," said Briony. "Tobias mentioned it."

"She has?" Kay asked. This was a surprise. She hadn't seen that coming at all. "An internship at Tobias's company?" Clever girl for managing to snag one of those.

"I noticed that she got on well with one of the bartenders at your wedding," said Max.

"You mean Luke?" Savannah stifled a yawn. "She's fond of him, I know."

"You *know*?" Briony asked her.

Savannah giggled. "No. There's nothing going on between those two, I'm sure of it. Izzy's mentioned him a few times, that's all." She yawned again.

"Are we boring you, darling?" Max asked, with a grin.

"No! No. I love that you all did this for me, and I really needed time away with you girls. I'm having trouble sleeping at the moment. I can't lie on my back at all, and I need to go to the toilet every half an hour. It makes for a lot of broken sleep."

Luke and Izzy?

The idea cut through Kay like a guillotine. Her gut told her it was pure conjecture, with no basis for truth, but a niggling thorn in her side made her wonder.

She looked on while Savannah and the others laughed.

She felt alone, even though she was sitting here in a room with them all. She felt apart from them, from life, as if the disconnect in her life, between what she once wanted and what she now had, was too large, and too ugly. She couldn't lie about her life, or her happiness, for she had clearly failed.

The rest of the day unfolded slowly and she managed to keep an upbeat appearance.

Much later on, Savannah called Morris, her chauffeur, to pick her up because it was Jacob's bedtime, and Savannah was mindful of being there for him. She had insisted on dropping Kay home, but Kay had made an excuse to stay back and offer Max some advice on her share portfolio.

"Thank you, girls," said Savannah, as she was ready to leave. "I've had a brilliant time. It should tide me over for a few months, when I'm hands deep in diapers."

"Lovely," said Max, not without a hint of sarcasm in her voice.

On his return to work, Luke discovered that he could only do half-days at work because he just got so tired as the day wore on. His entire life had changed so drastically within the space of a month. And his future too.

It wasn't just the recovery and the adjusting to meds, and dealing with having only part of his thyroid working. The whole business with Kay preyed on his mind.

And he couldn't get a hold of Xavier. Where was that guy when he needed him? Feeling at a loss, and not used to needing someone to sound off on, he sat at his desk, flicking through books on self-healing and veganism. These days he surfed the internet looking for recipes that would help his energy levels and food that would help him to become healthier, than surf the net looking for sites for sale. The work on the Canal Street site was still going ahead, but he had to seriously think about putting his plans on hold for Miami and LA.

Unable to concentrate, he walked into Marie's office, and eased himself into the chair opposite her.

"How are you feeling?" she asked. "Because you don't look too good."

"I've felt better."

"You came back too soon," she told him. "Take another few weeks off, Luke."

"I could," he agreed. But his malaise wasn't due entirely to his health issues. It went way deeper and he couldn't concentrate much. His heart wasn't in the business, and this was a first for him.

"Take a few more weeks off. I can handle things at this end, and if I'm stuck, I know where to find you."

"Maybe I will go home. I'm pretty useless here. I can't even keep an eye on Canal Street. So much for building that empire." It sounded tempting, goofing off work again. But his apartment was empty, and there was no Kay coming around in the evenings to check in on him. She had vanished from his life, and he missed her like crazy. It was his fault completely, and he wasn't sure how he could fix it.

"I've got a handle on Canal Street. I'm getting daily updates from the guys, and I've been over a couple of times this week," Marie told him.

"You have?" He had no idea. He'd barely been able to focus on his emails. Amanda called more often than she had before, and Maggie had sent him a couple of texts asking how he was. He had ignored them.

But Kay? He'd heard nothing since that day.

He waited for Marie to say something. The women

talked, and he was sure they'd spoken. He coughed lightly. "Seen Kay lately?"

Marie sat back in her chair, her expression softening. "I have, actually. We went out for dinner last week."

"You had dinner? Both of you, together?" The idea was hard for him to get his head around, that these two women were meeting without him. They wouldn't even have known one another had it not been for him and now they were best friends all of a sudden. "How is she?" he asked, brushing dust off his jeans.

"She's looking for another job."

He jolted upright. "She's what?" She loved her job. She spent enough goddamn hours there every day. "Why?"

"She said something about losing a project, some major client account her boss took away from her."

"He did what?"

"She said something about one of her co-workers going behind her back and doing a dirty on her."

"Fucking asshole," he hissed. She'd worked damn hard. He thought back to when she was checking on stuff on her laptop, while he took a shower. He scratched his chin. The days' old stubble was rough against his fingertips. These days he couldn't even be bothered to shave daily.

"What?" Marie asked, sharply. "Who?"

"The bastard who snitched on her. I bet it was Geoffrey."

"She didn't say."

"She's a hard worker, and she tried to do everything. I know she did."

"I take it you haven't apologized to her yet?"

He felt hopeful. "She's waiting for me to apologize?" If that's all it was going to take, he'd do it now.

"I have no idea. She refused to talk about you. It was the

one condition she made, otherwise she said she wouldn't meet me."

He slumped back in his chair. He'd assumed as much.

"Why can't you be happy with the good things?" Marie asked. What could he say? He stared back at her, knowing he wasn't going to tell her about his past. She didn't need to know and he didn't need to explain her why he messed up the good things that came his way.

"I'm team Kay, if you were wondering," she said, when he rolled his shoulders and didn't offer an answer. "She's been one of the better things to happen to you in years, ever since I've known you."

If there was anyone he owed an explanation and an apology to, it was Kay, but he didn't know how to put things right. He'd said too many vicious things for an apology to smooth everything over. For a man who always knew how to get what he wanted, he was suddenly lost.

CHAPTER FORTY-TWO

"You said you needed my help?" Kay looked at Savannah, puzzled. Savannah and Tobias's bedroom was pristine. Everything had been packed into neat boxes.

"The removal men are coming tomorrow," said Savannah, placing her hand on her back.

"Then what do you want me to do?"

Savannah walked over to the bed and sat down. "I want you to tell me what's going on with you."

Kay walked towards her cousin, and feigned a surprised face. She was about to deny anything was wrong when Savannah beat her to it.

"Because I know it's something, and I don't want to spend an hour listening to you pretending that everything is fine," said Savannah. "Jacob and Tobias are out and it's just you and me. I won't get a quiet moment like this to myself for a long time, so you'd better hurry up and tell me."

It was no use. She'd been baited. She hadn't done as great a job in hiding her feelings at the baby shower as she thought she had.

She wasn't sure where to start, or what to say. Shame

made her suddenly hot, and anxious and she could feel sweat dampen her armpits. Savannah angled her head, frowning slightly. And she already looked worried—not relieved—that Kay was about to tell all. Her expression made Kay falter. "It's—I—uh..."

It was hard. "Please stop looking at me like that," she pleaded.

"Like what?" asked Savannah, genuinely surprised.

"As if you're already judging me."

Now her cousin looked *really* worried.

"I don't want you to break your water."

Savannah chuckled. "It's fine. It'll save the doctor inducing me."

The mood lightened a little, giving Kay the spurt of courage she needed. "I never went on the man-free diet."

"I had a feeling."

"Am I that transparent?"

"You have a tell. You avoided me."

"I was genuinely busy."

"It never stopped you when you were halfway across the world," Savannah replied. "We talked more when you were in Hong Kong than we have living in the same city."

Kay's mouth opened. "Shit," she said. Savannah was right.

"Plus, I have a sixth sense about you and these things. So..."

Kay relaxed. Her shoulders easing down slightly as the tension oozed out of her tight muscles. "You never said anything?"

"I knew you'd say something when the time was right, and when I saw you well up at the baby shower, I knew it had to be something big, something even you couldn't bring yourself to talk about. Maybe even..." her words trailed off, and Savannah stared at her, "Maybe it might be something you were ashamed about."

Freaking hell. Savannah did have a sixth sense about these things.

"Tell me it's not Dean."

Kay tilted her chin up. "Dean?" Her lips twisted, and then she pressed them together. "It's not Dean." She noted the relief on Savannah's face.

"Why would you think it's Dean?"

"Because he always had a way of reeling you back in."

"It's not Dean," she said, firmly.

"Thank heaven for small mercies."

Kay blinked, wondering how to start explaining how she had ended up here. Why—after being used by Dean, and being thrown to the side by Xavier—why she would then choose to go after a man who had warned her from the start that he was not looking for a relationship.

"Someone from work?" Savannah asked. "Is that why you're leaving?"

"No," she replied quickly. "God, no. Nobody from work."

"Someone I know?"

"Yes."

Savannah looked worried.

"It was at your wedding, in the evening at the reception." Kay replied, slightly confused, and trying to read Savannah's expression. She had been anticipating a shaking of her head, and exasperation, not this. Not a dour face, expecting the worst.

"At our wedding," Savannah sighed, as if it had been the worst day of her life. She lowered her gaze to her knee, and it was a few seconds before she was able to say anything. In those few seconds, Kay's insides bobbed up and down furiously, as if she'd been on a rollercoaster ride. "Xavier," she said, huffing out a breath. "I thought I warned you about him."

"Xavier?" Kay asked, incredulous.

"*Not* Xavier?" Savannah looked curious, a small frown line appearing on her brow. "Then who?"

"Luke."

"Luke?" Her eyebrows lifted. "But ... how... where...*when?*"

"It was ... we got to talking," Kay replied. "He made me laugh, made me a cocktail, he was easy to talk to."

"At the wedding?"

She nodded.

"You let me believe you were taking my advice and steering clear of men and lying to me?" This time Savannah shook her head, but she seemed to be amusingly exasperated. "Why did I ever think you would listen to me?"

"I wish I had now." Kay's voice turned quieter. If only she had listened to her cousin, she would have saved herself a ton of heartache. She would have spared herself the humiliation of having someone tell her she was a pity-fuck. She wouldn't have ended up being a trophy wedding guest. But even as she tricked herself into believing this, she remembered how tempting Luke had been. Who was she kidding? He'd been a towering inferno of sexiness that she had found particularly potent. She could never have walked away from *that*.

"You're not together anymore?"

"No."

She found herself telling Savannah about everything, but leaving out the terms of their arrangement, that it had purely been a hookup in the beginning. She sensed that

Savannah would see her in a different light if she told her that she'd agreed to meet for no other reason than to have sex. Just thinking and talking about it out loud made her feel dirty. It wasn't only to Savannah, she felt that there was no way she could ever bring herself to tell anyone.

So she told her about his cancer, and that his mother had died when he was in his teens, and that he was a difficult man to love. But it was the news of the cancer that caught Savannah completely by surprise.

"I didn't know," Savannah exclaimed. "Tobias hasn't said anything. Poor man."

"Don't tell anyone," said Kay, remembering all too late that Luke didn't want any of this to get out. "Please don't. I don't even think he's told Xavier."

She couldn't even bring herself to explain that the thing that hurt her the most, not only what he called her but the reason he took her along to the wedding in the first place. "I got it wrong. I assumed he wanted me to meet his family," she said, "But he told me later that it was because he wanted to show his ex that he had moved on. I thought he genuinely started to like me, and that I meant something."

Savannah looked confused. "He had to take you to a wedding for you to think that? Didn't you sense that before?"

Kay made a grating noise in her throat, as if it was too difficult to explain herself. There were days when she looked back on her reasoning and couldn't explain it to herself.

She'd wanted a fairytale, and he'd given her ashes.

But it wasn't his fault.

It was hers. For going along with a man like that in the first place.

"I've learned my lesson."

Savannah looked at her silently.

"I have," she insisted. Being man-free was the way to go. She needed a huge change in her life. A new job and no man, not for a good while.

Of course she had learned her lesson, otherwise why else was she ignoring Dr. Santini's calls? They had ended up talking one time when she left the hospital, and he'd been most interested to hear that she was an investment banker. She suspected that his recent calls to her, on the pretense of needing financial tips, was a ruse to get her to go to lunch.

Nope. No way. The old Kay wouldn't have thought twice about it, but the person she was now longed to be single again. She wanted a stress-free life devoid of all drama.

"Oh, by the way," she said, suddenly remembering, "Arnold says 'hi'. He asked me how you were doing, and he wanted to pass on his good wishes for the new arrivals."

"Awww. He's so sweet," replied Savannah, her face brightening at the news. "I must try to get him to visit in a few months' time."

"He's not so bad," Kay agreed. She had time for Arnold these days. She *made* time for him. No more did she rush to work, and spend long hours there. In fact, helping Engelmann out had its rewards. She got to leave work early, often walking past Geoffrey's desk with a huge smile on her face. Nobody at work knew that she was looking to leave yet, and she intended to keep it that way. "But he's not so happy these days."

"Oh?" Savannah looked concerned.

"He says his employer isn't giving him a pay rise, and they're being stingy with their holiday." She paused, a new idea coming to her. "Couldn't he do something for you at your new place?" she asked, thinking out aloud. "You've got an elevator at one side of your mansion, maybe he could help out there."

"A concierge in our home?" asked Savannah, as if the idea was crazy.

"Maybe not."

"But I could definitely put him to good use." Savannah must have liked that idea, because her eyes widened and Kay could almost see the cogs turning in her brain. "I don't need a nanny, though I'm going to have to fight Tobias over that one for now, but I could do with a handyman around the house."

"Around the mansion," Kay corrected her.

"I wonder..." And she appeared to be hatching up a new plan. Then she turned to her suddenly and asked, "Why were you so upset, then, at the baby shower?"

"Because...I thought he might be the one, and he so badly wasn't. I just feel so humiliated, and so stupid. It's embarrassing."

"Would you ever give him another chance?"

Savannah didn't know the full story. So there was no point in discussing it further. "No. Like I said, I've learned my lesson."

"It's just that..." Savannah hesitated. "That's not the impression I got of him."

"No, me neither. It's amazing how someone can turn out to be so different."

"He sounds as if he needs help."

"I hope he gets it."

CHAPTER FORTY-THREE

He was going to win her back, only, he didn't know how to, just yet. "I'm probably the most-hated man on your list, but I need to talk to you. Please, Kay."

"Not probably, you *are.*"

"Look, I don't blame you for hating me, but please can we meet even if it's just for five minutes?"

"I don't have anything to say to you."

"But there's a lot I need to say to you."

"You already did."

"No. No I didn't. That was me just being...being a total loser." He couldn't excuse himself from the way he'd treated her and the things he'd said, and he had said plenty. The last time had been low, even for him. But he'd been hoping she might have understood him now that he had revealed all his past. After Maggie and Amanda left, his emotions had gotten the better of him, even after all these years he still got sucked back into that soulless abyss he'd tried so hard to climb out of.

He needed help, he knew that now.

"I feel so low. I hate how I've treated you, you have no idea, Kay. Please give me a chance to say what I need to."

"There's nothing you can say to me that will make me change my opinion of you."

"You can't just leave like that."

"I can do whatever I want. You do. You *did*."

"I mean, without me apologizing." She wasn't making this easy for him at all, nor would he have expected her to. "Please see me just the once, and then you can tell me to go to hell." He'd never had to beg a woman before, and he wasn't used to it, but he couldn't let this one walk away, not without hearing what he had to say.

When he didn't give up, she finally relented. And this was how Luke found himself in the lobby of Kay's investment bank, one evening at the end of her work day.

"Thanks," he said, when she finally came downstairs. He stood around in the shiny chrome and marble area, bedecked with oversized plant pots, and stern looking security guards. Somber, suited young men and women rushed in and out of the sparkling clean glass doors, like a trail of ants.

"Shall we go someplace?" he asked, suddenly hopeful that she was wearing her coat. He'd been expecting the worst—that she would only give him a few minutes of her time before returning to her work. But she looked as if she was ready to leave for the day.

"No."

Her cold and flat reply knocked him back slightly. "Okay, well, thanks for agreeing to see me."

"I don't have long." She glanced at her watch. He lowered his head, and looked down at her. Dammit if she didn't look as sexy and as hot as ever in her dark business suit. "I know you hate my guts and you never want to see me again, and I know I have a lot of making up to do."

"Nothing you do or say will ever make up for the way you've behaved."

"Then give me a chance," he pleaded, staring at the face he hadn't seen in ages. He missed those lips, those eyes, her softness, and her concern. He missed her. All of her.

"This is pointless. It really is." She was shaking her head now, a sense of irritation clouding her smooth face. And those lips. She was wearing lipstick, a different shade to the one she usually wore.

"Then why are you here?" he asked. She'd agreed to see him.

"Because you sounded desperate and because you annoyed the heck out of me on the phone. Please, let's just say our goodbyes and be done with it."

"What if I'm not ready to? Look, Kay. I know I've been a complete idiot."

She said nothing. She didn't agree, or disagree, and it was bad because she seemed so resigned about it. "Don't think I haven't appreciated anything you've done for me. The truth is, I've never had anyone who has been there for me the way you have. I'm used to people letting me down. It's become my default expectation of others. It's what I expected from you. Only, you never did that to me, even when I treated you like shit, you still came back."

Her eyes flashed at him, a burst of anger behind those brown irises. "I'm known for that. I told you, I've never been good with men. Seems like I attract all the losers within a one mile radius. But you..." She was angry, her face twisting, her voice sharp—the way she had never been with him before. "You've been the worst. It's been enough to turn me off men for a good while."

Shame rolled over him like a tractor, bulldozing him to the ground. He was desperate to make amends, desperate to make her understand but she didn't seem interested. She was cold, and distant, and the warmth he had often seen in her eyes when they met, had been extinguished.

He wished he could turn back time, wished he could take back the words he had said to her. The truth would have come out eventually, but he could have delivered it more softly—the suicide, the seduction, the betrayal—things which had made him *him*. Instead, he'd pushed her away.

But it was all he knew because there was safety in being alone, in not having anyone else to rely on.

"I can change, and things can be different between us."

"You sound like how I was, months ago," she said. "I used to think things would change between us; that we would move on and have a proper relationship one day."

"It's not too late."

"It is for me. I can't do this anymore."

The muscles in his face tightened. This wasn't how it was supposed to end. "Don't dismiss me as easily as I dismissed you."

"You have a nerve to ask me that," she shot back.

"I know. I'm trying to make amends. I still want you in my life."

"I don't. It stopped working for me even before you got ill."

He looked at her in shock, smarting from the verbal punch she'd delivered. He hadn't been expecting smiles and laughter, but he'd hadn't been prepared for this, or her level of animosity. He'd been a shortsighted fool.

"Look, you've obviously had some sort of epiphany," she continued, "and I get that you've had lots of time to think about things, but so have I. I know you're recovering from an illness, and there's never going to be a right time to say it, and I haven't said it. I just went quiet hoping you'd get the hint, but I realize it isn't the right way to finish things. And that's why I agreed to meet with you now."

"Don't do this."

"Hear me out. At least give me that," she said. "You've been able to say and do as you please, you've been cold, and callous, and you've constantly told me exactly what we have. What we *had*. I know. I *know* that now."

He flinched when she talked of them in the past tense. "We can make this work," he insisted.

"I don't want to make it work."

"Night, Kay," two men walked past, one of whom tapped her on her shoulder. The guy next to him was the one he recognized as that schmuck Geoffrey.

She nodded her head at them, saying nothing, but he knew her well enough now that he could read her expression. She was being wary, and wasn't at all enthused to see them.

"Is that your boss?" he asked.

"Yes. With Geoffrey."

"Thought I recognized the shitbag. I've heard you're looking to change jobs," he said, hoping to redirect her anger.

Her eyes narrowed and she leaned towards him slightly. "Why don't you announce it even louder? I haven't told anyone here, yet. I have to find a job first."

What an idiot. He placed his palm against his cheek, feeling mortified. "Sorry. I wasn't thinking."

"You often don't."

He let that one sink in, and nodded in agreement. "I've been a lot of things, Kay. And there are a lot of things I'm ashamed of," he said, keeping his voice low. "I've used you as I pleased, without any regard for your feelings. But we had an arrangement, and back then, when I didn't know any better, I just went along with it. I wasn't expecting much from it, and I thought it would fizzle out, like things often do for me."

"That's all in the past now. Can we not ever talk about that arrangement again?"

"Yes," he said. This could be construed as progress. She had suggested the very thing he had wanted to see her about; forgetting what they had before, and starting over. "Let's leave that in the past where it belongs. Maybe we can focus on the future."

"Future?" she scoffed. "We don't have a future." She looked towards the entrance then glanced at her watch again.

"Don't say that," he said, touching her arm and trying to bring her focus back to him, to them, to this. "We can make this work. I know we can."

"You're being hopeful. I'm being realistic." She gave a cruel laugh. "Oh, how the tides have turned. I used to be in your shoes once, wanting what you do now. It's such a weak, pathetic place to be in." He couldn't read her expression, couldn't tell if she was relieved or sad. But her words had cut through him like a knife, and he stared at her knowing he was losing. That he had maybe already lost weeks ago.

"I was going to split with you before," she told him. "Actually, it was the day before your surgery, before I even knew you had cancer."

He tried to think back through the fog of the recent weeks, back to the day when the doctor had told him. "But you came to see me in the hospital," he said slowly.

"That's right. I was going to split with you then...I mean, *extract* myself from this arrangement. You only *split* if you've been in a relationship." She slapped her forehead in mock disbelief. "How stupid of me to think that."

He clenched his jaw, fighting back a retort. This wasn't a fight where he got to prove that he was right, or had the upper hand.

"I cared about you," she said. "You made it hard for me care, but I did it anyway. I did it because I wanted you to get better, and especially after you told me about the things in your past, the things that have scarred you so deeply—"

"I'm not scarred," he shot back.

"Aren't you?"

He exhaled loudly, not wanting to talk about that. "What stopped you, from splitting with me then?"

"Marie. She told me you were ill, and that you were in the hospital awaiting surgery, and so I couldn't. I couldn't split with you when you were already down."

She would never have, he knew that. She was selfless, and loving, and caring. A Florence Nightingale with the body of Marilyn Monroe. He'd fucked up big time. "I bet you wish you had."

"I do. I've thought about it many times," she replied, nodding. "Being with you was the worst thing I ever did to myself, but I'm not that type of person who can do that to someone—even if that someone has already done that to me —treated me badly. It's a weakness I have, which is probably why I let men walk all over me."

"You don't let men walk all over you. You're leaving work, you're looking for a new—"

"You've been speaking to Marie," it wasn't a question, more of a dismissive, passing statement. "I'm going to leave this place," she said, lowering her voice to a whisper, "because I will no longer tolerate not being valued at work, and for that same reason, I can't ever be with you again, because to do so would demean me."

He lowered his head in shame. "I'm going to change. I have issues, you told me that. I accept it now, and I'm going to get counseling."

"Good luck with that."

"I can't do this anymore." She splayed out her hand. "Whatever this is." She looked around, and he could sense that she was uneasy having this conversation here of all places.

"Let's go somewhere where we can talk privately," he urged.

"There's no need. I think we're done."

"Please, Kay," he begged, almost reaching for her hand. But he composed himself and shoved his hand into his pocket. "I can't get past this, knowing what I said to you. I need to make it up to you. I *will* make it up to you."

"You don't have to make it up to me. I knew exactly what I was letting myself in for, maybe not when I first met you on the island, but back home, in your bar, when you spelled things out for me. I knew the score. I knew what *this* was. And the truth is, I'm done with that kind of messed up relationship."

"Is this why you agreed to meet with me? To make it official?"

She looked up, perplexed. "You deserved an explanation in person." Her cellphone beeped, and she looked at it, typed a few things, then slipped it away quickly. "I have to go," she said.

"Now?"

"I'm meeting a friend."

The way she said it, he had a feeling she was seeing someone. "A friend?"

"'Bye, Luke. I think it's best if we just go our separate ways. I'm a different person now. I can't let myself be treated like that."

"What do you want?"

"I want the fairytale. "

"I can give you the fairytale," he replied, thinking, as he said it, how odd it was for him to say that.

"You don't believe in fairytales."

"But I believe in you, and I believe in us."

Her mouth twisted, as if she was going to say something but had decided against it.

"What?" he asked, desperate to know. "Say it."

"You...You're ..." She shrugged. "Maybe you have had time to think about things."

"I have and—"

"I'm glad you're getting counseling," she said, cutting him short.

Before he could say anything, her gaze drifted to behind him, and she waved. His heart took a deep dive, the type of dive a plane would take when its engines misfired and it was about to crash. He turned around only to someone walking towards her. A guy. And he looked familiar. And the fucker was smiling at Kay.

"I have to go," she said, looking impatient to leave. He examined her face, needing to read, to understand what the fuck this was. She looked uneasy, or excited. He couldn't tell which. "You're seeing someone?" he asked, shock spinning inside him like an angry twister.

"Dr. Santini," she said, turning to go.

It took a few seconds before the name meant something. "You're seeing my *consultant?*"

"I wish you all the best, Luke, I really do," she said,

flashing him a rare smile; something he hadn't seen from her in a while. And then she was gone.

Dr. Santini hadn't even noticed him. He was too busy grinning away at Kay. They shook hands, awkwardly at first, before she leaned in and kissed him on the cheek.

Everyone in the lobby faded into the background, and all Luke could see was Kay and Santini. His mind blanked and he forgot to breathe.

She had moved on.

He had barely recovered, and she had already moved on.

CHAPTER FORTY-FOUR

Dr. Santini looked taken aback when she kissed him on the cheek, hooked her arm in his and walked out.

Once outside, she pulled away, as if he'd given her an electric shock. She didn't want him to get the wrong idea. "I'm sorry I made you come here. I was running late."

He looked pleasantly surprised. "It's not a problem. I was waiting around the corner," he replied. "I hopped into a cab."

That explained why he got here so fast. But it had worked to her advantage. What better way to make Luke see that she was done with this, than to show that she had moved on? "I can only spare half an hour," she told the doctor, wanting to quickly undo the damage that her crossed messages might have caused.

"Shall we go for a drink, then?" he asked.

She hesitated. She'd been hoping to see him in the lobby, so that she could speak to him there for a while sitting on one of the plush sofas at one end. The lobby was safe, and didn't give ideas. He was hitting on her, or trying to. She knew.

"Uh...I don't know," she said, slowly. She wasn't keen on going for a drink, or a coffee, or dinner. He'd pursued her, not relentlessly, not crazily, but with a few phone calls over the past few weeks. Hadn't helped that she'd been especially generous the last time, talking to him for a long time, after that argument with Luke. Loneliness did that sometimes, and their conversation had moved on from stocks and shares, and the markets, and economy, to personal things.

She was afraid now, now that she had met with Luke, and her emotions were in turmoil again, that Dr. Santini would want to delve more down the personal route then simply wanting investing tips from her.

"Surely a drink or two won't hurt?"

She knew otherwise. A drink or two was exactly how things had started the last time. "I really can't."

He looked disappointed. "You're always working so hard, Kay."

She examined his face, but she still had Luke's face imprinted on her mind. At one time she might have even considered Dr. Santini to be handsome. He was handsome, and clever and sexy; the perfect combination. Like Luke had been once. And so far, he had been incredibly attentive, and nice, and interested. Just like Luke had been, and still was.

Dr. Santini was the type of man to give her the happy-ever-after she'd dreamed of.

Just like she had hoped Luke would have, once.

She was starting to mesh the two, starting to think of her conversation with Luke just now. Starting to get sucked back into it. Into him.

She couldn't go there. Would not let herself. "I can give

you some general investment advice and tips," she said. "And it will be just for the one drink."

"One drink. I appreciate it."

As he hailed another cab, she glanced over her shoulder a couple of times, and thought she saw Luke standing there, watching them. When she blinked, he was gone.

CHAPTER FORTY-FIVE

She had been at the hospital soon after the twins arrived, and had cried, and hugged and been swept up in the joy of the moment. Having new life injected a burst of happiness in her own life.

Even if Savannah had allowed Tobias to get a nanny, there would have been no point. She practically lived at the Stone's new residence for the first two weeks. She stayed over some nights because there was room, and because Savannah was tired, and breastfeeding, and because Jacob's excitement never let up; because Tobias and Savannah were so hands-on with their boys, and there was so much going on.

Being here was so much better than sitting in her own apartment. Time, at the sprawling Stone mansion, flew by.

She was there when their families came to see Lewis and Samuel. She was Savannah's wing woman when her mother-in-law, Millicent came over, and then her own mother and Savannah's parents. She was there when Xavier and Izzy turned up.

Apparently they had been away earlier to the

Hamptons for a weekend, and it was official, they were an item now.

It was towards the end of June when the job she had desperately wanted, came through. After four rounds of interviews, the company—previously one of their main competitors—came through. They wanted her, and offered her the job. She was due to join in a few weeks' time. Breaking her good news to Remington had given her a long overdue sense of satisfaction, and telling him she'd been taken on as an executive director, had left him speechless, something she had never before witnessed.

She had parted ways with her current company only last week.

With a month stretching out in front of her, a much needed month of rest, and recovery, she had decided to stay in New York for a week, before taking a couple of weeks off on vacation.

Savannah and Tobias were going back to Kawaya, the private island on which they'd gotten married. Jacob's school had ceased for the summer holidays, and they were going to spend the summer there, and they had invited her along.

She was thinking about it. Not sure whether she wanted to return to the island where such bittersweet memories lay.

"When are they going to wake up?" Jacob asked, for the third or fourth time since she'd arrived. He was in the nursery, and the two boys were lying in their own cots. "Shhhh, Jacob," she said, putting her finger to her lips.

"I want to play with them before everyone gets here."

"Oh, sweetie. We should let them sleep as much as they can. Your mom and dad need the rest."

While everyone had come to see the new arrivals in the hospital, the proud parents had asked for a few weeks before they had visitors at their home while Savannah was still recovering from the birth.

But with the boys now almost a month old, Tobias and Savannah had opened their house to close friends and family so that everyone could come and meet the new Stone brothers.

Savannah's parents and Kay's mother had been here for a few days already, and Tobias's parents had just arrived when Kay went in to let her know.

Savannah was getting changed. "Don't leave me alone with Millicent," she begged. "The last thing I need is for that woman to be standing over me and watching while I feed the babies. She'll be here any moment now and guaranteed, one of them will wake up and need a feed."

Kay's face twisted in shock. She couldn't imagine letting anyone see her do that, if she ever miraculously found herself in the position of having a baby.

"I'll make sure I herd her out," Kay promised.

Tobias was the gracious host, and there was plenty of food and drink. Arnold, who now worked for them, moved around the house as if he was the head butler.

She stayed in the background, talking to people, being a second-hostess of sorts. Jacob seemed to hang around her more, until Xavier and Izzy turned up. They made polite talk, baby talk, and they commented on how they hadn't all gotten together like this since Tobias and Savannah's wedding.

"We were just talking about you," said Xavier suddenly, when she turned around to look.

Luke appeared from out of nowhere, and the unexpected sight of him made her heart stop.

Because Izzy was there, and because he greeted her with an affectionate kiss on the cheek, he did the same to her. "Hey," he said softly. She hadn't seen him for almost two months. He looked the same, but not the same. His face seemed thinner, and his eyes were gaunt, and lined. He seemed to have aged five years in the last month. He didn't seem as strong, or as vibrant as the man she remembered, and the sight of him wreaked havoc with her emotions. They continued making small talk. Continued as if nothing was amiss. Nobody apart from Savannah knew about her and Luke, though everybody now knew about his cancer.

A couple of times she caught Xavier looking at her, not in his usual flirty manner, but as if he was watching her. Assessing.

Later, Izzy and Luke wandered away to get some food, Xavier didn't.

"Why do you keep staring at me like that?" she asked, starting to get irritated.

"Where's the doctor?"

"What doctor?"

"Luke's consultant."

Somewhere in the distant depths of her mind, she tried to work out how he knew about Dr. Santini. And why that had even come up in a conversation between Luke and Xavier.

But it was enough for her to know that it had.

She shrugged. "I don't know."

"You're not together anymore?"

She scowled, annoyed by the line of questioning. "I was never with him."

Xavier invaded her personal space, and it made her take a step back. Lowering his voice, he said, "Luke's never opened up to me about his girlfriends before, but he told me about you. I'm sorry it didn't work out."

She blinked.

And then Izzy returned with a plate of food, and the two of them got to talking again. She noted that Luke hadn't returned to the group. Feeling uneasy, and as if she was eavesdropping, she suddenly remembered to check in on Savannah, and excused herself.

Grateful to escape, she rushed upstairs, and headed off towards the direction of Savannah's room, when she saw Luke standing at the top, his hands resting on the bannister, looking at the sparkling crystal chandelier that was in the hallway. It was so big, that it was visible from the landing where they stood. She stared at him, hesitating, her feet forgetting how to move.

She had to get past him to get to Savannah's room, and it was too late to do anything but walk straight ahead. Even though she knew he had seen her bounding up the stairs, he didn't look her way.

"What are you doing up here?" she asked, finally speaking.

"It was getting noisy down there."

Kay agreed. "They invited a lot of people."

"Brave of them," he replied, still leaning over with his hands resting on the bannister, his gaze on the floor below. It was the perfect place from which to people watch.

"They probably wanted to get all the visiting out of the way in one go. They're going back to their island for a long vacation."

"Smart move." He looked up at her then. Straightened his body, and leveled his gaze at her. "You look well."

"Thanks." She couldn't quite say the same back. He looked better, but he didn't look 100%. It shocked her, because as the months had passed on, she had expected him to have returned to his usual self. He must have noticed, because he said something about the medication being difficult to get right, and that it was a question of trial and error.

Just seeing him like this made her feel down. Brought out her caring side, made her forget the hurtful things that had happened between them. She looked away, determined not to feel anything, trying to turn a blind eye to the way he looked, and the melancholy tone of his voice. But she couldn't look away for long. "Are you...is the cancer gone?" she asked, not sure how to say it. The idea that his cancer cells might have come back, suddenly frightened her.

"It's gone. I have checkups all the time, but it's definitely gone, for now."

For now?

He must have seen her concern, because he said, "It can come back at any time. Even with healthy people. I just try and make the most of each day."

Her heart softened like jello. He looked so vulnerable and so weak. Not the Luke she knew. The Luke she missed. He looked as if all his vitality had been sucked right out of his body, and all that was left was an empty man. She was tempted to buoy him back up again, to make him see that he was fine, to bolster him, because she couldn't bear to see him like this.

But she wasn't going to.

And though it was hard, she forced herself to hold back.

And yet she couldn't walk away either. She looked over his shoulder at Savannah's door, wondering, hoping that Millicent wasn't in there, irritating the hell out of Savannah.

She didn't have it in her to walk away just yet. It had been easier to stay away, but now that he was here, in front of her, that familiar pull of old kept her rooted to the floor. He had changed, he seemed softer now, almost resembling the man she had first met on the island.

But she had changed, too.

She was harder, not so forgiving, and much more protective of her heart. She wasn't going to rush back, not like Good-Time-Kay would have. She was no longer the woman to sidle up to him and bat her eyelashes, but neither was she a coldhearted monster. And with the passing of time, things softened.

Memories blurred.

Harsh words and actions were forgotten.

And some things still remained. She had never forgotten the trials of his teenage years. Had never been able to erase what must have been the shaping moments of his youth. Many times since that last time, she had been tempted to pick up the phone and talk to him; had been curious to know how his counseling sessions were going, and how he was doing, and each time she had managed to stop herself.

These days she prided herself on her self-restraint.

"How is Dr. Santini?" he asked, looking away again.

"Good." *I expect.*

"Savannah said you've got a great job with another bank."

"I have."

"Good luck. I hope you told your boss and Geoffrey to fuck off."

"Not in those words."

They both smiled. "You're way too classy for that," he said, a flash of something that looked like regret crossing his face.

"I don't know about classy," she said. "I prefer feisty."

"No," he said, softly, shaking his head, his eyes scanning every inch of her face as if he'd forgotten what she looked like. A rush of stirring jangled in her heart, upsetting her breathing patterns again.

"You've always been classy. Feisty too," he added, before his lips clamped shut, as if he was forcing himself to watch what he said.

"How's the counseling coming along?"

"It's enlightening."

Good, bad? What exactly did he mean by that? "Has it helped?"

"It's helped. At least, Amanda seems to think so."

This pleased her. If he could heal over his past, he could move on. She wanted that for him, she wanted the man underneath to be more like the man she had first come to know—sexy and nice, and hard to ignore.

"We went out for dinner with Kyle."

"Oh," she cried, pleased to hear that. "The couples dinner, you mean?"

He nodded, the tiny movement stabbing her with something she couldn't define. He'd said '*we*'. Who had he gone with? The question buzzed around her head like a noisy mosquito, hard to ignore and as irritating as hell.

"I..." He cleared his throat. "I have something of yours still lying around at work."

"Something of mine?"

"I bought you a gift, I just forgot to give it to you that time when I gave you the lingerie. It was still in my jacket pocket."

"You don't have to bother with that," she said, waving her hand, dismissively.

"I bought it for you. I'd rather you have it."

"It's not necessary, now. But, if you insist..."

"If you really don't want it, I'll return it."

Now she was curious. "You could return it and..." *And buy something for your new girlfriend.*

She wondered what this new woman was like. Lucky woman, obviously, to be enjoying the fruits of all that counseling.

"If you really don't want it, if you feel that strongly about it, I'll return it, but I'd like you to have it," he said.

"If you feel that strongly about it, if you really want me to have it, then I guess you can send it to me, but you didn't have to buy me two gifts. You didn't even have to get me the one." She was rambling. "I don't give to—"

"To get," he said, finishing her sentence for her. "I know. Truth was, I felt so lousy when you got me the cufflinks, and I got you nothing," he pulled out one of his shirt cuffs to show her the key-shaped cufflinks he was wearing.

Her heart opened up like a sunflower. "You must really like them," she said, feeling suddenly happy.

"They remind me of you."

They were smiling at one another, not the big flirtatious smiles-that-would-lead-to-something, type of smile, but a more relaxed one. As if they were getting used to and enjoying being together again.

She remembered the Luke she had glimpsed on the island, in the sultry heat of the night, underneath the starry sky, when he'd made her his variation of a cocktail, and she'd told him her fears about men. He'd been a good listener then, and he'd cheered her up. Already there was a shift in how they were around one another, and this felt easy, like the night after the wedding, when they were just talking, nothing too deep, but finding out about one another.

Seeing him again had brought back all those memories, and it felt new, and pleasant, and touched with a tinge of regret.

"Also," he continued, "I didn't want you to think that I was with you for one thing only. The lingerie was an impulse buy. It's what most guys buy their girlfriends. I wanted to buy you something meaningful, because by then..." he shrugged, then stared at the chandelier again.

"By then?" she said, softly, her ears straining.

But he pretended not to hear, and didn't finish his sentence.

People walked past, but she couldn't look away. It was only when she heard the knock, and "Are you decent?" in Millicent's clipped tones, that she was suddenly jolted into awareness. Her eyes widened and she looked from Luke to beyond him. Millicent had disappeared.

"I have to go," she said, rushing off. "I'll be back..." She wasn't sure if he heard that last bit.

She knocked on Savannah's door and then walked in before Savannah could answer. Her cousin was sitting in the rocking chair, while Millicent paced the room with a crying baby in her arms. "There, there," she said, as she tried to soothe him. Kay couldn't tell which of the twins it was. Miraculously, only Savannah seemed to be able to tell the difference between her boys.

"Oh, hey, Millicent," Kay said, plastering on a fake smile. "Lovely pearls." Millicent acknowledged her with a smile that was just as fake, before asking Savannah if she was going to feed the baby.

Savannah looked as if she was going to explode, prompting Kay to say the first thing that came to her. "Uh... Arnold uh... he was looking for you, Millicent."

"Me?" Millicent looked puzzled. "Whatever for?"

The baby cried even louder and Savannah reached out and took him.

"He said he found your…your…one of your pearls, I think."

Millicent's hand touched her throat. "I'm not missing any pearls." She huffed loudly. "I'd better go and see what he's talking about," she grumbled.

"Pearls?" asked Savannah, putting the baby to her breast while her mother-in-law flew off on her broomstick.

The room was suddenly silent. "I didn't know what else to say."

"You came just in time," said Savannah.

"I told you I would. I'll leave you to it," she said, anxious to get back to Luke, but when she walked back to the bannister, he'd gone.

CHAPTER FORTY-SIX

He had the gift couriered over a week later. She gingerly undid the packaging and took the delicate bracelet out of the box and examined it.

Whoa.

It looked like it was made from platinum, and engraved with the Cartier name, with what looked like tiny diamonds, given the way they sparkled. Tiny diamonds an inch apart all around it.

This was no ordinary impulse buy.

She slipped it on straight away, admiring it.

And then she hugged her hand over it, knowing that he had likely taken one last look at it, or had at least touched it before he'd sent it to her.

She had been thinking of him ever since the weekend. And now she wondered how much longer they would have carried on talking that day, had she not put on her Superwoman cape and rescued Savannah from Millicent.

She stared at the bracelet again, and wondered what would have happened if he'd given her the bracelet instead of the lingerie. Would she have taken it to mean that he thought more of her than just a sex object? Because that had been her initial reaction when she'd opened the bag and found the skimpy lingerie.

She sent him a quick text, thanking him, and telling him it was lovely, and five minutes later he texted back saying he was glad she liked it.

Her finger hovered over her cell phone button again, poised with another question, but he had clearly moved on now, and it was time that she did, too.

***

She liked it.

He knew she would.

Classy and chic, just like her.

It had been tough, seeing her again. When she'd gone off with that doctor, it had been easier to forget her, but then she'd showed up at Tobias's place. He knew she would have, it being a big day for the Stones to show off their new twins.

He almost didn't go, but Xavier had forced him to. Xavier who was so much calmer and laid back these days, had managed to get it out of him about Kay. He hadn't told him everything, hadn't in so many words talked about their arrangement, but just that they'd been together, and she had nursed him through his illness. That had been another thing Xavier hadn't been too happy about. "You're like a closed book, dude. It's bad enough I don't know who you're sleeping with, but getting cancer and not telling me?"

He'd left Tobias's place quickly, because talking to her, laughing with her, being around her, reminded him of what he had lost. She looked happier. She looked damn good, and he was conscious of the fact that he didn't. It wasn't easy getting his medication right. It wasn't easy recovering from cancer, and it wasn't easy trying to move on with his life.

And then Xavier had gone and told him that Kay had never been with Dr. Santini in the first place. And Savannah had casually mentioned that Kay was taking a break before she started her new job.

It got him thinking—because he also needed a break.

He could take a chance and risk it—and one of two things would happen. Either he'd piss her off so much that she'd think he was stalking her, or she'd actually listen.

And if she was on an island, where was she going to go?

CHAPTER FORTY-SEVEN

"You don't want to go to the waterfall, do you?" Jacob asked her.

Kay opened her mouth to say something, but she didn't want to lie. So she didn't say anything. She didn't have the energy, or the inclination to traipse to the other end of the island. And she'd been playing tag with Jacob in the pool for the past hour. "It's getting late, Jacob." The sun was starting to set. "I don't have your energy, sweetie. I need to recharge," she told him. "Maybe tomorrow. How about we go first thing in the morning?" She'd have more energy then, before the sun beat down.

"Okay," he said, easily pleased. "I'm going to check on my bros."

She sat up on the sun lounger. "I'm not sure that's a good idea, Jacob. Your mommy's trying to rest." Savannah was always feeding them, or changing their diapers. And when she wasn't doing that she was taking a nap with the babies while Tobias was probably taking care of business somewhere in the study. Thinking about it, she'd hardly seen him all day today. From what Kay could tell, this wasn't much of a vacation for either of them, but they seemed happy. "Try not to wake them up if they're asleep."

Jacob put his finger to his lips. "I'll go in stealth mode," he whispered. "Then I'll be invisible." She nodded, not completely understanding, but smiled and let him carry on.

She lay back, letting the silence swirl all around her. Kawaya was so different now with just the Stones and her on it, give or take the few staff Tobias had hired. They took care of the day-to-day maintenance on the island, as well as the cooking and cleaning. It was just as well, given that Savannah had still been adamant about taking care of the twins herself, and didn't have much time to do anything else.

Kawaya was definitely more tranquil this time around, for her at least. She needed this time to get over the chaos of the past few months. At the wedding, almost ten months ago, the place had been packed full of people, and the 24/7 party atmosphere had gone on for days. Now, as she turned and stared at the bar, everything stood desolate and empty. She imagined Luke standing there, serving people, being polite. Friendly enough, yet distant. She suddenly missed him and touched the bracelet around her wrist, remembering the good times.

Accepting Savannah's generous offer to join her and Tobias here, she had decided to come for a week, making the most of her break in between jobs. She envisioned a week of reading and relaxation, but Jacob—as sweet and as understanding as he was given his tender years—was full of energy. She was having trouble keeping up. What he needed was Izzy, or friends his age to keep him company. She was struggling already, and this had only been her second day here.

Apparently Izzy and Xavier had also been invited, but

the two of them had plans to vacation in Mexico this summer.

She sighed, wanting to stay out here, but knowing that it would be time for dinner soon enough. The twins' schedule dictated events, and Savannah preferred to eat after she'd given them their evening feed.

She quickly showered, and dressed, and joined them all for dinner at the table around the pool area.

"An early night tonight, I think," said Tobias.

"Are you on night duty?" Savannah asked. "I've expressed milk for the next feeding time."

"What's *sesspressed* milk?" Jacob asked, lifting his burger.

Savannah grinned, and looked at Tobias to reply.

"It's...uh..." Tobias was never one to be stumped for words, and even Kay was curious to hear his explanation. "It's milk that mommies have for their babies."

Jacob shrugged, suitably satisfied with this explanation, and bit into his burger.

"Jacob wants to go to the waterfall in the morning," Kay told them. "And I promised I'd take him. So don't get worried if we've disappeared. In fact, you two can sleep in."

"I don't know what that is anymore," Savannah grumbled. Tobias patted her hand. "You can have a sleep in, and I'll take care of the twins."

"They want what you haven't got," Savannah replied. "But just give them to me in bed and I'll feed them while I'm still asleep."

"Why don't you consider having some help?" Kay suggested, "Just so that you can have a bit of a break."

"No," Savannah replied, smiling. "I'm loving every sleep-deprived moment. Besides, Max and Briony are coming out next week."

"You said they'd gone skiing." Kay was sure this was what Briony had told her when she'd seen her at the gathering last week.

"They've compromised. Briony got first choice. They're skiing in Lake Tahoe this week, and coming here next week. Max wants to babysit."

"Ouch," said Kay, remembering the conversation with Briony. "Is this in order to get more practice before they decide whether they're going to adopt or not?"

"Next week will be crunch time, according to Briony," Tobias said. "She's going to use that week to decide. I personally think she wants to do whatever makes Max happy, but she's going to get her hands dirty, and see if it's the right thing for her."

"Oh, she'll get her hands dirty," quipped Savannah. "She'll have a pretty good idea after an hour with the twins."

"Hmmmm." Easing back into her chair, Kay took a sip of water, thinking about it, and what a life-changing decision it would be for those two. Compromise, and change, and going with the flow, wanting what made your partner happy—those seemed to be the basis of a good relationship, along with mutual love and respect, longing and desire. She looked away. Complicated, that's what relationships were. Maybe she wasn't cut out for them. She ate silently, lost in her own thoughts as the Stones laughed and talked about the day's events. Looking at their beaming faces, she dared to hope. Relationships weren't impossibly hard, not if you found your soulmate; Tobias and Savannah were living proof of that. They made it look so easy.

Conflicted, she stared at the sea. The light of the moon danced across its surface, and it was eerily silent again everywhere.

"Time for a movie," declared Tobias.

"Time for popcorn!" exclaimed Jacob, jumping out of his seat.

"It's going to be a Marvel film, isn't it?" Savannah asked.

"We can watch Wonder Woman, mommy."

"It's not the same as a rom-com, honey," said Savannah. "I'm outnumbered already."

"Haven't you already had your rom-com fix for today?" Tobias asked her.

"You watched a girlie film without me?" Kay asked.

"You were lying on the beach, reading, or something," Savannah replied. "I didn't want to disturb you."

"Don't feel outnumbered," said Tobias, rising from his chair and resting his hand on Savannah's shoulder. "We're going to have to make some girls next time, just to even the numbers."

"That's a lot of leveling to do," Savannah replied, her eyes twinkling.

"I'm all for it." He gave her a kiss, and the intimate moment between them made Kay look away.

"Are you coming?" Savannah asked her, making her turn her attention back.

"Not yet. I'd like to sit out here for a while. I'll come in later."

"Okay." Savannah cleared her throat. "You're sitting out here for a while are you?" she repeated, in a slightly louder-than-usual voice.

Kay looked up, puzzled. "If that's okay with you." For a moment Kay wondered what was wrong with Savannah, but put it down to lack of sleep and baby overwhelm. "I won't be too long. It looks like a nice evening." She looked up at that stars, so bright in the inky satin sky. "We can watch a rom-com in the other room, if you want."

"Maybe not tonight," Savannah replied. "I should spend some quality time with Jacob and Tobias, once the twins fall asleep."

When she disappeared into the main villa, Kay walked over and sat on one of the sun loungers. Looking up at the sky, she took a deep breath. This was beautiful, and peaceful, and perfect. She gazed out at the sea, at the lit up beach area with its fairy lights. Savannah had liked them, and Tobias had asked that they be put up again.

It was beyond pretty. Turning her head, she glanced at the bar area again and memories of Luke came flooding back.

Holy shit.

She blinked, and her heart almost jolted right out of her rib cage. She blinked again, then jumped up in shock. "You?" she exclaimed, staring at the vision behind the bar.

This wasn't real. It *couldn't* be real.

There, in his signature black T-shirt, was Luke. She battled shock and surprise and a tiny ball of excitement as she walked towards him, still shaking her head, still blinking and expecting the mirage to vanish any minute now. She told herself she was suffering the effects of jetlag, and she was overtired, and ... losing her mind.

But he stood there, smiling back at her. The image refused to disintegrate.

"Luke?" she asked, tentatively, resting her arms on the bar, needing something solid to grip onto, something real, while she struggled to make sense of this.

"Hey," he replied.

"What are you doing *here?* When? How?" It was too much to take in. She stared at him, losing all sense of reason, and logic. Every bone in her body numbed.

"Sorry to mess up your relaxed evening. I didn't know

when to come out," he said, as if he hadn't just upturned her world. Those lips, those eyes, that face—staring back at her, as real and as handsome as ever. A swarm of butterflies fluttered around in her stomach, and in the back of her mind she was still trying to process the information, still trying to get a handle on the shock of him being here. Luke Hunter, cool and undeniably sexy, stared at her with an intensity that shook her to her core.

"Come out? From where?" She looked behind her, expecting to see some magical, mystery box he might have been hiding in.

"I didn't mean to startle you," he said, in his familiar, understated way. She snorted. Her heart beat furiously, and her insides shook as if they were having their very own surprise party. She was pleased, and angry, and excited all at once.

"Say something," he said, when she was speechless again.

"I...I don't understand...you...here...Savannah never said..." she grappled for words, then took a hold of herself. "*What* are you doing here?" Max and Briony were coming, and Izzy and Xavier had been asked. She suddenly wondered if the stay at the island had turned into a couples' vacation, and nobody had told her.

"Savannah and Tobias asked if I'd like to come out."

"With who?"

"Excuse me?"

"Who did you come with?"

Her question seemed to confound him. "Just me."

Just him. She let out her breath.

"I made you a cocktail," he said, sliding the cocktail glass towards her.

That got her started. "Don't go getting any ideas—"

"I'm not." He shook his head. "I promise you, I have no intentions. This is for old time's sake. I swear. I would never..."

She left the cocktail glass untouched while blood coursed through her veins, making her dizzy. Determination steeled her. She was going to take a stand. He obviously had come here alone, for a reason. Well, she wasn't going to fall for any of it. But he looked better. At least he seemed to look better, it was hard to tell in the soft glow of the fairy lights. "Did you get your medication back on track?" she asked, concerned as always about his health.

"I did. Thanks for asking." He folded his arms, forcing her attention to those muscles again. She deliberately looked away, refusing to admire them.

"I'm back at the gym again, and back at work. Marie sends her love, as does Amanda."

Her eyes widened to saucers and she turned to look at him again. "They *knew* you were coming here? They know *I'm* here?"

"Yes."

Indignation swept over her like a tidal wave. "If you think you can just turn up unexpectedly and pretend that everything is fine, you are severely mistaken."

"It doesn't mean anything, me coming here, and you being here," he told her, in a calm manner. "Tobias said I looked as if I needed a break, and he invited me. Savannah let it slip that you'd be here this week."

"And you decided to come *this* week?"

"Yes."

Why did that not make her as angry as it should have? "Why?" she demanded.

"Because I needed to get away, and seeing you again seemed appealing."

"But I ... I...this was meant to be *my* vacation before I started my new job."

"It's a big island, Kay. I can stay out of your way if you want me to. If you still hate me as much as you did before."

She didn't have a ready answer for that. "When did you arrive?" she asked.

"In the early hours of the morning, before you got up."

"And you've been hiding all day?"

"Tobias took me snorkeling at the other end of the island. We chilled, catching up on things."

Her lips pressed together. "Tobias and Savannah sat with me having dinner knowing that you were skulking around the island? Did Jacob know?"

He shook his head. "I don't think that little dude can keep a secret, but I'm happy to take him to the waterfall tomorrow, if you don't want to."

She wondered how much of her conversation he'd heard, and how long he'd been skulking around. "Have you been stalking me?"

"Only since towards the end of your dinner." He paused, his eyes dancing with amusement. "This brings back memories," he said, "You and me here. If I could take back time, I'd do it all differently."

"You can't." She lifted her head, curious anyway. "What would you do differently?"

"I'd appreciate you more, be more grateful for you, recognize everything you did for me. But more than that, I wouldn't push you away all those times you tried to get close to me."

She folded her arms.

"I pushed you away, Kay, because I didn't want to get hurt again, and you threatened me more than the others."

"Threatened?" she asked. She didn't want to give him

the time of day, but she was curious to know how he'd felt threatened.

"You understand me more than anyone in my life ever has."

She slid her fingers towards the cocktail glass, and circled the stem. "I *tried* to understand you."

"You *do*. And you put up with my foul moods, and all those nasty things I said. You understood what I was trying to do, and you didn't let me. You should have walked away, but you didn't."

"It was Marie's fault."

He shook his head. "I think we both know that—as subtly persuasive as Marie is—you and I aren't the type of people to go and do something if we don't want to. You looked after me because you're a nice person. You have a big heart. You cared for me."

"You're a hard person to care for," she said, lifting the cocktail glass. "It hurt to be around you, sometimes. It hurt to care for you, to—" *Love*, she almost said. She put down the cocktail glass without lifting it to her lips. "To try to get close to you."

"And yet you stayed, right up until the end."

"I was always ready for a good time, remember?" she said. "And before you got ill, we did have some really good times."

"That's not true, and you know it. Sure, we had good times, but that's not why you stayed around, after I got ill. Don't pretend you did it for a reason other than because..."

"Because?"

"Because I meant something to you," he said.

"We exchanged bodily fluids," she flung back at him, wanting to taint what they'd had, not dress it up the way he was trying to. "So yes, you could say we had some sort of connection."

He looked defeated, as if she'd thrown a knock-out punch at his face. "Don't make it sound vulgar. We were starting to become more than that."

He'd realized, had he? He'd realized too damn late. "But that's what it was," she insisted. "You told me many times about your rules, and what you didn't want, that you didn't do romance, and all that..." She tried to think of the word he'd used, "You didn't want the emotional *fuckery*," she said, using her fingers to make air-quotes. "Remember that? You pushed things too far, and I've had enough. I deserve more."

"I *did* push things too far, and you were right to have had enough, and you *do* deserve so much more. You deserve all the good things life has to offer."

"Is that why you're here?" she asked sarcastically. "To give me a few good things, for old times' sake?" He didn't like that. Oh, she was loving this. Seeing him be the one who chased, who wanted more, and who felt the hurt.

"I'm here because this is my last chance to explain myself to you. I figured you'd have nowhere else to run on an island. No Dr. Santini to whisk you away."

She peered at his face. "Is Dr. Santini as big a threat to you as Dean was?"

His hands went to his hips. "I *am* working through my issues. Maggie cheating on me had an effect, I know that now. I was completely head over heels in love with that girl." His confession felt like a thousand pin-pricks across her skin. "But I'm over it. It took me meeting you to realize that."

She turned away. It was all getting too heavy, and too much.

"Listen to me, Kay. *Please*. I know I was a douche bag to use you as—"

"As your bullet-proof vest?"

"I was going to say riot-shield."

"Neither of them are complimentary," she pointed out.

"But they serve a useful purpose. They save people. *You* saved *me*."

She wasn't sure what to make of it—his appearance, and what he was saying. But, like last week, it was nice to see him again, to be talking again, to address things.

Get a handle on it, she told herself. She couldn't let the shock of seeing him unexpectedly move her into doing something irrational. Out here, under the starlit sky, with the silver sea just behind her—well, it was the type of place to make her not think straight. She had already suffered enough with him. She had wrongly believed she could make him love her, and now she was afraid of making the same mistake again. "If you think you can win me back, you're wrong, Luke. You can't."

"I know," he said, walking out of the bar and coming towards her. "I don't intend to make you do anything you don't want to. I never have." There was something in his expression she had never seen before, not even when he had been lying in his hospital bed. It looked like vulnerability; not quite defeat, but a letting go of the hardness which had been such a big part of him.

She stepped back, determined not to feel anything, trying to turn a blind eye to the soft tone of his voice. This man had cost her her self-esteem, her career, and her big client deal.

All for nothing.

This man whom she had thought, once upon a time, that she could tame, had now come to her looking fully tamed. For all his pain, and messed up past, she had recently seen shimmers, and glimmers of hope, of the type of man he *could* be, but she had been hurt too many times, and this time she wasn't going to back down.

She wanted more. She didn't want a hookup. It had taken a while for her to see that, and it had cost her more pain than she had envisaged, but she didn't need the sex, or the intimacy or the attention. What she craved, what she *had* craved all along, was to have someone to care about, and to have that person care about her.

With Luke, it always felt as if she was the one doing all the caring. As if she was the only one hurting, and loving, and having feelings.

"I would rather we stayed friends," she said, ignoring the way her heart was starting to thump inside her rib cage. It was nerves, and the shock, that was all.

"Friends? Of course. I hope we'll always stay friends." But the words didn't line up with the way his jaw clenched.

She needed to make sure he understood her, that there was no miscommunication. The man had flown out here for a reason, and she wasn't going to let him charm her panties off this time. "That arrangement," she said, looking around and lowering her voice, "It wasn't the first friends-with-benefits-hookup I've had. You weren't my first."

That seemed to piss him off. "Okay," he said, the muscle on the other side of his jaw twitching.

She wasn't exactly telling the truth, either. He might not have been her first tawdry little secret, but he'd been the first man she had wanted something with. The others had been mere stones along the pathway, but Luke Hunter could have been the final destination. There had been times when she had believed that she could fix him, heal him, be his salvation—and that he would never want to let her go.

After all, what woman didn't want to be *the one* for her man?

"But you were my first," he said.

That stumped her. That swarm of butterflies in her stomach started to spin around like crazy. "Your first what?" she whispered, while her heart thump-thumped with abandon.

"The first woman to reach inside," he tapped his fisted hand to his chest, maybe it was to his heart. That wasn't a Luke move. Was he *really* indicating his heart?

"Friends," she said, the word absurd, and deflecting from the moment. She couldn't go there, back into that hothouse of complications and misery and bliss—the rollercoaster of being involved with Luke again. He was trying to reel her in again, and she refused to be reeled in.

"Friends, always," he said, in that honeyed, husky voice of his.

Holy freaking shit.

CHAPTER FORTY-EIGHT

They talked for hours into the night. Even the staff had long retired by then. He'd gone inside and brought out a blanket, then laid it out for them to sit on over by the sand, with the sea a few yards away.

He'd moved the conversation away to other things—safe topics, about her new job, and her plans for the rest of her vacation—because talking about things between them only resulted in Kay putting up her barriers again.

Other topics worked.

Her frostiness had slowly melted away, and that was a good sign. But he hadn't come here with any indecent intentions. He wanted the real deal because she *was* the real deal. He had realized it in a roundabout way, via cancer, and much soul-searching, and losing her, but he liked to think it still wasn't too late. He'd been prepared for her to tell him to get lost, to go to hell, but she hadn't.

"We should go to bed," he said, grateful that they had talked. She'd sat on one end of the blanket, and he'd respected her personal space, and sat at the other. This wasn't going to be a continuation of what they had before, if she wanted it, if and when she was ready, this could be a new start.

"Go to bed?" she asked, giving him an odd look.

"Not...not *that*. Just...sleep...in separate beds, in separate rooms."

"Obviously. Where's your room?" she asked, as they started to walk towards the main villa.

"Right down at the other end of the corridor. I specifically requested it."

"That was wise."

"Tell me about it," he agreed. They walked in, and the next few moments stretched out in awkward silence. "Well, goodnight," she said, as they came to a stop outside her room.

"Good night, Kay." He stifled a yawn. "I'm tired, sorry."

"It's a long flight. The jet lag takes a while to wear off, and you've been snorkeling," she reminded him.

"I rested up after that, and then I spent some time with the twins before dinner."

Surprise lifted her brows. "You were with the twins?"

"And Tobias," he clarified. "He said it would give Savannah a break."

"Where was Savannah?"

"Watching a rom-com."

She laughed. "The cheeky little vixen." She stared up at him again. "You and Tobias looked after the twins? What did you do? Watch them sleep?"

"They woke up when I switched the baby mobile on by mistake. But we gave them a bath, and that seemed to calm them down."

Her mouth fell open. "You gave the babies *a bath?*"

He nodded. "I gave Lewis a bath. Tobias had Samuel."

"How can you tell which is which?"

"You can't tell?"

"Not unless they're wearing monogrammed clothing."

That made him chuckle. "Lewis takes a hold of your finger. He's a real grabber."

"A real *grabber?*"

"You never noticed?"

"I'm better at looking after Jacob," she replied, wincing. "And even then, I'm not so great."

"You don't know what you're missing. They're a handful, but they're damn amazing. They *react*. Like you give them a finger and Lewis will put his teeny weeny hand around it. It's freaking awesome."

"*Freaking* awesome," she parroted, obviously noticing that he'd used her phrase. Pretty soon he was going to end up finishing her sentences. "I didn't know you had a thing about babies."

"Me neither. It kind of took me by surprise, too." It had actually shocked the shit out of him, since he'd never been around babies, and had no experience of them. But those fragile little things, a bundle of limbs and eyes and lips, had suddenly made him protective, and soft, and turned him into a complete wuss. Even Tobias had commented on it. Truth was, he'd never allowed himself to think about anything other than his business empire. Women and sex had been secondary, and there had been no need to think beyond that.

"Who would have thought Luke Hunter would be taking care of babies?"

"A baby," he said, correcting her. "I only had to look after one. I don't know how Savannah does it. I'll show you how to tell the difference between them tomorrow, if you want." He paused because she was looking at him all shiny-eyed. "Are you okay?" he asked, because she suddenly looked like she wasn't. Before she could reply, she tip-toed up and kissed him lightly on the cheek, for some crazy, unexpected reason.

"What was that for?" he asked, his insides tingling.

"For no reason," she said, sniffling. She cleared her throat. "For being brave, I guess, because it must have taken some guts to come out here, not knowing how I would react."

"I'd take a bullet for you. This was nothing."

"A bullet?" she asked, sounding surprised. "That's a bit over-dramatic, isn't it?"

"But true." Because he would. He'd do anything for her.

She leaned forward again, tip-toeing up again, and kissed him, this time on his lips. And just as quickly, she backed away.

But she'd set his pulse racing, and his insides raging. Before he could ask her what *that* was for, she told him, "I'm glad you're here. I've been thinking about some things, and I was hoping that in time we could move—"

But he didn't let her finish. He only needed to hear the first four words. In one swoop, he leaned in and kissed her; it was almost a celebratory, seal-the-deal kiss that deepened and lengthened as the delicious seconds ticked by. He'd been dreaming about those plump lush lips of hers for ages.

She moaned into his mouth, resting her hands on his shoulders before throwing them around his neck. And then his hands were on her bottom, then down to her thighs. She jumped up, and wrapped her legs around him.

The speed of it left dust trails in his deeply aroused mind. She clung to him, spurring him on with her delicious noises, and the feel of her body pressed so snugly against him was starting to arouse him. His hands skated to her back, and he grabbed her butt, squeezing it gently.

"Wait," she said, then opened the door to her bedroom. Somehow they made it inside, closing the door with her back.

If it wasn't for the fabric getting in the way, he would take her like this, with her up against the wall and her legs wrapped around his waist. Give her that slow comfortable screw up against the wall, only there would be nothing slow about it. The vision was like dynamite to his fire. She pressed against his erection, driving him giddy with desire.

Moving to the bed, he threw her down, then climbed over, retaking her mouth and tasting its sweetness again. Her hands came up around his neck and she pulled him close, their tongues dueling for dominance, until he hit the tipping point, the one which if crossed would be hard to come back from. He pulled away, gazing down at her with his heart racing as if it had been injected with steroids.

She lay on the bed, flushed, her eyes shining, then propped herself up on her elbows. "Freaking hell," she said, in that breathless just-kissed voice of hers, "I thought I'd gotten you out of my system."

"Thought?" he asked, his hopes rising. She hadn't told him to get lost yet, and he was waiting for her to land back down to the ground from their kissing-fix. Actions spoke louder than words, and the two of them had this amazing chemistry, their bodies connected, and the sex was off-the-charts-hot. But he didn't want to go down that route again; he wanted a deeper connection, a meeting of minds. He didn't want to rush it no matter what his body said, or hers.

"I didn't come here to ...to do *this*," he said, then lay beside her on the bed. She lay down too, and he took her hand, interlacing it with his. "Is this okay, or too much?" He wanted to hold her, but not come on too strong. The balancing act was killing him.

"It's okay."

They stared at one another. "I really only wanted you to hear me. I swear to you I never intended for us to end up kissing like this."

"I started it," she reminded him.

"So you did," he replied, somewhat relieved. "I wouldn't have started it, even though I've been dying to do that from the moment I saw you."

"You reined it in, huh?"

"With great difficulty." Even this, lying next to her and going no further, was getting impossible. He was going to have to leave soon. "I wasn't sure how you would be."

"Hmmmm."

She wasn't giving anything away, but if that kiss was any proof of her feelings, it was a good start. "I'd give anything to have you back in my life, so I guess I'm left here waiting for you to decide on what you want."

"We could take it slow," she said, sounding unsure.

"Slow is good." She was starting to consider taking him back.

"Uh-huh, slow would be good." She didn't sound convinced, and he didn't feel it was entirely true, but if they could convince themselves...

He needed her to know, in case she woke up tomorrow and came to some sort of decision which didn't include him. At least he knew he'd told her. "I'm in love with you. I don't know when it happened, or when I realized it, because this is something new for me, these feelings I have for you. I think its love because you're all I think about." He gazed at the ceiling, not wanting to see or hear, or sense the rejection, which even now, despite the heat rolling off their bodies, he was afraid of.

She made a noise, a tiny sound in the back of her throat.

Something he couldn't decipher. He had to wait it out because, after the way he'd treated her, and now with him turning up out of the blue, she was probably still in a state of shock. The kiss wouldn't have helped, and it might have confused her even more. She needed time, and he was in no rush. "I wanted one last attempt to explain myself. Maybe even win you over. I only came because Xavier said you weren't with Santini."

"I wasn't. We were never together. He only wanted investment information. I mean, he wanted more but I didn't."

That hurt. Like a hunting knife through his gut. She hadn't been interested in the doctor, and that counted for something. He turned his head and stared at her. It was going to take a gargantuan feat of self-control for him not to lay a finger on her tonight, or, god forbid, start kissing her again, because he wasn't going to be able to hold back. "If I'd known you weren't with him, I would have hand-delivered the bracelet to you, not sent it via courier." He touched her wrist, his fingers sliding over the gift he'd bought her.

"You stayed away because you thought I was with Santini?" she asked.

"What else could I think after seeing you with him? I wanted to see you again, but I was scared that you might tell me to go to hell forever. Santini was an extra deterrent."

"But you're here now, and this is good," she told him, "Us talking like this. It's a start, maybe."

"I hope it is. I have lots I want to tell you, things I discovered about myself in the counseling sessions."

"Oh," she said, turning to her side and propping herself up on her elbow. "It really helped?"

He nodded. "Amanda says she'd like us to meet for dinner."

"Who did you go with last time? You said you met with her and her husband. Who was '*we*'."

"Just the three of us."

She leaned forward and kissed him. Those soft lips sent a signal straight to his groin. He almost let his hand fall to her breast, but stopped himself. "We can't do this," he said. "I meant every word. I will make it up to you—the things I said, the way I behaved. But I want to get to know every single thing about you first."

"Okay," she said, lifting her hand to his face and stroking it. Then she leaned in as if she was going to kiss him again, then groaned as she stopped herself, their lips just an inch apart. "This isn't going to be easy."

"The best things often aren't," he murmured in agreement, then climbed off the bed. "I need to take a cold shower."

"I'll take one with you," she said, mirroring his movement and standing in front of him.

He took her hands in his. "That's not how it works, and you know that." As if he'd let her get into the shower with him. Cold water or not, they'd soon make enough steam if they weren't careful.

She bit her lower lip, the movement telling him this was just as difficult for her as it was for him. Her reaction had been everything he had dreamed of.

He'd once believed that romance was an illness, that caring for someone made him weak, and that falling in love would be something he would never do. Kay had discredited all those notions of his. He owed her more than she would ever know.

This was a start, returning to Kawaya, her listening to

him, giving him a chance. Sharing a kiss. He couldn't have asked for more than that. Actually, he could have, but making love was way down on his list of winning Kay back.

Right now, he was a torrent of emotions. Hot and steamy thoughts raced through him, because it was impossible to be with this woman and not feel those things, but there was also something else—something steady, and warm, and constant; a fledgling feeling that hinted at a possible future with this woman.

"You'd better go and take that solo cold shower," she said, "And I'll do the same."

A smile danced on the edges of his lips. She was a tease, but she was *his* tease. "'Night," he said, unsure of whether to kiss her or not. He backed away, choosing safety instead of blue balls.

"'Night," she said, as he walked out of the door. "Are you going to come with me and Jacob to the waterfall tomorrow?"

"Do you want me to?" he asked.

"Are you going to answer every question of mine with that?"

"I don't know, should I?"

She narrowed her eyes at him. "I'm sure Jacob would like it."

"Then I'll come, but only because Jacob wants me to."

"You great big liar," she said softly.

"See, you do understand me."

He went to bed, thinking of her smile, and her words, and what he hoped would be the start of something new.

The Tobias Stone Foundation was hosting its annual Christmas party for the adoption centers in New York and this year it was held later than usual, a few days before Christmas.

Tobias and Savannah had invited a few of their friends along, and Kay had jumped at the opportunity. She and Luke had decided to make a quick appearance before they caught their evening flight to Pennsylvania. They didn't have long to spend here but she'd been keen to come.

Savannah had explained that one of the largest toy stores in the city was closed to the public and Tobias's foundation invited children from the local adoption centers to come here for a big party. As per Tobias's wish, every child left with a Christmas gift of their choice.

Savannah started walking towards them as soon as she saw them. "It's crazy out there," Kay replied, when Tobias's security men ushered her and Luke to safety. She was glad to be inside. It had been her first proper glimpse into Savannah's world. Huge crowds had formed outside the store with reporters and cameramen swarming like flies near the entrance.

"Nice to see you," said Savannah, welcoming them both.

"It never used to be this mad before," muttered Tobias, looking out from the glass doors. "I blame it all on my wife." He nodded at Savannah.

"Trust me, I had nothing to do with it."

"You married the elusive billionaire," Luke countered.

"That's right," said Kay, jumping into the conversation. "And Tobias gave you your happy ever after."

"I disagree," said Tobias. "*She* gave *me* my happy ever after." Savannah blushed, and rolled her eyes in response. Tobias winked at her before bending over to lift one of the twins out of the stroller. "You remember this was how it all started," she said.

"How could I ever forget?" Tobias stood up with his son in his arms—which one, Kay wasn't sure.

"How what started?" Kay asked, curious.

"Us," Savannah stated. "This is where we first met."

"I thought you worked for him?" At least that's what Savannah had told her.

"I did work for him, but a couple of weeks before that, Jacob wandered into this store without realizing it was closed to the public. That was two years ago."

"Two years," said Tobias, grinning. "It seems like yesterday."

"No it doesn't," said Savannah, swatting him playfully. "We've had so much going on in our lives since that time."

"Jacob peeping through the doors and looking in is an image I'll never forget," said Tobias, sighing as if he was reliving the memory.

"And his personal assistant hating me on sight is an image *I'll* never forget," Savannah recalled, making a face.

"Candi, wasn't it?" Kay remembered the upstart with airs bigger than royalty.

"Candace," Savannah corrected.

"Why did she hate you on sight?"

"I have no idea. Maybe because I didn't fit, or because Tobias had taken a liking to Jacob."

"I was trying to get him to come inside and play," said Tobias.

"Candace probably saw you as a threat," said Kay, hazarding a guess.

"I doubt it," Savannah replied. "I was hardly a catch."

"You were to me," Tobias told her.

"Not then. We were struggling. I used to dress so shabbily, and I had to go to the food banks so that we could eat."

"Never again," said Tobias, putting his arm around Savannah and hugging her. Samuel, in his other arm, played around with Tobias's tie.

Kay flinched at the idea of what her cousin had endured back then. She'd never liked Candace much, and knowing this only made her want to rip her eyes out. "That little bi —" but before she could finish, Luke interrupted her.

"Hey, Samuel," he said, holding his arms out. The baby gurgled in response. "You want to come to me, don't you, little buddy?" He reached for the baby and took him from Tobias.

"You're a natural," said Savannah.

Kay held back as a funny strange sensation took a hold of her gut and made it go all gooey. Watching Luke with the twins seemed to have jumpstarted her maternal feelings.

She'd never had them before, not until he'd come into her life, and she tried to work out where they had appeared from at all. Maybe it had been the pregnancy scare, followed by the disappointment of knowing she hadn't been pregnant at all. And during the summer, when Luke had turned up unexpectedly on the island, they'd ended up looking after the twins on a few occasions.

Something about seeing that big, gorgeous man of hers with a baby just turned her insides to mush.

It was insane.

And yet the past six months had been nothing short of insane, but the happy type of insane—the one which rocked her world but made it better.

"Where are your other boys?" she asked, looking around, and finding it strange that Tobias and Savannah didn't seem at all flustered.

"There," said Savannah, pointing towards the middle of the floor where a huge Christmas tree sparkled. "Oh, goodness Tobias, would you look at that?" They all turned to look at Jacob crouching beside the stroller and pointing to the tree—as if his little baby brother had any idea what it was. Xavier was with them.

"Why didn't we bring the double stroller?" asked Tobias.

"Because Jacob insists on pushing it, and I didn't think it would be a good idea for him to push one of those inside the store," said Izzy, appearing from nowhere. "Hi," she said, acknowledging Kay and Luke.

"Hi," said Kay, then, "Are you still working as a nanny?"

"Not in any official capacity, but if I'm around, I can't resist helping out with the little guys. Aren't they adorable?" She held out her arms to Luke, to take the baby from him.

"Do I have to give him up?" he asked.

"Only because Jacob wants him to see the tree. Can I take Samuel if I promise to bring him back?"

Luke begrudgingly handed the baby to her. Izzy left, and walked over to the boys, and Xavier left them and started to walk towards her and Luke. "Hey, guys," he said, shaking hands with Luke and kissing Kay on the cheek. "You finally turned up. I thought you'd gone straight to the airport."

"Our flight isn't until later," said Kay.

"Of course," said Savannah. "You're going home. Say 'hi' to Aunt Sylvie."

"I will," Kay told her.

"It's going to be a huge surprise," said Savannah, winking at her.

"She has no idea," agreed Kay. She and Luke were taking the flight home to see her mom and spending Christmas with her. For once, she didn't dread going home. For once, she relished seeing the look of content on her mother's face when she turned up unannounced with Luke by her side.

Her mother already knew about him. She'd come over for Thanksgiving, and Kay had introduced her new boyfriend to her mom then, but having Luke come and spend time with her mom back in the house Kay grew up in somehow made their relationship more official. She knew her mom was desperate for her to settle down, but the truth was, it didn't matter to Kay. She had her man, and she was happy, and things between her and Luke were moving along beautifully.

She looked over at Jacob again. "Is that..."she peered, craning her neck. "Is that Arnold?"

"I couldn't invite all of you and leave him out," said Savannah.

"That's nice. It's like he's part of the family."

"He might as well be."

"I need to go and see how he is," said Kay. She hadn't seen him in a while, and both their lives had changed so much.

"Are you ready, dude?" Xavier asked as soon as Kay was out of sight.

"Ready for what? The private jet?" Luke asked, teasing.

"No," Xavier retorted, shaking his head. "You know that's not what I'm talking about."

Luke knew full well what he was talking about. The private jet he'd recently bought wasn't the only big news. He'd bought it on a whim, and he wasn't in the habit of acting on whims. Up until meeting Kay he'd had a much more logical approach to things. But taking his sister's advice, and with a new outlook, he'd found himself driven more towards wanting to enjoy life, rather than working every minute of every hour of every day.

Kay applauded his new attitude, as did Marie. Buying the jet hadn't been the major life decision. But buying an engagement ring had. He'd known for months that Kay was the perfect woman for him, but he needed to be sure that she felt the same way about him.

The thing that had done it wasn't her telling him she loved him every day, but her casually mentioning that she liked the idea of having a baby one day, maybe in the not too distant future.

"I know what you're talking about, pal," Luke replied.

He was starting to get restless and they'd only just arrived here.

"You're really going to do it?" Xavier quizzed him.

"Of course I'm going to do it."

"No regrets?"

"None whatsoever."

"'Cos that's not the sort of thing you get cold feet over, right, dude?"

"I've got no doubts." He'd managed to keep it a secret from Kay, but mostly everyone knew: Tobias and Savannah, Izzy and Xavier, even Max and Briony, who he'd seen sitting around playing games with a bunch of children.

Even Kay's mother knew. He'd called her up and asked for her permission first, wanting to do things in the right way. Sylvie had started to cry, and that had gotten him choked up with emotion. He'd promised her that they would visit her on their return journey, another surprise that Kay knew nothing about.

In fact, the only people who didn't know about the proposal were Kay and Jacob. Jacob, because he couldn't keep a secret, and Kay because in a woman's life, this was one of the ultimate surprises.

He couldn't wait to see the look on her face—not when she boarded the new plane, but when it didn't touch down in Pennsylvania; when the journey took much longer than expected and touched down in Lapland the next day.

"She still doesn't suspect?" Savannah asked, joining in.

"She has no idea."

"I wish I were a fly on the wall," she said. "Promise me you'll tell me everything when you come—" But she stopped talking when a visibly shaken Briony came up to her, with Max following close behind.

"What's wrong?" Savannah asked.

"Nothing's wrong," Max replied, putting an arm around her girlfriend's shoulder.

"It doesn't look like it's nothing," said Tobias, looking a little concerned.

"It's nothing," Max insisted. "Come on, Briony," she whispered, trying to soothe things over. "You'll upset the children if they see you like this."

"Upset which children?" Savannah asked, looking around.

"We were playing Snakes and Ladders with a group of children over there," said Max, nodding at an area behind her.

"Who the hell plays Snakes and Ladders nowadays?" Xavier asked, a little too loudly.

"And what happened?" Savannah asked, ignoring him.

"Nothing..." Briony's voice wobbled. "Nothing really happened, but...it's just sad. It made me feel so sad when she kept a hold of her brother's hand the entire time."

"Who?" Savannah asked, looking completely confused.

"That little girl and her brother, over there," said Briony, looking at them. "The girl with pigtails and the brown dress." They all turned and looked.

Luke had no idea what was going on. He didn't know Max and Briony too well, only what Kay had told him, so he was completely confused now. He cast his eye around the store, trying to locate Kay, and found her standing near Santa's Grotto, still talking to Arnold.

"She's what? Five or six?" Briony asked Max. "And she kept a hold of her brother's hand the entire time, like they needed each other, like they didn't have anyone else. Isn't that sad?" Briony's face had turned pale.

"That is sad," said Savannah softly.

"She's so young, and he's so young," said Briony,

clasping her hand to her chest. "I can't bear to see them looking so sad."

"They were sweet," Max acknowledged.

"I want to take them home," Briony said, suddenly. "I want...I want to adopt them."

Max's mouth fell open. "We're going skiing the day after Christmas Day. You were adamant that we'd go, remember?"

"I don't care," said Briony. "I can't go skiing knowing they don't have a home."

Max gave her a tight hug. "Darling, this isn't a pet shop. We can't just pick a couple of children and take them home. There are processes and rules and—"

"I won't ..." said Briony, shaking her head. "I won't be able to sleep tonight. I won't be able to forget their faces."

"You don't know what happened," said Savannah. "It's best not to speculate."

"But why can't we adopt them?" Briony asked, looking at Tobias.

"Because there are checks and processes, and people in the list before you," Tobias replied. "But ... let me speak to a couple of people in charge, and see what we can do, providing it's the right thing for those children."

Briony's eyes widened.

"I can't promise you anything," Tobias said quickly.

"But it's a start, right?" Max asked.

"Let's leave it with Tobias," Savannah suggested, "And maybe we can discuss this properly later on."

"We should go and finish the game," Max suggested.

"Okay," said Briony, looking somewhat cheered up.

"Can you pull strings?" Savannah asked Tobias, when they had gone.

"I'm not sure, but I'm going to try."

"They'll end up with two children and a dog," Savannah mused.

"Their family will have tripled, just like ours." Tobias remarked, putting his arms around her.

Luke listened, not saying a word. He still wasn't entirely sure what that was all about.

"Should we get ready to go soon?" Kay asked, suddenly appearing by his side. "It's such a shame because I could easily spend all evening here."

"We can leave later. We've got time."

"Are you sure?" she asked, looking confused. Earlier, he'd told her they could only stay for about an hour.

"I'm sure. I got the times wrong. We've got a few hours left yet."

"Great." She kissed him on the lips and vanished again.

They were leaving a couple of hours later than he'd initially told her because he wanted to take things slow; maybe a scenic tour around the city before they reached the airfield. He was getting goosebumps just thinking of the evening he had planned. It was Kay's expression he wanted to savor, the look on her face when he showed her the new jet, and then again when he told her where they were *really* going. More than anything, he couldn't wait for her reaction when he proposed.

He'd have to tell her about the new destination at some point during the 10-hour flight. They'd have to christen the bed, first, and that would definitely take up a few hours.

A proposal in Lapland, on the snow, under the kaleidoscope of the polar lights and surrounded by fir trees. He wanted to see her face light up. It was what he loved, making her eyes shine, making her happy, giving back everything she had given him.

She'd told him once that it was her idea of heaven,

sitting under the stars and making plans for the future. They'd seen plenty of stars during their time in Kawaya, and now he wanted to see the beauty of the aurora with her; they weren't stars, but lights, under a different type of sky, and now at last, he and Kay could make plans for *their* future.

Thank you for reading THE HOOKUP! I hope you loved reading Luke and Kay's story, as well as catching up with your favorite characters from earlier books. If you haven't yet read the first series from which this book was born, you can read an excerpt from THE GIFT at the end.

If you loved Luke, you'll love Elias, the gritty underdog from THE WRATH OF ELI.

Elias Cardoza gets a shot at the world heavyweight title, but nobody expects him to win.

Harper, a journalist from the local paper, has to shadow him for a month. She's out of her depth in the dirty boxing gym with her manicured nails and perfect hair trying to cover a story in which she has no real interest.

Eli despises her on sight. She's a distraction he doesn't need.

SIGN UP FOR MY NEWSLETTER to find out when new books release!

http://www.lilyzante.com/newsletter

I appreciate your help in spreading the word, including telling a friend, and I would be grateful if you could leave a review on your favorite book site.

And now, you can read an excerpt from THE WRATH OF ELI and THE GIFT next.

Thank you and happy reading!
Lily

Eli

It's not often that Lou calls me into his office in the middle of a sparring session. I figure it must be important, something to do with the fight.

"What is it?" I say, still wearing my boxing gloves.

"There'll be a journalist hanging around here for a few weeks. They want to do an interest story on you."

"A what?" My guard is already up. A journalist? What the hell for?

Lou stares back at me, his saggy, wrinkly skin hanging from his face. At times he reminds me of a turkey. " This is publicity. You don't have Garrison's pulling power. We need this."

The hell we do. I shift uneasily from foot to foot. "I don't need it."

"You do need it. It's the Chicago Daily Herald, kid. You should be honored."

"So?" I say, with a careless shrug. "So what?"

"So shut the hell up and pretend nobody's around."

I stare at Lou in disbelief. I'm training for a shot at the World Heavyweight title next month against Trent "The Tank" Garrison, the current champion. Nobody expects me to win; I'm the underdog, and a long shot, and I got this chance by pure luck.

But Garrison has everything to lose.

I have nothing.

The last thing I need is a journalist hanging around here watching me and asking stupid questions.

"How long?" I ask.

"Up until the fight."

"A month?" I shake my head. "What the fuck are they hoping to do here for that long?"

"Calm down, Eli. Quit getting so riled up."

"But, *a month?*"

"They're writing an interest piece spread over a few days of the fight. Be grateful."

My face twists. This is bullshit.

"They want to write about your training regime, see what you're made of. You should be thankful, kid."

Thankful is the last thing I feel when my manager's telling me that some nosey parker is going to shadow me for an entire month during the run up to the fight.

Hell no.

"I don't need a distraction."

"Ignore him. Pretend the guy, whoever he is, isn't around. You do that to most people most of the time anyway."

I ignore the snide comment. "He better not come to the training camp." It's the week before the fight. Lou's taking me to Dwayne Bank's house for my most intensive training yet. I spar and fight and hone my technique here in the boxing gym where I've been coming for the last six years, but Lou says the final weeks we're going to build my strength and stamina at Dwayne's place. Apparently it's in the middle of nowhere, and a four hour drive from Chicago.

"Okay. Done. Don't let this get in your way. You're Chicago's New Hope, Eli," he reminds me, "You have other things to think of."

That's exactly my fucking point.

Chicago's New Hope.

I grit my teeth. They're calling me that because Garrison is from the Bronx. Whoever coined this phrase is being nice, but I'm not stupid. Behind my back I know what everyone thinks.

I'm a poor bastard who doesn't stand a chance.

I tap my gloves together, because I'm itching to get back to the ring. Santos is waiting. "Is that it?"

"Can I count on you to be nice?" Lou asks.

I take a deep inhale because his request still pisses me off. "This isn't school, Lou. I don't have to be nice to anyone." Not that I was nice to anyone apart from Nina, much. Even my foster parents, and there were many over the years, struggled to cope with me.

He wants me to say 'yes'. The hell I will. I need to focus. I need to keep my wits about me and my eyes on the prize, and the prize is the title of the world heavyweight champion. It doesn't matter how I got this chance—sheer luck many have said, even directly to my face. *You won't last more than two rounds,* others have told me. But I have a chance at this, and I'm going to prove everyone wrong.

I remember one of the caretakers at Grampton House. Dennis Swain was his name. I used to shiver when he walked past us. Nina would tug at my hand and keep me close by her side.

I grind down on my teeth and shake my head. This fucking random and unwanted thought has sliced into my brain when I least expect it. Sweat drips down my neck and back. "I'll try."

Lou nods, more in relief than anything else. "Now get back to the training. We need you ready for the big night."

"I am ready," I mutter under my breath, as I turn to leave. I was born ready. Born to good-for-nothing sack-of-shit parents. My sister and I deserved better. When I win, when I get the money, things *will* be better.

I climb back into the ring, bristling with rage, and a few seconds later, my clean left hook sends Santos flying to the ground.

Harper

"Elias Cardoza?" I frown, because the name is vague enough that I've heard it, but I can't put a face to it. "Is he a popstar?" I ask Merv.

My boss huffs out an irritated breath. "He's a boxer, right here from Chicago. How can you not know that?"

"Because I don't watch boxing."

Gerry tries to hide his laugh, but I catch it.

"You need to start watching this guy. Everyone's got an eye on him, and he hasn't lost a fight this year." Merv pauses for effect, but I stare at my nails, noticing that the color has chipped and I'm going to have to run into one of the nail salons during my lunch hour to get it fixed. Or maybe not. I have an article that needs to be finished in the next hour.

"Are you paying attention?" His tone is harsh. It's like he's still pissed that I got this job instead of his nephew.

"I always pay attention." I force a smile because I know this annoys him even more. I swear to God, I don't know how come I'm still in this job two months down the line. This guy is looking for any excuse to fire me so that he can tell everyone how useless I am. Only, I've not given him the chance because, despite my designer suits, and matching bags and shoes, I can still deliver nitty-gritty news when I need to. I never miss a deadline and it surprises many people. They think I'm an airhead, and I'm so not. This is what Merv thinks. I feel as if he's constantly trying to test me, but my father's on the board—which is probably another reason for Merv hating me—and he can't really fire me.

"That's your next assignment. Think you can handle it?"

I have a million reasons why I don't want to handle it. I don't know the first thing about boxing, and I hate the idea of it; two grown men knocking one another to pieces. It's barbaric and shouldn't be allowed. But I smile sweetly, because this asshole of a man finds things he knows will test me.

"Of course I can handle it." Then I wonder what Gerry's doing in here, and why Merv is only addressing me about it. "What about Gerry?" I ask, nodding in his direction. Gerry's a senior editor here, and sort of like my mentor.

"Gerry suggested it would be an interesting story for you to do. You can shadow Cardoza for a month in the run-up to his fight."

"A month?"

"You can get up to speed with boxing, while writing an in-depth piece on him," Gerry explains. "It will be a good experience for you, especially since this fight is going to be huge. Cardoza's not going to win, obviously, but we'll get a lot of interest because he's a local guy. Garrison is the clear favorite, and the bigger draw, no question about it."

"But a month?" I ask, thinking back to the Rocky films and images of a dirty and dingy little gym rush to my mind. I don't particularly want to shadow a boxer in a place that smells like a boys' locker room all day long. Why couldn't I cover a gala fundraiser event or something more interesting?

"I want you to immerse yourself in this guy's daily routine. Our angle of interest is that Cardoza's a local boy. They call him Chicago's New Hope and, trust me, we wouldn't be doing this if he wasn't from here. This kid has come from nowhere, and if he goes on to win the fight it's going be a huge upset."

Gerry interrupts with a smirk. "He's not going to win," he says, smugly. "Cardoza got this fight because the other guys got disqualified."

Merv frowns. "He might surprise us." Gerry shakes his head again, as if this is ridiculous.

Merv laughs. It's the usual part-condescending, part-being-polite laugh he usually reserves for me, the one where I can't tell if he's being a dick, or if he's suddenly remembered that my dad sits on the board and it's because of him that Merv has to be nice to me.

"You start tomorrow. It's all been arranged with his manager, Lou McNeilly. He's the trainer manager, and he owns McNeilly's Gym."

"Tomorrow?" I ask, feeling slightly anxious. They've

definitely thrown me in at the deep end. I have a lot to research, especially since I have no clue who this guy is.

"You'll do," Merv says, resting his head in his hands, arms wide open as he rocks back in his chair. "You'll be fine."

I don't bother to question what he means by that, and I especially don't like the way he looks me up and down; as if he thinks I don't know that he's checking me out again. He's a sick and dirty old man. So many of them are. I shudder, and thank my lucky stars that unlike most people, I don't have to work if I don't want to.

At least I show up to work and do the work. Truth is, I don't want to rely on my father all my life. I want to make it on my own. He helped fund my Ivy League education and, yes, he bought my apartment in one of the most affluent parts of the city, but that's what all parents do. I can't help it if my parents helped me.

"What does he look like?" I ask. Merv throws a folded paper across the desk. I stare back at a guy who looks angry. But then my heart skips a beat as I rake my eyes over his chest. I skim over the article headline and see that this is a shot of him in the ring after he's won a fight. He's wearing a don't-fuck-with-me glare, and his hands are down by his side, his eyes a riot of fury. My heart skips a beat because this guy has abs that are so beautifully sculpted that I'm tempted to trace my finger over the paper.

I would have probably done that had Merv the Perv not been watching me.

"I think she likes him," Gerry says, grinning.

"He looks familiar," I say, trying to cover my embarrassment. He doesn't look familiar at all, and I can't believe I've almost drooled over the paper.

"Get to know him, Harper. Make him trust you." These are Merv's parting words to me.

"Looking forward to it?" Gerry asks when we leave the office. He's always checking to see if I'm okay. At first I thought it was because of my dad, but the more I get to know him, the more I realize that Gerry's making sure I settle in okay. Maybe he's trying to make up for Merv's thinly veiled hatred of me. In any case, Gerry reminds me of a kid who always wants to please his mom, or his school teacher, except that he's in his late forties, I'm guessing, and he's been here longer. Yet, for some reason, he seems slightly in awe around me, and I don't know why.

"It's a bit sudden," I say. "Telling me the day before I start."

"That's because we had someone else in mind."

"Then why am I running with this?" There are others here with so much more experience than me.

"This will be good for you. Merv reckons you might be better in getting more information out of Cardoza." He coughs and looks embarrassed. "As opposed to a guy, but I have no idea why he'd think that, especially in this day and age."

Merv the Perv. I wince. "I know nothing about boxing," I say.

"You're not on your own, Harper. Maybe we can get together for lunch or something once you've settled in? You can let me know how you get on."

"Sounds good."

I go back to my desk and prepare to get better acquainted online with Elias Cardoza.

Screaming children wreaked havoc in the toy store, and their cries of laughter rang straight through Tobias Stone's ears.

Not much excited him these days but it was hard not to get caught up in their excitement, hard not to feel their joy, hard not to hear their high-pitched shrieks. Hard to dismiss the wonder on their faces as they played with the display toys and stared wide eyed at the shiny new boxes that were displayed so enticingly on the shelves.

It made him feel better about himself and made Christmas more bearable to know that he was spreading a little happiness. Or rather, his foundation was. The huge toy store had been closed to the public for the evening while the Tobias Stone Foundation invited children from the city's adoption centers to visit the store and select a toy of their choice.

But he was also aware that he'd had to miss an important meeting that had suddenly come up. Luckily Matthias was standing in for him but he would need to return to the office soon. His multi-million dollar hedge fund didn't stop running just because Christmas was coming.

His eyes darted around the place, and he glanced at his watch again, getting anxious and needing to leave. Contemplating his escape he looked towards the exit and saw a child peering through the glass doors.

"I'm going," he told Candace, his hard-as-nails assistant.

"Not yet, Tobias. It's barely been an hour. Smile." She flashed him her false one. "At least make it look as if you're having a good time."

"I *am* having a good time but I'm in the middle of important negotiations, in case you'd forgotten."

It was all very well hosting an evening for children from the city's adoption centers—and it made him feel good about himself for a change—he still had a business to run.

"People need to see your face, Tobias. It's good publicity for you to be seen mixing with all sorts of people— especially these poor kids at a time like Christmas. It adds credibility to your philanthropy."

He didn't mind giving his wealth away. If anything, he thrived on it and there was no way that he was going to get through his millions in his lifetime. He didn't spend too extravagantly. Even though he enjoyed the finer things in life he worked damn hard and preferred to remain low-key, as much as was possible for a man with his wealth and history. While giving away his wealth made him happy, making money did too.

"If we could just have a few shots of you with the children, Sir," said the photographer herding a group of children together and leading them towards him.

"What a brilliant idea," agreed Candace and took his arm. "How about near the tree?" She led him over to a beautifully decorated Christmas tree lit up with warm, golden colored lights.

"Smile, everyone," the photographer ordered.

"Is this necessary?" Tobias asked, giving the man a tight-lipped smile.

"Smile," said Candace smiling through her gritted teeth. Tobias obliged as a group of young children, barely reaching his waist, gathered around him as though he was Santa Claus.

"You are so kind, Mr. Stone," gushed one of the women from the adoption centers as she gave him a dazzling smile. "This is so very generous of you, taking the time to give these children a Christmas present." He nodded at her, barely hiding his look of unease. While he liked giving his wealth away, being thanked for it made him uncomfortable.

"Would you mind if we had a photograph taken together?" She stepped up alongside him. "Vanessa? Hurry up!" She called out to her colleague, another matronly woman who looked as though she'd be more at home baking pies. "We can put this in our newsletter," she explained. "People might be more interested to read it if they see your picture." She smiled sweetly.

Tobias returned a fast smile, conscious of time slipping away. It would be the morning of the next day in Hong Kong and he was anxious to sit in on the negotiations. "Thank you, ladies, but I must leave." He broke away from the group, determined to disappear before Candace asked him to do something else. She was like a fiery Doberman, silky, fast, super alert and she made sure he was seen in the right places with the right people at the right time.

"You're still making the most eligible bachelor lists," she told him. But he had no interest in these things. He preferred to pay for sex, seeing it as nothing more than a transaction which required payment. There was no emotional attachment that way.

"I'm leaving," he growled; he'd been here an hour already but as he turned around and headed towards the exit, he saw the same child still peering in. "Has nobody let him in?" he muttered and strode up to the large glass doors of the store. "It's a win-win deal, Tobias," Candace had told him. "You buy those poor kids a toy, and come out looking like a saint." Tobias grimaced at the thought. He wasn't a saint. Not by a long shot.

But that wasn't the reason he'd gone along with her idea of giving Christmas gifts to children less fortunate. He'd done it because for the longest time he'd hated Christmas and had avoided the festivities. Christmas was about being with loved ones and Tobias was alone.

It could have all been so different.

This had been the second year they had run this event, and this year he'd even been looking forward to it. But he was now anxious to return to the office even though it was past eight o'clock. Apart from work, Tobias didn't have much else to occupy him. His millions couldn't buy him peace, love or happiness, though whiskey and Naomi made the world tolerable.

He walked up to the door and the sight of the child looking through the glass, wide-eyed with wonder, reminded him of himself; of how he'd been at that age. He had been dirt poor once and remembered the time when he used to stare at other kids who had the things he never had.

"Where are you going?" Candace tottered up on her heels behind him.

"I'm letting him in."

"But we're closed to the public this—"

"Where the fuck is his mother?" Tobias snarled. The

security guard nodded at him, as Tobias flung the door wide open and peered at the child who stared back at him with fear in his eyes.

Immediately his hardness melted. "Do you want to come inside?"

The child's body language perfectly illustrated his dilemma. One foot was poised as if he was ready to enter but his solemn face indicated no immediate desire to make a move.

"Don't just stand there," Tobias said. "If you want to come in, then come in." He looked around for signs of the boy's parents and saw a woman with her back to the child, talking on her cellphone. She turned around just at that moment, her gaze landing on the child, before moving to him. She rushed towards them and stopped at the door, just behind the boy. The child stared at his mother but said nothing.

"Jacob, we can't—"

"Can I have a look? Just a look. Please, Mommy?" Tobias watched the exchange; the woman appeared to waver and then stared at Tobias. "Are you open?"

"Yes." He pulled the door wide open and moved away.

"Pleeeease, Mommy? Just a look?"

The woman appeared to consider it. And the longer she took, the more the child's anticipation grew. It annoyed the heck out of Tobias. "Why don't you let him in and put the kid out of his misery?" He gave her the once over, taking in her scuffed shoes and the huge tear in her tights.

"He's not miserable." The woman retorted.

"He doesn't look too happy to me."

She narrowed her eyes at him. "Ten minutes, Jacob. No more." The boy smiled so brightly that it brought a smile to Tobias's tight expression. He remembered that look, and wished he still could feel that level of excitement about anything. Even winning new deals and reaching the next milestone in his business had lost its sparkle. Nothing mattered much, anymore. Christmas, with its gaudy commercialism, packaged and dressed up in dazzling bright baubles and sparkling lights, had lost its allure for him years ago because now it reminded him of the life he could have had. He would still have been insanely successfully, disgustingly rich, but he'd have had someone to share his wealth with.

Now he carried too many memories of the wrong kind.

He watched as the woman—the boy's mother, he presumed—stepped aside warily and looked around the store. Candace sidled up to him. "We're *not* open to the public, Tobias," she seethed. "You can't just let any strays in. This is specifically for kids from adoption centers."

"It doesn't matter," he replied, noting that the boy wore a coat that was obviously one size too small for him.

The boy's mother walked up to them. "Is something going on in the store?" she asked.

"We're not open to the public," Candace replied.

"You're not? I'm sorry, we'll leave."

Tobias walked over to the boy who was happily sitting on the floor playing with an Iron man figure and a fighter jet.

"So you like Iron Man, huh?" Tobias asked, crouching down.

"Who doesn't?" replied the boy, with the fighter jet in one hand and the figurine in the other.

"Did you write your letter to Santa?"

The boy nodded, his eyes sparkling.

"What did you ask for?"

"Coloring books."

"Coloring books?" asked Tobias in surprise. "So you must already have an Iron Man?"

The boy shook his head.

"Would you like to have Iron Man?"

The boy stared down silently and shrugged.

"Did you know that tonight is a very special night?" Tobias asked, eager to get the boy talking. "You can pick anything you want from here and it will appear under your tree on Christmas Day."

The boy frowned as he stared back at Tobias. "You're not Santa."

"No. I'm not, and I'm sure you'll get your coloring books from him. But, see all of these children here?" The boy looked around and nodded. "They're all going to pick a toy and they get to open it on Christmas Day. You can, too."

The boy looked at the floor again, as if he didn't trust him. Just then Tobias's cell phone rang and he answered it, standing up slowly.

"It's not going too well." Matthias told him. "Are you coming back to the office? There are a few things we need to discuss."

"I'll be back. Give me twenty," replied Tobias and watched as the woman rushed over to her son and told him they had to go. He hung up and walked back to Candace. "Why did you do that?" He growled at her. "How much trouble is one extra child going to be?"

"If you let one in, you won't be able to stop the rest." But Tobias was too busy staring at the child. He saw the boy's face drop, saw him leave the toys he'd been playing with and get up slowly.

"You're too uptight," he hissed and walked over to the mother and son. "You should let the poor kid stay."

"He's not a poor kid," the boy's mother returned. The child was silent.

"Looks to me like he wants to stay."

"But the woman said—"

"I don't care what she said."

"Tobias, let me handle this." He felt a tightness in his chest as Candace turned to the woman. She put on what he now knew to be her best and most false, over the top persona and explained. "Tonight is a charity event hosted by the Tobias Stone Foundation for a few of the city's adoption centers. This store is closed to the public for a few hours. Why don't you come back tomorrow? You can shop all you want then."

"I saw you on TV," the boy said, shyly.

"I don't think you did, honey." The boy's mother gave Tobias an apologetic look.

"I did, Mom. He *was* on TV." For the first time Tobias tried to hold back a smile. The woman slipped her hand through the boy's. "Come on," she said, obviously not believing a word. "Let's go."

"I did, Mom." The boy turned to him. "You were on TV, weren't you?"

But the woman appeared to be in a hurry. "I'm sure you did, honey. Come on. We need to get back." He watched as they walked away and then the woman bent down and pulled something out of her bag then handed it to the boy. When the boy put it to his mouth Tobias realized it was an inhaler.

He glared at his assistant. "Was that really necessary?"

BOOKLIST

Honeymoon Series: Take a roller-coaster journey of emotional highs and lows in this story of love and loss, family and relationships. When Ava is dumped six weeks before her Valentine's Day wedding, she has no idea of the life that awaits her in Italy.

Honeymoon for One
Honeymoon for Three
Honeymoon Blues
Honeymoon Bliss
Baby Steps
Honeymoon Series (Books 1-3)

Italian Summer Series: This is a spin-off from the Honeymoon Series. These books tell the stories of the secondary characters who first appeared in the Honeymoon Series. Nico and Ava also appear in these books.

It Takes Two
All That Glitters

Fool's Gold
Roman Encounter
November Sun
New Beginnings
Italian Summer Series (Books 1-4)

The Billionaire's Love Story: This is a Cinderella story with a touch of Jerry Maguire. What happens when the billionaire with too much money meets the single mom with too much heart?

The Promise (FREE)
The Gift, Book 1
The Gift, Book 2
The Gift, Book 3
The Gift, Boxed Set (Books 1, 2 & 3)
The Offer, Book 1
The Offer, Book 2
The Offer, Book 3
The Offer, Boxed Set (Books 1, 2 & 3)
The Vow, Book 1
The Vow, Book 2
The Vow, Book 3
The Vow, Boxed Set (Books 1, 2 & 3)

Indecent Intentions: This is a spin-off from The Billionaire's Love story. This 2-book set consists of 2 standalone stories about the billionaire's playboy brother. The 2nd story is about a wealthy nightclub owner who shuns relationships.

The Bet
The Hookup

Indecent Intentions 2-Book Set

The Seven Sins: A series of seven standalone romances based on the seven sins. Emotional, and angsty romances which are loosely connected.

Underdog (FREE prequel)
The Wrath of Eli
The Problem with Lust
The Lies of Pride
The Price of Inertia
The Other Side of Greed
The Seven Sins Books 1-3

A Perfect Match Series: This is a seven book series in which the first four books feature the same couple. High-flying corporate executive Nadine has no time for romance but her life takes a turn for the better when she meets Ethan, a sexy and struggling metal sculptor five years younger. He works as an escort in order to make the rent. Books 4-6 are standalone romances based on characters from the earlier books. The main couple, Ethan and Nadine, appear in all books:

Lost in Solo (prequel)
The Proposal
Heart Sync
A Leap of Faith
A Perfect Match Series Books 1-3
Misplaced Love
Reclaiming Love
Embracing Love
A Perfect Match Series (Books 4-6)

Standalone Books:

Tomorrow Belongs to Us
Love Among the Ruins
Love Inc
An Unexpected Gift

ACKNOWLEDGMENTS

As always, I would like to say a huge 'Thank You' to my amazing group of proofreaders for their patience and support, and for calmly accepting my ever-changing deadlines. These ladies check my manuscript for errors, typos, inconsistencies and strange words and phrases which often find their way into my story.

Without them, I wouldn't have the confidence to release each book and I am eternally grateful for their help and support:

Marcia Chamberlain

Nancy Dormanski

April Lowe

Dena Pugh

Charlotte Rebelein

Carole Tunstall

I would also like to thank Tatiana Vila for creating my awesome covers:

www.viladesign.net

ABOUT THE AUTHOR

Lily Zante lives with her husband and three children somewhere near London, UK.

Connect with Me

I love hearing from you – so please don't be shy! You can email me, message me on Facebook or connect with me on Twitter:

TikTok | Instagram | Website | Facebook | Twitter | Email

tiktok.com/@lilyzantebooks

instagram.com/authorlilyzante

facebook.com/LilyZanteRomanceAuthor

twitter.com/lilyzantebooks

goodreads.com/authorlilyzante

bookbub.com/authors/lily-zante

amazon.com/author/lilyzante